Ashara sat up █████████████████████████ the almost-comple██████████████████████ the back of her mind. Now that the basic construction was in place, she realized she'd seen its like somewhere before.

An image rose to her mind, from an old record of the days when the Towers served the great Domains lords, making terrible *laran* weapons for them—*clingfire*, bonewater dust, and more.

A weapon? Could Corus have taken a commission to build a weapon, *right here in Varzil's Tower?*

Ashara forced herself to calm as she gathered up the diagrams and strode along the corridor to Corus' private suite. A tendril of *laran* told her he was there, awake and alone. She knocked and a moment later the door opened.

"Corus, I must speak with you." She held out the plans. "I must know what this is and to what use it will be put. It's a weapon, isn't it?"

He watched her, his eyes glowering in the candlelight. "Ashara, I warn you, you have no need to know these things."

"*What kind* of weapon?"

Corus slammed one palm on the arm rest and got to his feet. "If I told you, what would you do with that information, eh? Whose cause would you serve? You know nothing of the world beyond the Towers. I am your Keeper, not the other way around."

"*Varzil* was my Keeper!"

Corus back-handed her across the face and sent her staggering. The surface of his mind, perhaps affected by the blocked sexual energy, seethed like a pot about to boil. Reflexively she reached out, caught a fragmentary image. Her eyes widened in shock.

A Cataclysm device, like the one that destroyed the Lake at Hali . . . !

THE RENUNCIATES:

During the Ages of Chaos and the time of the Hundred Kingdoms, there were two orders of women who set themselves apart from the patriarchal nature of Darkovan feudal society: the priestesses of Avarra, and the warriors of the Sisterhood of the Sword. Eventually these two independent groups merged to form the powerful and legally chartered Order of Renunciates or Free Amazons, a guild of women bound only by oath as a sisterhood of mutual responsibility. Their primary allegiance is to each other rather than to family, clan, caste or any man save a temporary employer. Alone among Darkovan women, they are exempt from the usual legal restrictions and protections. Their reason for existence is to provide the women of Darkover an alternative to their socially restrictive lives.

AGAINST THE TERRANS
—THE FIRST AGE (Recontact):

After the Hastur Wars, the Hundred Kingdoms are consolidated into the Seven Domains, and ruled by a hereditary aristocracy of seven families, called the Comyn, allegedly descended from the legendary Hastur, Lord of Light. It is during this era that the Terran Empire, really a form of confederacy, rediscovers Darkover, which they know as the fourth planet of the Cottman star system. The fact that Darkover is a lost colony of the Empire is not easily or readily acknowledged by Darkovans and their Comyn overlords.

AGAINST THE TERRANS
—THE SECOND AGE (After the Comyn):

With the initial shock of recontact beginning to wear off, and the Terran spaceport a permanent establishment on the outskirts of the city of Thendara, the younger and less traditional elements of Darkovan society begin the first real exchange of knowledge with the Terrans—learning Terran science and technology and teaching Darkovan matrix technology in turn. Eventually Regis Hastur, the young Comyn lord most active in these exchanges, becomes Regent in a provisional government allied to the Terrans. Darkover is once again reunited with its founding Empire.

*THE BLOODY SUN
HERITAGE OF HASTUR
*THE PLANET SAVERS
SHARRA'S EXILE
*THE WORLD WRECKERS
*RETURN TO DARKOVER

THE DARKOVER ANTHOLOGIES:

These volumes of stories edited by Marion Zimmer Bradley strive to "fill in the blanks" of Darkovan history, and elaborate on the eras, tales and characters which have captured readers' imaginations.

DOMAINS OF DARKOVER
FOUR MOONS OF DARKOVER
FREE AMAZONS OF DARKOVER
THE KEEPER'S PRICE
LERONI OF DARKOVER
MARION ZIMMER BRADLEY'S DARKOVER
THE OTHER SIDE OF THE MIRROR
RED SUN OF DARKOVER
RENUNCIATES OF DARKOVER
SNOWS OF DARKOVER
SWORD OF CHAOS
TOWERS OF DARKOVER

(*forthcoming in DAW Books editions.)

Snows of Darkover

Edited by

Marion Zimmer Bradley

DAW BOOKS, INC.
DONALD A. WOLLHEIM, FOUNDER
375 Hudson Street, New York, NY 10014

ELIZABETH R. WOLLHEIM
SHEILA E. GILBERT
PUBLISHERS

First Printing, April 1994

1 2 3 4 5 6 7 8 9

DAW TRADEMARK REGISTERED
U.S. PAT. OFF. AND FOREIGN COUNTRIES
MARCA REGISTRADA
HECHO EN U.S.A.

PRINTED IN THE U.S.A.

Contents

Introduction

This is the twelfth anniversary of my career as an editor of Darkover anthologies. In that time I have printed the first stories of many young writers who have gone on to write in their own worlds. Several of them are now successful novelists with many novels to their credit (Mercedes Lackey, Diana L. Paxson, Susan Shwartz); some have just sold their first novels after years of selling short stories (Elisabeth Waters, Deborah Wheeler); and many of them have a long string of short stories sold to various markets. Of the 84 people from whom I have bought Darkover stories for previous anthologies, at least 10 have published books and 24 more have other short stories in print.

One of the most gratifying things to me (besides the privilege of discovering so much new talent) is the high percentage of "my" writers who continue to write for me, both in the Darkover and SWORD & SORCERESS anthologies, and in *Marion Zimmer Bradley's FANTASY Magazine*. This volume, for example, includes stories by Mercedes Lackey, Diana L. Paxson, Elisabeth Waters, and Deborah Wheeler.

Indeed, "my" writers were instrumental in helping me to get my magazine off to a good start. And for that, as well as for the many wonderful stories they have given me to read over the years, I thank them.

The Yearbride

by Lee Martindale

Lee describes herself as "female, fat, 43 and fabulous!" and adds that her husband's description of her is "red-headed hell on wheels." Sounds like quite a marriage. She lives in Dallas with her husband, two cats, and various computers. She says they have no children, but "there's a black German shepherd puppy in my distant future."

She has previously sold nonfiction, but "Yearbride" is her first fiction sale.

"I am sorry, my husband, but I simply do not understand. Why must you take another wife?" His bride's voice held so sad a tone that Dyffed thought his heart would throw itself from out of his mouth if he tried to open it.

"Lass, I told you before," he said after a long time. "Such is the way it has always been." Taking the young woman's hand and cradling it in his own, he looked at his bride and found himself close to weeping. It had been Dyffed who brought her to Rockraven from her father's house in New Skye, to be fostered between Midsummer and Midwinter and approved by the women of the Clan. Dyffed standing with her before his father as she vowed a long life and many children to Clan MacKenzie. Her first child, his strong son, slept in the cradle near the hearth. And now it was Midwinter Festival again.

"Yes, my husband, you told me before. Please tell me again."

Dyffed looked with love at the woman whose voice was now steadier. But she did not see; her face was turned away from him. And for the first time in over a year and a half, her thoughts were closed to him as well. "I wish there was time to, my love. But we must go. They will be blowing the summons soon."

He watched her nod, then rise and move with the slow grace he found so enchanting to the cradle where their child still slept peacefully. She looked from the child to him, and was drawing breath to speak again when the sound of a horn came faintly from below. Her eyes momentarily widened with fear, but she composed herself, expelling the breath slowly and without sound. She caught up a festive wool wrap and held it toward Dyffed, turning her back as he draped it over her shoulders. His hands lingered in a momentary caress of her shoulders. "I do love you, Caitlin," he whispered into her hair.

"And I will always love you, Dyffed," she whispered before squaring her shoulders and moving to the door.

Fires burned in the giant stone hearths at either side of the Great Hall, and holiday smells of spicebread and resin branches seasoned every breath. Musicians played for couples and groups who danced in front of tables laden with goblets and platters. As Dyffed entered the room, he saw the celebration as it had been all his life. But Caitlin, on his arm, saw something else. Something interwoven with the threads of merriment. Here and there, men and women looked at each other with love and sadness. Hands clung together as if the owners of those hands were loath to let go before it was necessary. She saw, then, that she was not alone in her sadness, and she somehow felt a little better for it.

The MacKenzie stood, pounding on the table and shouting good-naturedly for silence. He looked around the room with obvious pride until all were quiet and every eye was on him. "Well, my people, Clan MacKenzie has survived another year. Let us drink to it!" Goblets were raised and shouts filled the room.

"It has been, all in all, a very good year for us. We have suffered our share of bad times, of course. This year saw the passing of old Morgan, the healer, and Donal the Younger caught in that icefall in the spring. Melora, may the Gods give rest to that pretty child, dying in childbed. We drink to their memories and wish them peace." This time the goblets were raised in silence.

"But new ones came among us as well. Dyffed brought us a new wife in Caitlin, who gave us Dyffed's son Bran. And Kenel brought us Cassilda, who gave us fine twin daughters just two tendays ago. Let us drink to the ongoing strength of the Clan!" More shouts, louder this time, as toasts were drunk.

"And so we come to Midwinter again. The harvests have been bountiful, our craftsmen have labored long to give the Clan a wealth of tradegoods, and we can be grateful that this winter is far from the worst Darkover has seen. All things are in order, and now it is again time to turn our attentions to the people of the Clan." The old man paused, grinned at those around the tables, then took another pull at his goblet.

"It is for the strength of the Clan and the well-being of those who come after us that our women bear children to as many men of the Clan as they may. Therefore, as has always been, the Head of the Clan shall pledge a woman to a man as yearbride to husband. For the next year, it is her duty to share his bed, his hearth, and his meat. It is her duty, if the Gods will it, to bear a child to him. It is his duty to care for her and provide for her needs. So it has been since the beginning, and so it shall be in the year to come."

The MacKenzie motioned for his steward, who brought a large leather-bound book and laid it unopened on the table. All around the Great Hall heads nodded, thinking how, most of the time, the ledger was opened to record which stallions were put to which mares and other common-day business. But this was Midwinter Festival, and recordings of another sort had been made that morning. They watched, as they always did, smiling at their leader standing as if studying the cover for a traditional amount of time. At the same moment as every other year, he looked around the room in mock surprise. "But I should not be keeping all these eager folk waiting, now should I?" he laughed, and opened the ledger to a ribbon-marked page.

He began calling the names of the men among his people, beginning with the oldest. When called, each man escorted his wife to stand before their lord, then returned to his chair. The MacKenzie would give a list of the children the woman had thus far borne to the Clan and by whom they were fathered. He would then name the man to whom she would be yearbride. That man would come and lead the woman to the seat beside him.

In the case of the older folk, Caitlin noticed, the partings were usually friendly and without tears. They were, she decided, used to the arrangement and, in some cases, glad to be assigned new mates. As the folk became younger, however, the good-byes grew sadder and the kisses and touching more prolonged. The MacKenzie seemed to take it in stride, diverting his attention elsewhere if the couple clung together for a moment.

"Dyffed, my son, come before me," he said at last. Caitlin rose and took Dyffed's arm, glancing once at him and smiling slightly. When he leaned down to kiss her, she heard him whisper hurriedly into her ear, "Father already told me. You have no need to fear. He is a good and gentle man and will love you well." His lips touched hers, and she suddenly stood alone.

"Well, my child, I suspect all this is strange to you," the MacKenzie said, not unkindly, "but you will come to know in time how much it benefits us all. Kenel, come forward and claim your yearbride."

After the feasting, couples were escorted, one by one, to the women's rooms. Caitlin was not surprised to see Dyffed's belongings gone and Kenel's in their place. Bran's cradle was also gone—moved, according to custom, to the nursery for the next few days.

The two young people, alone for the first time, looked at each other for an awkward moment. Then Kenel reached out and gently took Caitlin's hand. "I know how much you love Dyffed," he hesitantly began, "and it is the same with me. I cannot conceive of loving other than Cassie." There were tears in his eyes, and his new yearbride saw no reason to hide her own any longer.

So it was that each found strong arms in which to mourn the loss of their loves, and sometime in that Festival Night, before the Bloody Sun rose, the need for comfort brought their bodies together.

It was as it had always been, they decided, and how it would always be.

Cradle of Lies

by Deborah Wheeler

It just so happened that, of the many stories I received this year, several—including three of the stories which I eventually could keep, and some others which I didn't—featured Varzil, nicknamed "the Good"—a character I've used before in TWO TO CONQUER and whom I may some day use again.

Deborah is one of the first writers I discovered, and one of the best. She lives in southern California in a household which includes a Rolfing expert and a Ph.D. in laser spectroscopy, as well as my two honorary grandchildren, Sarah and Rose. Her science-fiction novel, Jaydium, *was published by DAW in May 1993. I had the privilege of printing her first story, and she's gone on to make many other sales. I couldn't be prouder of her if I'd written them myself.*

As the funeral procession wound through Hali, Ashara Alton thought there was no more fitting tribute to Varzil the Good than the mysterious, cloud-filled Lake which he had restored. The Keepers of half the Towers on Darkover had come to honor Varzil and now, to the solemn, measured rhythm of the dirge, they bore his silk-shrouded body to the ancient *rhu fead* where his bones would rest, along with the other holy things, until the end of time. A few wept openly, others masked their grief behind stony expressions. Many of the great lords had set aside their feuding for these days of mourning. Varzil had touched them all with his wisdom, healing the wounds of war and chaos, even the devastating effects of the Cataclysm that had destroyed the Lake.

I had not thought to follow him so soon. Ashara pulled her mourning robes closer as she walked in her proper place as Underkeeper of Naskaya Tower. To most people she seemed a slip of a girl, barely taller than a child, with delicate features and eyes so pale they seemed almost colorless. But Varzil had seen through her frail appearance.

"Your body may be small, but your spirit is pure blue fire," he'd told her when she first came to Neskaya Tower.

Remembering, Ashara stumbled on the matrix-smoothed pavement. Her heart brimmed with pain, a heaviness too great to bear. . . . The moment of weakness passed in a heartbeat. Ashara drew upon the training Varzil had given her, her and her alone, to fulfill her promise, he'd said. To become the first woman Keeper of Neskaya.

"They'll fight you, the other Keepers," he'd warned her. "You must prepare yourself constantly, without mercy, to be even stronger than they are."

I am your successor, Varzil, and nothing they can do will take that away from me!

The evening after Varzil's funeral, every Tower worker present, from the oldest Keeper to the youngest novice, gathered in the central hall of Hali Tower. Ashara, seated with the others from Neskaya, kept her eyes downcast, but her nerves tingled with the assembled *laran* power. Deep within her, something ached to reach out, grasp that power, and bend it to her will. It was, Varzil said, the same instinct that would someday make her a Keeper, one of the most powerful the Domains had ever known.

Arnad Delleray, Keeper of Arilinn, rose to his feet. Torchlight glinted off his silvery hair. The oldest living Keeper, he had been most bitterly opposed to Varzil's plan to train women as Keepers. As he addressed the convocation, he betrayed no hint of any grief. All the tributes had been spoken, all the rites performed. He reminded them of the historical uniqueness of what they were to do. Traditionally, each Keeper chose his own successor, tested him, trained him.

As Varzil trained me! Ashara thought.

"Now it lies before us, acting as the united voice of the Towers, to choose a new Keeper for Neskaya," Arnad said.

Ellimara Aillard of Corandolis Tower rose to her feet and the room rustled as people turned to look at her. She was not only Keeper, but *comynara* in her own right, and no one dared challenge her privilege to speak. "It is known that Varzil chose and trained but a single Underkeeper. Surely he intended her to take his place. It would be presumptuous for any of us to question that judgment."

A murmur rippled across the room. Ashara's *laran*-aided senses caught hushed comments. "She can't be serious . . ." "What did you expect? She's a woman, too." "The only woman Keeper—and likely to remain so, if you ask me!"

Arnad swept the assembly with a stern glance and they quieted immediately. "Who wishes to speak on this question?"

"I do." Mikhail Storn-Aillard, Keeper of Comyn Tower, got to his feet. He wore his dark red hair long, curling over his shoulders and blending with his beard like a living mantle. "Varzil was an innovator, always questioning and trying new things. Who else could have reversed the effects of the Cataclysm and restored the Lake? Who else could have brought the great lords together to talk of peace? Yet even Varzil realized that not all experiments succeed and new ideas take time to be accepted. I believe that training women as Keepers is one of them. Our cousin Ellimara—" referring to their distant kinship, "—is living proof that a woman can serve in this way. But just because one woman is talented enough, does not mean that *all women* are qualified. More than that, we are not here to debate the role of *all women*." He took a deep breath, puffing up the considerable bulk of his chest. "We are here to discuss who would best serve Neskaya as Keeper."

The response was so loud, Arnad had to lift his voice to call for order. Around the room, several people had risen to their feet, waiting to be acknowledged to speak. Ashara was one of them. She held herself proudly, chin raised. Arnad's eyes rested on hers for a long moment. Then he turned away and nodded to one of the Arilinn monitors.

Ashara's hands curled into fists as she sat down. Clearly, she was not going to be allowed to speak. *Or believed, no matter what I said.* With a growing sense of futility, she listened as the discussion proceeded to possible candidates. Some of them, she realized, had less training than she. None of them had worked directly with Varzil.

Ashara glanced at the other workers from Neskaya and shuddered. How could she have been so blind, not to see it before, the fear of change, the smoldering resentment that she, Varzil's favorite, had advanced when they had not?

She forced her thoughts back to the debate. Tramontana Tower had several Underkeepers, including a man past the usual age of advancement. Corus MacAran was from a good family and Mikhail of Comyn Tower vouched for his competence.

Ashara turned cold. She'd met Corus once or twice and found him to be ambitious and more interested in getting her to bed with him at Midsummer Festival than in the quality of her *laran*. And he was not even here—no one from either Tramontana or Dalereuth had been able to make the long journey in time.

They would prefer a man they have not seen and cannot question to a woman who stands before them, ready to pass any test they set for her!

Ashara could not longer hold herself still. She rose to her feet again, trembling slightly with the effort needed to maintain control. She did not know it, but her powerful *laran* made her glow slightly, like an activated matrix. The room fell silent and everyone looked in her direction.

"I cannot allow this," she said in her clear, light voice. "Not without speaking the truth." Once she'd begun talking, the words seemed to flow from her. Her trembling eased.

"Varzil is not here to tell you what he wished. Believe what you will, he intended for me to be Keeper at Neskaya after him. But if it is not to be, I must accept the will of this council and serve in any way I can . . ." She paused, her pale eyes flickering from face to face. "But not under Corus MacAran. He may be proficient enough as an Underkeeper, but he knows nothing of what Varzil was trying to accomplish at Neskaya—and if he had any gift as a Keeper, he would have been one in his own Tower long before this!"

Mikhail jumped to his feet, his voice thundering through the hall. "Is there any question now that this girl is unfit to be a Keeper?"

Within a few moments, Corus MacAran was confirmed as Neskaya's new Keeper. Word would be sent to him over the matrix relays to depart at once.

Raimond Lindir, Keeper of Hali, rose to speak. A tall, thin man, he was so fair it was easy to believe that *chieri* blood ran strong in his family. Ashara knew him only from the relays and had admired his detachment and proficiency. "We cannot afford to discard a *laran* talent like Ashara's. With proper training she might become a great asset. If there is some difficulty of her continuing at Neskaya under Corus MacAran, she may remain here with us at Hali."

"We have no other Underkeeper," said one of the Neskaya technicians. "To lose Ashara now would leave us greatly understaffed."

"Then you will return to Neskaya to serve under your new Keeper," Arnad of Arilinn told Ashara sternly. "And we will hear no more prattle about your childish whims or secret ambitions, do you understand?"

Ashara bowed her head in apparent submission. Anything she said now would cost her not only Neskaya, her home, but a place in any Tower.

Varzil, I will not betray your dream! I will find a way, I swear it!

Once he had established himself at Neskaya Tower, Corus MacAran summoned Ashara to the laboratory which he had taken over for his private work. She expected a difficult interview, but to her surprise, he was courteous, almost affable. "You're one of our strongest matrix workers and I need you for my special project."

Ashara said carefully, "I'm scheduled to supervise the newer technicians on the relays."

"Forget that, it's just routine. I'll assign someone else to do it. I want you to take charge of this section." He indicated a table heaped with papers.

Her curiosity aroused, Ashara bent over the top diagram. She understood the antiquarian notations well enough, but she'd never seen anything written in them before. They seemed to describe part of some larger device.

"What is it?" she asked.

"Oh, you'll see when it all comes together," Corus said. The edge in his voice told her that if she asked too many questions, she'd quickly find herself removed from the project.

Varzil would not have treated me like a child, she thought, bowing her head. *And the day will come when you will not, either.*

Ashara sat alone in the darkness, to all appearances, as cold and unmoving as the bare stone of the walls of her narrow room. Around her, the Tower's living quarters lay silent, sleeping. Only Ashara kept her self-imposed vigil, drilling herself in the focusing techniques Varzil had taught her.

At first, Ashara did not stir at the sound of knocking at her door. Then, she blinked, settled her awareness properly in her body, unfolded her legs, and went to the door. Bellisma, the young novice who worked with her on Corus' project, stood there, trembling so violently that the candle in her hand spattered drops of wax on the stone floor.

Ashara's heightened perception quickly took in the swollen energy channels in the younger woman's body. "Blessed Cassilda protect us, what has happened to you?"

"I—" Bellisma slumped silently. Ashara caught her and dragged her to the bed. The candle fell and guttered out, but Ashara needed no light. She bent over the barely-conscious girl, skimming her hands over Bellisma's torso. The congested channels pulsated, glowing dull, dark red. Bellisma's heart fluttered like a caged bird's.

Ashara clamped her lips together. She knew what had happened. Bellisma was a pretty girl, physically mature for her age. Ashara had seen the way Corus looked at her, had heard him speak about what a waste it was to remain celibate while not working the great energon rings. "This nonsense about 'keeping virgin for the Sight' is nothing but superstition," he'd said.

And now the girl's awakening sexuality completely obstructed the very same channels that should be carrying her *laran*. Powerful energies, deprived of their natural flow, threatened to overload vital organ systems. She was only ill now, but if she tried to work in this condition. . . .

Silently Ashara gave thanks that her childish appearance had deterred most advances; she'd been fortunate that her cycles had not yet begun and perhaps never would, thanks to the strenuousness of her training.

Clearing the girl's blocked channels was simple enough, any properly trained monitor could do it. But that would not end the problem, Ashara knew. The austere discipline Varzil had demanded of the Tower was slipping away. No wonder Bellisma had come to Ashara and not to her Keeper for help.

I cannot risk this child's life, Ashara thought, aware that she was taking on herself the responsibilities of a Keeper. Varzil had shown her how *laran* might be permanently diverted, although he'd warned her never to try except in dire emergency.

When she'd finished, Bellisma's channels flowed as clear and steady as a child's. Now it would be a simple matter to teach her to avoid any sexual arousal, so that even a deliberately erotic caress would seem as appetizing as three-day-old porridge.

I have no choice, Ashara told herself. *Varzil would understand.*

Bellisma murmured and rolled over, instantly asleep. Smiling, Ashara stretched out beside her, and they lay together, side by side, as chaste as the moonlight.

Ashara often stayed in the laboratory after the technicians had left, checking the linkages and the unfamiliar design of the batteries. The Tower monitors insisted on examining her regularly, concerned with how little rest and food she took, but Ashara always amazed them with her continued health. These days, they acted as if the entire Tower needed nursing.

Ashara had other things to worry about. Gradually the form of the device took shape and she still couldn't figure out what it was for. The *laran* batteries were strangely configured, clearly not meant for any ordinary storage function. She identified mechanisms for the transmission of a short, immensely powerful burst of energy—but for what purpose? When she asked Corus again, he put her off, nor would he say where he'd gotten the designs or for whom the project was being built.

One night Ashara sat up, poring over the diagrams for the almost-completed device. Something nagged at the back of her mind. Now that the basic construction was in place, she realized she'd seen its like somewhere before.

An image rose to her mind, from an old record of the days when the Towers served the great Domains lords, making terrible *laran* weapons for them— *clingfire,* bonewater dust, and more.

A weapon? Could Corus have taken a commission to build a weapon, *right here in Varzil's Tower?*

Ashara forced herself to calm as she gathered up the diagrams and strode along the corridor to Corus' private suite. A tendril of *laran* told her he was there, awake and alone. She knocked and a moment later the door opened.

"Ashara ... it's late," he said, standing back to let her enter. She saw, in a glance, the red, swollen channels of his lower body. What he was thinking, to allow himself to get into such a state?

"Corus, I must speak with you." She held out the plans. "I must know what this is and to what use it will be put. It's a weapon, isn't it?"

Corus turned his back on her, crossed the room, and sat in his richly upholstered chair. "I knew I was taking a chance, including you on this project. I thought that once you'd settled down.... Go to sleep, do our work, and leave the decisions to those who are wiser than you."

"It *is* a weapon," Ashara repeated evenly.

He watched her, his eyes glowering in the candle-light. "Ashara, I warn you, you have no need to know these things."

"*What kind* of weapon?"

Corus slammed one palm on the arm rest and got to his feet. "If I told you, what would you do with that information, eh? Whose cause would you serve? You know nothing of the world beyond the Towers. I am your Keeper, not the other way around."

"*Varzil* was my Keeper!"

Corus back-handed her across the face and sent her staggering. The surface of his mind, perhaps affected by the blocked sexual energy, seethed like a pot about to boil. Reflexively she reached out, caught a fragmentary image. Her eyes widened in shock.

A Cataclysm device, like the one that destroyed the Lake at Hali ...!

"No!" She cried out, horror-struck. "You cannot do this! I'll warn the other Towers—"

"And who will believe you? No one else even suspects. Half the device is here, half still safe at Tramontana. And if we don't build it, someone else will, someone with no scruples about how to use it!"

She got to her feet, the plans still clutched in her fist, and said stiffly, "Then I will destroy what I have built, rather than see such destruction unleashed."

"You! You're incapable of seeing sense in this matter!" He stormed toward her as if he would strike her again. "You will leave this Tower immediately, watched every moment until you pass the gates. That is my command as Keeper of this Tower. I will no longer tolerate your constant questioning and insubordination. If this is how Varzil trained you, then it's a good thing he's dead!"

Ashara shook with outrage as he ripped the diagrams from her fingers. Temptation flooded through her, to reach out with her Alton Gift, force his mind open before hers. It would be as terrible as any rape, against everything she believed in, everything Varzil had taught her.

But Ashara did not give in to her fury. Varzil's training held firm. She allowed herself to be escorted down to her room, where she packed her few belongings. An hour later she found herself wrapped in a travel cloak, sitting on an old white mare. The air was still, but a light sprinkling of snow covered the ground. A few clouds scudded across the night sky, glowing softly with the light of three moons.

Ashara raised her head. Corus thought he could humiliate her by packing her off in the middle of the night in total disregard of her rank and birth, without even a decent chaperone. He thought she'd go crawling back to her family and a marriage to some upstart desperate enough for an alliance with the Altons to take her.

"No," she said softly, like a vow made in her heart, "I will not go back to Armida. To Hali, where Raimond Lindir offered me a place. Whatever happens, Varzil's dream must not die!"

Numb with cold and exhaustion, Ashara stood at the gates of Hali Tower an hour after sunset. It took her a few moments to summon the strength to pull the bell rope. There had been days on the trail when only her rage at Corus MacAran and the other fools of the Tower council kept her alive and moving. She'd walked the last miles on her own feet after her mount collapsed.

Now she lifted her small chin and addressed the sleepy-eyed porter. "I am Ashara Alton, Underkeeper of Neskaya Tower, and I have come to serve here at the invitation of Raimond Lindir."

The motherly woman who supervised the housekeeping bustled Ashara into a heated room, plied her with food, and settled her in bed under three feather comforters, refusing to hear a word of explanation.

As Ashara slept, her mind wandered in the gray formlessness of the overworld. Here she felt no pain, no hunger or thirst or bone-weary fatigue. Her body seemed as light as a feather. In the distance, she saw a human figure, hauntingly familiar, moving away from her. Instantly she recognized Varzil.

It was dangerous to be abroad in the overworld, but even more so when one was exhausted and heart-sore. Ashara longed to follow Varzil and be with him, to see his face and hear his voice one last time. If she tried, she knew, she might wander there forever. She held still by only the frailest margin of will. In desperation, she imagined herself in the midst of a blue flame, cut off from all temptation.

Walls of cold azure fire burst into being around her,

deepening in hue with each passing moment. Ashara clung to them, as if she could make herself one with their frigid beauty. An instant later, Varzil's retreating form was lost to view. She drifted back to her body.

The next morning, Raimond Lindir received Ashara formally. He commented that the roads were not safe these days, with the Hastur lords rumbling rebellion and war so close at hand. "I had not thought to welcome you so soon," he said without the slightest trace of emotion. "Neskaya's loss is Hali's gain."

"I shall strive to be worthy of that trust," she answered.

"Whatever reason Corus had for dismissing you, I cannot so lightly overlook the appearance of disobedience. You will have to earn your right to the position you formerly held. I can grant you only a technician's status."

Ashara held her face expressionless. What did she expect? And yet, Raimond spoke of *earning her right*. So be it, then. She would show him what kind of Keeper Varzil had trained.

In the days that followed, Ashara recovered her strength and poured it gladly into whatever task was set before her. For the first time since Varzil's death, she began to think she might be happy. Raimond Lindir was a very different sort of Keeper from Corus. He didn't waste time on distracting emotions and she never caught even a whiff of sexual interest from him. It was as if he had been made *emmasca* after the old traditions.

Ashara continued the training exercises Varzil had taught her, often staying up very late, deep in breath-control trance. To avoid any inadvertent energy leakage, she set up a *laran* barrier around her room. One night, when she'd been at Hali Tower only a few months, she sensed nothing amiss until a voice rang out down the corridor.

Instantly alert, Ashara grabbed a thick woolen shawl and jerked her door open. Cheria, one of the young monitors, darted toward her, unbound hair streaming down her back. Her face was flushed, her eyes rounded with fright.

"Ashara!" she gasped. "Help—you must come!" With a desperate backward glance, she raced on toward the next room, sounding the alarm.

Ashara paused, reaching out with her *laran* senses. Now, with her barrier down, she felt Raimond's polished mind as he assembled the Tower into a circle.

Ashara had not gone more than a few steps down the icy corridor when a ripple of inhumanly powerful mental energy slammed her against the wall. She staggered and barely caught herself from falling.

Blessed Cassilda! She'd never in her life felt anything like that—*laran* with no taint of human personality, a warping of the basic forces that held matter together. She scrambled to her feet and raced downstairs.

His face frozen in concentration, Raimond bent over the great matrix screen which was the heart of Hali Tower. Around him, pale and eerie in its blue light, sat the two Underkeepers, technicians, and senior monitors.

Ashara slipped into place across the circle from him and clasped hands with the workers on either side.

Without warning, the psychic firmament flexed once more, as if nature itself were being uprooted. Ashara's breath was squeezed from her lungs and her vision darkened. Stone walls cracked and splintered. The Tower seemed to sway on its very foundations.

With a few practiced breaths, Ashara settled her

body into a trance state. For a moment she seemed to hover above Hali Tower. She looked down on it and the glimmering Lake, the village where fires had broken out and men scrambled like frantic insects to put them out. She shifted her vision; colors blurred into shadow. Neskaya Tower burned in the far distance like a torch of sorcerous flame.

A crackle of lightning shot out from Neskaya Tower in the direction of Thendara. Corus must have brought the pieces of the Cataclysm device together; he'd spoken of using it in a cause. For an instant, Ashara wished she'd paid more attention to the politics of the day. Varzil had thought them important; he'd said something about a Hastur lord at Thendara—

It didn't matter now. The lightning arched above her, swelling and branching. More and more tendrils shot out from its trunk, curving down toward the earth. Where each slender branch touched the earth, a noise like thunder rolled through the air. Rock crumbled to powder, trees and buildings to smoke.

Ashara, with her trained sensitivity, felt the collapse of the very forces binding matter together. The Cataclysm device, like a monster out of legend, seemed to gain new intensity from each disintegration.

Around her physical body came wails of terror and despair. Dimly she heard the other workers gasping, sobbing. Someone screamed and a body thudded to the floor. Only Raimond held firm, desperately trying to keep his circle together. But his *leroni* were slipping away, his own powers too weak to hold them.

Raimond! Ashara *reached* for him and, after a startled instant, he linked his mind with hers. She searched the Tower for those whose will and reason had not been broken by the awesome psychic forces raging overhead. She found a few—less than half—and brought them into the circle. Quickly she gathered their *laran* energies, weaving them together as she would a skein of finest silk, spinning a web of protection around the Tower.

The rumbling retreated to a muted, barely audible sound. The stone floor steadied under her feet.

"Thanks be," someone murmured. "We're safe."

The circle began to break up. "No!" Ashara commanded. "It must be destroyed!"

"That?" Raimond stared at her, his face white, mouth stretched taut. "How? It's beyond any of our powers. I can't—"

"But I can!" She would have to link with other circles in other Towers, too far for ordinary *laran* to reach. Yet there was another way. . . .

Ashara gathered the *laran* energy from the Hali circle and burst into the overworld in a blaze of shimmering blue fire. Gashes of lurid red and black cut through the usually featureless gray landscape. Hills and crevices of blood-soaked dust surrounded her. To one side, Comyn Tower in Thendara writhed and shrieked as if it were a living thing. Inside, its defenders flared and died like embers. Their screams echoed through her mind.

Opposite it, Neskaya Tower blazed, spewing forth supernatural fire. Everything it touched turned to ashes and then to nothingness, worse than any *clingfire*. Ragged holes appeared in the very fabric of the overworld. Then the attack lessened, as if the device were recharging.

Ashara!

Behind her stood a young woman she instantly recognized as the mental image of Ellimara of Corandolis. She reached out her hand. Ashara took it and felt a surge of power—Ellimara and all of her circle that yet remained.

With all her inborn talent and skill, honed by desperation and years of rigorous training, Ashara visualized a Circle extending the length of the Domains. She had been right to move the struggle to the overworld, for here distance meant nothing. She found herself surrounded by human forms, some solid, others flickering and insubstantial.

With a Keeper's firm touch, she bought them all into the circle—Arilinn, Nevarsin, far Dalereuth, and Tramontana. Even Mikhail at Comyn Tower answered her. The next instant, they stood, hands and minds joined, around the inferno that had been Neskaya. With a quick, sure touch, she shaped their forces into a net, then a blanket, and cast it over the Tower.

For a moment nothing happened, then Neskaya erupted in an explosion of raging, mindless energy. It seared Ashara's psychic form and threatened to blast through the shield. Ashara tensed, but her circle held.

Suddenly she felt the shift in the device's focus. No longer was its destructive force directed at Thendara, it was now aimed directly at her circle.

The foundation of the overworld quivered like a living thing and the blanket which Ashara had visualized began to tear and shred. Promontories of flame burst through it, leaping into jagged white lightning as they rampaged outward.

Hold! Ashara cried, even as the fabric of the blanket disintegrated into tatters. Fire raced along the circle, seizing the men and women. Their psychic bodies blurred until all Ashara could see was a skeleton outline of their glowing *laran* channels.

Screams pierced the air, cries of stark agony. Arnad of Arilinn winked out of sight, his aged heart unable to withstand the strain. Mikhail of Comyn Tower arched backward, his physic body laced with red like molten metal. Something deep within him exploded. His body blew apart into scraps of ashes.

Ashara desperately tried to reform her circle. Not even Varzil himself would have had the power to hold them together. But the next instant, a pattern leapt to her mind. Around her, some *leroni* struggled and died while others continued, strong but fewer each passing moment. The key was right in front of her—the pulsing red sexual energy blocking their channels. The Cataclysm device was somehow tuned to that energy, perhaps a bizarre reversal of the process of life creation. Every sexually active man or woman who'd worked on it and now battled it was drawn into its perverted pattern.

Only I can withstand it, Ashara realized. *I and others like me.*

Instantly she sorted through the giant circle, seeking those workers who, through training or personal choice, had remained chaste. Their minds joined hers in a blaze like purest blue fire. She formed the energy into walls of solid, impenetrable ice, blocking the Cataclysm device's lightning on every side.

Moment after moment, the fire grew less fierce. Then a tremendous explosion rocked the overworld, contained within the blue ice crystal of Ashara's circle, and gradually died away into silence.

Days later, Ashara awoke, shivering, in her room in Hali Tower. Cheria, the young monitor, bent over her with an anxious expression. Ashara sat up and tried to speak. She was too exhausted to form words, too exhausted to reach out with her *laran*. But not too exhausted to realize that of all the Keepers on Darkover, all that remained were Ellimara of Corandolis, part-*chieri* Raimond Lindir, and herself.

The other Towers did not argue for long, even what was left of Neskaya. The choice was to accept

Ashara's terms or their own slow death. They could limp by for only a few years with their Underkeepers, doing mostly low-level work. It would take far longer for the widespread destruction of the Cataclysm device, even contained as it was, to be reversed.

"I will train your new Keepers," Ashara told them, "but I will train them *in my own way*." They had all agreed to send her their best novices—young girls only, as she demanded.

But, Ashara reminded herself, the memories of men were as short as their gratitude. Look at how quickly they'd abandoned Varzil's teachings, when it was expedient to do so.

I will not allow that to happen again. Varzil might die and be forgotten, but I will not!

She would train virgin Keepers for as long as she was able, and after that, she would build a new Tower in Thendara. Ashara's Tower. From there, she would find a way for the work to continue until no one dared question her methods.

She could not know it would take the death of Cleindori Aillard, hundreds of years in the future, to reverse the harm she would do.

Power

by Lynne Armstrong-Jones

Lynne is in her thirties, has a small son and a fairly young daughter, and lives in Canada. In addition to being one of the more prolific writers I know, she teaches English to adult students, and she has recently begun studying karate.

She is also working on a novel, though with such young children it will be some time before she starts circulating it to editors. Not too long, we hope.

She was too old for this. Of *that*, she was certain.

Her heart pounded, pounded, thudded against her rib cage, while her burning lungs screamed for air. Yet she continued, for she had no choice.

Her tongue fought against the dryness inside her mouth, her throat so thick she couldn't swallow. She stopped, one hand against the trunk of a small tree. Gasping, she sucked in the precious air, almost sobbing. A shaking hand wiped at the sweat on her brow, then moved downward, pausing at the feel of the silk pouch around her neck.

Her starstone. Once almost a part of her; no, it *was*—had indeed been—a very part of her. A door to the overworld, to her power, to her identity as Ginevra, the skilled and respected *leronis*. And then, as she'd aged, it seemed her *laran* had dwindled.

She bit her lip, fighting the tears that blurred her vision, the lump that sought escape from her aching throat. Blinking the tears away, she watched helplessly as the two children were carried off: The children, her charges, the ones she most cared about!

"No," she whispered. "No. I can't *let* them!" Already her fingers caressed the starstone, her eyes closed as her mind reached out, out—and found only the blackness of nothing.

"No," Ginevra whispered again, this time struggling up to watch the fleeing forms of the kidnappers.

No. If she had to die trying, she would. Little Eduin and Carletta would *not* become pawns in this cursed battle! Gritting her teeth, she clutched her robe in sweaty fingers and stepped gingerly among the trees, gray eyes never straying from those silhouettes ahead.

Despair became anger; anger at the *doms* for squabbling continually for control of the area, anger at the kidnappers for seizing the precious little ones, anger at herself for losing the power she'd developed and used with such skill only, it seemed, a few years before.

But the energy of anger lit something inside her; a spark became flame, and she hastened in her pursuit. Her fingers clutched at the starstone once more, almost as though they refused to accept the message of uselessness playing over and over in Ginevra's mind. Helpless, helpless ... hopeless. ...

But fury had her grinding her teeth, shaking her head. No! It would not be! It *could* not.

The jolt almost knocked her to the ground. She put a hand to her head, the other seizing a nearby trunk for support. What—?

Ginevra scanned the dark skies, but the sparkle of stars and the gleam of the fourth moon said it had *not* been thunder. Her fingers moved to her starstone. The energy was *here!* Dwindling ... dormant ... *dead,* she'd thought. And yet now a hint, a murmur of life.

Yes! Her fingers curled around the stone, and she squeezed her eyes shut. Did she have the power? Could she?

No! Forget all that. Just concentrate, *focus* . . . let all concerns drift away until there was just . . . *laran* . . .

She could see *them* now, the *laran* serving as her vision. Two large men, two children. A face, an achingly innocent face, peering over a broad shoulder, wide eyes closing sleepily despite the constant jostling. And the other, the elder, carried roughly, dangling over the shoulder of the other man. Limply. Too limply. Oh, blessed Avarra, let her be all right!

Ginevra fought, seizing every spark, every ember of energy inside. *Chiya, hear me, feel me*—In the vision, she saw the child move against that shoulder, heard—felt—the groan, the whimper as consciousness returned. Then—silence. Darkness. No sound, nothing but blackness . . .

She opened her eyes, closed them, disoriented. Fatigue settled across her shoulders like a heavy blanket, weighing her down. She'd lost the rapport!

She had to find them. *Had* to! Teeth clenched once more, she pulled her cloak around herself, setting off in the direction her *laran*'d said they'd taken.

An old, useless woman. That's all I'm getting to be! Little more than head-blind. . . .

After a time, she could make out a soft glow. Evidently they'd stopped. Breathing heavily, she stepped quietly in that direction. And, by the light of their fire, she could see them. *Arrogant bastards!* So confident they knew they had time to stop and *eat!*

She closed her eyes and drew a long breath, letting it out very slowly. *What* could she *do?* One woman, alone and nearly head-blind, facing two large and armed men. If *only* she still had her *laran*. If only . . .

Suddenly Ginevra stood taller, straightening her

cramped shoulders and tossing her hood back with a
snap of her neck. She pulled her starstone from beneath her blouse and held it in the palm of her open
hand.

She stepped into the light, eyes hungry for the sight
of those children. Little Eduin, asleep yet on a blanket
beside the log where the smaller man sat. And Carletta,
seated forlornly across, beside the taller kidnapper.
Ginevra took another step, her gray eyes locking with
the deep blue ones of the girl. *Read my eyes, chiya!
See my message!*

The larger man stood slowly, pausing to spit upon
the ground. Brown eyes returned Ginevra's stare defiantly, confidently. The large man smirked, nodded in
his companion's direction. "Well, then, Greg, it seems
we have a new hostage! Or do you think she's just
looking for company?"

"No! Wait! Listen, Dev! She's got a starstone! She
must be the household *leronis,* Dev!" And, in a more
hushed voice, he added: "In the name of Zandru, Dev,
she's got *laran!*"

Dev shifted his weight to his other foot, spat again,
shifting his gaze from Ginevra to his companion, then
back to the woman.

"An old thing like this, Greg? C'mon!"

"It's true," piped a young voice from beside him.
Carletta rose to her feet, but Dev shoved her back
down roughly.

"I am Ginevra, the household *leronis* of *Dom*
Lennart. In the names of Avarra and Evanda, I demand
the release of the children." Her voice was soft,
gentle—yet strong with command.

Dev looked at his companion, who nodded urgently.
But he turned once more to the *leronis.* "It's been said
that there *is* no *leronis* in Lennart's home. There was

once, but her skills dwindled and grew cold, they say. If you be she, we've naught to fear, old woman."

She took a step closer, eyes never leaving those of the large man. "I am the *leronis* of *Dom* Lennart. Do not seek to defy me."

"Listen, Dev! Listen to her! I—I've seen what *laran* can—"

"Shut up! Shut your face so I can think." Dev turned his gaze once more to the woman.

His eyes glowed still with smugness. Yet, for just a moment, she'd seen him start, then hesitate. She licked her lips—

SNAP!

And they were jumping, startled once more, this time even little Eduin's eyelids shooting upward.

"A catman," Ginevra declared quickly, "under *laran* control. Should you refuse my demands, I'll have him attack!"

But now Dev was glancing again at his trembling companion, who was already loosening the boy's bonds.

"No! She's bluffing. Our information said she's beyond being a threat."

"Then what was that—that *noise?*"

"Something. *Any*thing. Just a—an animal—"

"Yeah, Dev. Like a *catman!* I'd rather face all of Zandru's hells!"

And Dev had to step around the fire, his back to Carletta, to stay his companion's hands.

CRACK!

Closer this time.

"Dev! Listen!"

"I heard it, you fool. Let go my hand!"

Ginevra pulled her gaze from the girl's, sending her most penetrating stare in Dev's direction. "Do you wish a demonstration of my power?"

"NO!"

"Yes."

The two men glared at each other, then Dev met the *leronis'* eyes. "Yes," he repeated.

Ginevra lowered her gaze to her starstone. "Death to the girl," she said softly. "Death is preferable to what you kidnappers have in store."

And silence surrounded the little group, but for only an instant—A gurgling, strangling sound came from Carletta, who suddenly slumped, falling to her side as a trail of crimson oozed from her lips.

"No!" Eduin struggled to reach her, but could not break free of his bonds.

"I can do the same with the catman," Ginevra said softly. "But I will do so only once you've released the boy to me. Otherwise, I'll simply kill him, too. What would your master, dear *Dom* Arran, say if you returned with the children *dead*? He might just be angry enough to kill you. Or perhaps I'll simply do that myself. But ... no. I *did* promise the catman. ..."

Dev let Greg pull him away from the area. The *leronis* could hear the whinnies of the mounts in the distance. She listened to the sound of their hoofbeats growing fainter, thinking with satisfaction of the reaction of their master as they returned empty-handed.

It took a moment before the little boy's whimpers penetrated Ginevra's thoughts. "Oh, *chiyu!*" She hurried to his side to release him.

"Is it safe now, Ginevra?" asked the other young voice.

"Yes, *chiya*. Quite so."

She looked in the girl's direction, seeing not a dirty, tired child, but a quick-witted young adult-to-be who'd someday do well for herself.

"Ow," moaned the girl, "I wish I hadn't bitten my lip *quite* so hard."

"Ah, *chiya*, but if you hadn't, they'd not have *believed* us!"

She helped Carletta to her feet, then embraced both children. "And thank you for thinking quickly enough to throw those stones while his back was turned! They made wonderful 'catman footsteps'!"

The girl smiled. "Thank *you* for being the most skillful *leronis* I've ever known!"

Ginevra sighed. Whatever she was didn't matter. Her dear ones were safe!

Upholding Tradition

by Chel Avery

I should have known somebody would sooner or later call my bluff. When asked for an update of her biography this year, and told that otherwise I'd make up something, Chel replied that she was really curious about what I'd make up about her. So she didn't update her autobiography and blithely told me to invent something. But while it's a temptation to make up something really outrageous, and say she's a Franciscan ex-nun who's teaching judo—or herding dragons—in Timbuktu or Borneo, I'm sure many of you remember I've printed her fiction before, enabling me to go back and look up what I said last time.

Of course, she has moved from Pennsylvania to Virginia, so I really don't know precisely what she's doing now. I think, however, that if she were herding dragons I would have seen something about it in the tabloids.

Leonie of Arillin received the Heir of Hastur in her private chambers. He was, after all, her own twin brother.

Lorill stood awkwardly in the doorway. The Keeper of Arillin was perhaps the only person in all the Domains, save his own father, who was not in awe of him. In years past, Leonie would have rushed to meet him with kisses and laughter and a loving embrace. But now she was Keeper in the most powerful of the

Towers, draped in Keeper's crimson that warned all around to keep their distance, to take care not to violate her with even the most casual touch or familiarity. Except for the lightest feather stroke of her fingers on his wrist, Leonie had not touched Lorill in more than three years. Each time he saw her she seemed more distant, more inaccessible. Had they ever even laughed together since the first time she passed through Arillin's Veil?

Leonie did not rise from the straight-backed chair in her austere chamber. She looked directly into her brother's eyes as only a Keeper or near kinswoman would dare to do, and Lorill observed, abstractedly, that she was still a stunning beauty, in the impersonal way a formal tapestry or carved ebony panel might be called beautiful.

In her lap lay a bundle so tiny it belied the great furor it had caused in the Hastur chambers at Comyn Castle, a wee infant, making soft smacking noises in its sleep. Leonie's voice was low and modulated. "Welcome, brother. May I guess the purpose of this visit?"

"I think, even without the benefit of *laran,* you would not have to guess much to know why I have come. Our mother's women are all humming like bees about the scandal at Arillin. Tell me it is not true."

"I cannot tell you what is true and what is false without knowing what you have heard."

"I have heard that Leonie of Arillin has taken into her personal care an infant girl, which she proposes to raise as her own fosterling, within the very walls of Arillin Tower. About the parentage of this child, I have heard many things, all of them fantastic, most of them scandalous."

Leonie's reply was haughty. "The stories of idle Comynara and the squawking of laying hens are none of my concern. Nonetheless, I assure you, brother, the mother of this child is well born, a *nedestro* daughter of Hastur by a highborn daughter of Aillard. Need I say more?"

"You have said enough to let me guess the rest. If the mother is who I believe, and you know I have reason to be interested, then the child is six-fathered, by a pack of bandits of the Kilghard Hills."

Leonie did not even flinch at this worst of insults. "And what if she is? Why is it such a scandal for a child to be fathered by bandits on a daughter of Comyn, yet if her mother were common and her father were Lord Alton or a Ridenow, or you yourself, there would be no shame? Notice would be taken whether she was being raised by decent folk, and if there were doubt, some fosterage would be arranged with one of our lesser septs. When she reached a certain age, a *leronis* would happen to pass through her village and observe her potential. And if she had *laran* and showed promise, she would be admitted to Neskaya Tower, or a small dowry would be settled on her so that she might be married to a landholder or an officer in the Guards. Why should she be cast aside when it is her father, rather than her mother, who is lowborn?" Though the words were stern, even angry, Leonie's careful control did not waver. She might have been speaking about which fruits would next ripen in the greenhouse.

Lorill took a seat by the fire, a luxury his sister did not normally allow herself in her own rooms. It must have been laid for the child's sake, but he was glad to see a little comfort in Leonie's austere life, even if it was only a fire in the hearth. "You misunderstand me, Leonie. I have no wish to cast aside the child or punish her. On the contrary, I propose sending her with one of my men who is returning to his holding near Armida.

He is married *di catenas* to a fine woman who has no children of her own, and she would care well for this little one."

The babe awoke and began to fret. Leonie rang a bell and a plump, matronly woman came to gather up the child. Lorill wondered how it had been possible to find a woman able to pass through the Veil of Arillin who was willing to serve as a wet nurse. Well, Leonie's influence was far reaching, perhaps even more so than his own.

When the woman left, Leonie rose from her chair and walked to the fire, gazing into its flames. After a while, she turned back. "Thank you for your kind offer, Lorill. I am glad you would do well by this child, but I have other plans. I intend to keep her myself."

Lorill ignored her tone of dismissal. "Leonie," he said gently, "you must know how preposterous this is. It has not been done, not ever. We are progressed far beyond the dark days when a Keeper was surgically neutered and bound to her station for life. If you long so much for a child, give up your post, and I will arrange a marriage for you. But a Keeper cannot foster a child. It has never been done."

"It shall be done. I will do it. I have no wish to leave Arillin, but I do wish to foster the babe. May I remind you, a Keeper is responsible only to her own conscience."

"So it is true. I am not contesting your right. But why, Leonie? What is your reason? You are respected, admired, even feared. Will you trade all that for a whim? At least tell me why."

Leonie sat silent. She wished she could make Lorill understand, wished his *laran* were stronger so he would know telepathically, without explanation, wished she had not been trained to hold herself in such

strict reserve that she could not somehow spill forth
her feelings and make him see.

"To be a Keeper," she spoke slowly, "is to learn to
be . . . not human. To withdraw so much that I have no
desires, that the desires of men and of women cannot
touch me. It means giving up so much. I have let go of
the warmth and love of others my age. But a child does
not threaten the *energon* flows in my body. It does not
threaten the purity of focus in my mind and nerves that
a Keeper needs. A child is possible for me. And *this*
child, this child was entrusted to me by one who could
not bear to keep her and who could trust no one else.
I believe it is well done that she stay with me."

Lorill sighed. "I wish I could be so sure. Leonie,
don't you understand, a mistake at this time would be
more than just a mistake? The old traditions are in danger. There are people on our world who have come
from the stars with customs and powers that threaten
our way of life, that threaten the very Compact. They
have gone among the Aldarans, and at Caer Donn they
have built what they call a "spaceport"—a great complex of buildings, higher than any Tower or structure
in Thendara. I have only seen them from a distance,
but they are wonderful and terrifying, not like anything
else I have ever seen. My plan, when my time comes
to succeed Father, is to bring them to Thendara, where
we might better shape the role they play on our world.
But think, sister, how our people will see new ways, be
tempted by new things, and may no longer trust
Comyn Council or the Towers to lead them. And if
they see the Hasturs themselves breaking tradition,
what will they think then? You are a Hastur and
Keeper of Arillin. It is a sacred trust. Please, set this
notion aside before the rumors spread further still."

"I am weary of sacred trusts. I have already given
my whole life and the greatest part of my humanity."

Leonie's voice was controlled and deep, but with an edge of anger. She stood silent for a moment, and Lorill watched her pull air deliberately into the deepness of her lungs in one of the most rudimentary exercises of *laran* control. "I will think about it, Lorill," she said finally. "I can promise you that much." She walked from the fire to his side. "Will you stay to dine with me?"

"No, I must return quickly." He rose to leave, then turned back. "Does she have a name?"

It took Leonie a moment to realize he was asking about the child. "I have named her Ferrika."

Lorill smiled. "When we were children, that was the name of your imaginary friend."

"And I always said, if I had a daughter, I would name her Ferrika."

"No Hastur ever bore that name."

"One does now."

Alone in her chamber, Leonie wished she felt half the certainty she had portrayed to Lorill. Could she do it? Could she live the life of a Keeper, set apart, impersonal, surrounded by mystique, and yet mother a child? If she could, why had no Keeper done it before?

Yet, when she held little Ferrika in her arms, she felt alive in a way she had forgotten over the many years of her strict Keeper's discipline. Something cold in her drained away when she cuddled the warm, squirming bundle or felt Ferrika's sleeping weight in her arms. Why could she not have this? The price she paid to be Keeper was so high. Was it not only fair that she have this one joy in her life?

She slipped quietly into the adjoining room where the still form of what once had been a young woman lay in *laran*-induced sleep. Passing her hands a few inches above the body, Leonie monitored it, satisfying herself that no infection or decay had set in, that the wounds were healing cleanly from the drastic alterations Leonie herself had performed illegally—no, not illegally, she reminded herself. The Keeper of Arillin is a law unto herself, and need answer only to her own conscience.

In sleep, the face that was once beautiful, and was still heartbreakingly young, held little of the anguish that had marked it so deeply a few tendays earlier when Leonie had consented to meet the distraught young noblewoman in Arillin's receiving room.

Then, this poor child had been many things that she was no longer. A woman. Pregnant. Bearing a name that was honorable, though recently tinged by scandal. Miserable and on the verge of suicide. It was the threat of suicide, and Leonie's sure knowledge that the girl meant it, that had finally persuaded Leonie to grant her request and perform the forbidden neutering procedure so she no longer need fear the unwanted attentions of men, so she no longer need fear seizure and rape. But not until after the child was born.

"I will never bear the name of Elorie Lindir again," the child-woman vowed. "I want to forget. Can you take away even the memory of what they have done to me?"

"Only at the cost of your *laran*. Would you live head-blind only to forget?"

"Yes," the girl insisted, but in the end, Leonie had consented only to a compromise. Memory and *laran* were dulled, but not beyond recovery.

"It is drastic enough to alter your body beyond ever living again as a woman, beyond ever bearing another child, beyond knowing love."

"Those are all choices you have made," Elorie reminded her.

"But not irrevocably. And having known their price, I do this to you only with regret and in great doubt. I do it in compassion for your pain, even though you will have none of the rewards I have had. But I will not also destroy forever the part of your mind that makes you who you are, that will let you understand the choice you have made, if a time ever comes that you regret it."

"Such a time will never come. Never, never."

Leonie sequestered the girl at Arillin, waiting for the birth of the baby, then, when Elorie lay spent and exhausted in her childbed, Leonie gave her what she had pleaded for with such great anguish, at the same time dulling her memory so that she would not be haunted more than she could withstand by bitter memories of rape, rejection, and the birth of a child never seen.

And in exchange, Leonie had kept the child for herself.

Later, when the nurse returned little Ferrika, Leonie walked with her back and forth before the fire, humming a little song her own nurse had often hummed to her, and which she had forgotten until that day.

It seemed to Leonie that so much had changed. She let the infant grasp her finger, delighting in the strength of the tiny fingers. So many simple things, things she hadn't noticed, held new delight. The warmth of the fire, the softness of the marl fur that lined her shawl, the taste of the ale and nutcakes brought for her dinner.

She touched her finger to the tiny button nose that promised, someday, to tilt upward. In training to be Keeper, she had learned to be strong, not to mind little discomforts, not to be distracted by small pleasures, but surely, it wasn't necessary to forget all the common delights that made life satisfying. Surely she could both be strong and know joy.

Surely she could be both Keeper and foster mother.

When Ferrika slept, Leonie gave her back into the care of the nurse and joined the others of the First Circle as they gathered in preparation for the night's work. She sensed a hush as she walked into the room. It was the silence not merely of stilled speech, but of quickly stilled thoughts.

So, they were talking about me. No need for this sudden silence, though. It is not as if we have any secrets at all from each other.

Indeed, she had known for several moons that Mario, the young technician who now stood to offer her his seat, had loved her with a remote and hopeless passion. She was only distantly conscious of her own beauty, and of its effect on some of the men at Arillin. Mario was not the first nor, most likely, the last to succumb, but the sacrosanct aura that surrounded her, like her crimson robes, kept them at a distance, kept them exercising careful control over their feelings, and she was able to ignore them, so their love was never more distracting than a light snowfall on a warm day.

Alida Ardais, First Technician, made no pretense of hiding anything. She was a few years older than Leonie, and only her impatience with a Keeper's sequestered life, and her preference to move in and out of the affairs of both the Towers and the Domains, had kept her from becoming a powerful Keeper in her own right. She spoke with authority. "Leonie, until now you have been the most powerful and least questioned Keeper in living memory. If you persist with this ridiculous undertaking, you will jeopardize your own reputation and Arillin's place as first among the Towers. I would not presume to criticize you, but . . ."

Leonie cut her off. "If you would not presume to criticize me," she said impatiently, "then don't." Again, a hush fell over the room. Leonie thought, *I must make them understand, or at least get them to accept this new step. But not until I can better understand it myself.*

"Shall we begin?" she asked, leading the way to the adjoining room that housed the ninth level matrix they used for mining ore.

The night's work progressed in routine fashion. Leonie wove the gathered minds together and focused their joined concentration through the matrix for the single-purposed accomplishment of their task. But she was remotely aware that the effort was more wearying than usual, that instead of the sharp clarity she usually felt, there was fuzziness in their connection. Young Mario's longing for her love, usually so easy to ignore, niggled at the edges of her attention, as if her mental feet were hobbled by mismatched shoes. When Donal, their monitor, broke the circle a half hour earlier than usual, she found herself wondering if she might have to send Mario away, rather than bear the weight of awareness of his forbidden love.

Alida grumbled about their poor performance of the night. "What's wrong with us? Donal, is someone sick?"

"No," Donal replied. "Everyone just seemed too tired, especially Leonie. It happens. Don't worry about it."

Leonie didn't wait to hear Alida's response. She picked up a piece of fruit to eat in her room, said good night, and went to bed.

She woke up mid-dream to the sound of Ferrika crying. The nurse was picking her up to take her away.

"I'll feed her, Lady, and when I bring her back, I'm sure she'll sleep quietly."

But Leonie could not get back to sleep. Her dreams oppressed her. Something about Elorie Lindir's pain, about Mario's longing that he was trying so hard to suppress, about caged birds beating their wings against the bars and breaking their feathers.

When the nurse brought back the baby, Leonie said, "Give her to me. I'll have her sleep here in my bed." She sensed the nurse's disapproval, but the woman would not speak against a Keeper. She set Ferrika in the bed, and Leonie lay beside her, sensing the simple infant feelings, the satisfying aftertaste of milk, the deepness of sleep. Slowly, Leonie began to sink into drowsiness, her dreams returning. The birds stopped beating in their cages, folded their wings at their sides, huddled together on their perches, preening their feathers. Her sense of Mario returned. Almost cozily, she felt his tenderness toward her, his joy in her face, in their psychic rapport. . . .

Leonie jerked awake. *Merciful Avarra, they are all right to be worried!* As a Keeper, she had been trained to screen out all awareness of sexuality, all feelings of passion, all thoughts or feelings that could possibly disrupt the energy pathways in her body that she used to channel the powerful psi flows during matrix work. She had been ruthlessly trained into absolute control over her every thought, feeling, sensation, just as those around her had learned never to intrude on her peace with outward touch or inward thoughts about her. But what was happening to her now was more insidious than anything she had been prepared for.

It was not that having Ferrika with her threatened in any way her ability to exercise full control. But she was losing her will to use that ability, she no longer *wanted* to screen out awareness of Mario's love, she no

longer wished to be impervious. Where before she was
without interest, now she cared to notice the warmth of
the fire, the softness of fur, the tenderness of a man's
thoughts. . . .

Her power was fully intact. Her will to use that
power over herself, over her own thoughts and feelings, was fraying, softening.

*This is something no Keeper should ever learn
about.*

Sadly, and with a sense of doom, she rose from her
bed and carefully lifted the sleeping Ferrika, ruthlessly
refusing to let herself dwell on the warm weight in her
arms, as she carried the infant to her cradle.

She reminded herself that she had not wept since the
day she first wore crimson.

"Thank you for returning so soon, Lorill."

"She will be well cared for in the Alton Domain.
You need have no fear for her." The nurse was mounting a horse behind a middle-aged couple who beamed
proudly. The man still wore the kind of boots preferred
by the Guard and carried his sword like a professional.

"Do you really believe, Lorill, that protecting our
traditions, without change, is so very important?"

"Maybe not forever, but for now, yes. These coming
years, with the Terrans among the Aldarans—we know
so little of them—we are at such risk of losing our au-
tonomy, our very identity. We need something stable to
hold onto. The Keeper of Arillin is one of our points of
stability. Whatever it costs you, Leonie, it is worth the
price."

"I hope so, Lorill, I truly hope it is worth the price."
She caught her last glimpse of Ferrika as the nurse
wrapped her in a thick blanket. "Because the price is
high."

As she watched them ride away, she had a moment

of foreknowing of Ferrika moving forward into a future she herself could know nothing of, moving into a knowledge of the world that Leonie would serve all her life without ever really understanding. And Leonie wondered if instead of upholding tradition, somehow she was helping to bring on its doom.

She remembered a proverb her mother was fond of quoting about the difference between humans and beasts: "Only men laugh, only men dance, only men weep." The Keeper of Arillin did none of these things.

She drew her red robes closely around herself as she wrapped her mind in a mental barrier against distractions. She walked through the Veil of Arillin and moved back toward the life she had been trained for.

The Place Between

by Diana L. Paxson

Everything Diana Paxson writes is good—which is why I've chosen her to collaborate with me on the novel of Roman Britain that I've been writing for much of my adult life. Diana writes much more meticulously researched historical material than I do—and I had literally been working on this particular book so long that I could no longer see THE FOREST HOUSE for the trees.

Diana's age, at the moment, I've forgotten—she seems young compared to me; but then, everybody is young compared to me, except maybe Lester del Rey. This present story deals with the period of CITY OF SORCERY, and with a Terran expedition commanded by a Free Amazon. But although many—too many—of the stories I have read have dealt with this much-attempted theme, she's the first person who ever did it well enough that I really wanted to print it. (If I had a nickel for every unoriginal and wholly uninspired Free Amazon story I've read, I could publish a lot more of the good ones.)

Diana lives in Berkeley, California, about a mile from me, and has many books both in and out of print. She also has two adult sons, Ian and Robin.

Lian n'ha Galia bent over the power-pile of the crawler which had been the sole transport of the Terran Institute of Xeno-Archaeology's expedition to search for a legendary Trailman Shrine.

"Now do you believe me? There's a distort in the rods, and no spares nearer than Thendara!" Tony Righteous, the expedition's transport engineer, stood back and wiped his hands on his coverall. "It will be completely dead by dark." He squinted at the horizon. The light of the red sun was always dim, but the twilight had certainly increased since they started looking at the crawler. "It's this rotten climate; colder than Satan's hind end!" The duralloy boomed hollowly as he kicked it.

Lian watched him tromp through the dirty snow to the hillock where the others were making camp. There was a friendly orange flicker as someone started a fire. Beyond it, the rays of the setting sun painted the surrounding mountains in garish shades of purple and rose. As trail-boss for the expedition; she wished they had brought chervines or ponies—something she could understand. The longer the journey went on, the less she knew what she was doing here.

Her eyes narrowed as she glimpsed the grizzled head of the Volsung Scholar Wandirr Gar'hi—leader of the expedition, Director of the Institute of Xeno-Archaeology, and the employer to whom she had sworn her oath. How could she tell him that the expedition for which he had prepared for so long was over?

Ill news grows no fresher with keeping—a favorite proverb of her armsmistress surfaced. Her lips twisted in something that was not quite a smile, and she moved lightly across the broken ground to the fire.

"One would have thought that a *Terran* engineer could at least tell us what is wrong with his machine. . . ."

Lian recognized the cultured, lazy tones before she

saw the man—Vasco-Mikhail Donato, the expedition's Armsman. She moved faster.

"The personnel for this expedition were chosen with care, Donato, all expert in their own fields," rumbled Wandirr Gar'hi. "No one here has any reason for sabotage."

Tony had the knowledge, but too much pride. Sara Jordin, the botanist, did not possess the expertise. Scholar Wandirr had planned the expedition, hoping for proof of a lost technology behind the legends of Power Places among the Trailmen. Lian's eyes flicked from the Director to Deuu, their guide. Technically his race were humanoid, though their small size, furry bodies, and primitive culture made them seem more alien to Terrans than Wandirr, or even the botanist's assistant, Tee. For untold generations the Trailmen had been confined to a few densely forested valleys between the Hellers and the Wall Around the World. Deuu would not have known how to disable a machine if he had tried.

And what about me? she thought then. *Would I try to stop this expedition if I knew what it would find?*

"I don't know what went wrong, but I'm going to find out!" Tony exclaimed. "I can stay here with the crawler while you folks hike back to Thendara for a new machine, or if worst comes to worst, for spare rods."

"*Are* we returning to Thendra?" asked Donato.

"That is indeed the question," said Wandirr gently.

"Return? What's wrong?" Sara Jordin turned from the specimens she was packing.

"Please, Scholar Jordin, and you also, Master Tee—I think I must ask you to join us." Wandirr gestured toward the space beside him.

Sara grimaced at the slushy ground, spread her rain-shield near the fire, and sat down. Tee padded cheer-

fully after her and curled itself nearby. Unlike most
sentients, Tee's people had maintained a horizontal
body posture. Basically saurian, they were also
hexapodal, so that Tee's appearance suggested a very
flexible Terran crocodile with a shorter, less fero-
ciously toothed head and an extra pair of four-digited
arms.

Sara, being small for a human, said she enjoyed not
having to look up to her assistant. Tee had, in addition,
an excellent instinct for locating rare plant species and
hardly any sense of caution, much less fear.

Wandirr signaled to Deuu. The Trailman picked up
several pieces of wood and built them into the fire, balancing them precisely and waiting until they had
caught before returning to his place in the shadows.

"This trip is Jonahed, sir!" Tony's politeness verified
his conviction. "Send someone back for more transport
or go yourself. You can try again another time."

If there was another time, thought Lian. Rumor had
it that Wandirr had had to fight his competitors at the
Institute as well as the more xenophobic members of
Comyn Council for this final chance to make his name
immortal.

"Well, Sara, what do you say?" asked Wandirr.

"It's all one to us—" she shrugged. "Tee and I could
keep busy for a year just studying this area. I move
that we wait here."

Wandirr nodded and looked across the fire to Deuu.
"And if we wait the time it would take for someone to
go to Thendara and return? Will we be able to reach
the holy place then?"

Deuu's fur rippled in denial. "Here the year-place—
is only at sun-turn. Here-time, you outworlders—" he
gestured as if the word also meant something outside
of nature, demonic, "you go back. Only the People can

see the Shining-Place. Others are burned by the Maker of Power."

Lian's neck hairs prickled as she recognized the creature's sincerity. Vasco-Mikhail Donato's hand shot out to grip Deuu's shoulder. "You want to keep it for yourselves?" Deuu whistled in alarm as he jerked him closer, holding him dangerously near the fire. "Well, it won't work. Avarra and all her works belong to my people, not yours!"

Lian was already beside him when Donato looked up. Her sword arm tingled as she met the Armsman's pale eyes.

"And what do you think you're doing, Amazon?" Donato's tone was lazy. "You're a cold bitch, but you don't scare me!" With apparent casualness he set Deuu down, but his eyes did not leave Lian.

She met them without flinching, having discovered on their first day out that Donato was the old-fashioned type of Darkovan male that had prompted so many of the "Free Amazons" to renounce men. Did he see her as a warrior, or as a tall, sturdy girl with close-cropped brown hair and an unwomanly stare? She forced herself not to reach for the staff which was really a sheath for her illegal full-length sword.

"Go or stay, we still need our guide," she said evenly. "Don't break him!" Bitch or not, no man had beaten her since she used to practice sword-play with her twin brother, before the blood feud that had destroyed the rest of her family brought him down. She slid back into her place while Donato ostentatiously wiped his hands. The glow that had flared in Wandirr's eyes at the confrontation faded, and he sighed.

"I am old. Another year when the time is right to find the 'Shining-Place' I will not be here. We will go on."

* * *

By the next morning, the crawler was an immobile monument to Terran pride. Deuu touched the inert metal gently, then drew his hand away. Lian, watching, wished she knew more about the aboriginals who lived in the rain forests beyond the Hellers. Could fear have driven one of the others to sabotage the machine, or was it Donato, driven by the Darkovan suspicion of all advanced technology, who had done the job?

Lian shifted her pack and looked at the others, wondering how many of them had motives which were as well disguised as her own. She remembered her final interview with Mother Callea.

"I shudder to think what could happen if some of the devices from the Ages of Chaos got into the wrong hands," the old woman had told her. *"Or this thing they seek could be still stranger. When she came back from seeking the City of Sorcery, Rafaella n'ha Doria reported tales of artifacts in caves beneath the ice from a time before humans of any kind came to this world. I am told that there are people in the Empire who would sell their own mothers for a new technology."*

"But aren't such things the business of the Comyn? Why should we be involved?" Lian had asked. Her main fault, and her strength as well, was her instinct for action. But the expedition already had an Armsman, a bastard Comyn who had served in the City Guard and was clearly meant to be eyes and ears for the Council.

"Because if this place truly has something to do with Avarra as the legends say, even the Towers may not understand it. The forge-folk kept the matrix of Sharra hidden all those years; who knows what secrets the Trailmen may hold? The Council, of course, would like all that to be forgotten, and so they dare not send a leronis. But you may be sure that this Donato will be reporting to one of the Towers."

For a few moments, then, Mother Callea had stayed silent, aware that she had not really answered Lian's question.

"You will not be there for the sake of the Comyn, or the Towers, or even the Guild," she had said then. *"Those Who Hear have had little to say to us for almost a generation. But word has come to us now—the priestesses of Avarra, too, believe that this place may be a long-lost stronghold of the Goddess, and if so, someone who is sworn to the Sisterhood must be there. . . ."*

"Well, *trail-boss*, are you coming with us, or are you going to stand all day with your feet in the muck and your head in the clouds?"

Lian spun to face Donato, with effort straightening from her instinctive swordsman's guard. Blandly she met the other man's stare.

"*You* are the Armsman here," she said softly. "Lead on." With something like disappointment in his eyes, the warrior turned. Lian looked after him, noting the easy strength in his walk. He certainly had all the Comyn pride. *The pride,* she thought, *for which my brother died. . . .*

The others were still milling about. She pulled herself together. If they did not get going soon, it would not matter whose secrets were revealed.

"All right, check your packs and tighten your bootseals. Let's move along." Sketching a salute to Wandirr, Lian took her place at the rear.

For several days they marched without incident through a waste of ice and boulders beneath lowering clouds that hid the horizon. Deuu scuttled along ahead, shivering, obviously longing to descend to his forests once more.

On the fifth day the monotony of the landscape was shattered by a gorge which tore the surface of the land as if giant hands had tried to pull the planet in two. Scarp and slide fell away to shadowy tree-choked depths. The opposite rim was lower, the country beyond it a jumble of forest and glacier scoured hills. Somewhere within them lay their goal.

"I guess it didn't matter about the crawler," Tony Righteous said bleakly. "We could never have gotten it across *this*."

"How are *we* going to get across it?" Sara peered over the edge, shuddered, and drew back again.

"Come!" Deuu motioned impatiently. "No good to cross the Wound in dark."

Only after one got up the nerve to drop over the edge of the gorge did it become apparent that there *was* a path, so treacherous that it required the use of mountaineering gear. Deuu clambered ahead, using hands and prehensile toes with equal facility, and Tee slithered excitedly after him, but the rest of them were roped together and made their way carefully downward in disjointed sections.

When Tony's feet went out from under him, it was Lian who took the shock, nearly becoming part of the slide of mud and stones which disappeared below. Swearing, Donato secured the rope and hoisted himself back to where Tony lay just as Lian eased herself down beside him.

"You clumsy Terran bastard, I told you to watch that ledge!" Donato hissed. "Get up—we can't stay here!"

Tony rolled his head to one side, white-faced beneath the freckles and grime. "I can't use my foot!"

"I don't care if your leg is broken. Move!" Donato's auburn brows pulled together, force radiating from him like heat from a fire. "We can't lose any more time!"

"Leave me here," moaned Tony. "This planet hates me ... leave me alone!"

The others were watching them, pale faces appearing to float in the mists below. Lian cut the rope that bound Sara to Tony.

"Take the others on ahead, Donato," she said quietly. "I'll bring Tony along." She ignored the Armsman's reddening face and the protest he suppressed as Wandirr shouted his aproval, and bent over Tony. "It's not far to the bottom," she said, "and it get easier on the other side."

This was not strictly true, but Lian's skills enabled them to catch up with the others. By the time they got out of the gorge, Tony was only favoring his foot a little and protesting that Sara's side trips in search of specimens would delay them more than his sprain.

"Let both of them stay in a base camp here!" exclaimed Donato that evening as Lian struggled to coax a pile of damp twigs into flame. "We have already been delayed too long. This thing, whatever it is, can only be seen at the solstice, yes? If the Trailman is telling the truth, we have only four days to reach it! And unless we keep to our schedule, our food won't last long enough for us to get there and back to Thendara again."

Lian looked up from the infant fire, trying to read Donato's expression. Why was *he* so concerned? Even if there was a weapon in the legendary shrine, the Comyn Council would forbid anyone to use it. Wandirr was the one for whom this expedition offered a last chance at immortality.

The old Volsung sighed. "I know ... I know ... but I do not wish to divide the party—there are too many unknown dangers here. Let us rest now. In the morning things will look brighter, and we will find a way."

But in the morning, Tony Righteous was dead, and

the time they had hoped to save they spent in burying him.

The engineer had been found sprawled facedown a little way from the camp. The ground here was too broken for Lian to tell if anyone had followed him from the campsite, but surely he could have called for help. Yet the body had lain like a practice dummy with the stuffing gone. Was this an attempt to discourage them, as the disabling of the crawler had been? Or had that been the accident, and was this death the work of someone who wanted desperately to reach their goal?

But the next disaster could not be blamed on anyone in the expedition. They were climbing one of the ridges, picking their way doggedly through the cruel rocks and clinging to Deuu's promise that the Shrine was only two days away. But the Trailman had not anticipated the thing that screeched from the crevice ahead of them.

"Banshee!" The name came out in a terrified squeal as Deuu dashed back toward the others. Lian reached out to him as he passed Wandirr, but got only a touch of wiry muscle knotting beneath smooth fur before he scrambled onto a boulder, keening despairingly.

Behind him, something huge and roughly feathered burst from the rocks, talons slashing far more quickly than a creature that size should be able to move. Donato evaded its first rush with a leap backward, swearing as he tried to bring his ice-axe into play. Lian, with a moment longer to prepare, cursed the law that forced her to conceal her full-length sword as she pulled her long knife free.

Sara, flattened by Wandirr against the rocks, cried out as Tee scuttled forward, gurgling with the sound that for its kind represented glee. Its toothed jaws crunched, and the banshee roared in pain, convulsed, and sent the little saurian flying. Donato swung at the creature's side, but the steel blade, improperly angled or perhaps defeated by the thick feathers, only sheared away an outer layer. It reared, wings buffeting, as Donato swung up the axe to try again.

Lian moved softly across the treacherous surface, allowing her weight to fall only on tested ground. She focused on the swaying horror above her, her mind assessing coldly the relative dangers of beak and talons while her soul reached out for the energy that would let her actions flow in harmony, the secret disciplines of the Sisterhood of the Sword.

Donato shouted and sprang forward, his sword gleaming dimly as it swept toward the banshee's neck. The beast's blind gaze swung in their direction, and in that instant Lian flowed forward, swordarm and body coordinating in one smooth motion that eased her between the flailing claws and drew the blade back and around in a continuous swirl that passed through the wattled throat and sheared off the banshee's right wing.

She waited, knife poised once more in readiness, while Donato hacked at the banshee's neck and it crashed to the ground, rocked up in agony, then fell once more, thrashing with steadily decreasing vigor as its stinking blood gushed onto the ground.

"What are you? They told me you were Darkovan, but the women of your world are not taught so to use the sword!" Wandirr settled back on his haunches and stared at Lian with golden eyes to which some of the sparkle had returned.

"The Renunciates are the only women on our world who are permitted to bear arms, and those only such as the men believe will not threaten their superiority," Lian said bitterly. Long ago the Sisterhood of the Sword and the priestesses of Avarra had joined together to form the Guild of Renunciates, and they re-

tained the skills of both, but they were not encouraged
to flaunt them.

"It seems to me you used that long knife of yours as
well as any sword," Wandirr said, smiling.

Lian shrugged uncomfortably. The Scholar's well-
meaning compliments were opening too many old
wounds. Why indeed should she be forced to hide her
skills to pander to some man's pride?

They had set up a makeshift camp in the first level
space beyond the cul-de-sac in which they had fought
the banshee. Donato and Sara, her eyes red with weeping, were preparing a grave for Tee. The swordsman
paused a moment to look at Lian, his gray eyes kindling momentarily with something between antago-
nism and curiosity. Then he returned to his labor.

But Lian did not need *laran* to guess what he was
thinking. Some people admired those Amazons who
were fighters or thought them romantic. Some feared
them. Some, and Lian suspected that Donato was one
of them, found their very existence a challenge.

"The question that still puzzles me," Wandirr drew
Lian's attention again, "is why I was not told of your
skills."

"Does it matter?" she asked uncomfortably. An oath
once given must be served until its term was done, and
she could only pray that it would not conflict with her
deeper loyalties. "My word binds me to your service.
Just consider that you have one more arm to defend
you than you knew."

She was grateful when Wandirr forbore to press her
further, and after a few minutes she climbed to her feet
and went to help with the burial. When the job was
done and Sara had gone to stare into the fire as if it
held some answer to her pain, Lian found Donato at
her side.

"Interesting." As usual, the Armsman's sardonic

smile made it hard to interpret his words. "I have always wanted to see a Free Amazon in action. Against a beast, at least, I think you are probably as good as a man."

Lian looked at him tiredly, reading his meaning plainly now.

"But intelligence should be allied with skill," Donato went on. "When we come to the Shrine, we may learn if you know how to use another kind of power."

"If there is anything there," Lian replied. The *leronym* of the secret sisterhood swore that the potential for *laran* was in her, but none of them had been able to awaken it. She had always believed that any talent she might have had been focused in her skill with the sword.

"Oh there will be—there *must* be!" Donato said softly. His mocking farewell followed Lian. "Good night, Amazon!"

Lian continued to walk toward her bedroll, but there was to be one more conversation before she could sleep. As she settled into the bag, she saw Deuu materialize from the darkness, and sat up again.

"Warrior-woman fight well . . . in old-time, the People fought monsters. Weak now. Is ice, snow, that kill us now . . . hunting grounds smaller, every festival. . . ."

She started to protest, but the Trailman was gone. She slept badly, haunted by visions of dark-robed women surrounded by clouds of calling crows. It seemed to her that they held a mirror before her, but when she bent to look into it, a banshee's hideous blind head snarled back at her.

Lian squinted up into the silvery mists, thinking that for a moment the clouds had seemed to thin, then sank back again on the rock she had chosen when they stopped for their nooning. *I'm letting fatigue get the best of me,* she thought wryly. *The weather beyond the Hellers doesn't change!*

Deuu hunkered down nearby and on impulse she spoke to him. "Do the clouds ever go away here? Have you ever seen the sky?"

Deuu's expression grew inward. "From the Shining-Place we see Deep Heaven on the Day of Festival. That-time only wakes the Maker of Power. We come too soon, too late—nothing there."

Lian nodded. "A while ago, you said this place would be dangerous to those who were not of your People. What did you mean? Does someone guard it? You know your elders gave permission for us to come."

"Spirits guard," he said softly. "Only People know to see. When great-times come again, Shining gives us power. When power comes, great-time is here. . . ." He got up and stalked away, and Lian realized she would get nothing more from him now.

Considering, she realized that this was the most the Trailman had been willing to say to any of them, and it was doubly remarkable that he should be willing to talk to a female. Had it been because she championed him against Donato or because she slew the banshee?

Someone shouted. Lian was already on her feet as she took in Sara's shocked face and the outrage in every line of Wandirr's body. The Volsung was facing Donato, who held the bag containing their food concentrates with one hand. The other gripped a small stunner.

Donato! Ever since the man had learned Lian was trained in combat his manner had threatened challenge, but why was he holding the stunner on Wandirr, and what was a stunner doing on Darkover anyway? Anger began to kindle within her as she halted before them, her hand on the hilt of her blade.

Donato's eyes flicked from Wandirr to Lian and back again. Wandirr struggled for words.

"The concentrates—"

"The food must be rationed." Donato's crisp speech echoed Wandirr's growl. "We are behind schedule. If we do not make up the time, we will neither find the Shrine nor get back to the pick-up point. Therefore we will eat only when I say, and whoever cannot keep up will be left behind."

"That is ridiculous!" Sara Jordin cried. "Tony and Tee are dead, and we have all the concentrates they would have used!"

Donato shrugged. "We still must reach the Shrine."

"Doesn't Scholar Wandirr have an even greater interest in reaching the Shrine than you do?" Lian said very quietly. "He is the legal commander of this expedition. Surely he should decide what we will do."

Donato's little smile did not reach his pale eyes. "Is he?" He shook his head. "I question not his interest but his competence. And as for legality, the authorization for this expedition—"

"Came from Imperial HQ, on behalf of the Institute for Xeno-Archaeology, which put *me* in command!" Wandirr found his voice at last, but the Armsman's voice bit through his growl.

"Neither Empire nor Institute could have authorized you to put a foot down here unless it was in the interest of both the Terranan and Comyn Council, or didn't you ever dare to wonder why everything was suddenly so easy when you'd been struggling for support for so long?"

"And that is why you will not oppose me, Rununciate." As Donato turned to Lian, his lazy voice made an insult of the word. "My commission comes from the same Comyn Council that guarantees the charter of your Guild House, and it authorizes me to take command if I think it necessary. Therefore, your responsibility is to *me!*"

Lian stared at him. Her oath to the Guild charged her to protect and abide by its laws, but those rules included loyalty to one's employer. No one had ever told her what to do if they disagreed. Unbidden, her fingers had gone to the hilt of her blade, and with the touch an old memory surfaced.

The fighting skills she had learned from her brother had given her an edge when she came to the Renunciates, and the old armsmistress, delighted to have so apt a pupil at the end of her days, had shared with her some teachings not given to the others, old ways inherited from the Sisterhood of the Sword.

"All woman go down to the gates of death in childbirth," her teacher had told her, *"but we who live by the blade face life and death in the way of women and of men as well. We exist on the edge between the two as the leronis lives between the worlds. And so, in our way, we also serve Avarra. It is Her truth that you must seek, between all the laws with which men, or women, seek to bind you—the truth that you see in the bright blade of your sword. . . ."*

Lian took a deep breath, centering herself as she did before a fight, and let it out again, feeling her soul still to an icy calm. That was the goal she was seeking, like the legendary Camilla n'ha Kyria, who had not needed *laran* to be the greatest warrior woman of her time. There were rumors that in the end even Camilla had gone to learn sorcery among the Sisters of Avarra, but Lian did not believe them.

She needed nothing and no one. What real difference did it make whose orders she obeyed so long as she was faithful to her word?

"We all want to reach the Shrine. The credit for any discoveries will go to Scholar Wandirr, no matter who leads us there." Her hand dropped from the hilt of her blade.

It was not quite a concession, but it was enough for Donato. He laughed, then began shouting crisp orders to Sara and Deuu to move on.

As Lian took her place at the end of the line, she reflected that her only other choice would have been to fight Donato there and then, and in country like this the party could not afford to lose either of its defenders. But though Lian could find no flaw in this reasoning, as she saw the defeated curve of Wandirr's back she could not help feeling that she herself had also been betrayed.

"Is this all?" Sara Jordin's soft whisper voiced what was in all of their minds as they peered at the deeper blackness of stones bulking against the dim pre-dawn sky. They had reached the holy place in darkness, after a nightmare race through the edge of the Trailmen's country in which more than once it seemed certain that Deuu must have led them wrong. The forest was before them. Behind them the glacier reared up in a pale wall. The fires of the Trailmen sparkled like red eyes in the rocks to either side.

"Be still! They will fear gods punish because you are here—" Deuu eyed the other Trailmen as if he expected them to attack any moment with stones and spears. Then he had gone off to show them the Elder's safe-conduct, a strange affair of beads strung on an interlace of twisted thongs, and to try to persuade them that the presence of strangers would not immediately provoke the wrath of the gods.

"What do *you* think the Shining Place is?" Lian

asked, trying to distract them from speculation about whether or not Deuu's persuasions would succeed.

"I don't care!" Sara replied bitterly. "The journey itself was my purpose, and my work is done. I have found two new species of *ericacaea*, which I will name after Tee."

"For me, this is the goal," Wandirr said after a few moments had passed. "Now that I am here, none of our sufferings matter any more." His voice was hoarse; he continued to look toward the shadows that hid the Shrine. "The chanting I hear from the Trailmen fires confirms what I have always believed. This is a holy place, and somewhere among those rocks is a statue or some other relic from the ancient days. When I see it, I will know if they had a culture of their own or guard some secret the Comyn have forgotten. I will write a monograph for the Institute, and the discovery will bear my name."

The light was growing, glimmering through the mists in haloes of lavender and pink as the red sun rose above the blanket of clouds. Now Lian could see that the slope ended in an amphitheater of rocks so weathered it was impossible to tell if they had been shaped or placed there by Nature, surrounding a few meters of flat, slabbed, stone. Beyond them a crevice in the rocks was still in shadow.

One by one the campfires winked out. Deuu trotted back and stamped out their own fire. After that, they sat in the cold shadow of the glacier, breath puffing out in chill clouds, waiting for full day.

"And what about *you*?" Sara asked Donato. "Why are *you* so eager to find out what the light will show?" The Trailmen had begun to chant softly, a wavering, oddly rhythmic song that suited the desolation.

Donato grimaced at the sound. There was tension in

the set of his shoulders, and even in the poor light Lian could see the glitter of his eyes.

"I think it is a weapon from the Ages of Chaos," he said at last. "The Trailmen have no culture of their own, but our own legends tell us of marvelous things—weapons that even the Terranan would fear."

"Would you destroy a holy place so that greater destruction can be done?" growled Wandirr. "Our permission from the Elders and your own Council was for study only. If we take anything from this place, we will break our word!"

"Listen, old dog! When the fate of a world is at stake, lesser oaths are expendable!" Donato shifted position impatiently as the tempo of the chanting quickened. Wandirr made a deep angry sound but did not answer him.

Oath fights against oath when visions clash, thought Lian, *and what is the Shining Place to me?* The proverbs her armsmistress had quoted still haunted her, and one came to her now. *"A test of loyalty is a mirror in which each one sees her soul. . . ."* When I see it, she told herself, *then I will know.*

She took a deep breath, then another, seeking clarity. The Shrine would force her to make a decision whatever its secret proved to be. She must achieve calm so that her actions would flow from harmony. That much the Sisterhood had taught her. She refused to worry about its other teaching—that sometimes the best action was to do nothing at all.

Imperceptibly, her body eased into the position of meditation. The chanting of the Trailmen and occasional low-voiced comments from her own party became part of the background, like the gray rocks and the shifting clouds. She let her awareness expand to include the weight that bound her to the earth, the movement of the air, and subtler characteristics of time and place for which there are no words.

As the light grew brighter, the clouds swirled in patterns of crimson and gold. The rhythm of the chanting was broken by an outburst of excited chattering as for an instant the vapors parted and the sky glowed a deep lavender blue like a jewel.

Lian realized that the first part of the morning had passed. It was full day, but all the moving clouds let through was a shifting, opalescent light in which the rocks seemed to become as insubstantial as they. Again and again they parted, and the silver in the clouds gave way to flashes of pure gold.

"Look!" cried Sara. Something was sparkling in the rock itself now, a pattern of light that flickered, disappeared, glowed again, strengthening with the movement of the clouds. "Oh ..." she breathed. "It is so beautiful. ..."

"Those are schematics!" Wandirr exclaimed, but to Lian it was like the pattern of lights in a matrix crystal, and she felt the same stir of nausea as when they had made her look into one long ago. Could some gigantic starstone have been buried here?

Now every rock glowed with moving lines and swirls of pale fire. Lian shook her head, feeling increasingly ill. The Trailmen were screaming and singing, hiding their eyes. Yes, surely something was waking here. Energy pulsed around them as the light flared. Now only the space between the rocks was dark—seeming blacker by contrast with the brilliance around it.

Donato stood up, staring at the dark mouth that gaped in the stone. "It's in there—I know it! And when I claim it, they will give me my birthright; they will have to acknowledge me Comyn then!" He started forward, his eyes shining with reflected fire.

Donato had reached the base of the tumble of rocks and made a first step onto the slanted slabs that faced the crevice before anyone moved. Then Wandirr cried, "Stop!" and leapt after him. Donato whirled, knocking the old Volsung aside with a sweep of one arm and drawing his stunner. Wandirr pushed himself up, stiffened when he saw the weapon, and called out to Lian.

But she was already on her way, her sickness overwhelmed by the rush of adrenaline, for what Donato wanted would shatter all loyalties.

"Put that thing away!" she stood between Donato and Wandirr. "You break the law twice over, showing that weapon and disrupting the ceremony."

Donato focused fully on Lian, and smiling faintly, slid the stunner back into its case as Wandirr backed across the slabs to the slope. For a moment Lian thought that she had won. Then the Armsman's hand moved to the pommel of his sword and he stepped backward onto the flat stones. His smile had broadened, but it held no amusement.

"Oh, no—You will not give orders to *me*, not here, not now! I am your superior by right of birth and rank and sex. You owe me obedience. And if you will not give it—well, you have forfeited whatever protection your womanhood should give you. I disposed of that fool of an engineer, and he was merely an inconvenience. I have much better reasons for finishing you!" His blade slid from its sheath and swung up to guard.

Lian stared at him, consciousness struggling with a useless appeal. Donato was imperiling himself and every treaty Comyn Council had made—with the Trailmen, with the Terranan, even among the Domains! The other part of her mind coldly assessed the Armsman's stance and the way he held his sword, marshaled her knowledge of the man's condition and the temper of his soul.

He was an aristocratic duelist, trained by the best masters in the Guard at Thendara, Lian thought as she slid the long sword from its hiding place in her staff. He would have won often enough to give him confidence as well as pride. She wondered if Donato held strictly to the classic moves or if he had developed a style of his own.

Then all calculation was extinguished as she stepped onto the stone and into a blaze of light. Donato danced toward her, radiance reflecting from his extended blade. Lian was half blinded as the rapier struck, but her body was already curving aside, and as she turned, her own blade swept from its resting position across her shoulder in a smooth arc against which the rapier glanced harmlessly.

Donato spun swiftly away, auburn brows lifting in momentary surprise, his sword immediately in position again. For a few moments the two faced each other, Donato made more cautious by his first repulse, Lian seeking a way to disarm him.

Pulses of light were flowing continuously through the rocks around them. Lian felt their energy tingle in her flesh, their patterns imprinted her retinas. There was purpose there, no random effect of the nearing sun. Dizzied, she stumbled, and Donato was upon her in a smooth lunge that carried his blade to the place where Lian's throat had been.

Avarra help me! the stumble had become a roll. Metal chimed as the two blades kissed; voices sang through the stones. Finding her feet, Lian swayed to the flow of power. The wind of a cut that had passed too close ruffled her hair; the needle-point of the rapier scored her thigh. Donato laughed exultantly, leaping across the stones, lost in his own mad dream.

Lian spun away from him, gasping. The sun was flickering through the clouds almost constantly now, disorienting her thinking as it transformed her surroundings.

Link yourself with the power that surrounds you. Servant of Avarra, be Her sword! And finally she understood. Opening herself to the glory around her, she let the flow of power carry her forward, long sword lifted high—

—and the burgeoning brilliance before her dazzled her eyes and her brain, and she understood what this place was for.

"Donato!" she cried. "Get away from the opening!" Already she was whirling toward the rocks with the same speed with which she had pursued her foe.

For a moment Donato watched her, and in that moment she saw the exultation with which her brother had always met danger blazing in his eyes. Then he turned back to the crevice, reaching as if to grasp whatever was within. His cloak glowed as the uncurtained heavens at last let through the full light of sun, and then suddenly he was a dark silhouette against an explosion of brilliance that answered the sunlight from within!

His shout was swallowed up in the delirious babble as the Trailmen hailed their deity, and Lian never knew if it had been a cry of ecstasy or of pain. His arms still outstretched, Donato turned into a form of fire, his sword a brand of living flame. The rocks shuddered as if something long-buried were striving for life again, and Donato fell.

"Merciful Avarra!" Lian whispered.

She had not killed him, and yet he was gone. She had walked the sword-edge; her brain felt burned from the inside. She was still half-blinded when the first veils of cloud began to cover the hole in the heavens once more. Blinking, she saw the colors dim and trails of fire dying across the stones.

One by one her companions clambered down to

stand beside her, staring at the charred thing that had been Donato.

"It *was* a weapon after all," said Wandirr harshly.

"No," Sara laid her hand on his arm. "It was beautiful."

Lian rubbed her eyes, seeing as an after-image a woman's shadowed face, ancient and beautiful. "For Donato it was a weapon, as for you it was beauty. Life or death, fire or ice, Avarra's mirror, the place between."

"And what was it for them?" Wandirr asked her then.

Lian looked at Deuu and the other Trailmen who were gathering around them, and suddenly the patterns of energy that had flowed through her reformed in words. "Don't you understand? This is literally a Place of Power. . . . Deuu, do your people know of other places like this one?"

"In the great-days," the Trailman answered. "Not now."

"I think that if you looked along the edges of the glaciers you would find some. They gather the heat of the sun, but the conduits are blocked. The people of the Towers might be able to help you to get it flowing once more. It could melt the ice, make more lands for your folk to live. Darkover is getting colder, but the Terranan tell us this has happened many times. I think the mirrors were made to get your people through such world-winters long ago."

"How can you know that?" asked Sara.

Lian blinked stupidly. She knew it . . . as she knew that Wandirr was already planning his monograph; as the news was racing through the crowds of Trailmen; as Sara herself was already wondering whether they would let her study the return of vegetation as the glacier was pushed back. As she recognized, at last, the pain that had festered beneath Donato's pride.

She understood then that to look into Avarra's mirror was not an escape from sorrow, but an acceptance—of everything. She had been right to fear the wakening of her gifts, but she was no longer the same person who had been so afraid.

Lian brushed wetness from her cheeks—of course, the ice was melting. Then she remembered the Trailmen had not yet used the Mirror, and realized that what she felt was tears.

Kadarin Tears

by Patricia Duffy Novak

As I've said many times, one of my favorite themes for these anthologies is a continuation of the lives of characters of whom I'd written before. We've printed many stories by Patricia Duffy Novak, both in these anthologies and in my magazine; this one deals with characters from STORMQUEEN, and is handled with her usual delicacy and subtlety. Readers will recognize Coryn and Renata and Allart from STORMQUEEN, and from at least two previous stories.

There is nothing much to say about this story except that it was the first of the longer stories I chose for this volume.

Patricia Duffy Novak has a Ph.D. in Agricultural Economics and makes her living as an Associate Professor of Agricultural Economics at Auburn University, where she is also working toward an M.A. in English.

There is a saying in the mountains: To have no son is a sorrow, to have too many is a tragedy. And Cyril, Lord Ardais, had six strong sons.

Ari Hastur, the youngest Keeper of Hali Tower, came out of sleep reluctantly, his mind screaming in fatigue, each bone aching with the effort of rising. But there was someone at the door, an annoying presence, insistent.

All right, all right. He swung his legs free of the blankets and balanced on the edge of the bed, head in hands. His temples ached with a dull, pounding throb, eroding his concentration. Still, with a flick of thought, the barest mental touch, he gleaned the identity of his visitor.

Dyan? Why was his friend standing outside the door of his suite in broad daylight, while all sensible matrix workers were asleep? Ari struggled to wake completely, then touched his friend's mind and said through the link: *I am awake, Dyan. Come in.*

The door swung open and Dyan Syrtis came into the room. "Gods, you look awful," Dyan said after a moment's silent appraisal. "What have they been doing to you?"

Ari groaned. He knew the sight he presented: face too white, eyes too dark, hair uncombed and disheveled. Leander Aillard, the Tower's senior Keeper, had set him on a grueling schedule. "Leander's put me to a circle of eight. Altons, all of them. The energy pounds through me until I think I cannot endure it!"

Dyan put a cautious hand on Ari's shoulder, the lightest of touches. Ari forced himself not to flinch under the pressure of his friend's hand; that was another thing about his training: he had become so sensitized that he did not like to be touched. He had been told that in time he would master this problem, that he would not spend his whole life shrinking from the touch of his closest friends. But he would never again be able to tolerate casual contact with strangers. That was the price he must pay.

"Leander means no harm," Dyan said gently. "It is just that—" Dyan shrugged. "Well, with Lord Coryn gone, *you* are the Hastur now. Leander is a competent matrix worker, but he is not a Hastur."

"Sometimes I wish I wasn't one either." That

thought had been with him often lately. He had come
to Hali unwilling, but had, in time, found a sort of
peace there. But now, with Coryn gone, the pressure
for him to take over all of Coryn's duties was almost
overwhelming.

Ari lowered his eyes, feeling again the guilt that always came with the memory of his father's sacrifice,
the destruction of almost unimaginable *laran* powers to
save Ari, his only son, from a deadly trap. "I know
what my father gave up for my sake. Do not think I am
ungrateful. But sometimes I fear I can never replace
him, and it is hard to walk in his shadow."

Dyan inclined his head. "In more ways than one it is
a pity he is gone."

"Why, what do you mean?" Ari asked, catching the
ominous undertone of Dyan's remark.

"I mean that if Lord Coryn were still in the Tower,
there would be more protection for the Hastur lands."

"Protection? But there is peace."

"For now, but how much longer? I've come to say
good-bye. Word has come from Ardais. I am to leave
Hali at once."

The last vestige of fatigue left Ari; his friend's announcement was like a pan of cold water tossed at his
face. "Recalled? But why?"

"There is talk of war."

"War?" Ari repeated. "But there is no cause!"

"Oh, there's been some sort of border skirmish between some minor nobles. Nothing of consequence,
but cause enough if an excuse for war is sought. Old
Cyril of Ardais sits in the mountains with his sons, an
old wolf with his pack, ready to rip the throat out of
the Domains. And look: Allart Hastur of Elhalyn has
no heir, Felix Hastur of Hastur will certainly never get
one, your uncle Regnald Hastur of Carcosa has lost his
only *laran*-gifted son, and Coryn Hastur of Hali has se-

cluded himself in Aldaran, his talent ruined. What better time to strike? Old Cyril has too many sons and those sons need land. They will not be dainty about how they take it."

"You don't sound like a very loyal paxman, Dyan," Ari said.

"Syrtis is an Ardais possession now, that is true. But less than a score of years ago, we were Hastur vassals. Even though our loyalty was traded away to settle some debt or obligation, still we have no love for Cyril and his ambitions."

Ari's head throbbed. War. He could not even imagine it, although he had heard stories from his foster mother, the Lady Renata Aldaran—terrible tales of destruction and death from a war that took place before he was born.

And Dyan—Dyan was oathbound to Ardais, forced to leave Hali Tower. And that, to Ari, seemed the unkindest blow of all.

"I will miss you, Dyan," Ari said softly, taking his friend's hands in his own. Not the light touch of telepaths, but a firm clasp that was painful to Ari's hypersensitive awareness. "And may the Gods look after you."

"May the Gods look after us both," Dyan answered grimly. "If there are any Gods at all."

In Aldaran, high in the Hellers, the afternoon sun cast long red rays along the mountain slopes. A beautiful afternoon in late summer. Warm. Untroubled. Perfect for sitting on a balcony of Castle Aldaran, far from any strife or problem.

And yet—

Renata cast a glance at Coryn, who sat across the table from her, his face turned partly away. A breeze ruffled his silver-flecked copper hair and, as he pushed a few loose strands from his eyes, the sunlight shone brightly on the copper bracelet he wore about his wrist. Part of a matched set. She herself bore the other.

As she watched, he twisted the bracelet absently, rubbing the skin of his arm. *As if the metal burns him,* she thought. *Or perhaps it is the marriage itself that galls.*

He turned to face her then, his gray eyes cool and unreadable. But they were almost always so lately, irrespective of his mood. "It is only the metal," he said. "I am not used to wearing it. All those years in Hali Tower I never wore a metal ornament of any kind. Metal conducts electric impulses. Do you know me so little, Renata, to think I find our marriage a burden?"

"Who knows what you think or feel, Coryn," she said in despair. "Certainly not I."

"I am sorry to be such a poor husband to you, Renata," he said. Then he rose and walked to the balcony wall and stood there, staring out across the valley. Was he angry? Was he hurt? Did he feel anything at all? A few months ago she would not have believed she would ever feel so locked out, so lonely in his presence. Why had he started to change, to erect barriers against her?

She was of the Alton-kin, with the power to force aside those barriers. Indeed, she had done it once, a year ago, when he lay stricken, nearly head-blind, after taking the full back-blast of a level five matrix, saving her son and his own from a treacherous attack. But he had been weak then, vulnerable, and heavily drugged. If she tried to force rapport now, when he was strong and resistant, she might kill him in the process. Even if she succeeded, what would she gain? Certainly not his love or trust.

Miserable, she sat watching him, not knowing what

to do, whether to go to him or go inside, whether to speak or be silent.

But he spoke first. "Horsemen," he said quietly. "They are already at the gate."

"Who?" She rose and strode rapidly across the space that divided them, then gazed downward, following the direction of his outstretched hand. At first she saw nothing but a blur of dust, then she discerned the riders. Three of them. Dim shapes, dark against the hillside.

"The lead rider carries a flag with Hastur colors," Coryn said.

Although she could not yet see the flag herself, her heart sank. Coryn's eyesight was unnaturally keen, and she had no reason to doubt his word. "Your brother has sent for you after all," she said. They had been married six months, but Coryn had never asked his brother's permission to be wed. In the eyes of the lowland, their marriage could not be legal without Lord Carcosa's blessing.

Coryn shook his head. "Not my brother. And even if it was, who would care for that? I've told you before, I do not care a whit for Regnald's opinions—or his lands. As for permission, he would not grant it, so I do not ask. But this is not Regnald. There is a crown on that emblem. Allart's men."

"Allart's men? But why?"

"I suppose they have a message Allart could not trust to the relays. Why else would he send a party? And see, the men themselves are not dressed in Hastur colors, but rather in mountain garb. They have come in secret, Renata, or their arrival would have been reported before this by your own people."

"Well," she said with a sigh, "there is nothing for it but to go and see what they want. But I am sure of one thing, this is not good news."

He followed her into the castle, and although he did not touch her, she was all too conscious of his presence, of the unresolved problems that hung over them like storm clouds over the Hellers. But there was no time to think of that now, no matter how her heart might ache.

Although Renata's son, Brenton, had for a year held the title of Lord Aldaran, the Hastur men would not tell their mission to him. Instead, they met privately with Coryn and Renata. "We have come," said their leader, after a few hasty pleasantries had been exchanged, "to beg Lord Coryn to return with us to Thendara. We have an aircar on the other side of the Kadarin River, waiting for him."

Renata was stunned by the request, but Coryn's face betrayed no surprise. "Allart is my liege," he said. "He has no need to beg. I am his to command."

The Hastur man spoke again. "Your pardon, my Lord, but there is more you should know. Ardais has recalled all his men from Hastur lands. There is talk of war."

Renata saw the color drain from Coryn's face and her own heart went cold. She knew old Cyril and his sons—their lust for land. The steep slopes of the Hellers gave her own Domain some protection from Ardais' greed, but if he marched against the lowlands, and won, could Aldaran long remain neutral?

She had seen war once, when Rakhal of Scathfell marched against her late husband Mikhail of Aldaran. She had seen it and dreaded seeing it again. She put her mind in light rapport with Coryn's, a conversational level of communication, all he would allow. *But what could Allart want with you, Coryn?* she asked. *You are no soldier. And you can no longer be a Keeper for a telepathic circle.*

Coryn looked at her and she saw in his eyes a terrible pain. *You are wrong, Renata,* he said through the link. *We were both wrong. The power was not destroyed forever. It came back. I have been half-expecting some sort of summons. Allart would know. That damnable* laran *of his—*

He opened to her then, fully. She felt for a moment that impossibly gentle mental touch, a touch that always reminded her of the lake at Hali, a lake that was neither water nor cloud. Then she read in his mind the agony of his last months at Aldaran. He was a Keeper, still under oath to King Allart, bound to Hali Tower as surely as any man is bound to wife. He had stepped aside only when he believed his powers lost forever, burnt out by the matrix backlash. He had never asked Allart to release him from his oath, thinking there was no need. He had married her believing he would never be Keeper again. But he had healed. And no matter how much he loved her, once again he was pure Hastur, bred for the task of wielding enormous matrix tools, a *laran* talent in desperately short supply.

For Renata the impending war momentarily faded into insignificance. She clung to Coryn in the link. *And you have kept this from me? I would not hold you here against your will. You must resume your place at Hali if that is what you want.*

He snapped the link abruptly, sending no answer. She wanted to put her head in her hands and weep, but of course she could not, not in front of Allart's men. "You must go if Allart needs you, Coryn," she said out loud, more for the sake of Allart's men than for Coryn. "He would not call for you on a whim."

Coryn nodded softly, then spoke to Allart's men. "Give me a moment to say good-bye to my lady. Then I will come with you."

After the men had gone, he took her hands in his.
"I'm sorry, Renata," he said. "I should have told you,
but truly I did not know what was to be done. Whatever I decided, an oath would be broken."

"And what do you want, Coryn?"

"I will not lie to you, beloved. I cannot tell you because I do not know."

She laid her head against his chest. The gold silk of
his jacket was cool against her cheek, but she could
feel his heart beating, firm and strong. He was such a
small man, so slightly built, that from a distance he
seemed like nothing of consequence, nothing at all.

She closed her eyes. She might lose him to Hali
Tower; she saw that possibility and accepted it. Worse,
far worse, was the thought of losing him in this war.
Her heart had broken once when she was a girl, shattered so thoroughly she had believed she would never
love again. And perhaps, she thought, that would have
been wisest after all, never to give her heart again,
risking everything on one man's mortality. "Keep safe,
beloved," she said. "Come safely through whatever
trouble engulfs the lowlands. And then we will worry
about the rest."

Ari strode rapidly down a corridor of Coryn Castle,
praying he was not lost. The castle was confusing.
Winding passages that seemed to lead nowhere. Hundreds of people coming and going, many with various
degrees of *laran*, largely untrained. And human servants everywhere, underfoot, intrusive. Ari sighed. He
did not like it here, but for the moment, there was no
choice.

He arrived at Leander Aillard's quarters and stood
outside the door. *You summoned me?*

Leander himself, a tall broad-shouldered man with
dark hair, opened the door and stepped into the hall.

"Come," he said to Ari. "Your father is here. I am to take you to him."

Ari stood stunned for a moment before following Leander down yet another snaking corridor. Coryn? Here? But why? *No one ever bothers to tell me anything,* he thought grimly, masking his thoughts from Leander. *It's "Ari do this" and "Ari try that" with no consideration for my feelings at all. Now they have brought Coryn here without telling me a word about it.*

When Leander and Ari arrived in the Carcosa suite, Ari saw his father sitting on a couch beside King Allart. The room was warm and pleasant, and the two men seemed to be conversing amicably, as if Coryn's presence at Thendara was nothing more than a holiday visit. But, of course, Ari knew it was no such thing.

At Coryn's feet was a long, wooden box, the kind that might be used to hold a sword. "Hello, Ari," Coryn said, looking up. "Greetings, Leander."

"Please, sit," said the king, motioning Leander and Ari toward some chairs. "We have much to discuss. I have brought Coryn here for a purpose, something that concerns us all."

King Allart's expression turned suddenly grave. "You know the situation with Ardais. One need not have the gift of precognitive *laran* to see that a full scale war would destroy us all, leaving nothing but barren lands and death. Ardais, naturally, would wish to minimize the destruction to the lands he hopes to gain. We have agreed to settle our quarrel with a Tower battle."

Ari sucked in his breath. A Tower battle! But that was hopeless! The Ardais Gift was a catalyst *laran*, a gift that could be used to awaken the potential of latent telepaths. That Domain was full of powerful telepaths, so many that, before the end of the truce, Ardais matrix workers had been scattered hither and yon across the

Domains, lent out because there was not enough work for them at home. King Allart must be mad to attempt such a thing as a *laran* battle with Ardais.

"Do not look so stricken, Ari," the king said. "The Ardais have many strong matrix workers, that is true. But no one there has the Hastur Gift."

There it was again. That burden. "My Lord," Ari said, "you do me honor. But I alone cannot stand against the full power of Ardais."

"Nor would I ask you to do so, Ari. There is another Hastur who will share the burden."

"But there is no other trained Hastur—" Ari began, then saw how the king's eyes were fixed on Coryn. "Father? But how? You can't—"

"I can," Coryn said. "The Gift was not lost forever after all."

Both Ari and Leander stared. "Is it true?" Ari finally said. "Are you Keeper once more? But still, even with your powers, we are gravely outmatched."

Leander's lips compressed into a thin line. "What the boy says is true. Lord Coryn's recovery is a welcome surprise, but still we are not equal to the Ardais."

"A few weeks ago I would have agreed with you," King Allart said. "But you know my peculiar *laran*, the gift of seeing all possible futures. Through this *laran* I saw a way."

"I do not have Allart's Gift," Coryn interrupted, leaning forward slightly, toward Leander and Ari. "But I also see a way to defeat Ardais."

Coryn reached for the box at his feet and opened it. Inside, against a background of purple velvet, a sword lay shining. But this was no ordinary weapon. In the hilt, surrounded by gems of various colors, a starstone gleamed. An enormous stone, the size of Ari's fist.

As Coryn's hand grasped the hilt of the sword, he seemed to rise, towering above the rest of them, a giant. Ari blinked, seeing a double image: the real man and the illusion.

Then Coryn lay the sword back in the box and shrank to normal proportions. "This weapon," he said, "can cut through the Ardais defenses, laying open the force field around the matrix workers."

"But for what purpose?" Leander asked. "If we send ground troops into the breach, we have violated the contract of Tower battle."

"Not troops," Coryn said. "While Ari breaks the barrier with that sword, I will teleport to Ardais."

Ari heard the first half of Coryn's words in shocked silence. Bear that sword? He did not want to lay so much as a finger on a weapon of that power!

Leander turned a cool gaze toward Ari, who wanted to shrink into the carpet. "The boy is Hastur, but does he have the strength for this?" He turned to Coryn. "And even if he can break that field, what can you do in Ardais Tower, one man against dozens?"

Coryn's face settled into determined lines. "I will extinguish the Tower matrix with my bare hands."

Leander made a strangling sound. "You are mad," he said. "The accident at Aldaran destroyed your reason."

"I am not mad, Leander," Coryn said, "that accident taught me something about this process. At Aldaran, I extinguished a level five matrix and nearly died in the effort. I did not know then how to go about it properly. But I am Hastur, the energy can flow through me, if I do not fight it, and if I can keep my mind clear enough to direct it away."

Leander's face was a composed mask, expressing neither acceptance nor disbelief. "I will support you in this, if you are determined to try," he said, "but only because I see no better way." Leander rose, and bowed, and took his leave.

"Father," Ari said after Leander had gone. "Is there truly a chance you will survive?"

Coryn spread his hands. "There is a chance," he said softly, "but not a great one. Alone, uncontested, I believe I could do it, but under conditions of siege, well, that is another matter."

As he spoke, Coryn fiddled with the clasp of the bracelet on his wrist, the bracelet that was never supposed to be removed, even in death. "Whatever happens, Allart," Coryn said, "have this sent to Renata."

The king took the bracelet from Coryn's hand. "As you request, Coryn. And I pray you live to reclaim it."

Ari saw how careful Coryn and Allart were to avoid each others eyes. *It's Allart's* laran, Ari thought. *Coryn does not want to know all of what Allart sees.*

"The world goes as it will," Coryn said, his eyes dark against the pallor of his face.

And the world, thought Ari, had become a grim and hostile place. Only a week ago he thought his gravest problem was the schedule Leander had set for him. Now the Tower days seemed like an extended holiday. In spite of all his training, he did not feel ready for the task his father had given him, wielding that terrible matrix sword. Nothing in his life had prepared him for this. Nothing.

Ari held the sword lightly and felt it pulsing, like something almost alive. Beside him, not touching him physically, but blended in a soft *laran* link, stood Coryn. Around the two of them, a circle of twenty had convened. Leander Aillard, the senior Keeper, held the first place. Two other Keepers were positioned at either side of him, to help him direct the flow toward the center, to Ari and Coryn. Among the other *leroni* in the circle was Allart Hastur himself, who had once, Ari had been told, been trained as a technician at Hali Tower.

Leander and the other Keepers were dressed in the traditional red robes, but Ari and Coryn wore black leathers, soldiers' garb. They were not Keepers now, but rather warriors in the strange battle that would unfold.

Ari was to go through the overworld with Coryn, but remain physically at Thendara. Coryn would teleport in flesh as well as mind, to walk physically through the circle at Ardais once the defenses had been breached.

Vaguely, Ari was aware of the buildup of energy in the circle, engulfing him, pouring over him, building, building. He tried not to think about his own fears as he seized the hilt of the sword and felt himself rise into the grayness. In the overworld he was a giant, enormous, towering above the gray plain, dreadful matrix-sword in his hand. In the distance, he saw Castle Ardais and strode rapidly toward it, each stride carrying him miles and miles along the gray path.

As he reached the castle gates, he saw a shadow hurtle past him. Coryn. It must be. He raised the sword against the castle wall, brought down a blow, felt a crack, a sundering.

Why, this is easy, he thought in wonder, and raised the sword again.

Then he staggered back as the Ardais *leroni* regrouped. He felt a blow to his head that sent his senses reeling, yet he struggled forward just the same, trying to raise the sword. But he was not strong enough. He reached for energy from the circle, pulling, pulling, drawing the energy in. Still he could not raise the sword.

If all had gone well, he would not have been aware

of his physical body. But he was aware of it, in a strange double consciousness, and could feel the sweat springing to his brow.

He must raise the sword! Everything depended on him cracking the barriers. He pulled harder on the energy links.

We cannot take the strain. Leander's voice intruded in the grayness. *The circle is breaking. Come back or we will lose you.*

Ari froze for a moment. No, he could not come back. The force field was not yet broken and Coryn was caught somewhere, neither here nor at Thendara.

Come back. Come back. Leander's voice, louder at first, then fading. There was no time to think. Ari gathered all the energy left in the circle and leapt, pulling his body forward through the overworld. With a jarring thud, his body and mind rejoined in the gray fog. Then he felt himself rush past the dream-Tower and fall through the mists toward the real castle. As he fell, he raised the sword, two-handed, swinging it over his head in a wide circle. Shutting his eyes and letting his *laran* guide him, he brought the sword forward, felt it contact a resistant surface. Marshaling his strength in one final effort, he pushed it through.

The next thing he knew, he was on the floor of a matrix chamber, staring into the dazzled eyes of Dyan Syrtis. Odd, he thought, so odd to be at enmity with Dyan. But there was no time to think about that. In front of him, the central drama was unfolding. Coryn was walking through the middle of the circle. Each step seemed to cost him an agony of effort as he slowly advanced toward the matrix screen.

Ari could feel the ripples of alarm spreading among the Ardais circle, could feel the outpouring of strength directed at stopping Coryn.

The images were like those in a dream. Coryn, arms outstretched, reaching for the matrix, moving slowly as if he were passing through water. The Ardais *leroni*, eyes half closed, faces dazed, not seeming to move or breathe. Beside Ari, on the floor, lay the matrix sword, now burned and lifeless. But it did not matter; even had the sword remained intact, he did not have the strength to lift it.

And he saw, too, that all of Coryn's strength was needed to fight the Ardais circle; Coryn would not have sufficient freedom of will to contain the backflow. They would all die. Everyone in this room. Ari was grateful then that the link with Thendara had been cut. He and Coryn would die, but Allart would live, and the war with Ardais would end.

No!

Whose voice was that? Just as Coryn reached the matrix screen, the Ardais circle rippled, the energy collapsing, dying. And Coryn was free, unencumbered, draining the matrix power into his own body, letting the energy flow through him to dissipate harmlessly in the air.

The matrix banked and died. Coryn staggered. Someone screamed. *It's over,* Ari thought numbly. *Over.* Then he closed his eyes and saw no more.

He woke in a strange room. "You're alive, then," said a familiar voice. "For a while I had my doubts."

"Dyan!" Ari struggled to rise. "By all the Gods it is good to see you! But where am I? Still at Ardais? Am I a prisoner?"

"You are still at Ardais, aye. But we have reached a truce with Thendara. We had no choice. You defeated us in the Tower battle, although we never thought you would."

"And my father?" Ari asked. He had seen Coryn stagger, fall. "Is he all right?"

"Appears to be. He was in here a few minutes ago. Said he'd be back when you woke."

Ari saw the grimness of Dyan's face and wondered at it. "But it's over now, Dyan. No one died. The land was spared. Why do you look so glum?"

Dyan's face turned red and Ari thought for a moment that his friend was on the verge of tears. "It's my fault," he said. "I broke the circle. I couldn't stand to see Lord Coryn die. He was my Keeper. I just couldn't—" Dyan broke off. "I am a traitor now, don't you see?"

Ari remembered the voice. The plaintive cry before the circle collapsed. "Then, I owe you my life too," Ari said. "Even if you had not faltered, Coryn still would have extinguished the matrix. Only everyone in that room would have died in an explosion because he would not have been able to drain the energy properly."

"Better honorable death than life as a traitor," Dyan said. "I have dishonored my family, my name. And you see, everyone will think I was a coward, afraid to die myself. But it was not that. I honestly did not know how far the backlash might carry. But I could not let Lord Coryn come to harm."

There was a noise at the door and both boys glanced up guiltily, ashamed to be overheard.

"It's all right, Dyan," Coryn said, as he walked into the room. "I understand and I am grateful. And you must not despair for your name or your family. I have spent much time in the relays speaking with Allart. We have concluded a deal with Ardais to purchase Syrtis for the Hasturs, returning that estate to its proper fealty. You will be Allart's vassal from now on."

The darkness faded from Dyan's face. "And you would do such a thing for me? My Lord, I am too overwhelmed to thank you properly."

Coryn touched Dyan lightly on the arm. "You have, truly, no reason to thank me at all. Rather, it is I who must remain in your debt."

Then he turned to Ari, smiling broadly. "We are all of us proud of you, lad. All would have been lost had you not cracked that force field."

Ari felt himself blushing, embarrassed by the praise. "When will I be going back to Hali?" he asked. "I do not wish to linger here."

"Leave as soon as you can travel," Coryn said. "Dyan may escort you there, if he wishes."

"Yes, sir." Dyan's face lit with a wide smile.

"Then I will bid you both farewell," Coryn said. "For now, my own road leads elsewhere. May the Gods grant you peace."

"Farewell," Ari echoed. And he did feel, now that he thought about it, a certain peace. The gift he bore could indeed be a burden, but he had held a matrix sword in his own hand and used it to save his land from a terrible destruction. He was not his father; he might never equal Coryn's powers as Keeper. But that didn't matter. He was himself. He was Hastur. And that was enough.

Renata did not know what compelled her to ride that morning, heading out alone toward a fork in the Kadarin River, where one arm flowed westward and the other to the north.

The world was quiet around her, the sun barely risen above the horizon. In the far distance, on the other side of the river's northern fork, she saw the peaks of Ardais, and wondered what transpired there.

She'd had no news from the lowlands; the relays had been deathly still, nothing but static. Three nights ago, there had been a wild disturbance, senseless, like a power surge. Then nothing again. Nothing.

Renata dismounted and let her horse graze in the long grass. The river sparkled in the morning sun, gold and white. She had heard a story once when she was a girl that the Kadarin River came from the tears of the *chieri*, exiled in the Yellow Forest, crying for the death of their race. At the edge of the river, she knelt and dipped her hand in the water, letting the cold drops fall from her fingers. Kadarin tears. So much sorrow. So much death.

She turned her face toward the sky. Why was she here by this river, alone? What mad compulsion had brought her out this morning? Her son, her ladies, would be beside themselves if they knew she traveled unguarded where any bandit or marauder might take her.

If Coryn returned, he would come from the other direction, from Thendara. Not from Ardais, along this road.

If he returned.

In the far distance on the Ardais road she saw a cloud of dust, such as a rider might make. *I should go,* she thought. *I mustn't expose myself to any danger. For Brenton's sake, I must survive.* But she did not move. She remained riveted to the spot as the rider came closer.

This is madness, she thought. Now she could see the horse, a dark animal of mountain extraction. And the rider, some sort of mountain man clad in leathers and fur. A bandit, perhaps. Who could say? And still she waited, her heart beating harder in her chest.

Renata.

Yes, this was madness. She was hallucinating his voice.

Then she saw the gleam of the sun against the rider's coppery hair. *Coryn, is it really you?*

No other.

She stood still, rigidly unmoving, at the edge of the river, watching as he rode forward, came into view, then finally swung himself from the horse.

He did not smell good. The dirt and sweat of his journey clung to him and his clothes were stained. She had never seen him in such a state. But she didn't care. She let him hold her, lost for a wonderful moment in the joy of his return. Then she saw, there on his right arm, the band of pale flesh where a bracelet used to be. Her heart froze. He had not come home to her; he had come to bid her farewell.

As if in answer, he held up his arm, pointed to his wrist. "I told you I was a poor husband, Renata."

She pulled away from him, not daring to meet his eyes. "Coryn, I would not wish to hold you against your will. You must go if that is your desire."

"My love, before you cast me out, perhaps you will hear the story of how I lost the *catena*. Although, in truth, it is not lost. Allart has it."

"Allart? But why?"

"Can't you guess?"

"Is it because of your brother? Has he has declared our marriage null?"

"No, no." Coryn shook his head. "Regnald had nothing to do with this. I took the thing off willingly enough."

Renata gripped him hard by the shoulders. "Coryn, do not jest. What happened to that bracelet?"

He was smiling now, openly. "I had to take it off to work in the circle. Either that or have my hand burnt off at the wrist. In spite of the vow I made you, I chose in favor of my hand. Oh, and by the way, the war is over."

She felt her breath expel in a long gasp. "Truly, Coryn?"

"Truly, love." He embraced her then, in mind as well as body, a harmony of joining. There were no doubts. He would stay at Aldaran for as far into the future as either of them could see.

"Allart released me from the Keeper's oath," Coryn said, when they emerged from the link. "I find I am not indispensable after all. A blow to my ego," he grinned, "but I will survive. Ari has the full talent—and perhaps something more. A courage I never possessed. He is young and willing to take the burden. In war, or other trouble, Allart will call me. Otherwise, I am free to live my life as I choose."

"But what happened with Ardais?" Renata asked. "How could the war be over so soon?"

"Ah, now there is a tale worth telling," Coryn said. "But I want to wash first and change out of these disgusting clothes. I smell worse than a *cralmac*. Do not deny it, Renata, or I will never believe another word you say."

She smiled. "No, I do not deny it."

He took her arm and started to walk with her, away from the river, toward their grazing horses. "And are you truly willing to forgive me about the *catenas* bracelet? I suppose I could have gone back to Thendara to get it, but that seemed an unnecessary bother. Allart promised to send it along."

"Zandru take that stupid piece of copper," Renata said, laughing. "I'm sure I don't care what Allart does with it!"

"And here I thought you would never forgive me.

How unfairly I have judged you!" He squeezed her hand.

He helped her onto her horse, then mounted his own, and together they rode toward Aldaran. Behind her, Renata saw the Kadarin River now gleaming a reddish gold—like copper wire—in the late morning sun. Were there tears in the river? She did not know. But if indeed there were, then perhaps, perhaps, they were tears of joy.

The Awakening

by Roxana Pierson

Roxana Pierson's first stories for us were both short and funny; this one is neither very short nor particularly funny, but it's good enough that I could not resist it. It deals with the very much overdone theme of a Free Amazon returning many years later to her home; while I usually find such stories infinitely resistible, this one struck me as sensitive and very much worth sharing. As a general thing I tend not to like stories portraying Free Amazons as lovers of women—there have been too many of them—this one kept me curious all the way through. It wasn't the same story I'd read hundreds of times.

This represents a new departure for Ms. Pierson, because instead of doing what she's successfully done before and could have successfully done again—I never get enough stories that are both short and funny—she tried a longer story where the competition is much tougher. And it worked.

The sun was just breaking through the dark blanket of dawn when Carilla pulled Greylock to a halt. The horse gave a tired snort and she patted the heavily muscled neck affectionately. She said, "You're getting old, boy, just like me."

Below, the long narrow valley of Snow Haven stretched out into the mist, the serrated edges of the surrounding mountains stark against the reddening sky. It was hard to believe so many years had passed since she had left home. Only yesterday, it seemed, she had slipped away into the dark and rain, wondering what would become of her. Still, time had passed, and just as she had changed, so had Snow Haven. Even from here she could see that the estate had fallen into disrepair. The roof of the Great House sagged and the moat her grandfather had ordered dug to discourage Ya-Men attacks was thick with overgrown weeds.

"That's some spread," Lori, her riding companion, observed. "I didn't even know your people were Comyn."

Carilla shrugged. "They're only a minor family. Certainly, nothing to brag about."

"Maybe not to you, but compared to my family they might as well be Hasturs. You might have warned me, you know."

"Don't be angry," Carilla said. "Are you sorry you came?"

"You act like *you're* sorry I came. The whole way here, you've hardly said ten words."

"I . . . have a lot on my mind. Maybe they won't even recognize me," Carilla said softly. She regarded her scarred, weathered hands thoughtfully. The slender, red-haired girl who had taken such care to keep her hands milk-white was long gone. In her place was a hardened warrior, a battle-weary swordswoman with spiky iron-gray hair and a broken nose permanently humped from years of fighting. Hardly the sort to catch a man's eye, she thought ruefully. Indeed, the thought had not even crossed her mind for so many years Carilla found it odd that she should think of it now.

"I don't see why you want to come back at all," Lori replied petulantly.

"I have my reasons." Carilla sat back in her saddle

and stretched. Kicking her feet loose of the stirrups, she hooked a knee over the saddlehorn and fished a long, slender cigar out of her belt-pouch. Lighting it, she inhaled the fragrant herbal smoke deeply and passed it to Lori, saying, "I showed you the message from Ranarl. He's been our *coridom* for years. He and his wife, Mara, were the only people who were kind to me after ... well, you know. ...." Carilla's voice trailed off. Long ago, she had told Lori the sad tale of her childhood; there was no use repeating it. "Anyway," she added, "I owe them something. If he thought there was trouble enough to warrant contacting me, I thought—"

"What?" Lori cut in sharply. "That your family would welcome you back? That's crazy."

"Maybe so," Carilla answered thoughtfully. "But when you get older, Lorilla, you feel different about things."

The younger woman snorted contemptuously. "Don't pull that 'old' stuff on me. After what they did to you, *I'd* certainly never speak to them again. I thought all along you were crazy to come back."

"Then why did you come?" Carilla said crossly.

"Could I let you travel through these mountains alone? I am your sworn *bredini,* after all, or is that the problem? You're ashamed, aren't you?" Lori accused. An angry flush spread to the roots of her hair. "You don't want your precious family to know you are a lover of women—and a lowly land-grubber woman, at that. That's it, isn't it?"

"No, that's not it! And if you can't understand, maybe you shouldn't have come," Carilla snapped back.

"If I had realized I was such a burden, I wouldn't have," Lori replied with equal vehemence. Her soft, young face twisted into a pout that Carilla knew from long experience spelled trouble. At this rate, it would be days before Lori would speak to her. Not for the first time, she chided herself for choosing a lover young enough to be her own daughter.

"Look," she said wearily. "Coming back here isn't easy for me, you know. Maybe I should go down to Snow Haven by myself. Why don't you wait for me back at the travel shelter? It's not a long ride—I can probably make it back there before dark."

"If that's what you want."

Carilla chuckled impatiently. "It's not what I want, but I suspect it's what *you* want. I'll see you there, then."

"Have it your way." Lori's horse whinnied in protest as she turned it sharply. As she rode off, she shouted over her shoulder, "If you're not back by morning, don't expect me to wait!"

"Don't do me any favors!" Carilla shouted back in turn. She sighed heavily. The girl was so young. How could she possibly make her understand? Things were so different when she was Lori's age. Pregnant and alone, she had soon been forcibly recruited as a camp-follower of a local mountain lord's army. For two years, she'd eked out a nightmarish existence of near-slavery. The work was ceaseless, the food scanty, and the cruelty of the soldiers unrelenting. Not surprisingly, when the birthing came it was so long and difficult the child died and Carilla nearly followed it. She had lived, but the midwife warned her: no more children. It had not been a difficult prescription to follow; she was cured of men forever.

It was the midwife who had told her about the Renunciates, but another year passed before she managed to find her way to them. She would never forget how frightened she had been that they would not want her—it had been difficult to imagine anyone wanting

her. No, Lori could never imagine what sort of hardships she had endured. Still, now that she was almost
past the age of childbearing, she sometimes wished she
had a daughter to whom she could pass on her hard-
earned knowledge. Lori, she supposed, filled more
needs than one.

Well, she had other things to worry about now. She
dug her heels into Greylock's flanks. All the better,
perhaps, that Lori wouldn't be present to witness the
humiliation that might await her. She had no illusions;
if her father lived as long as a Hastur, he wouldn't
change.

Ranarl met her at the gate. He was old now, but he
still had the powerful build that had made him a cham-
pion wrestler in his day. Before she could stop him, he
bowed low. "*Vai domna, vai domna!* You are here at
last! We did not think you would really come."

"Enough, enough!" Carilla said with a laugh. "You,
of all people, needn't bow to me! And, as you can see,
I am no lady!"

Amazement spread over Ranarl's seamed face as he
took in her closely cropped hair and battle-stained
clothing; his eyes lingered disapprovingly on the long,
slender knife hanging at her belt. Finally, he said
thoughtfully, "So I see. . . . Who would ever have
thought such a thing? We often wondered what became
of you."

"What else could I do?" Carilla said matter-of-
factly.

Ranarl shook his head and said, "It's a sad day when
women would rather carry swords than babes."

Carilla opened her mouth to defend herself, then
swallowed her words. Ranarl meant well; it was point-
less to hurt his feelings by arguing. Instead, she said,

"What of my family? Your message said I should come as quickly as possible."

"It's the *Dom;* he's dying. I thought you should see him." Ranarl shook his head sadly. "Your mother died three years ago, but I doubt you heard."

"No, I didn't know Mother was dead," Carilla said huskily.

"Nothing's the same here now. *Dom* Garyth's mind wanders, and now. . . ." Ranarl's voice trailed off.

Carilla sighed. There was Ardais blood in their family. It was far removed, but whenever her mother had been angry, she had accused her husband of "having the same crazy streak as all your relatives." If there was anyone who was half-cracked, though, it had been Carilla's older stepbrother, Felix. Her father's firstborn by a previous marriage, Felix could do no wrong; even as a small child she had known it was useless to go to her mother with the black eyes and bloody nose Felix inflicted on her regularly. "You must have done something," her mother would always say.

"Boys will be boys," her father would concur. "Just stay out of his way. No young man wants a baby sister tagging along all the time."

Then her mother would add sadly, "If I'd only had sons instead of just you, everything would be different."

But there had been no "staying out of the way." Wherever she was, whatever she was doing, any time Felix caught her alone, he had tortured her. Even when he had used her pet cat for archery practice, her father had laughed and said, "Well, he's got to practice shooting at something, you know. There must be fifty cats out in the barn. Go get another."

It was Felix and that rough crowd he traveled with that had been responsible for the "trouble" that had ended her childhood so abruptly. Despite her precautions, they had caught her alone in the barn one fall afternoon and dragged her up to the hayloft. She had prayed that she would die, prayed that, at least, no pregnancy would result; her prayers had not been answered. Frantic, she had tried every abortifacient she had ever heard of, from herbs to riding wildly. Nothing had helped. When her pregnancy could no longer be concealed, she had thrown herself on her mother's mercy. Neither of her parents believed her story.

She had left that same night. Only Ranarl and Mara had shown her kindness. The *coridom* had insisted she should take her horse, Dance, and Mara had prepared a basket of food. At the last moment, Ranarl had even pressed coins into her hand. "You're going to need a bit o' coin, girl," he had said, wiping tears from his eyes. "It's not right, what happened—I know what that brother of yours is like, don't think I don't—but there's no changing our lord's mind. He's a hard man, and that's all. I hope you find someplace safe." Only later, had Carilla realized what a chance they had taken.

"My lady," Ranarl said hesitantly. "You have traveled far. Will you not at least stay the night?"

"The night? I think not." With an effort, she dragged herself back to the present. "But I wouldn't mind some food, and Greylock could use a good feed. It's a hard trip up here. The riding was so rough after Scaravel I wondered if we would get here at all."

"I'm not surprised. The weather's been bad this year; hardly a day goes by without snow. I'll see he's taken care of, and as for yourself—Mara has been cooking from dawn to dusk. We have few servants now, as you'll see, so she does everything in the house. I think you will find many things have changed since you left."

* * *

Mara met her at the door. Dusting floury hands on her apron, she swept Carilla into her arms. Weeping, she said, "I'm so glad to see you. We were so afraid you wouldn't come." She held Carilla at arm's length and exclaimed, "You've grown into a fine woman. A fine woman!"

Carilla tearfully returned the embrace. Mara had grown so thin and fragile, she barely recognized her. "I came as soon as I could, but I don't understand. . . ."

"You will. Ranarl will explain later, most times he keeps *Dom* Garyth company. Your father doesn't get out of bed much anymore. Ranarl does just about everything, inside and out, I'm afraid. Most of the servants ran off to join the last war—you know how it is up here in the mountains—and now, there's no one left. We do the best we can, but it's not easy." She shook her head dolefully. "Well, I shouldn't bore you with our problems. Everyone's the same, these days. We thought you should see your father before he dies, but have a bite to eat first. Come, sit here with me in the kitchen where it's warm if you don't mind."

"Of course not!" Carilla laughed. "I'm hardly dressed for a formal dinner."

"Oh, you look just as your mother did when she was your age. Of course, she didn't wear a sword, but there now, times change, don't they!" Taking Carilla's hand, Mara led her down the long, dark hall toward the cheery glow of the kitchen. The old woman seated Carilla at a rough wooden table close to the fire and poured a mug of steaming herb tea for each of them. For Carilla, the kitchen brought back childhood memories of stolen hours spent with servants who paid her more attention than her parents.

Mara set out platter after platter of food, chattering all the while. "I hope you've found some happiness, child. But you're ... you're not married, are you? I mean ... you don't look like—"

"Hardly!" Carilla exclaimed. She laughed ruefully. "Marriage isn't everything, you know." She dug into the food eagerly. However, she couldn't help noticing that the chicken was tough and scrawny, the nut-bread largely devoid of nuts. With a sinking sensation, she realized that Mara's thinness might not be due just to old age.

"Oh, don't say that," Mara said. "Every woman wants to be married. It's just that ... well, things didn't work out that way for you. Well, well, the world goes as it wills and not as we wish. I guess we never do know what the Gods have in store for us, do we?"

"I guess not," Carilla said thoughtfully. Her life had taken many a strange turn, and perhaps this was the strangest of all. Who would ever have thought she would be welcomed home again?

Her father's chambers were smaller than Carilla remembered, but still impressive despite the cobwebs that hung from the ornate carvings. Indeed, everything looked as though it could use a good cleaning; the room smelled of old age and sickness. Taking a deep breath, Carilla entered, her footsteps echoing loudly.

"Good evening, my lady," Ranarl said. Hurrying forward, he bowed low to Carilla. "Your father is most anxious to see you." Quietly, he added, "I gave your horse a good feed. Don't worry about anything. And don't be upset if the old man doesn't recognize you; sometimes he doesn't even know me."

"It's been so long," Carilla said. Suddenly, she felt like a child again. She had always been forbidden to enter this room unless ordered—and that usually had meant a punishment of some kind. Her heart skipped a beat as she saw the withered form almost lost in the massive bed. Surely, the bony fists that lay clenched on the blankets did not belong to the husky, broad-shouldered warrior she remembered?

"You must be tired, my Lady," Ranarl said. "Please, seat yourself." He indicated an over-stuffed chair beside the bed.

Carilla sat down gingerly, perching stiffly on the edge. Her father didn't speak, and neither did she. Finally, Ranarl said, "I'll have to wake him. He falls asleep right in the middle of speaking sometimes, so don't be surprised." Smiling encouragingly, he propped the old man up on his pillows. "There's someone here to see you—someone we've been expecting."

"Eh?" *Dom* Garyth's eyes opened a crack to stare suspiciously at Carilla. "Who are you?"

"Don't you recognize me?" Carilla asked softly. Somehow, the fact that he didn't recognize her hurt more than open hostility would have.

"Eh?"

"I'm Carilla. I've come back; don't you know me?"

"Carilla! You?" *Dom* Garyth laughed sourly. "Don't play me for a fool. My girl had hair like spun copper." He eyed Carilla's hair with distaste. "She was a beautiful lass, that one. Always happy to see me, she was—not like that fool of a Felix. I took her everywhere with me until she got too big. Girls are like that, you know. Once they get to being women, it's best for a father to keep his distance."

"What . . . what happened to her?" Carilla had to take a deep breath to still the shaking that threatened. It was easier to go along with her father's confusion than argue; she didn't need *laran* to recognize the pity in Ranarl's eyes.

"What happened?" Her father gestured vaguely and shrugged his bony shoulders. "Just up and ran away one night."

"Why?"

"Why? Who knows? She was an ingrate, that's what."

"Did you have a . . . ah . . . disagreement. Didn't you . . . tell her to leave?" Carilla asked cautiously.

"Tell her to leave? I might have. I didn't mean it though. The house was empty after she left. Empty. . . ." Tears coursed down the old man's withered cheeks unheeded. "You see how it is, nothing here now. Everything's gone. When Felix comes home, he's going to get a piece of my mind."

Clearing her throat, Carilla said, "Mara told me Mother passed away. I'm sorry." Cautioning her not to mention it, Mara had also told her that Felix was long dead, killed in a duel over a woman.

"Eh?" Her father's head jerked up. "What's that?"

"*Domna* Garyth," Carilla repeated, more loudly, this time. "I'm sorry to hear she's dead."

"Oh, aye, she's dead. Buried her up on the hill."

"I . . . I haven't been up there yet. Ranarl said . . . ah . . . things aren't good here."

"Good? You call this good?" The old man gestured wildly. "Look at this place! Not fit for a peasant. The bandits have been here time and again. Between them and Felix, they didn't leave enough to feed a mouse. You'll find slim pickings here, my girl. Slim pickings."

"Ranarl said there was trouble, but I never expected this."

"Ranarl? What does Ranarl have to do with anything?" Behind her father, the *coridom* rolled his eyes skyward as the old man's voice rose. "Felix did this! I warned him again and again—if you keep gambling and womanizing I'm going to cut you out of my will. Heir or not. He stays out to all hours, can't even remember the last time he bothered to come home." The *dom* shook his head sadly. "Be back when he needs money I suppose. That's what usually brings him home. Well, he'll be in for a surprise this time. Slim pickings, that's what. Slim pickings."

"You already said that," Carilla said. "Don't you know that Felix is—" she clamped her lips shut as Ranarl gave her a warning look, pressing his finger to his lips.

"Felix is what? A fool? Don't you think I know that? Still, he's the only son I've got and . . ." He leaned close to Carilla and gave a leering wink, "He's a fine young stallion—reminds me of myself. Young man's got to sow his seed, you know. He'll settle down, just wait and see." His face clouded over. "Not like that girl of mine. Wild young filly took off for parts unknown; never heard from her again. Broke her mother's heart, she did."

Carilla clenched her teeth to keep back the angry words. Crazy or not, she wanted to hit him. Rising, she said abruptly, "I have to go. Ranarl, will you show me out?"

"Go, go!" The old man ranted, throwing up his hands. "What do I care? Nobody comes here unless they want something, but there isn't anything." He cackled mindlessly.

"I'll see you out, *Domna*," Ranarl said quickly.

When they were safely out of hearing, he said, "You see how it is."

"He's as witless as a *cralmac*!" Carilla exploded.

"Sometimes he has periods of clarity and then . . . well, I think maybe it's better this way."

"I don't see why you bothered to send for me," Carilla said tiredly. "There's nothing I can do here."

"That's not entirely true. There's something in your father's study I need to show you."

Memories welled up as Carilla followed Ranarl into the dusty old room with its rows of leather-bound

books. How often she had perched on her father's lap
while he tallied up the estate accounts! And ridden the
hills at his side—he had been so proud of her horse-
manship skills. How could she have forgotten that?
With a pang of guilt she realized they had enjoyed an
unusually close relationship until that fatal day; her
trust in his affection had only made his rejection hurt
all the more. And all these years, she had refused to
think about it—until now.

Ranarl fitted a key to a drawer in her father's desk
and lifted out a small, iron-bound box. "This is yours."

Carilla recognized her mother's jewelry box immediately. She opened it slowly and lifted out a necklace
heavy with precious gems. This, too, she remembered;
her mother had worn it every holiday. To her surprise,
the whole jewelry collection seemed intact, although
how they had managed to keep it from being sold or
stolen she couldn't imagine. At the bottom of the box,
there was a small scroll bearing her father's seal, and
to her astonishment—his signature ring.

"It's for you," Ranarl said.

"I don't understand."

"Read it."

Carilla bent over the yellowed parchment. Tracking
the spidery letters with her forefinger, she slowly read
it aloud. Reading had never been one of her talents, but
she could muddle through when she had to.

"You understand it?" Ranarl asked.

"He left me Snow Haven, if I read it right," Carilla
said slowly. "I don't understand."

"There isn't anyone else. And I think he was sorry
for what happened. He penned this in one of his last
lucid moments. Mara and I, we tried to find you then,
but we didn't even know if you were still alive."

"How did you find me?"

"One day Mara went down the village to help in a

birthing, and the midwife turned out to be a Free Amazon." Looking embarrassed, he added, "Her ... ah ... clothes were like yours, and she was the talk of the town for days. Mara thought, well, midwives mostly know each other, Amazon or not, so she asked. It took time, but one day we heard a rumor that you were alive and well in Thendara. We were so happy!"

"What made you think I would come back?"

"We ... hoped. I didn't know what else to do, and the land is yours. So far as I know, there aren't any relatives left who could lay claim to it."

Carilla sank back in the chair, her head whirling. She had often wondered where she would go, what she would do when she grew too old to fight. Lately, she sometimes thought those days were not so far away. How she dreaded the thought of becoming a burden to the Guild House! But now.... They had long talked about acquiring land to start a horse-breeding business, but estates were usually inherited, and ownership hotly disputed. Up here in the mountains, however, the sword ruled, not the Comyn.

Did the Renunciates have the strength to defend Snow Haven? she wondered. As soon as her father died, they would probably be attacked from every side. In fact, it was a wonder Snow Haven had survived intact this long. Carilla's mind raced. She had saved something from her years of service and with the money her mother's jewelry would bring there would be enough to buy stock and equipment. So far as help was concerned—she knew dozens of women who would be glad for a chance to start a new Guild House. In this isolated place, there might not even be a need to ask permission. It was almost too good to be true.

Carilla sank back in the chair. Rubbing her hands over her face, she said, "This is all something of a shock; I don't know what to say."

"Don't think too long, my Lady," Renarl warned. "We are all old up here. If you delay, there's no telling what might happen."

"My thought as well," Carilla replied slowly. "Still, I'll have to discuss it with my Guild-sisters and look into the law. I'll need a lot of help if I'm to run an estate like this—I'm afraid I know more of war than peace."

"You'll have it as long as I live," Ranarl replied gravely.

Carilla replaced the contents of the box and closed it tightly. Slowly, she rose and gazed out the window. The light was fading. More time had passed than she had realized; Lori would be worried. She turned back to Ranarl. Barely able to speak over the lump in her throat, she said, "I should have come back sooner."

"It would have been a great help." Ranarl's eyes filled with tears. "I probably shouldn't tell you this, but ... Felix was a monster. Toward the last, even the *dom* couldn't control him. He ... he beat the old man half to death one day—that's what started his mind wandering, I think. Maybe it was a blow to his head, or maybe just the shock, I don't know. Other times, he locked the old man in his room and forbade us to go near. I'm ashamed to admit it, but we were all frightened of him. If you hated your father for ... for putting Felix first, I think he lived to regret it." He hesitated before adding, "Your mother did, too. The money Mara gave you that night—your mother gave it to us and made us promise not to tell you. She was afraid of your father."

"I ... I never knew." Carilla swallowed heavily. She had always wanted revenge, and now all she felt was emptiness as the rage she had so carefully nourished for years drained away. She felt suddenly giddy and light-headed. Even the faded colors of the study were richer, the yellow light of the candle brighter, as though she had somehow stepped outside of herself. For the first time, she realized that even if her life had followed the usual course of marriage and children, she would never have been happy with that narrow existence—and the Gods only knew what sort of idiot her father would have chosen! The event that she had always considered a tragedy had been a blessing in disguise. In a moment of perfect clarity, she saw how she had used her anger to fend off any threat of attachment. She had always complained about every little thing and wondered why even her Guild-sisters often avoided her. Lori, too, she had loved at a distance; why had she never seen that?

"I . . . I don't know how to thank you." Tears streamed down her cheeks as she embraced Ranarl, and the old man looked away, embarrassed.

"There, there," he said huskily. "We'll have none of that. I'm only doing my duty, you know."

"I would have died that night, if you and Mara hadn't helped me."

"It wasn't right, what your father did. I wished I could have done more, but I'm sworn to him."

"I know you took a risk just doing that much. Did he ever miss Dancer?"

Ranarl smiled. "We told him she jumped a fence. Your father was very busy with the estate—as he always was in those years—and he didn't pay much attention."

"I always wondered." Carilla gathered up the box slowly, carefully tucking it inside her tunic. "I'm afraid I have to go. The friend who rode up with me is waiting back at the travel shelter. It's not far, but she'll be worried if I'm not back before dark."

"It's good you have a friend," Ranarl replied thoughtfully. "It's a long way to come by yourself."

"Yes, it *has* been a long journey," Carilla said with a sigh. "But it's over now." She had so much to say, so many plans to make. She would make Snow Haven a prosperous estate again, breed horses, train swordswomen. . . . Her whole life lay ahead of her, a new life, free of despair and rage. And best of all, Lori was waiting for her.

Safe Passage
by Joan Marie Verba

Joan Marie Verba, whom I've met, or rather brushed up against at a convention or two, lives in Minneapolis, the climate of which, I seem to remember, is much like that of Darkover. In addition to several stories for these anthologies, she has written two nonfiction books—I think, about astronomy. (Better her than me; I looked into several of my first husband's astronomy texts and found them too mathematically complex for my limited mathematical talents.)

Orain wiped his mouth with his hand. Yes, that was blood on his lip. Touching his forehead gingerly, he felt an egg-shaped bruise beginning to grow. Bending stiffly, he scooped up a handful of snow and held it to his head. He staggered to a tree and sat between two large roots, resting his back against the trunk.

Mhari, his chervine, nosed out grass from underneath the snow nearby. One look at her told him that the bandits had indeed taken everything—his pots, his food, his bedroll, his extra clothes, and, most important of all, the money he had accumulated all summer walking from one village in the Hundred Kingdoms to another. For many years, he had made an adequate living selling wares to farmers, hunters, and craftspeople in the summer, and returning to his home town of Nevarsin in the winter when the roads became impassable. He loved the wandering life and made many friends on his travels. But through luck or chance, never before had he met bandits that had stripped him of everything. Maybe he was getting too old for traveling, he thought as he touched the bump on his head. Maybe he should have gone off the road when he had heard others approaching, as he had done for safety many times before. But the sun had been shining, his spirits had been high, and he had thought that surely nothing bad could happen on such a fine day.

Now clouds covered the sun. Snowflakes began to flutter down. Painfully, Orain got to his feet. He walked over to Mhari and took her halter, the only thing the bandits had left. He stepped back on the road.

Which way to go? This was an unfamiliar road, recommended to him by friendly villagers in the last place he had sold his wares because of rumors of fighting—an old blood feud—on his familiar path home. To his left was the way back to the village, more than a day's walk. The other way was completely unknown, except that he had been assured it would eventually meet up with the main north-south road to Nevarsin. He knew there was no shelter for a long way on the stretch of road he had just traveled, so he gambled on finding shelter soon and took the unknown path.

Fortunately, the bandits had not taken anything from the pockets inside his coat. He switched the halter from one hand to the other as he put on his mittens, and then again as he put on his hat. The snow became thicker and the wind struck his cheeks. He pulled the scarf around his neck to its full width to cover his nose and mouth, but the cold still clawed at his eyes. He bent his head and pressed on, hearing Mhari's breath huffing and puffing behind him.

The wind became more bitter as he walked. Tears

from his eyes froze on his lower lids, frost formed on his lashes. More than once he stopped and took off his mittens for a moment to pry his lids open. His teeth chattered and his body shivered. Not even force of will could bring it under control.

At last, the track turned. Mhari stumbled down the steep incline after him. He saw the dark wall in front of him only an instant before he collided with it. Stunned, he rested his face against the wooden boards. When he had recovered a little, he moved around until he found a door. The latch was merely a leather loop around a wooden peg; he fumbled with the thong until it came loose, pushed the door with his shoulder, and stepped inside, pulling Mhari in with him.

He stood shivering as his eyes got used to the dimness. Eventually he saw some light coming through cracks in the walls and ceiling. He was in a barn. A great mound of hay was stacked to one side. On the other were a number of wooden stalls. Orain could hear the scuffling noises of the animals moving within. He smelled the horses as well as hay and manure.

He led Mhari to the nearest stall, which was empty, and tied her to a post there. He used some hay to brush her coat, then put a stack of hay near her to feed on. He walked to the door to push it shut again, and burrowed into the nearest mound of hay. Soon, his shivering stopped. He slept.

He woke to the sound of footsteps sliding on the wooden floor. A slurred male voice said, "Say, where'd you come from? Ooh, look at the horns. You got horns, there, horsie?"

Orain parted the hay around him in time to see a young man in disheveled clothes walk up to Mhari. The chervine, used to strangers touching her, continued dipping her head in the water trough as the man awkwardly stroked her head. The man flinched with every twitch of Mhari's head, as the horns wavered near his face.

Cautiously, Orain crept from the haystack. Every crackle of the straw sounded like an explosion to him, but the man did not turn as Orain tiptoed across the wooden floor. Orain grabbed him from behind, pressing his thick arm against the man's neck until he fainted from lack of air. Slowly, he lowered the victim to the ground. Spotting leather thongs hanging from a ring, he bound the man's hands and feet, took a kerchief from his pocket, and tied it over the man's mouth. Stepping back to see the man's face, he recognized one of the bandits who had robbed him.

Orain stepped to the door. The new snow shimmered brilliantly in the light of the early morning sun. He shaded his eyes and squinted to see where the man might have come from. Some distance away was a decaying stone house—not a villager's shack or a great mansion, but a house that a minor lord might have built for himself, to house his family and small staff of servants. Nothing was moving in the snow-covered yard, or behind the panes of the windows that he could see.

Orain turned back to Mhari. He could take her now and proceed up the road, hoping to find a friendly village where he could work for enough food and supplies to get him to Neversin, but if no such village was nearby, he would freeze or starve before finding one. No, he needed at least a hunting knife and a bedroll if he was to make any progress toward his destination. Crouching low, he scurried across the yard and ducked under a window. Cautiously raising his head, he cupped his hands around his face and peered inside. The room was empty. Head down, he padded to the doorway. The door was cracked open; he pushed it gently and it swung inward, hinges creaking softly.

His heart raced as he stepped inside. Cocking his
head to catch any sounds, he heard no voices, but he
did hear the snoring and moaning of people in sleep.
Treading the wooden floor carefully, he went to the
room to his left. Peering inside, he saw several men
sprawled on the floor. The odor of sweat and stale li-
quor reached his nose, as well as the pungent smell of
vomit. A man groaned and stirred in sleep. Orain flattened himself against the hallway until the sound died
away.

Peeking in again, he saw that his bedroll and pack,
and even some of his unsold pots and pans had been
stacked in a far corner. In order to get there, he would
have to tiptoe past the sleepers. An extra blanket had
slipped off one of the men near the entryway; Orain
reached in and wrapped himself up in it, covering his
head with a corner. He stayed close to the wall as he
made his way across the room. If a sleeper opened an
eye and saw him, he might think Orain was merely a
companion who had gotten up to find a place to relieve
himself.

Hours seemed to have passed before Orain reached
the other end of the room; his way had been hampered
by sticky wine on the floor, and by sleepers flinging
arms and legs in his path as they stretched in their
dreams. But at last he was bent over the stack of booty.
Orain wrapped one pot in the bedroll—he wished he
could take more, but more than one would have
clanged against the others—took his pack with his
hunting knife, and stuffed his moneybag into his coat
pocket. All else of his he sadly left behind.

He shed the blanket at the room's entrance and ran
across the yard to the barn. His arms laden, he pushed
the door open with his foot, stepped across the
threshhold . . .

. . . and promptly tripped over the man he had tied

up. The man had worked his gag loose and was struggling to free himself. Sprawled on the floor, Orain picked up his one pot and swung it over, hitting the man in the head. The blow only stunned him, but that gave Orain enough time to gather his possessions and move out of the man's reach. Scrambling to his feet, Orain went over to Mhari. He pulled down more leather thongs from the hook. After bundling his pack and bedroll and pan, he tied them all onto Mhari's back.

Meanwhile, the man, hands and feet still bound, called out to Orain. "Please! Take me with you! I'm not one of them! I came here to get a horse and escape!"

Orain paused in his task to take a long, good look at the man. "Seems to me that you were one of those who robbed me."

"Because they made me! If I hadn't, they would have killed me! Please! I'm Jarrel, son of Lord Valdrin! He'll reward you handsomely if you bring me back to him!"

Orain turned back to Mhari. "I thought that Lord Gareth ruled here."

"No! No! The river takes a turn and so we're still in Lord Valdrin's realm!"

Orain turned a skeptical eye toward Jarrel. "In all my years of traveling, I've met smooth liars before son, and you're not even close to their level."

"No! Please!"

Orain untied Mhari from the post and took her reins. "Please, as in 'please untie me so I can beat and rob you again'? Sorry, no."

"I swear! By all the Gods, I swear!"

Turning to the young man, Orain tried to appraise his expression. Then he shook his head. "If you really came out here to escape, and not just to water the horses . . ."

Jarrel's expression changed momentarily; Orain knew he was on the right track. He continued ". . . then you will free yourself from your bonds eventually. The bandits inside the house are drunk and asleep. You'll have plenty of time, if you don't cry out."

With the light bundle on Mhari's back, Orain knew that the chervine could carry him easily. He swung up and pressed his knees to her sides.

"I'm your only chance to get away!'" Jarrel pleaded. "The others have a sorcerer with them! They'll find you! They'll hunt you! I have a starstone in my pocket! I can help us hide from them!"

"I'll take my chances." Orain guided Mhari to the door carefully; the chervine obediently stepped over Jarrel. The young man screamed after him, confirming Orain's suspicions. He heard other voices answering Jarrel's as Mhari trotted out of the yard.

At first, Orain guided Mhari on the road northeast. Orain reckoned that even roused by Jarrel, the hungover bandits would take some time to come to their senses sufficiently to saddle horses and organize a search party. Still, once he was well out of sight of the homestead, Orain guided Mhari eastward off the road. The chervine could easily pick a path over woodlands that horses would find difficult, and if Orain kept generally to the east and north, he would inevitably reach Nevarsin.

He urged Mhari to keep a steady pace until noon, when he stopped to rest and eat. As he was cleaning up, he heard Jarrel's voice shouting, "Hey, pot-man! No escape this time! This time you're dead!"

Orain scrambled onto Mhari's back. To the west, he saw a knot of horsemen through the trees. He knew that any tracker could trace him easily through the new snow, but for horses to follow him through this rugged terrain was nothing less than ... magical. He gritted his teeth and urged Mhari forward. He knew little of sorcery, of the *laran* arts, of the starstone, but he did know that he would not surrender to them again. Maybe they would catch him again, beat him again, rob him again, perhaps kill him. But he was not going to make it easy.

If this had been familiar territory, he could have guided Mhari to a ravine or steep gravelly hill that a chervine could surely cross and a horse surely could not. All he could do now was dig his heels into Mhari's sides, urging her to gallop, letting her pick her own path. Straight ahead was a thicket. Mhari's antlers barely cleared the lowest branches of the overhanging trees; Orain ducked to keep the leaves from slapping his face. They pushed through the bushes and weeds; suddenly everything went dark. Orain clung to Mhari's neck as she plunged down ... what? He could not guess.

They were not falling. Mhari's pace slowed. Orain could feel her picking her way down an incline he could not see. He rubbed his eyes, alarmed by his sudden blindness. Had Jarrel used sorcery against him?

Then Orain saw a thin shaft of light. Looking up, he could see fissures in a stone roof. Slowly the darkness became dimness and he could see the cave around him. Mhari continued to descend along a narrow path. A rock wall loomed up to their left; a deep ravine yawned to their right. Mhari's hoofbeats echoed in the chamber.

Hearing distant voices, Orain turned to the cave entrance.

"You can't get away from us by hiding in bushes, pot-man," called Jarrel. "We ..."

Horses and men screamed. Orain heard the thud of

solid hitting solid, the scrape of sliding rocks and gravel and the desperate clawing of humans and animals trying to gain a hold on an unforgiving cliff face. The cacophony of sound echoed off the cave walls, then diminished as gravity took hold and dragged the pursuers into the depths.

When it was again quiet, Orain took stock of his surroundings. The path Mhari found was too narrow for them to turn; there was no room even for Orain to step off the chervine and walk alongside her.

"Help," Jarrel wailed.

Orain turned and saw a shadow against the rock face. "I'm sorry," he called softly. "I can only move forward myself."

"Please," begged the young man.

"If you truly have command of sorcery, now is the time to use it," suggested Orain.

"I made that up to get you to untie me."

Orain nodded to himself. "I thought you might have. And told me a tale about being Lord Valdrin's son."

"A lie. Please," he urged. "I can't hold on much longer."

"I couldn't reach you even if I tied all the thongs I have together and threw a line to you. All I can do is go forward and see if I can find a spot wide enough to turn around."

"Hurry."

Orain urged Mhari forward at her own pace. He half-hoped not to find a wide spot, because the bandit would certainly rob him again once free from the fear of death. Then again, Orain needed to find his own way out.

At last, Mhari stepped on a ledge. Orain turned and heard other voices at the cave entrance. He froze. If these were more bandits . . .

A sorcerous blue light illuminated the cave. Five

men stood just at the edge of the abyss. One knelt and held a hand down to Jarrel.

"No tricks when you get to your feet, bandit," said the rescuer. "There are twenty more of Lord Gareth's men just outside."

Jarrel scrambled to solid footing and pointed at Orain.

"Him, too! He's one of us! He forced me to steal! Kidnapped me from my home!"

Orain remained still. Sorcery or not, he did not think they could reach him if he stayed where he was.

The rescuer snorted at Jarrel. "You must be the one who claims to be Lord Valdrin's son. Too bad you got greedy and strayed from your own land. Your companions would still be alive if you had known of these caves, and we would not have caught you if you had not left such a wide track through the snow." The speaker pushed Jarrel out of the cave. Then he turned to Orain. "Come out, traveler. You're safe now."

The man with the stone in his hand that radiated the blue light turned to his companion. "Rhodri, I recognize this pot-seller. He came to my village once a year when I was a youth."

With more light to see by, Mhari reached the cave entrance quickly. Lord Gareth's men followed him outside.

Rhodri looked up at Orain and patted Mhari's side. "You have a good companion here. And here, too," he added, pointing to his head. "Not many escaped both the strength and the wiles of these bandits. If a beating does not work, all they have to do is mention sorcery and their victims do as they wish, not knowing that sometimes even sorcery may be outwitted. I have followed a trail of victims from here to the river."

Orain nodded. "Aye, and I know it."

Rhodri reached for the reins of a nearby horse. "We

can take you as far as the borders of Lord Gareth's land. Then you'll be on the main road, and I strongly recommend you keep to that from now on."

Orain smiled. "I will, and you can believe *my* oath on it," he said, following the party out of the forest.

Garron's Gift

by Janet R. Rhodes

Janet and her husband John live in Olympia, Washington, and play bluegrass music; he plays guitar and she plays the autoharp. They have also started a vegetable garden. Janet has a degree in microbiology and has been studying alternative healing therapies and, more recently, herbology.

She has worked for the Washington State Department of Ecology for almost twenty years now. Fortunately, they shift her to a new project every four years or so, so she doesn't have a chance to get bored.

She has sold short stories to three previous Darkover anthologies and to Marion Zimmer Bradley's FANTASY Magazine.

The morning wind blew cold, plunging under Melitta's heavy skirts and nipping at her legs with icy teeth. She replaced the lid on the cookpot and stood to draw her cloak more snugly about her body. Though lined with marl fur, the garment did little to keep out the morning chill. Fall in the Hellers! To the northeast, Mount Kimbi stood stark and purple with distance. Dropping her gaze from its heights, she saw that her brother Stefan, her junior by three years, slept still, huddled in his blankets against the morning's cold. Of their two escorts, Lerrys, too, was sleeping and Rafael had disappeared, she supposed to heed nature's call.

Melitta sighed. If it were not for Ysabet's baby, she and Stefan would be at home in the Great House, warmed by the fires carefully tended in each room. But their older sister had need, and here they were!

Suddenly a weight pressed her foot into the light covering of newly fallen snow. An earthy odor swirled up to greet her. "Ugh, get off!" Melitta gasped, turning, pushing with her hands, twisting the imprisoned leg. "Get off my foot! Off, you clumsy beast. Off!"

When the chervine calf shifted, Melitta quickly pulled her foot back and out of the way. But the calf still strained against her, bleating now, a cry of sad entreaty. She pushed again, finally setting it off balance. The calf hobbled backward, and she stood, brushing mud from her hands. Ugh! She found the discarded shirt they used for cleaning and wiped off the worst of the dirt before she turned back to tend the kettle of porridge. Melitta steadied the pots—in addition to the porridge, she had set a pot of water to boil for *jaco*—concerned she might have bumped into them while turning the calf away. What odd behavior for a chervine, she thought.

A cold wetness brushed the back of her hand. Melitta jumped as the chervine calf tried again to push past her. "Now, what in all the Domains!" She grasped an ear and pulled, turning the animal's head and aiming it toward the other pack animals. "There is your mother, now go!" The calf hobbled a few steps toward its mates, then turned back to Melitta and the fire, its large, dark eyes staring at something behind her. It moaned, a low mournful sound. Abruptly, the chervine surged forward. "Ohhh." This was just too much. She jumped to turn him from the

fire and the kettles, shouting at the same time for
Lerrys and Rafael to help her.

The calf shoved and Melitta fell backward, entangled in its legs. She heard a clatter, then the hissing as
of green wood added to the fire, and knew the cookpot
had spewed porridge into the flames. Melitta found
herself in the snow, the chervine, bawling hysterically,
on top of her. She called out, and Lerrys answered in
his rough, guttural voice. Then the calf planted a small,
sharp hoof in her stomach and stood.

Peering beneath the chervine's belly, Melitta saw
Lerrys on his feet, knife in hand, preparing to defend
them. Within heartbeats he had reached the fire and
dragged the calf off Melitta. "*Damisela*, are you all
right?"

"Fine. No. Dirty, but not hurt. Maybe my pride. The
calf—" She looked up. The animal had scrambled
around the fire and was heading toward the bundle of
blankets that hid Stefan from view. "Stop him!" she
cried to Lerrys. He ran, intercepting the calf before it
reached Stefan, who slept on in spite of the restless
lowing of the calf and its mates.

Lerrys put all his weight against the calf, which continued to push towards Stefan. Suddenly, he fell backward over Stefan's legs, and the calf tumbled on top of
him. Beneath them, the boy squirmed and yelled, his
shouts muffled.

Melitta rushed to help. Where *was* Rafael?

A movement in the trees lining the clearing drew her
gaze, and the missing escort broke from cover, rear-
ranging his clothing as he ran. "Hurry," she shouted.
"Hurry!"

The calf had stumbled out of the tangle of blankets
and was struggling to elude Lerrys, who hugged the
beast to himself with both arms. Melitta rushed to aid
Stefan.

The youth stared about with sleepy eyes. "What is happening?" he asked, his voice indignant rather than pained. She sighed. Now at least she had no fear of returning to the Great House with her father's heir maimed for life.

Melitta went to aid Lerrys. Even with both of them pushing, the calf stood immobile, bawling its frustration. To Melitta it seemed the beast was calling to her brother. Could Stefan have reached out to the animal with *laran?*

Threshold sickness? No! He was too young. She shivered, remembering the violent upheavals within her own body as the sexual and psychic energies developed. Her brother was too young for his *laran* to awaken. Anyway, they were on the trail, bound to Ysabet's for the birth of her second child, and Melitta had none of the medicine called *kirian* to treat him. And no time to search out a *leronis* to test him, she concluded, surveying the clouds, violet with their burden of snow, piled up against Mount Kimbi.

"Well, are you not going to help?" she asked Rafael, when the man finally reached them. "You have no idea how ridiculous I feel fighting a losing battle with a calf."

Rafael grinned. "I will gladly help, *damisela.*" He reached out his hands, then pulled them back. "But I know not where to push. All the available hide seems to be taken."

She made a rude noise of exasperation.

"Perhaps if we all crowded together and herded the calf," said Stefan, who had roused himself at last.

The four closed around the calf, preparing to force it back to join the other chervines, when all at once, the beast ceased its struggles. The foursome stumbled and would have fallen in a heap, except that they clung to each other like trees in the wind.

The calf turned, trotted over to its mother, and started nursing. Every so often it stopped to butt its dam's udder as if to say, "More, faster, I am hungry."

The sight reminded Melitta of their porridge in the fire. "Ah, no!" Stefan followed his sister as she retrieved the blackened kettle. What had been their porridge burned now with the dull red of dying flame. "Zandru's hells," muttered Stefan behind her. "That was not breakfast!"

Silently, Melitta nodded. This day had not started well at all. They had at least one more night on the road before reaching Ysabet's, and snow was on the way. She wished that one of them had the weather sense, but that was impossible. Of the four of them, only Melitta herself had any *laran* at all. And the woman who had tested her, the *leronis* Mahari from Tramontana Tower, had said it was minimal. This was just going to be one of those days, she decided. Stepped on toes, burned porridge, and an errant calf. Well, it could have been worse; they could have awakened to hip-deep snow.

She sighed. There was no time to cook more porridge. The pot of water was still hot, so she stirred in nut flour mixed with dried fruit. This gruel was ready when Rafael and Lerrys joined them at the fire after tying the calf to its mother's harness to keep it out of harms way.

After eating, the four saddled the horses and loaded the pack animals. Lerrys and his black mare took the lead, heading eastward on the trail. Stefan followed on his copper mare and Melitta on her bay. Rafael pulled in at the tail of their line on his gelding, the lead-rope for the pack animals tied to his saddle. The crispness of early morning had already faded. Melitta hoped they would reach the estate by the next afternoon. Just one more night on the road, please, Evanda. Ysabet is so close to birthing. . . .

They had been traveling for several hours when Melitta heard Lerrys laughing. There was no mistaking his hearty guffaws. Stefan, who had drawn up to ride beside the man on the wide trail, reined in so quickly his mount was forced onto its haunches. While Lerrys continued forward, chuckling, the boy guided his horse backward along the narrow way until he came abreast of his sister. Stefan's face was dark, his bushy eyebrows pulled together in a frown, and he was muttering to himself.

"Do you want to talk about it?" she asked.

"Was not my fault the chervine spilt the porridge."

"I never said it was. Sometimes, when we start into the threshold sickness, funny things happen." He scowled and she asked, "What did Lerrys say?"

"He had no right to talk to me that way."

"What did he say!"

"That I must be like Ysabet or Raynald. But I want no rabbit-horns following me out of the forest, nor colts trailing me into the house. I remember Mother telling Raynald he must live in the barns if he could control his *laran* no better. Melitta, I want not to live in the barn!"

Melitta suppressed a smile. Their family was kin to the MacArans and, like that clan, had the gift of rapport with hawk and horse and hound. "At least your gift seems not like Edric's. We need no scorpion ants crawling in our bedding." But then he shuddered and threw her such a wretched glance that she felt responsible for his pain.

Late in the afternoon, the four riders reached the crest of a ridge they had been climbing since midday. They pulled up, Lerrys and Stefan in front, Melitta and Rafael crowding behind. Ahead of them and to the north, Mount Kimbi rose above the trees. Below them, the trail zigzagged down a steep incline until it disappeared, lost in the forested floor of a deep valley. Here and there sunlight glinted from a stream.

The animals seemed eager as they started the descent. The horses danced restlessly; their ears stood straight up and twitched from side to side. The chervines called to each other with quick little lowing sounds. The trail, bearing to the north, appeared to lead the party to the base of Mount Kimbi itself.

As Lerrys reined his black into the first switchback, the mare balked, snorting its displeasure. The horse peered back at Lerrys and snorted again, nostrils flaring wide, as if to say, "Do you really want me to turn here?" Lerrys pulled on the reins, drawing his mount's head hard to the right. The horse danced sideways toward the unbroken undergrowth at the end of the track, as if it insisted on continuing northward. Lerrys gave a strong kick and struck with his lash at the same time. The horse rebelled, rearing, then backing into the brush on the uphill side of the trail until it came up against a tree. Lerrys, caught between his horse and the tree, grabbed an overhanging branch that threatened to sweep him off his mount. Just as he came off the saddle, the horse bolted. After several strides, the black slowed to a walk, then turned to stand in the middle of the way, staring at its rider, ears pricked forward.

Melitta followed the horse's gaze. Lerrys had pulled himself up so his hands and arms supported his weight on the branch and the limb pressed against his belly. With his legs swinging three feet above a snowdrift, Lerrys muttered words that Melitta was, thankfully, too far away to hear.

Finally, Lerrys seemed to make up his mind, for his expression shifted, and he took a deep breath. A moment later, he had dropped from the branch, lurching forward awkwardly as he landed, as if his right foot had caught on a rock or fallen limb. Shaking his head, Lerrys started to rise from the ground, and fell back, grimacing.

"Are you all right?"

Lerrys peered up at her, a perplexed look on his face. "I thought so, but—" He gestured toward his right leg. "I have done something to my ankle," he said, his voice rising. While the others tethered their animals, Lerrys apologized for holding them up.

"Forget it," chided Rafael. "Things happen."

Stefan agreed. "Especially on this trip," he added.

Rafael and Stefan supported Lerrys on either side, while Melitta retrieved his mare. The black eyed her warily, front legs splayed, tail held high. As she grasped the reins, the horse snorted and took a backward step. Talking quietly, she finally drew the mare back to where the others waited.

They helped Lerrys mount, then gathered up their own horses. Rafael and Stefan walked their horses ahead along the track, which ran southward on this leg. Lerrys followed. Melitta, who brought up the rear, saw that he left his right foot out of its stirrup.

The horses had to be urged along the track, and the chervines themselves lagged on their lines. Melitta prodded her mare forward with hands and heels and voice. At last, the trail doubled sharply back on itself. As Lerrys rounded the bend, Melitta's bay broke into a canter without warning. The jolt threw her off balance and they crowded into the black mare before she regained her seat and control. "Sorry," she murmured, then, "What are you doing?" she yelled to the bay as it nipped the black mare's flank. The black kicked out at Melitta's bay, causing Lerrys to groan as the movement jostled his injured foot.

Some minutes elapsed before Melitta and Lerrys got both mounts under control. By then Lerrys was clearly in pain, his face gray and glistening with sweat. But he shook his head when she suggested they stop to check his foot and bind it if necessary.

The travelers continued down the track, moving deeper into the valley, alternately pushing their mounts forward on the southward tracks and restraining them when the way led to the north. Lerrys joked once that their beasts seemed to have a peculiar liking for Mount Kimbi. Nevertheless, it was tiring work and full dark was sweeping down the valley as the weary travelers made camp in an old three-sided travel shelter that stood by the stream Melitta had spied during their descent. She welcomed the brook's calming song.

Rafael tethered and fed the chervines and the horses, while Stefan gathered wood and mosses for a fire. Lerrys had dismounted with a grunt of pain, and Melitta offered her shoulder for support as he hobbled to the shelter.

Though he contended he was well enough to care for himself, Melitta insisted on helping him remove his boots. She cried out in dismay upon discovering his right foot was so swollen the boot would not come off. Was it better, she worried, to cut off the footware or to leave it on to support the injured ankle? Fearing the inflammation would cause damage if the boot were not removed, she finally cut it off, trying not to cringe sympathetically as Lerrys hissed painfully. Then Stefan brought snow and they packed it around the injured ankle. Lerrys muttered to himself. "I cannot believe I did this," he said, over and over again. But Melitta saw that he finally relaxed, the stiffness of pain borne in silence ebbing as the snow did its numbing work.

Too tired to wait for water to heat, the four travelers sat in the shelter and gnawed on dried fruits and meats. At last, they rolled up in blankets, the banked fire warming their feet, their heads far within the shelter's protection.

As she lay in the world between waking and sleeping, Melitta listened again to the stream's peaceful song and wondered at the odd behavior of the chervines and horses. What was she to do about Stefan! Finally, she slept.

Melitta traveled the gray paths of the overworld in her dreams. A child cried in the distance. She searched through the mists, drawn by the sounds, until she came upon a small figure. The child was, she judged, no older than Ysabet's Donal, who was two. Melitta reached out to comfort him, but he moved a step backward, eyes wide in surprise, eluding her grasp. "Why are you crying?" she asked.

He turned and gestured at the emptiness behind him. Then the grayness moved and shifted, until animals— hounds and marl and rabbit-horns—formed out of the mists and gathered around him. As she watched, he stretched out his arms and grabbed handfuls of fur, willynilly, holding the beasts even closer to his small body. His cries turned to giggles, then laughter as more and more animals appeared, until they crowded around both of them. Soon, the animals swarmed over the child, pressed against her, making it difficult to breathe.

The child. He will suffocate! She pushed and shoved, and tried to create room for both of them in the malleable spaces of the overworld. She was gasping for air, her body laboring with short, panting breaths. With her mind, she painted an image of the sunlit conservatory in the Great House. She always felt refreshed there, as if the plants revitalized the very air! The fabric of the

overworld rippled and stretched. The child—she must
make sure he was safe. She probed the mists for the
boy. But he was gone. Gone!

Melitta called out. Again and again she shouted, until her throat felt dry and raw. But the child had truly
vanished along with the animals. What had gone
wrong?

Desperately, she fled the overworld for the chill of
the fall night. Melitta came to herself with a start. The
dream had been so real. She still felt the pressure of
warm bodies crowded around her, still smelled the
aroma of soiled dirt and closed barns on a hot day.
What had happened?

Too nervous to sleep, Melitta sat up in her blankets
and stared into the darkness. From the other side of
the dying fire, a pair of cat's eyes glared back at her.
The horses and chervines stamped restlessly. Should
she awaken Rafael? Before she could call out, the eyes
blinked once, then disappeared. Melitta scoured the
bushes with her gaze, watching for the eyes to reap-
pear. But she saw nothing. After a while, the animals
quieted, and Melitta snuggled into her blankets. A disturbing question followed her into sleep: What of the
child?

In the morning, they awoke to the quiet hissing of
falling snow. A thin blanket already covered the cold
ground. The bloody sun of Darkover was a glowing
ember behind the screen of snow-laden clouds. *Avarra
have mercy on us!* cried Melitta silently. If the snow
continued to fall throughout the day and into the night,
travel would be impossible for days. They would miss
Ysabet's birthing. A prickling at the back of her neck
made her uneasy. It was the type of feeling she had
when a summer storm was about to break.

Stefan's cry of surprise and frustration attracted her
to the line of riding and pack animals. When she and

Rafael joined the youth, he showed them the broken tethers.

The chervine calf and its dam were gone!

And Stefan pointed out tufts of hair—wolf, by the look of it—on nearby branches.

Melitta's spirits plummeted lower. The chervines were lost in the storm or dead, food for wolves.

"I should go after them," said Rafael. Melitta could tell by his flat voice he knew a search was useless.

"No," she said curtly, then realized she sounded annoyed. And she was, but there was no need to take her anger out on Rafael. Softening, she added, "There is no time to go after them even if there were a trail to follow. Lerrys needs care and Ysabet's baby could be born any minute!" She gazed toward the east, through the swirling flakes: *Ysabet, please be late with this baby. Please.* Then, to make up for her abruptness, "I will tell Father that the chervine's loss could not be helped." Rafael looked relieved.

A grunt of pain interrupted them. Lerrys sat with his blankets pushed back, his right foot, dark purple with bruising, exposed to the cold air. Rafael brought torn strips of clothing, and Melitta wrapped it around the foot, while Lerrys gritted his teeth against the agony. It was all she could do for now. The man needed an herb woman or a *leronis* who had been trained to use her psychic skills in healing. Well, for that they needed to get to Ysabet's.

After a quick meal huddled over the fire in their warmest clothing, they saddled the horses and loaded the pack animals, spreading the missing chervine's load between the two remaining animals. The entire party, including the animals, seemed irritable. Even Rafael's normally stolid mare nipped him in the shoulder.

As they began the journey up the east slope of the

valley, the two chervines bawled their displeasure at the heavier loads. The horses continued to balk whenever the trail wound southward, and the riders had to urge them forward. On the northward tracks, the horses moved eagerly through the ankle-deep snow. Fortunately, the snow remained dry and powdery on the cold ground, and the road was not icy.

They rode onward, winding up the eastern slope of the stream valley in which they had camped, then up and over a ridge and down into another valley.

Ahead of her Melitta saw first Lerrys, then Stefan break out of the forest into the afternoon sun. She rode into the warmth followed by Rafael who had the pack animals' lead rope tied to his saddle. A rocky slope lay before them, the stones dry in the warm sunshine. Mosses and lichens had begun to make their homes on the rocks. Traces of snow lingered where the sun's rays had yet to reach under the trees.

The heat felt good on her neck. A pain had been pressing against the base of her skull all morning. Hour after hour it had worsened. Now the sun's rays warmed and loosened the knot of muscles there.

Lerrys shouted and pointed to a flat spot of ground beyond the rocks. Melitta waved him on. Carefully, she and Rafael guided their mounts to it. The horses nickered and snorted as their hooves slipped on the loose stones. When they reached solid ground, Melitta's bay stopped for a moment and shook, a shiver that cascaded from head to tail. Melitta tugged on her reins and the horse drew up to the others, Rafael right behind her. She noticed that the road forked here, one path leading eastward, toward her sister, the other northward toward Mount Kimbi. The mountain seemed to loom over them now, the purple starkness of yesterday morning resolving to ridges and rocks and ice. It was clear they would not reach the Castamir estate before nightfall. And Lerrys plainly needed the warmth of a roof and a bed. "What is up the northward track?" she asked.

Lerrys squinted and peered north as if he could see through the trees. Behind them, Rafael volunteered, "Some small villages, farms."

"An estate or two, further along," added Lerrys, his voice tight with suppressed pain. "I remember visiting your sister's new kin with your father. But I recall not how long we were on the trail."

The muscles at the base of Melitta's skull tightened. She thought she heard a child laugh in the distance and turned to follow the sound.

"What is it," asked Rafael.

"I heard someone."

"Where?"

Melitta pointed up the northward track. She sensed a tugging from that direction, almost as if a fishing net had surrounded the four of them, horses and chervines included, and was being drawn in. Closer and closer. The faraway child was giggling and babbling its child's language. "Do you not hear him?" Melitta asked. The men shook their heads.

"Perhaps," ventured Stefan, "it is the wind, or the snow falling from trees."

But Melitta was certain she had heard a child's laughter. She had thought, *Do I have threshold sickness? At this late date? Or is someone out there, just up the trail?*

"Well, what do you think?" she asked, rubbing the back of her head, wishing they had reached Ysabet's and sat by the fire drinking hot *jaco*.

"If you hear a child, then a house or village may be but a short ride north," offered Rafael. Melitta looked at the pain reflected on Lerrys' face and agreed they should try the northward road.

They rode north for an hour, then another. Melitta's headache returned and grew more intense with each step. The child cried and babbled and laughed at the periphery of her awareness. Each time their party rounded a bend in the trail, Melitta thought she would see him sitting in the middle of the track. Each time they rounded a bend, the trail lay empty before them. The way continued, always tending northward.

They had just finished a long, steep climb, Melitta entering a meadow just as the men reached the trees at its far edge. The two men sat on their horses, apparently waiting for her to catch up. Lerrys had his right leg hooked around the pommel, looking almost as if he were riding a lady's saddle. Melitta supposed it gave him some relief from the pain of his injury. Stefan appeared to be trying boyish stunts, making his mare rear and paw the air, childish playing that could cause injury to the horse and its rider. She urged her own mare to pick up its pace. *How could he endanger himself like that! Wait until she got within shouting distance—*

Suddenly, the constant pressure that had been drawing them northward shifted. The force of it jerked her sideways. The bay slipped and fell to its knees. At the first jolt Melitta had pulled her feet from the stirrups; now she jumped to the ground. The bay rose to its feet, tossing its head, then butting her in the chest— throwing her off balance so she stumbled—before giving a little jump and fleeing down the grassy slope. Stefan shouted and set his horse after the runaway mare.

"Help me up!" yelled Melitta to Rafael who had ridden up to her. She yanked up her skirts and reached out her hand. Before he could disagree, she added, "I am coming with you whether you want me or no.

I will ride a chervine if I must!" Rafael sighed and grasped her forearm to help her swing up behind him.

The net of energies that had been tugging at them for two days pulled them toward the banks of a wide brook that cascaded over moss-covered boulders. The horses bolted toward the stream. Melitta felt Rafael sawing at the gelding's reins, trying to slow the horse to a walk, but it was no use. She had an instant to see animals and birds of every kind beyond the brook—*kyorebni* and crows perched in the trees. Horses and rabbit-horns were there . . . and a mountain cat, lithe and nervous, its tail flicking, and her two kits. And beyond them, a hut made of stones—then the horses charged through the water.

As they rushed up the other bank, she saw a young child standing amidst the beasts. The horses and chervines were still running and Melitta feared they would trample the boy. She shouted and waved, and she heard the men yelling, too. Then the gelding stopped so abruptly that Melitta and Rafael were pitched off and landed among squealing animals. So many, many animals.

Rubbing her head where a bump was forming, Melitta glanced up to see that Lerrys had managed to keep his seat in spite of his injured foot. Nearby, Rafael scrambled up from the ground, slapping his clothing to rid it of the worst of the snow and mud, while Stefan stared at the milling mass of animals from astride his mare, expressions of both disbelief and relief on his face.

The boy! Where was the boy! Had he been hurt? But no, there he was, toddling toward Stefan's mare, as if he were walking amid the bustle of Midsummer Festival. Evanda and Avarra be praised—he was all right. In the midst of this chaos, the remnants of last night's dream floated into remembrance . . . a boy surrounded, nearly suffocated, by animals of every kind.

"*Damisela*, are you harmed?" asked Rafael, coming to escort her away from the press of animals.

"No," she said, "just a bit shaken." Then she gave a little start, and Rafael inquired of her health again in a gentle voice. "Our chervines—there!" she exclaimed. "And the feeling," she added, sounding puzzled. "The tugging, as of a net pulling us in. It is gone!" She stared hard at the red-haired boy.

"What do you make of all this?"

"What I think," she said, "but scarcely believe, is that little boy has *laran*, the MacAran Gift in full measure." She turned to Stefan. "I am sorry for blaming you, brother—" She would have continued, but a shout cut through the bedlam. Melitta turned to see a tall, gaunt woman bearing down on them, fury on her face and a heavy skillet in her hands.

"Who are you?" shouted the woman, panicked eyes searching the still milling animals. "Garron! You come here! This moment!" She reached forward and snatched the child's hand from Rafael, who was already bringing the boy to his mother.

The woman straightened, prepared, Melitta thought, to do battle, when she stopped suddenly and stared, first at Melitta's red hair—the sign of the noble-born of Darkover, the Hastur-kin—then at Stefan's.

"*Vai dom, domna,*" she stammered and curtsied. "What brings you here?" Then she seemed to realize better manners were necessary, because she added, "I, Renata, am at your service."

Melitta stepped forward. "*Mestra* Renata," she said, "we are in need of assistance for an injured man."

"I have little here to help him. There is a village a long day's ride north. Or the Castamir's, south and east of here, is a bit closer."

Melitta glanced at the gathered animals, which were just now settling down. So many *different* animals! Now that they were here, would she and the men be able to coax their horses and chervines to leave? "I believe that might be a bit difficult. Perhaps we may discuss the matter inside."

Melitta saw the woman pause and sensed that she fought conflicting emotions. But then Lerrys, who was dismounting with Rafael's help, groaned, the sound filled with pain, and the woman turned toward him, arching her neck to see around people and beasts, and her features softened.

"For your friend." The woman picked up the boy and motioned for them to follow. As they walked toward the hut, the child struggled in his mother's grasp, extending grimy hands to the animals clustered around them. The woman set her feet down carefully, searching for spots free of beasts.

Renata bid them enter her sparsely furnished home. Seeing a pot of vegetables set to boil by the fire, Melitta sent Stefan for food from their bundles to add to the fare.

Immediately, Renata set to straightening the blankets on the bed, but Melitta stayed her with a word. "No, *mestra*. We will make our beds on the floor." Renata watched, astonished, as Rafael helped settle Lerrys on blankets before the fire.

While they ate, Melitta told how they journeyed to see Ysabet, and of the troubles they had had on the trail. Of how they finally came to follow the forces pulling at them from the north, until they had arrived at this place. Hesitantly, Melitta told how she believed Garron to be the source of the *laran* energies that had harassed them for two days.

Renata denied firmly that Garron could do such a thing.

As they ate, beasts gathered at the open door, poking their heads in and looking around. When they took tentative steps inside the room, Renata left the meal to chase them out, hissing and flapping a towel in their faces. Startled, the animals retreated and she closed the door.

"And you think the child has not *laran*," chided Stefan, as Garron began to fuss and whimper, demanding someone open the door for the "an'mals."

Renata shook her head in disbelief. "I knew his father was of a Great House by his red hair and rich clothing," she said quietly. "We met under the moons at Midsummer Festival and I know neither his name nor family. I expected to live the rest of my life here, alone, where my parents raised me—they died some years ago. The child was a gift of the Gods to gladden my days.

"But *laran* at so young an age!"

"Did you not wonder at the animals?"

"There were but a few at first. Rabbit-horns mostly."

"And when the cats arrived?"

"I feared them at first, but they seemed almost tame, like stable cats."

"You are overly patient," said Stefan around the food in his mouth. "If Garron were fostered at our house, Mother would have him living in the stables, for all the animals he tracks in. My brother had only colts follow him into the house, and she made him live in the stables for a tenday."

Melitta glared at her brother. "The time has come sooner than you expected, is all. Perhaps you should come with us to the Castamir estate, there to find training for the child."

"I could not. To leave this place—my home."

"The boy desperately needs training."

"You do not realize how powerful his Gift is," said

Rafael. "Soon more than rabbit-horns and chervines will come. What will the northern villagers say when the milk chervines and woollies abandon their pastures?"

"And," added Melitta, "we likely cannot leave here—" Renata looked at her in confusion "—the animals were drawn by Garron. I doubt he will let them leave."

"You are a *leronis*," answered the woman. "You have a starstone. I see its pouch at your throat. Cast a spell that frees Garron from the animals."

"It is more that the beasts must be freed from your son."

"I believe you not."

Melitta bid Stefan ride to the main trail and back.

"You are not serious!"

"I certainly am!" she said. "And take the calf on the leading rope," she called as Stefan left, shaking his head.

Without a word, the others followed Stefan out of the hut, Renata holding Garron in her arms, Rafael helping Lerrys, who could not bear any weight on his right foot. Stefan saddled his mare, caught up the calf's leading rope, mounted, and headed up the path at a trot. Until the first turning.

There both animals stopped, legs splayed, and refused to move. Stefan kicked and shouted, until the copper mare bucked a little in rebellion. And, finally, he rode back to the hut, the chervine calf pulling ahead eagerly and trotting up to nose Garron's hand. Renata's wide-eyed gaze fell upon Melitta for a moment before she went inside the hut.

There was little more they could discuss. Darkness had followed Stefan up the valley, the four travelers were tired, and with little comment, the six bedded down for the night.

Melitta woke before dawn, a feeling of unease growing within her. Lerrys moved restlessly on his pallet. They had to leave! Ysabet's time was growing ever nearer and Lerrys clearly needed the attention of a healer. How were they to convince Renata to abandon her home? How did one explain to a two-year-old child that the "pretty horsies" had to leave?

Melitta was helping Renata prepare the morning meal when a cry sounded. Stefan had accompanied Garron outside, Melitta's brother to heed nature's call and the child to visit his playmates. When Stefan shouted for help, Melitta dropped the bowl, which shattered on the floor, and joined Renata in a race for the door, Rafael at their heels.

Beside her, Melitta heard Renata gasp. A huge wolf loomed over Garron, who clutched and pulled happily at the beast's fur as if it were a well-behaved hound. Melitta, fear rising within her like well leavened bread, felt the boy's mother move, ready to save her son from the wolf's claws. She placed a hand on Renata's arm, warning her to stillness. Frightened wolves were known to attack even grown men.

"We must think first," she breathed.

Behind her Lerrys spoke. She turned and saw that he had caught up a stick and used it to help support his weight. Slowly, slowly, he edged toward the wolf and the boy. By the time Melitta realized the man's intent, it was too late to stop him. Four pairs of eyes followed Lerrys as he limped forward in a line bearing slightly left of the wolf and the boy.

"Fool," murmured Rafael in an admiring voice.

Melitta clutched at Renata's arm. "What will distract the boy?" she hissed.

The woman appeared flustered for a moment only. "Another animal. A rabbit-horn, something small and cuddly."

Most of the animals had retreated, finding shelter in brambles and small bushes. Only the mountain cat and her two kits remained in the open, softly growling, tails twitching.

"Find a rabbit-horn, if you can," Melitta whispered, then approached the cats, step by step. All three turned their heads from the boy and the wolf to glare at her. Warily, they stood and she feared they would bolt if she advanced further.

Melitta turned and saw that the wolf's eyes tracked Lerrys. The beast stood on all fours now, a deep growl rumbling from his chest, Garron seemingly forgotten. Then Lerrys stumbled, and unable to recover his balance, fell to the ground. Melitta had to do something!

"Kitty, Garron," said Melitta in a low voice, trying to sound calm as her heart pounded in panic.

"See the kitty, Garron?" pleaded Renata. "Come to the kitty."

Garron yanked once, hard, on the wolf's fur, but the animal was intent on Lerrys, who struggled to stand. When the wolf failed to respond, Garron turned at last and his gaze fastened on the cats. He toddled forward. Behind him, the wolf crouched, preparing to pounce on the injured man. As soon as the child was a man's stride from the wolf, Rafael and Stefan rushed forward, waving their arms and yelling.

Renata fell on her son with a sigh, believing the crisis over, but Melitta again cautioned her to stillness. She spilled her starstone from its pouch onto her palm. Blue lightnings glittered in its depths. She allowed her mind to merge with the energies of the stone, letting her awareness stretch until it encompassed the child and the wolf. Finally, she saw the net of energies that emanated from the boy. Blue strands connected Garron with all the animals. Melitta tracked down the single line that ran from the boy to the wolf, reached out with her mind, and broke the cord.

The wolf, which had refused to retreat, suddenly flinched, then shook from head to tail, as if awakened from a dream. Then it spun about and ran.

"Well, Renata," said Melitta. "You and your child are safe for now. But what will you do when another wolf appears. Or banshees. What will you do then?"

"Banshees?" whispered Renata. "Blessed Cassilda!" She turned to Melitta. "It will take but little time to pack."

Melitta led their tired group up to the Great House. Servants ran to take the horses and pack animals, but quickly stopped and backed away from the band, shaking their heads, retrieving tools and holding them like weapons.

Melitta slid from her horse and shouted for someone to take it to the barns. No one moved forward. She glanced at the riders behind her, making a noise of frustration. During their journey, most of the beasts had slipped away to return to their forest homes. However, the mountain cat and her two kits still trailed after Garron who sat on Rafael's lap. Neither shouting nor rock-throwing had been sufficient to chase them away.

Well, she had no time to coddle servants. Lerrys needed medical attention and Melitta sensed that Ysabet was on the verge of giving birth. She pointed to the closest man and ordered him to help Lerrys into the house, then she handed over the bay's reins to a second man as she stomped past him. Stefan would have to take care of Renata and Garron.

Melitta rushed into the house and up the stairs to her sister's bedside. As soon as she entered the room, Ysabet and Brydar gave a great exclamation. For several heartbeats, the room was silent but for their hard breathing, then their cry was echoed by a newborn's first wailing. The midwife held a baby boy in her arms.

The Chieri's Godchild

by Cynthia McQuillin

Cynthia McQuillin was featured in my first anthology, and I remember I started off my introduction by asking: "Is there anything this young woman can't do?" At that time I was speaking of her artistic abilities. People who are fluent with artwork rarely make good writers; people who think in pictures, in my experience, are seldom fluent in words. There are famous exceptions, however; I just bought a cover for my magazine, along with her own story, by Janny Wurts; and I discovered that George Barr, best known as an artist, also had undiscovered writing talents. And my well-known favorite Darkover artist, Hannah Shapero, has, so I found out at Darkovercon 1992, written and is circulating a novel. Maybe I only think it rare because I have very little artistic ability.

Whether it's all that rare or not, Cindy undeniably has both. As I said, I printed one of her stories in the first Darkover anthology. That, too, if memory serves me, was about a chieri ... a theme which has seldom been well handled by other writers. But I think Cindy, (who is at present a member of my household and one of the few people about whom I'll admit her cooking is as good as mine—another of her many talents) definitely handled it well. Don't you agree?

* * *

Chiaryl felt a deep and inexplicable sense of sorrow as he watched Merilys, sure-footed as a doe, scrambling down the slope. It seemed such a short time ago that he'd found the human child crying over her parents' bodies, hopeless and alone in the depths of the forest he called home. They had been foolish to travel so far into the wilderness with such a small party; but from what he'd been able to learn from the girl, then a child of nine or ten, her parents had fled in fear from their own kind to seek refuge in the trackless mountain stands. They'd lost that gamble and the child would have been lost too, if not for Chiaryl's intervention. Now the *chieri* had begun to regret his decision to adopt this alien child.

The few remaining members of Chiaryl's powerful and once vital people had grown morbid and solitary over the long years, mourning the death of their species and their world. They were beings of transitory gender—one season male, another female, and still another sexless. They had grown fewer with the passing of time as the mating urge came less and less frequently, until finally no children were born at all. Perhaps it had been a secret longing for a child of her own that caused Chiaryl, then in her female phase, to adopt Merilys. It might have been kinder to let her die in the mountain snows or, since the *chieri* had felt compelled to rescue her, to have returned her to her own kind. Still, what was done was done. *She* had grown to love Merilys and now *he* had only himself to blame for the consequences.

"Chiaryl, look what Chacka has found for supper," Merilys burbled happily as she bounded up the slope toward him. She held out a huge brown mushroom. "There's a whole ring of them under the trees down there."

The *kyrri*, a creature akin to, but not as developed as the *chieri*, trundled up the hill after the girl. He'd had charge of her for almost six years now; and at Chiaryl's bidding he faithfully followed her about, half playmate and half nursemaid.

"Oh, such a grumpy bear," the girl teased. She rumpled the *kyrri*'s fur, so different from the silken smooth feel of a chieri's skin. Indeed, the two creatures were as different in appearance as they were in texture. Chiaryl was tall and elvishly slender with long wisps of silvery white hair, gray eyes, and a fragile appearance even during his male season. Chacka was tall and burly, with a plush white pelt and dark, piercing, animal eyes.

You should be kind to your companion, Chiaryl's gentle thoughts chided her. *He is less quick than you in many ways.*

"I'm sorry," Merilys replied, contritely digging her toe into the ground. "It's just that I'm so excited! I haven't seen any of my people for so long."

Have you been unhappy, little one? the *chieri* asked silently, his thoughts featherlike in the child's mind. He'd vainly hoped she might acquire the mind-touch so she could communicate with him in this intimate way, but she stubbornly clung to human speech. Now, he supposed, it was just as well.

"No, Chiaryl, I haven't been unhappy . . ." she said, sensing his hurt. "Surely you must know that I love you and Chacka. It's just that I hate being cooped up all the time, and there's no one to talk to." It was true; except for the brief summer season, Merilys was confined to the *chieri*'s cavern, which was heated by a natural hot spring through the deadly chill of winter. Though he and Chacka were able to withstand the cold, she could not. It was no wonder she reveled in her freedom.

Well, soon we shall have you back with your own kind, he returned kindly. He smiled wistfully, watching her shaggy mane of red hair fly as she jogged back down the trail. As usual, Chacka was right behind. And he had thought to keep her with him forever! Chiaryl shook his head sadly at his own folly. That desire had been born of loneliness and despair, he realized now. Even if she had stayed for the rest of her life, it wouldn't have been long enough, for the *chieri* were a very long-lived race. He would still have died alone. But he might have kept her longer if the Summer Dream Winds hadn't precipitated his rather dramatic change of gender a month or so earlier.

The hallucinogenic pollen of the blue flower his people called Dream Breath affected every living creature, even the *chieri*. The most remarkable side effect of the golden dust was sexual promiscuity, though it also intensified psychic ability. It had been a very long time since Chiaryl had experienced a gender shift when the winds blew. Perhaps Merilys' budding womanhood had stirred the change within him; but for whatever reason, it had happened. In that state of heightened psycho-sexual arousal he'd been unable to resist the mating urge. Chiaryl sensed the moment of conception with a kind of joyous wonder under the pollen's influence; but with the return of sanity came the realization that Merilys must return to her own kind to bear and raise her child. It had been ill done to keep her away from her own people for so long, and he realized that now.

Noting the cooling of the air and sudden darkening of the sky that heralded the onset of night, Chiaryl hurried down to join his companions. He found them busily making camp on a stretch of sheltered ground just off the rugged trail they followed. The *chieri* built a fire from the wood Chacka had gathered and began preparing a soup of the mushrooms, adding dried herbs from the stock he'd brought. It was good that they were near the human-held lands, he thought, for there was little warmth left to the season. Once the snow began to fall, Merilys would find the journey a hardship rather than an adventure.

Chiaryl found no rest that night though he tried; even the sedative herbs did nothing to soothe his restive mind. Finally, he rose and decided to walk for a while in the moonlight. Three of the four moons were in the sky; the largest hung very low on the horizon, just about to set. The *chieri* needed no light to guide him, though, able to see perfectly well by the psychic energy emanating from everything about him.

One with the life of his world, as well as the living things it nurtured, he experienced a sense of peaceful acceptance as he let his mind open to the peace of the night while he followed the soothing flow of a small stream that washed down the hillside. Chiaryl and his kind had watched as Merilys' strange new race bravely emerged from the vessel which had carried them so far from their home world. They set about conquering his world with a joyful kind of desperation that fascinated him. The *chieri* people, with their deep, abiding love of life, found hope rather than a threat in these strange invaders. Perhaps this was his answer, Chiaryl thought, as he circled back at last.

When he returned to their humble camp, he stood looking at Merilys where she lay snuggled in the *kyrri*'s arms. She still seemed very much like a child. How quickly she'd grown and matured; but they were like that, these humans. They grew quickly, died quickly, and bred promiscuously, all the while striving to grow in knowledge and skill as well as territory and power. Humans were a primitive and brutal race by *chieri* standards, and yet they bore a spark of that higher self which his people cherished. More than likely, though, it was their sheer vitality which would allow them to carve a niche in the hostile environment of this frigid world.

And now, Chiaryl realized, their vitality offered hope to his own dying breed as well. He smiled as he casually monitored the growth of his son within Merilys' belly. The two species were obviously compatible, as the conception proved; but would the offspring be viable? The embryo seemed strong and healthy to Chiaryl's tentative probing; and he gave every indication of bearing his father's psychic gifts, though he would bear the stamp of his mother in features and coloring. But that was just as well, the *chieri* decided, for if he were too strange the settlers wouldn't accept him.

Merilys began to stir in Chacka's protective embrace, and Chiaryl noticed wearily that the sun had painted the sky with its magenta dawn light. Sensing the girl's waking, the *kyrri* was instantly alert and unfolded himself from around her as she strove to sit up. Groggily she rose and went off to the stream to make her morning ablutions and relieve herself. It amused the *chieri* that she'd developed such a sense of modesty with him after all this time. Perhaps she still felt awkward because of the intimacy they'd shared under the influence of the Dream Breath.

During his nocturnal peregrinations, Chiaryl had discovered a human settlement nearby. He'd seen the palisade walls and crude buildings in the valley clearly outlined in the starlight. It seemed a large enough community to support an extra person, and was certainly well defended. They could easily reach the holding by early afternoon; but he was reluctant just to leave her with the first humans they found, so he told Merilys that he would go ahead of them that morning. They would follow when they'd breakfasted and broken camp.

Just as he'd assessed it the previous night, the holding was reasonably sized and well established. It occurred to him that this might be the very place Merilys' parents had fled, but the memories he'd gleaned from her certainly didn't seem to indicate it. Finding a spot where he could remain unobserved for a while, he settled in to watch the people coming and going, and attending to their chores. There were numerous children of various ages who teased each other as they fed the animals penned inside the barricade. Everyone he saw was well fed and appeared to be happy and healthy enough.

After a while, Chiaryl established light rapport with one of the women he'd been watching. She was busy washing out bedding and hanging it up to dry. He let his mind-touch seep lightly into her surface thoughts. She was slightly bored, but pleased that they would have clean bedding to sleep in. She went about her work with a light heart, as she anticipated the return of her husband and son that day. They'd been out on a hunting trip in the deep woods, hoping to add to the supply of meat the villagers were salting and smoking for the leaner days that winter would bring. The larders were fairly well stocked already, but any surplus would be welcome; it seemed there was never enough meat come midwinter. And besides, once the heavy snows began, the herds would seek higher ground where they could forage bark from the trees, and the rabbit-horns and birds would all be nestled safe in their dens; hunting then would be futile.

The woman had only one son; and though she had long wanted a daughter, she knew this could never be. Complications during her first pregnancy had left her unable to carry another child to term. *That was certainly promising,* Chiaryl thought. Not quite satisfied, though, he sampled a few of the other people, finding them all to be of similar temperament. Then, having learned what he'd come to learn, Chiaryl carefully withdrew back upslope to meet Chacka and Merilys on their way down. Naturally, Merilys had seen the settlement from above and was anxious to get there. She tugged at the *chieri*'s hand when he just stood there looking sadly down at her.

You go ahead, little one, he whispered in her mind. *Chacka and I must stay here.*

"You aren't coming with me?" she asked, suddenly at a loss. "But I thought. . . ."

No, he interrupted her stream of unspoken objections, *it would be better if they didn't see us, and you would also be wise not to mention who sired your child.*

"Then I'll never see you again." Her face crumpled into tears and she hugged him fiercely.

I will watch over you, he replied, *and your children's children as well.* His eyes glowed warmly as he gently pushed her away so that he could look into her eyes. *If you have need of me, I will know.* He opened her hand and, lightly kissing it, laid a small luminescent blue crystal in her upturned palm. *You have only to look into this stone and think of me and I will know.* As she looked into its depths, the stone began to glow; then it sparkled to life, pulsing with the beat of her heart.

I love you, her thought met his for the first time. *And I do understand, but I shall miss you and Chacka terribly.*

He touched her face lightly with the tips of his fingers and nodded. *There is a woman named Marja doing her wash below. Go to her and she will take you in. You have only to follow the stream.*

"Thank you," she whispered, breaking the contact that had become too painfully intimate. Then she turned and ran down the path, taking nothing with her but his parting gift.

Chacka moaned plaintively as he watched her retreat, then came to lay his hand on the *chieri*'s shoulder. *Yes, I know, old friend. We are again alone, but not without hope this time.* Chiaryl smiled to himself, thinking again of his grandchildren's grandchildren.

Fire In The Hellers
by Patricia Shaw Mathews

*Pat is another writer who has been with us since be-
fore I was a Darkover anthologist and whose version
of Darkover is about as close to my own as anyone's.
She says that she still lives in Albuquerque, is divorced
with two daughters who are now grown and moved
away (one in the Peace Corps—I at first wrote "Peace
Cops," an interesting typo in view of our current foreign policy), and she inherited their cats. When my
kids left home, the cats all went with them—Patches
with Beth, Mozart with Kristoph—and I was left with
only a toy stuffed cat (Victoria Regina) who never,
never claws the furniture or makes a mess on the rug.
I sometimes wonder if the disadvantages don't outweigh the advantages of this arrangement. Or do I
mean the advantages outweigh the disadvantages?*

*Pat said that "Brother Auster in this story is based on
and a tribute to the Reverend Mr. James Patterson Shaw
from Western Pennsylvania, 1911–1966, who went through
the worst of World War II as an unarmed Red Cross vol-
unteer rather than compromise his principles, and still
picked up a Silver Star for valor. Like many of his generation, he became a moderate in midlife, but never
changed his views on social justice. Like C.S. Lewis'
bishop, he may be preaching it in hell, where they need it
far more than they do in heaven. Rest in Peace."*

To which I can only say a heartfelt Amen.

* * *

The harsh, watery light of the boundary between late winter and early spring pierced the stone latticework on the wall above the cobbled walkway, stinging Father Master's aged eyes. The wind shifted fitfully, biting through the old monk's worn brown robes as he moved slowly along the walkway at the back of the line. Ahead of him, a double line of brown-robed monks shuffled along the snow-covered cobblestones, the youngest first, trying not to seem cold.

One tall, rangy, graduating novice walked as if neither cold nor heat had any meaning for him. Brother Auster, whose turn it was to read the sermon for the day.

"We have to do something about Brother Auster," Father Master heard Novice Master Randale grumble, just before they entered the tiny, frozen chapel. His normally soft voice was locked down in his throat as if to keep him from shouting. "We can't keep him here."

The Novice Master slowed his steps as much as he dared, then picked up his pace as a flurry of snowflakes dashed against his scarlet cheeks. His half-bald pate was white with cold; his bushy graying eyebrows were locked together in a frown. "He's a troublemaker."

The rough, backless benches were filling up as the red sun peeked out from behind a vagrant cloud to briefly warm the stone-carved entrance to the chapel. "You know that, and I know that," Father Master agreed. "But can we prove it? His record is as blameless as that of young Varzil yonder." A jerk of his chin indicated the young redheaded postulant at the beginning of the rapidly dwindling line.

Father Master moved his head slightly as the old monks before him filed into the chapel. The Novice Master took his seat, and the doorkeeper swung the heavy wooden doors shut behind them. The sounds of the ages-old Office of Evensong began, the clear soprano voices of the youngest postulants and students blending with the adolescent altos and the full range of men's voices in a chant that briefly brought tears to the older monk's eyes. One moment of peace, before that peace would shatter.

". . . and woe be unto those," Brother Auster declaimed, his right hand swinging outward a bit more than was proper for a monk, "who take part in this abomination called a Breeding Program!" His hands were huge and callused, with the powerful bones of a mountain man. "Woe unto those who drag pure young maidens and virgin boys from their parents' homes, to lie with their masters and whoever their masters shall choose, for they shall burn in hell forever!"

His betrothed? a postulant in his mid-teens mouthed at a benchmate. The Novice Master started to frown at young Varzil, then let the breach of discipline go by.

His little sister, a rawboned mountain youth mouthed back. *She killed herself rather than submit. She wasn't yet twelve years old.*

Oh. The Ridenow boy's refined, aristocratic face paled, and he looked up at the young preacher with mingled guilt for the deeds of his elders, and hope.

"Woe unto those who force their children to lie even with their own father's sons and daughters, for the sake of this," Brother Auster's long, mobile mouth twisted in contempt, "Breeding Program, for their sons and daughters will not forgive them; nor will God Above. Woe unto those," the young monk's voice rose to a shout, his broad cheekbones streaked with a hot red flush, "who lie with animals as with humans, so that a truthful man must call himself true brother to a speechless beast; for this is an abomination in the sight of men and God! The fires of hell shall consume all those—you know who I mean, brethren!—who do these things and who order them done, and the ghosts of their innocent victims shall not forgive these *Hali'imyn* their deeds!"

Brother Auster stopped speaking. His breath rasped in the chilly air, and his long, heavily knuckled fingers twitched silently. Boys in their teens and young men in their twenties looked up at him, a few hot with anger, but most of them hungry, as if for the truth none of their elders dared speak.

Massed voices now rose, harmonizing, in a hymn of praise to the beauty of love and creation. Brother Auster's brilliant blue eyes stared upward and to the left as the song passed over his sandy, tonsured, freckled head unheard and uncomprehended. "We have to do something about Brother Auster," Father Master admitted as the monks filed out of the chapel.

A reeking tallow candle guttered in the wind that blew through a crack in the shutters of Father Master's office. Novice Master Randale brushed a sprinkling of snow from his stool and sat down, a heavy black leatherbound book on his lap. Outside, the night wind whistled through the barren branches. "No breach of discipline at all," he said in disgust. "Saving a few minor offenses, most of them accidental. Talking too loud. An occasional uncharitable statement."

Father Master laced his thin, aged fingers together. "Who among us has not done the same?" he asked softly. "Does he take his penance like a man?"

The Novice Master shifted his weight on the wobbly stool and drew his arms closer to his body for warmth as a banshee cried in the distance. "Worse. He confesses immediately and takes it upon himself to discipline himself."

"An excess of zeal," the older monk murmured, running a blue-veined hand through what was left of the thinning white hair at the back of his head.

Novice Master Randale snorted rudely. "The boy's a fanatic," he said flatly.

"He's suffered much," Father Master put in, his voice mild. "What about his followers?"

Randale's plump lips tightened. "He urges them to greater strictness in keeping the Rule. No meat there. And his rabble-rousing sermons . . ."

"Are within strict doctrinal limits," Father Master confessed.

The two monks looked at each other in the dim, fitful candlelight. "He can't stay here," Father Master said at last. "But we have no cause to expel him."

"He's a gifted preacher," the Novice Master admitted, shifting his weight again. He rubbed one hand with the other. "And the abuses he speaks of exist. If I didn't fear repercussions against our Order, small and vulnerable as it is, I'd be tempted to send him out against the Comyn lords and let them destroy each other. Or perhaps he'll antagonize one of those half-nonhumans he was ranting about and learn his lesson."

Father Master shook his head. "He's from the Hellers, where nonhumans abound."

"Where the only good nonhuman is a dead nonhuman," Novice Master Randale said sourly. Then an almost vicious smile came to his lips. "Where they're farther from any sort of true religion than even Comyn, for at least the Comyn gods claim to be good. Well, three out of the four do, at any rate. But the folk of the Hellers, to a man, woman, and child, adore this female fire-demon. . . ."

Father Master caught his eye. "Don't oversell your case, Randale. Who knows?" He looked upwards.

"The boy might even convert those demon-worshiping mountain folk."

The Novice Master grimaced. "And the Hundred Kingdoms might unite and lay down their arms forever, too."

The red sun of Darkover had yet to rise for another hour, but Brother Auster moved through the refectory with bowls of porridge as efficiently as he had once tended cattle on his father's homestead. The soft voices of monks and students, freed during meals from the Rules of Silence, filled the room with an understated hum.

Auster's long-jawed face was dour, as always, as he laid the wooden bowls on his assigned table and sat for prayers.

"Aye, Brother Varzil," he told the young postulant who had blanched at his sermon the day before. "'Tis true what I said, every bit. May the Bearer of Burdens dump me in the Kadarin if I did ought but soften the tale for the tender ears of the wee lads yonder. 'Twas my own laird's deeds, no better than the rest but no worse neither, as drove me to this place for fear I would slay him the way yon maid I spoke of did slay herself." Auster's accent thickened as his rawboned face darkened. "'Tis a sin, as murder be a sin, and I do think day and night upon it." He looked up suddenly as a shadow fell across his table. "Aye, Father Master?"

The older monk was mincing around something unpleasant. Brother Auster sat, his hands folded quietly as the Rule decreed, wrestling with his short stock of patience. The old monk beckoned, spoke briefly to him, then mounted the lectern at the end of the dining hall. "Today Brother Auster, Novice in our Order, has been called to go forth into the Hellers, his native country, there to spread the message of the Bearer of

Burdens," Father Master said briefly. "Brother Auster. Do you accept this commission?"

Brother Auster, forewarned, rose. His blue eyes gleamed hot. "I do. 'Tis an honor," he said briefly, and sat down again.

The nobly-born boy stared up in outrage. "The Hellers! Why, that's . . . that's a punishment duty! And all you did was tell the truth. I can tell him some tales from my own house. . . ."

Auster's lips twisted. "Varzil, lad," he said, keeping his voice soft with an effort. "Ye think I dinna ken the cause o' them sending me into the hills? Fear o' the *Hali'imyn* and a vast dislike o' trouble. Dinna trouble yersel'; I go willingly."

Varzil's frown vanished. "I see. What a marvelous test of your faith, Brother Auster." His eyes were shining.

"Aye. 'Tis," Brother Auster answered, lips clamped around the urge to stop the boy's blather with one work-hardened fist. There was a lack of charity, Auster's hard-driving conscience reminded him, that was worthy of such a sinful, ill-tempered wretch as he was! For he had brawled, head-down in the beer jug, with the other lads at home. He had reived away other holders' cattle with his brothers; and the temptations to do all those things were still with him.

The vision of his betrothed, sold by her father to be a Comyn lord's concubine, rose before him, then his sister's still, white form as they laid her in the thin, hard mountain soil; and the hateful, sleek-furred beast that lisped the message of her death. His father's face, as stony as the land he held; his mother's worn and weary resignation.

He would go into the Hellers, back to his own people, even as these mewling *Hali'imyn*-fearing cowards had ordered. He would not preach armed revolt. But he would tell them plain that there was one God, who abominated what the Comyn lords were doing. Men of the Hellers were men of reason, who thought for themselves and would rise up for what was right.

"When I'm old enough," the young Comyn lad said impatiently, "I'll ask Father Master to send me out to join you."

Auster shook his head. "Sooner the Hundred Kingdoms will lay down their arms and make peace," he unconsciously quoted Novice Master Randale, "and the Comyn lairds turn to the path o' righteousness. There be your work, lad, if you set your hand to it."

Varzil bit his lip. "If anyone could make that happen," he said doubtfully, "I'll believe in miracles for sure."

Auster fixed him with a cold blue eye. "An' d'ye doubt the miracles, laddie?"

The bloody sun shone down on the tiny mountain village, glinting off a stray patch of ice-melons. As Brother Auster's mule plodded into the holding, the weary monk caught a glimpse of long, furry ears twitching in the melon patch, and despite himself, he smiled. Hard people of a hard land, his own were no tame sheep to herd!

In Dead Man's Crossing, one of the local farmers had rolled a barrel of firewater to the door where he was preaching, and had offered it freely to all comers, so he had preached to a congregation as drunk as monks at Midwinter Festival. At Crooked Creek, one of the locals had dressed up in a poor imitation of his robes and spent the night with a plump widow, passing the word around that Auster had done so. Near Bitenose Peak, an old woman had belabored him in public for disrespecting his elders. And at Mulekick Pass, a raucous heckler's daughter had turned her back and lifted her skirts to show him her opinion of his preaching. His people.

More, they took to his hellfire-and-brimstone message so readily, he ended up shouting at them "Dinna ye think I ken why ye take so well to these teachings? 'Tis the hope o' sinning all yer life an' staying warm i' the hereafter!"

"Ye needna' worry yerself about stayin' warm," a buxom farmwife shouted back. "All that hot air ye spout'll keep ye as toasty warm as a lamb by the fire! What's the Comyn lairds to us or we to them? Let them bide i' the lowlands with their kind and we gang our ain way as allus!"

Suddenly the sky darkened and the ground cried out. The hillside shook, and the skies in the south reddened as if the very world were on fire. Brother Auster gaped, then swung one long leg off his mule and dropped to the ground, face in the dirt. The hillside swayed back and forth as if the mountains were about to fall, and the world flared up in a flash of blue-white light so bright Brother Auster could see the very bones of his hands through his flesh. He lay, scarcely daring to breathe, as the land collapsed and re-formed around him in a burst of noise louder than a thousand rolls of thunder.

This is death, he thought, *and this is the damnation I have long preached and long feared, tha' will be done.* Around him, in his mind, he could hear a million frantic voices screaming "I believe; oh, great Bearer of Burdens, I have seen the fire and I believe."

A sob burst from his lips. *I didna' want ye to believe fra' fear,* his mind cried out, *but from the righteous rage at a' the evil done.*

The mountains shook again and settled into place, shaking themselves ever more lightly until the tremblors ceased. Brother Auster rose and shook himself

the same way, and looked around. The forest around
him was not on fire, for which God be praised, but to
the south and east, the sky blazed with a grimly unnat-
ural fire. In the distance, Brother Auster could see the
hellfires he preached raining down upon the land, and
his soul wept blood for the people trapped therein. His
people.

A black cloud roiling overhead opened enough to
rain down soot that dusted Auster's habit and his tonsured head. A few grim, frightened men ventured down
the road from the village beyond, armed with pitch-
forks and anything else they owned. "I believe,
preacher," the oldest of them said, raising a long cattle-
skinning knife, "but ye didn't have to go proving it on
our hides."

Brother Auster faced the old man's weathered face
and cold grey eyes calmly. "'Twas not I who brought
this on ye, but the lairds of the lands below. But if it's
a scapegoat ye're wanting, then my blood be on it. Or
would ye sooner I help fight the fires ye see below?"

As the old mountain man scratched his head, perplexed, Brother Auster looked up at the cloud, now
covering all the sky. Already the land was starting to
turn as cold as winter, though it was near to midsummer. Live or die, he would preach no more unless
asked, for the evils he had preached against were
gone—dead by their own hand. Now the world needed
a miracle. *Brother Varzil,* he thought as he waited for
the old mountain man to use his knife or not, *I'm sorry
I misled ye. There's no miracle in store for ye. I believe; oh, God, forgive my unbelief.*

But I do believe, the ghost—or was it the living
soul?—of the Comyn lad from long ago—answered.
*Not in your God, but in your Cause. And miracles can
happen if we make them happen.*

Nay, Auster thought with his last breath. *Only justice happens. 'Ware what you ask for, lad; ye might get it.*

Behind him, the lands that had once been the Hundred Kingdoms blazed in grisly glory.

A Matter of Perception

by Lena Gore

I met Lena Gore at the World Fantasy Convention in Georgia, approximately two weeks after I bought this story. She has a husband (an officer in the Coast Guard), one son, one daughter, one dog, and "the required two cats." She lived in California for 17 years, before her husband (and, perforce, the rest of the family) was transferred to Texas.

She was involved in a serious car accident in April, resulting in neck surgery in June, followed by extensive physical therapy. She tells me that any of the therapists who had not read my books when she started therapy were reading them by the time she was done— apparently she spent a good deal of her therapy time flat on her back reading one of my books. (I hope they were a suitable distraction from the pain—I've had physical therapy, too, and it is not exactly a fun experience.)

Lena asked me to put in a Thank You to the Physical Therapy Department at St. Mary's Hospital in Galveston, Texas. She says "Thanks to them I can walk normally and turn my head again. Their tireless efforts enabled me to make the trip to see you in Georgia." I am happy to do so. A good physical therapist is definitely to be valued above rubies.

* * *

Branith and Dora sauntered lazily down the hill in the hot sweltering summer sun. "Peel the potatoes, draw the water, feed the animals. I hate the country! I want to live in the city and go to parties and sing and dance," lamented Branith. "I'm almost seventeen, I have no *laran* yet and I refuse to marry a lack-a-wit farm boy. What kind of life would that be?"

Dora turned a baleful eye upon her sister, "You never want to do your share of the work, Branith. You always want to be Miss High-and-Mighty, marry a rich Comyn lord, and live happily ever after."

"What's wrong with wanting to be rich and have fun, Dora? You're such a plain thing, I'll bet *you* never think about beautiful clothes and handsome dashing men. All you ever do is talk to these stupid animals as if they really understand you. Here, you draw the water. I don't want blisters and calluses on my hands. No Comyn lord would want a lady with farm-wife hands."

"No Comyn lord would want a head-blind lazy ninny, you mean," replied Dora crossly.

Branith petulantly thrust the oaken bucket at Dora, then lifted her skirts and twirled about as if she were already in her dream castle.

The two girls were as different as night and day. Where Branith was fair, Dora was tanned from the sun. Branith's hair was silky blonde, Dora's mousey brown. Brainth's eyes were crystal blue, Dora's the color of mountain heather. Dora had *laran,* an odd mix of Ridenow, Alton, and Aldaran. Branith had none.

Dora snatched the bucket angrily. "You're such a lazy lack-a-wit yourself, Branith. I do all the work and you just preen about. Well, I hope you get your wish. A fine castle and a dashing Comyn lord with it. You're certainly no help here."

"You're just jealous," Branith snapped at her. "You'll never be anything but a milkmaid. You're always pretending to see things with your stupid *laran* that no one else can see. It's just your way to get attention."

"I do see things," Dora exclaimed heatedly. "Just because *you* don't see them doesn't mean they're not there."

Dora placed the bucket on the winch rope and angrily flipped the lever. The bucket fell swiftly to the bottom with a resounding splash. Fearing that the bucket had fallen off, Dora peered into the well. Ripples flowed outward from the dark water below. The water calmed and a pair of evil yellow eyes stared back at her. Dora screamed and fell back, clutching her hands about her head and nearly fainting.

"What's wrong now, Dora? Did you drop the bucket again? I hate fishing for that stupid thing. Get out of the way, let me see."

"Nooo!" Dora gasped, unable to catch her breath. "Eyes ... in the well. Horrible yellow eyes! Demon eyes! Don't go near it, Bran!"

"What are you talking about? Are you having an attack from the heat or is your *laran* running wild again? Let me see before you get us both in trouble with Father for losing another bucket."

Branith approached the well and peered down at the dark water. A joyous shout escaped her lips. "Help me, Dora! There's a man down there. He must have fallen in, and ... oh, he's so gorgeous!"

Dora stared incredulously at Branith. Grabbing the edge of the well, she forced herself once more to look over the edge at the dark water. A tremor shook her as the demon's head rose above the water, the stench of it nearly gagging her.

"Are you going to help me or not, dumbbell?" shouted Branith, angrily shaking her.

"I ... I can't, Branith. It's not a man, it's a demon!

Let's get out of here and tell Father. Please, Bran!"
Dora pleaded.

"Dora, you're crazy as a sun-stroked *cralmac*.
That's a man down there and you're going to help me
get him out, do you hear? Now grab that rope and help
me pull him up," Branith shouted, shoving her roughly
toward the well.

Dazed and wondering if Branith were right and she
really was going crazy from her *laran*, Dora shakily
grasped the rope. As she leaned over the well to grab
more rope, the yellow eyes glared back at her. *This is
probably just a hallucination from threshold sickness. I
can't give in. I've got to help Bran,* she thought.

All the while, Branith was busily pulling on the rope
and drawing the handsome, silent man upward nearer
and nearer to the top.

I wonder who he is? thought Branith. *Maybe he is
rich and lives in the city and just stopped at the well
for a drink and fell in. Oh, Goddess, I hope he's rich
and will take me to his castle to thank me for saving
his life.* Already she could see herself twirling across
the beautiful marble floor of a fabulous castle in the
arms of this handsome man.

He was at the top now and both girls reached to
grasp his arms to help him out. Dora retched at the
slimy feel and putrid smell of the creature's scaly skin.
Branith marveled at the feel of the rich silky fabric of
his sleeves, and the brocade and soft velvet of his tunic.

His flaming red hair framed a strong handsome face
with deep blue eyes. *Who said wishes never come
true?* Branith thought as a smug smile spread across
her face.

Stepping to the ground, the handsome man spoke to
Branith in a voice like dripping honey.

"My name is Jaramond Weatherby, and I thank you,

beautiful lady. How can I ever repay you for your
kindness?" he asked with a deep bow. "Would you
consider accompanying me to my castle for dinner tonight? It would be such an honor to have your beauty
to grace my table. It is not often that I have guests as
lovely as you."

The hissing guttural growls emanating from the
wretched creature frightened Dora half out of her wits.
She thought she heard it speak an almost unpronounce-
able name that sounded like Krakendrathlothtvayen.
What's happening to me, she thought. *Am I really losing my mind? Father will have to send me to a Tower
to have my* laran *burned away before it kills me. Lady
Evanda, I hope it doesn't hurt. I will be head-blind for
the rest of my life.*

Tears slowly trickled down her face as she watched
Branith walking away, arm in arm with the scum-
covered demon from the well, its barbed tail flicking
from side to side behind it.

Branith chatted gaily with the red-haired man as
they walked along the wooded trail leading into the
forest. Suddenly, the handsome stranger began to hurry
them along just a bit. A small spot of green scale was
just beginning to show on the hand now resting on
Branith's shoulder.

Poetic License

by Mercedes Lackey

Mercedes, who was just a folksinging young fan when first I knew her, is another of the fine writers of whom I had the privilege of printing her first story. Now she's gone on to many books of her own, including the very fine HERALD MAGE series, some of which strike me as having almost as much flavor of Darkover (perhaps because she deals with many of my own favorite themes) as my own or those of Diana Paxson. Betsy Wollheim and I have chosen her to inherit the Darkover series in the unlikely event that I ever become unable—or unwilling—to do any more of them.

Here we have one of the many, many Free Amazon stories I received this year. Most of them were either hackneyed or unspeakably bad; this was neither, and it's a pleasure to bring it to you, as always.

Tayksa's jaws strained as she tried not to yawn; playing personal guard to the newly-crowned King Varzil (known from the moment he engineered the Compact as "the Good") might be an honor, but it was a damned boring one. The throne room was a little overwarm as a concession to those who wore the light robes of *leroni* and that made her sleepier. There were no elaborately jeweled, heavily-embroidered robes of Comyn lords and ladies out there below Varzil's throne—not during this hour. The only spots of color were the oc-

casional merchant; the rest was a milling sea of
browns, grays, and subdued plaids. This was the time
Varzil set aside to hear the petitions and grievances of
his less-than-wealthy subjects. Assembled below the
throne were merchants, farmers, a Tower worker or
two, and even one lone Renunciate who came to request more aid for orphans of the war currently being
cared for by Renunciates—Maria n'ha Joyse, who still
wore her dust-gray robe of the Ladies of Avarra, although she had shortened it to tunic-length and wore it
now over the breeches of a Renunciate. This was a
much quieter crowd than the nobles tended to be, but
the eyes of the petitioners often flickered from the king
on his throne to the Renunciate guarding his right
hand. For this was Varzil's little way of showing that
the Renunciates were under his protection.

Once every five days, select members of the
Renunciate's Guild here in Thendara served as guards
to Varzil during the hour he took public petitions. This
duty was normally shared between the City Guard and
his own personal guards; the Renunciates replaced one
or the other alternately.

There were only so many of the Renunciates trained
to carry out such a duty; the Ladies of Avarra tended
to outnumber the former Sisters of the Sword, since the
latter profession had a shorter life expectancy than the
former. Tayksa and Deena were two of the group qualified. Still, with normal rotation, Tayksa should not
have been standing here more often than once every
four or five tendays, but given the past associations
that Tayksa and her partner Deena had with the king,
he usually requested one or both of them.

The king's tactic of making a visible presence of the
Renunciates and his backing of them seemed to be
working. There had certainly been fewer incidents

since Renunciates started showing up in the king's service on a regular basis.

Still, it was boring work; there was no doubt about that. Tayksa would far rather be chasing chickens on the farm than watching these sheep bleat their troubles to Varzil.

The petitioners were the usual lot, with all the usual pleas and gifts. An impoverished Comyn lordling of a minor sept of the Hastur clan asking for a dowry for a daughter—presumably her *laran* was not powerful enough to qualify as a dowry. A collection of shepherds petitioning against the enclosure of what had been common land. A falconer presenting the High King with a beautiful bird in gratitude for something-or-other. A fat merchant asking for a royal monopoly. A musician of some kind in Ridenow colors—

What's this?

Tayksa stood a bit straighter as the latest petitioner approached the throne. Musicians were by no means strangers to these audiences, but they were usually musicians without a place, starving and thin, and usually very young. This man was in late middle age, with silver-gilt hair and a look about him that said he had not been a starving young artist for a long time. Furthermore he clearly wore the Ridenow clan colors. Tayksa had never seen a musician show up in full livery before, and the harried expression on his angular face was also not one she normally pictured a minstrel wearing.

What was more, Varzil seemed to know him.

The man bowed profoundly, and Varzil smiled a warm greeting. "Anndra!" the King exclaimed, "What a pleasure to see you! Does your lord send you to me?"

"Nay," the musician said gloomily. "Nay, lord King. It is myself and my troubles that brings me to petition

you, Though those troubles may well involve my lord
before all is said and done."

Varzil motioned to the musician to come closer, out
of hearing of the rest of the petitioners. The young City
Guardsman to the left of the throne shifted his grip on
his spear nervously, but Tayksa remained relaxed.
There was nothing in the way this musician moved that
alerted her suspicions, and if anyone here would know
the way a potential assassin looked, she would be the
one.

After all, she used to *be* an assassin.

Cemoc, the king's paxman, took note of her relaxed
stance and shook his head a little at the worried
Guardsman.

"My lord King, I come to you with a problem that
could cost me more than my life," the musician
Anndra said unhappily. "It could cost me my reputation, which means far more to me than my life does."

Zandru's Hells, no wonder he looks bad. Both the
king and Tayksa nodded understanding, although
Anndra paid scant attention to her. His whole focus
was on Varzil. "The problem lies with Lord Ridenow's
youngest," Anndra continued. "The Lord entrusted him
to my hands for instruction in music, to be taught with
my three apprentices. The boy has ... average talent,
or a little less, but he and my Lord both seem to believe he is truly gifted." The man shrugged. "I saw no
harm in letting my Lord continue in his fond belief—
but the boy was impossible to teach, for he refused to
believe that he *needed* to learn anything."

"Well, Anndra, I cannot see how Lord Ridenow can
fault you for that," Varzil began, but Anndra shook his
head.

"That is not the problem, lord King. The problem is
that the boy is—is a thief. Not of things, but of ideas."

Varzil frowned. "One cannot put a name tag upon an

idea, Anndra," he said, his tone gently chiding. "You, of all people, must know that."

"*I* know that, my lord King, and *you* know that, but try to tell this to Lord Ridenow!" the musician said in despair, although his voice still did not rise above a controlled whisper. "My lord, listen to me, before you make a judgment that ideas cannot be stolen. This is how the trouble begins. I, or one of my apprentices, will begin a new ballad. Jehan will overhear it, and *immediately* go and make a botched and mangled version of his own. Then he will run to play it to his father— and once he has done that, *we* dare not perform our own songs, lest *we* be accused of stealing the boy's ideas! Perhaps he is not stealing ideas, precisely, but he is rendering them unusable by the rest of us!"

"Surely Lord Ridenow has more sense than to accuse you of that," Varzil said dubiously.

Anndra's expression of desperation deepened. "My lord King, it has already happened, and all that saved my apprentice was my declaration that I had set the other boy to making a variation on Jehan's theme. I do not know what to do. Already Lord Ridenow asks why I have no new songs for him. How can I explain that his son has stolen and ruined the ones I had been preparing?"

Varzil settled back into the soft cushions of his throne with a sigh and a deeply troubled expression. The folds of the red robe he had adopted as a reminder of his power as *laranzu* and Keeper settled about him. "Rafael Ridenow is a man of temper," he said slowly. "And a man who is proud of his blood. If it came to your word against the boy's—"

"I would lose—position, reputation, all," Anndra agreed miserably. "My lord King, what can I do?"

Tayksa guessed what was going through Varzil's mind, although she was no *leronis* to see his thoughts.

Lord Ridenow was powerful in his own right and took assumed slights personally. Varzil's new rank was a precarious one, based on a delicate balancing act among all the Lords of the Domains. He could take Anndra into his own service if Lord Ridenow dismissed him, but if he did, Rafael Ridenow might well see that as a deliberate insult and act accordingly. Of such trivial incidents wars had been made in the past, and probably would be again.

"Perhaps if we arranged for the boy to be elsewhere for a time," Varzil mused aloud. "I could ask for him to come to my court—no, that would not serve. Rafael would assume I wanted a hostage and refuse."

Tayksa cleared her throat delicately. Varzil shot a look at her.

"I take it you have an idea, *mestra?*" he said. The Guardsman looked scandalized, but Cemoc only smiled indulgently. Tayksa dared what few others would, partially by virtue of the fact that she had already saved Varzil's life twice. The king permitted a certain amount of impudence from her that he would never tolerate in anyone else. She kept her insolence to an amusing minimum, and occasionally took advantage of the situation to have a small say in small things. Both of them understood the game and enjoyed it.

"A true artist needs inspiration, my lord King," she replied casually. "And a young man needs experience to give him inspiration. What better inspiration for a heroic ballad, or even a series of ballads, than a journey of some kind? Perhaps a visit to the holy lake at Hali, to see what you restored, to see the *rhu fead,* the chapel, the Veil, and the holy things there at first hand? Surely that sight alone would be enough to inspire a mighty song. And it would be a pious thing for a young man of the Comyn to do."

Varzil stared at her for a moment, then his lips

slowly curved in a broad smile. "Surely," he agreed.
"And if, in addition, something in the reports from the
boy's escorts happened to trigger inspiration in Anndra
and his apprentices . . ."

"Then it would be obvious that it is the talent of the
musician that makes the song and not the idea," Tayksa
said smoothly. "Especially if the boy himself is not
particularly inspired by his experiences." She studied
her fingernails for a moment and then said casually, "I
think that my partner and I know that part of the country very well. And I think that I may well write the dri-
est dispatches in the world. So if my lord would care
to recommend us as the young lord's guides. . .?"

*It will get me out of this audience chamber for at
least several tendays! And Deena has been itching to
get out into the howling wilderness for a while.* Tayksa
did not quite shudder at the thought; child of the cities
that she was, she had learned to appreciate wild places,
and for Deena's sake she would put up with a bit of
camping in excellent weather, but it was something of
a struggle. If her sense of justice had not been so stung
by the poor musician's plight—

—and if Deena hadn't been threatening to go out
into the hills anyway—

*Well, if we are guiding a pampered son of the
Comyn, there will be good strong tents, soft beds, and
a cook to make the meals. That is more like my idea of
camping.*

Varzil's grin widened as if he read her thoughts. Perhaps he did; she was quite likely to be broadcasting
them to a telepath as sensitive as the High King. "A
very generous offer, *mestra,*" he only said mildly.
"Now, let me think; how can we plant this notion so
that Lord Ridenow thinks he thought of it himself?"
His smile continued as his eyes grew distant for a moment; then he snapped his fingers. "Of course!" he ex-

claimed. "How else but—a song? A song of yearning to make such a journey, and to see these things at first hand!"

Anndra blinked, looking perplexed. "But my lord King," he stammered, "What if the boy—" Then his eyes widened as understanding dawned. "Of course! If the boy steals it, Lord Ridenow will take it as Jehan's own wish!"

"And he will surely grant it," Varzil replied, nodding. "As any indulgent father would. And what harm could a boy come to on such a pious trip, with guards and guides of the best?"

Jehan had been a pain in the rump from the beginning of the journey to the end. Although this was one of the safest trips Tayksa had ever been on, the boy had evidently *thought* he was in imminent danger of losing his life every moment something went slightly wrong. Tayksa would have been heartily sick of the whining brat if she had not known the real purpose of this expedition.

As it was, although she had been cherishing secret amusement during the ride to and from Hali, she was mortally glad to see the towers of Castle Ridenow rising above the roofs of Serrais. When she looked back to see how the rest of the cavalcade felt, the veiled expressions of relief told her that Jehan's constant complaining had worn thin with them as well.

And it wasn't even a particularly hard journey.

As she'd expected, when Anndra made his song of yearning to see the holy lake, Jehan had plagiarized it, and Lord Ridenow had taken this for a sign that the boy truly wanted to make such a journey. Jehan had been trapped; he could not admit that he had gotten the notion for his song from his teacher, and he would not admit that such a thought had never entered his shallow mind, so will-he nill-he, off he must go. Lord Ridenow had, of course, petitioned Varzil for permission and additional protection for his youngest—Varzil had cheerfully granted it—and offered the services of "two of my former fighters who know the place well" as guides. If Lord Ridenow had been disturbed to see a pair of Renunciates show up on his doorstep along with the detachment of Varzil's guards, he had not shown it. Perhaps, given Varzil's well-known patronage, he had expected it.

It had, as Tayksa had hoped, been quite a luxurious little expedition. There were excellent tents and gear for all, and the best chervines to ride; one whole wagon was devoted to foodstuffs, a portable kitchen, and a cook to make them hot meals at morning and evening. Jehan himself got Lord Ridenow's campaign tent complete with a bathtub, carpets to soften and warm the ground, and ingenious collapsible furnishings. All in all, it was Tayksa's idea of the only way to camp, although Deena had grumbled under her breath about "soft living."

They had met with a few, entirely anticipated, hardships. Two storms had left them snowbound for a couple of days apiece, and an attack by catmen had cost them one of the chervines. But no one was hurt seriously; no one even missed a meal.

But the boy—she could *not* call him a man, even though he was well past his fourteenth birthday and wore the sword and airs of a man grown—had been miserable. During the storms he had been certain that Ya-men were going to descend upon them at any moment. While they lay snowbound, he had issued so many contradictory orders that the men ignored him altogether and obeyed their captain instead. During the attack by the catmen, he had hidden himself in the food-wagon and did not emerge until it was all over.

Even Tayksa, who considered herself cynical, had been moved by the mysterious, cloud-covered lake at Hali and the shimmering phantom of the holy *rhu fead* on the other side. None of them dared go too near, of course; only the Comyn dared set foot on the farther shore. But the far sight of the place gave Tayksa the shivers and moved her lanky partner to tears and a sigh of awe. Neither of them would ever forget the sight of the lake-bed drained and cracked by the Cataclysm, nor the memory of Lord Varzil standing beside the ruins of the *rhu fead,* his face white and unhuman beneath his crown of copper-red hair as he struggled to heal the lake with the powers of his circle of *leroni.*

Deena was even inspired to tell the boy of that time—how Varzil had stood there through three days and three nights, never eating, never sleeping, like a waxen statue, while power crackled bluely about him and no one dared approach him for fear of being struck down. How at the end of that time, the army woke to find the lake once more filled with a mist or cloud so dense that no one could see into it, restored to its former mysterious glory. At that moment, if Varzil had chosen to call himself Hastur, Son of Aldones, come to earth again, there was no one in all that army who would have been prepared to deny him that claim.

But he did not; he simply did what any other man, *laranzu* or otherwise, would have done at the end of a mighty labor. He ate hugely, went to bed, and slept for two days and a night. Nor did he make any other claims when he woke; he simply took his army and returned to Carcosa.

But Jehan had been as unmoved by the tale as he had been by the sight of the lake and the *rhu fead* itself. He was too frightened to cross to the farther shore; having viewed it all from a distance, he decreed his journey done and ordered the return.

And for all that he carried a harp with him constantly, Tayksa had never once heard him play or even practice much. He seemed content to use it as some kind of badge, claiming the power of "musician" without ever proving that he was one. Oh, occasionally he would take it out and perform some piece that was supposedly of his own composition, but as soon as it became evident that his enforced audience was hiding its boredom, he would stop, declare petulantly that his music was "obviously" unsuited for such coarse ears, and flounce off to his tent. And not once had Tayksa heard him try anything in the way of composition.

Deena once remarked with a cynicism unlike her usual self that Jehan was like a mocker-bird; without something to imitate, he had no songs.

Even Deena has noticed; now we'll find out if Lord Rafael can be convinced.

She had not expected to find out the end of the tale personally; in fact, she had fully anticipated that she and Deena would be given some kind of token reward for their service and sent packing back to Thendara. She had even made plans to lurk about the castle long enough to find out from Anndra himself what had transpired. But instead, before she had a chance to do more than dismount, she found herself whisked away into the depths of the castle and offered a hot bath, clean clothing, and an invitation to "participate in Jehan's homecoming celebration." Since the bath was something she had been longing for over the past several days, the clothing was perfectly acceptable by Renunciate standards, and the celebration was going to be interesting by anyone's standards, she gleefully accepted all three.

She and Deena were seated down among the servants, which did not perturb either of them in the least.

For up at the high table, sitting beside his father, was young Jehan. And beside Jehan was his harp. . . .

And standing beside the high-table, ready to play, were Anndra and his three apprentices.

At a nod from Lord Ridenow, the youngest of the boys picked up a *ryll* and began to sing and play—and before the song had gotten past the first verse and chorus, there was no doubt that it was inspired by the first of the storms the party had weathered. Tayksa was rather taken aback to hear her own words turned suddenly evocative and poetic; she would have been quite willing to swear that she had not the least bit of poetry in her soul, and yet here were her own dry dispatches ornamented and made lyrical.

When the first boy finished—and Jehan appeared completely oblivious to what was going on, for he applauded halfheartedly and then went right back to his meal—the second took his place before the audience. This time the story was one that Jehan *could* have composed, if he'd had the talent; the tale of a young man's first encounter with battle, fighting off the catmen.

"Too bad it didn't actually happen that way," Deena whispered to her partner. Tayksa hid a grin. She had carefully worded her dispatches so that Jehan's cowardice had not been noted, but from the whispering up and down the table, it seemed that the guards and servants who had made the journey with them were not being so reticent. Jehan had the grace, at least, to look shamefaced—there was applause for the performer and smirks for the subject when that song came to an end.

She saw now what was going on, though she expected Anndra to save the subject of the holy lake for himself. But no, his third apprentice, a young man just a bit older than Jehan himself, sang of the lake, retold the tale of Varzil's Labor, and sang movingly and emotionally of the awe the place had inspired in him. By now Jehan was sinking slowly in his chair; one more song and he might even crawl under the table.

Then Anndra stood up to sing, and Tayksa realized why he had waited until last. His song was a recapitulation of the first three, the thoughts of a man turned homeward, returning to a family beloved and a home familiar and dear. It was *not* a song that Jehan could have written; it required maturity for such insights. Tayksa saw, though, why Anndra had impressed Varzil so much—the man had a true gods'-gift for music. As he sang, she thought of her own home—the Guild House in Thendara—with longing; she thought of all her friends and Sisters there. And she thought of all those who would not be coming "home" again, those who had not survived the wars or the persecution long enough to see the Guild House become a reality. Her eyes were damp by the time Anndra was finished, and she was not alone.

The applause that followed was delayed by that moment of silence that is the artist's true reward; then the shouts and clapping filled the vaulted room to then rafters.

Anndra bowed once, slowly, then took his place again. His face bore no expression that she could see. She waited with tense anticipation for the climax of this little play.

"Well, Jehan," Lord Ridenow said heartily. "You have heard the songs that Anndra and his apprentices have made to welcome you home again—and I confess I could not wait to hear the songs that *you* composed about the things that inspired you on this journey. I had your harp brought down and tuned for you—give us one of *your* songs, son! If such secondhand inspirations were so breathtaking, surely your own music will be its equal!"

Huh. I don't think so.

Jehan did sink nearly under the table. He murmured something; evidently too low even for his father to catch.

"What?" Lord Ridenow said, sharply. "Speak up, Jehan—what did you say?"

Silence fell, an avid silence. Jehan pushed himself up in his chair a little, glowering sullenly, as if he had decided he could rescue himself by bravado. "I said that I don't have any songs, Father," he repeated, his words falling into the silence like pebbles into a well. "It wasn't like that at all; it was a horribly boring trip. Might I be excused? I'm terribly fatigued."

Lord Ridenow looked blank for a long moment; then Tayksa saw something she had not expected. His eyes met those of Anndra; she saw his lips tighten, saw Anndra nod briefly. Then he turned back to his son, who had been oblivious to the brief exchange.

His tone was even, but Tayksa read something in the Lord's lack of expression that did not bode well for young Jehan. "Of course, Jehan," he said. "Go right ahead. I have a great deal to discuss with Anndra and Captain Lerrys that I'm sure would only fatigue you further."

As the boy rose hastily, he exchanged another set of meaningful glances with the chief minstrel and the captain of the guards that had accompanied the expedition to Hali. Jehan either ignored the exchange or it completely escaped him.

Probably the latter.

Shortly thereafter, Lord Ridenow excused himself, and Tayksa noticed servants coming to fetch both Lerrys and Anndra.

I would love to be a fly on the wall at that meeting—

But the final resolution took place long after she and Deena left to return to Thendara. She was not to hear the true end of the tale until her next turn at honor-guard.

There was a lull as the petitioners sorted themselves out, and King Varzil spoke over his shoulder to the Captain of the City Guard, making certain that he spoke loudly enough for Tayksa to hear.

"So, Rafe, how is the young Ridenow working out?" Varzil asked with feigned casualness.

"Jehan? He's on punishment detail again, my Lord," Captain Rafe replied cheerfully, with a wink at Tayksa. "Boy wouldn't stop complaining, so we gave him something to complain about."

Varzil shook his head with a sigh. "Lord Rafael gave us his blessing to do whatever we had to in order to shape him up, Rafe, but try not to be *too* hard on him. He's been badly spoiled, and it's going to take him a while to grow out of it."

"If you ask my opinion, my lord—" Rafe began, then stopped.

"I value it, please continue." Varzil looked interested. "I'd heard you had some kind of plan or other you wanted to approach me about."

"Well, my lord, it seems to me that there's a-many of these spoiled young Comyn that could use some shaping up—and you said yourself you wished you had some way to bring them all to your Court so you could get their minds set on working together. Why not bring every boy about to turn fourteen here, and put 'em all in the Guard?" Rafe's face was turning pink with embarrassment, for he was by no means as comfortable with Varzil as Tayksa was, but he continued doggedly. "We'd shape 'em up, you can bet; they'd learn what a day's work was like, and they'd be living with each other day in, day out. Hard to declare a feud on a man you grew up with, eh?"

Varzil stared at his captain with open astonishment. "Rafe, you surprise me. That is a magnificent idea! I'll put it to the Council—I suspect we would have to institute some law that would safeguard the boys, forbid filing blood feuds or intent-to-murder on them until their terms in the Guard were over and the like—but I think perhaps I can persuade them. Perhaps if young Ridenow shapes up, we could put him in charge of these—we could call them, 'cadets'—"

Rafe snorted. "Him? Not likely! Best we can hope for is to grow him a little more spine! But the oldest Alton boy now, though . . . I served under him during the wars. . . ."

Rafe's expression grew thoughtful and Varzil chuckled. "I'll leave you in charge of planning this, then. When you have something concrete for me, let me know."

Rafe nodded, and Varzil raised a quizzical eyebrow at Tayksa. "Well, *mestra,* what do you think of the end of Jehan's musical career?"

"I think, lord King," she said delicately, "that Jehan as a musician has a great deal in common with the hautboy."

"Hautboy?" Varzil's other eyebrow rose. "How so?"

"The hautboy, it is said, is 'an ill woodwind that nobody blows good.' I think the same could be said of Jehan in many, many ways." She grinned, and Varzil returned the smile. "In the case of both, perhaps the best use of them is as—kindling. To inspire other fires to proper combustion."

"Indeed," Varzil chuckled. "Indeed."

The Midwinter's Gifts

by Jane Edgeworth

Jane Edgeworth says that she found these contracts in "a loose pile of mail while doing my cleaning yesterday." Sounds like a woman of my own kind; things around here are always disappearing into my desk or the clutter on the kitchen table, to be fished out by one of my housemates who is more methodical than I am—namely all of them. And since two of them are writers and the other a poet and songwriter, there goes my excuse that writers can't keep track of mundane details.

Jane says she'd be "interested in seeing what I could make up" in the way of biographical information. (She knows not what she says in leaving me an opening like that!) At risk of letting me say she's an amateur trapeze flyer and loves true crime, because it so aptly displays her ambitions, it would be better to stick to the facts; she's single and an unemployed alumna of Michigan State University. Her hobbies include, predictably, "reading, watching videos of obscure British TV series, and living vicariously through my writing."

Bet I could have made up something more interesting than that, but there's no reason biographies should be fiction. Jane thanks me for considering her piece. She says that ever since she wrote it, three years ago, she's wondered, " 'What in the world am I supposed to do with the thing?' I'm glad that someone else besides

*me will have a chance to read it; I hate to think of it
sitting all alone and neglected in an envelope in my
desk."*

*My pleasure; that's just why I love doing these an-
thologies.*

Rafael shivered slightly in front of the hearthfire. Such
heavy snows already! But then, these *were* the
Kilghard Hills, after all—he would be mad to think the
snow an unusual thing. Idly he listened to the relentless
winds outside. They were like beasts in pain, some
said, but Rafe preferred to think of them as sad songs
instead whose notes forever changed and which never
seemed quite finished. He stirred the soup in the pot
hanging over the fire—it would be done soon. It was
poor soup, much too thin. One scrawny rabbit-horn
was all he had been able to find. But he was thankful,
and it would be more than enough for one. He knew
that it was well-seasoned; his grandmother's training
had seen to that.

A particularly strong gust of wind rattled the small,
thickly-glazed glass panes of the cottage windows, and
Rafael shivered again. At least the chervine was well
tended to, fed and watered, so he would not have to be
going out into the storm for a while yet. He thought of
the beast, sleeping outside in the small stable. The poor
thing had to be cold even with the extra fodder he had
packed around it. And it would be lonely, too, without
the warmth and company of its mate. It would have to
warm itself tonight. . . .

As will I, Rafe thought. He looked up out the window and shook his head, reassuring himself. Of course
Darrel knows better than to travel in this, even though
I think he's mad sometimes. He smiled to think of his
bredhu, a man closer to him than a friend could be,
closer than a brother. They had been together six years,

a long time, and they were well-matched, people said. Well, those people who knew and liked the two of them and would not look the other way, seeing them together. Not many did this anymore, although they still gossiped. There would always be that; there was nothing for it. But this village was a small one; everyone who lived here was needed to help with harvests and animals and, more rarely, to protect the village against fire or enemies. Every able-bodied man was important, even if he was thought to be a little strange.

Only a harmless *ombredin*, that was what people said of Rafael. A little odd perhaps, but not womanly enough to wear skirts or even a butterfly clasp in his hair. . . . Rafael smiled secretly to himself: he had heard those particular words many times. Thoughtfully, he ran a hand through his thick hair, a plain dark brown very lightly streaked with red. True, it was just a bit longer than most men's—Darrel liked it that way—and if the truth was to be known, sometimes Rafael did wish for a woman's hairclasp. But a small bit of ribbon always sufficed, and no one was the wiser for it.

Rafael bent to pull a burning stick from the edge of the fireplace's flames and lit a nearby oil lamp. He had some close-sighted work to do now, and sometimes the fire was not quite bright enough. He laughed suddenly, a soft sound. If those loose-tongued gossips in the village could see him here sewing!

Of course sewing was a woman's job, but Rafe had never regretted acquiring the skill. He had made and mended a good portion of Darrel's clothes, as well as his own, and was secretly proud of his handiwork. Certainly it rivaled that of others he had seen. But, he chided himself gently, it never does well to be too proud of oneself. He unwrapped a hide-bound parcel, and unfolded the piece of work at hand—a finely-spun, white linen shirt with bands of brightly-colored leaves embroidered at the neck and cuffs. It was nearly finished now; he had been working on it in secret for weeks.

It had been easily hidden of course, with Darrel away so much. He was gone even now, earning honest money as a stable-groom at the large manor house at Armida. He came home only once every two tendays, and then only for two days at a time. It was precious time, and they treasured every minute of it. Especially days like the coming holiday—Midwinter's Day. The Midwinter holiday was a time of celebration for the peasants in the poorest towns as well as for the lords in their grand houses, with much dancing, feasting, and gifts. It was this shirt here, fit for a festival, which was to be Rafael's Midwinter Gift to Darrel. It was also going to be a gentle jest: a festival shirt was a traditional betrothal gift from a young bride to her husband. He had to smile. A fine bride he was—giving his mate a betrothal present that was six years overdue!

Rafael hunched his shoulders, moving closer to his task, and worked the needle rapidly with quick strokes of his fingers. How often Darrel had kissed those fingertips and softly teased him, saying that he should have been a lord in a great house, having such beautiful and delicate hands. Rafael had always laughed to hear that. Delicate looking they might be, but certainly not finely pale and soft, as a rich lord's! He had the same rough, reddened hands as any villager, the ones that came from working in the village gardens and doing his share of work on the periodic Autumn firebreaks. But this had never mattered to his Darrel. He had kissed his fingertips all the same, and never failed to make the joke.

He was always one to joke about nearly everything, especially the herb stall near the front windows of the

cottage, where Rafael's grandmother had sold her healing herbs and cooking spices. It was there that Rafael
could usually be found, arranging his wares in little
piles and tied bundles, or perhaps working at the dis-
tillery equipment set up on the floor or inspecting the
drying racks. Darrel had always found it somehow
amusing to watch his beloved sit on his knees in the
middle of the floor intently staring at this mixture or
that winding and bubbling through the glass tubing.
And it was more amusing still, to see him crawling
about on all fours in a field of grass, looking for more
chesari (there never seemed to be enough). Darrel always laughed to see that and affectionately called Rafe
a "choosy rabbit." He sometimes checked to see if his
lover was growing a tufted tail or fur on his ears.

Rafael wasn't cold anymore. He was warm enough
on his cushioned bench in front of the fireplace,
warmed through from both the glow of the fire and
from fond memories. How had he and Darrel gotten so
close? Had it always been so? Certainly they had always known and loved each other well enough as children, but there had always seemed to be something
more. Rafael smiled sadly. He had nearly been the one
to spoil it forever. . . .

It was high summer again, and he was fifteen. Darrel
had always liked this time of year best, when there was
always plenty to do. But if one tried hard enough, one
could always steal a few minutes away, to just lie
under the nut trees and do nothing at all but be sleepy.
And this was precisely what Darrel planned to do. But
never without his favorite company, of course.

Rafael was curled next to him, warm and comfortable in the crook of his friend's arm. But he was troubled this day. He had had much to think of. His
great-uncle, Rafe's only guardian save his grand-

mother, had begun the wearying talk of betrothals—
marriage again—when somehow the idea of life with a
woman seemed uncomfortable. It did seen a bit
insulting—he was fifteen now, nearly old enough to
choose for himself. Darrel was sixteen, and *he* had not
yet been betrothed, after all.

Rafael and Darrel had shared so many things, their
feelings and dreams. There had been intimacies between them of course—there was nothing odd about
that, at their age. Once it had been under the blankets
on a particularly cold night, and once there had been a
delightfully secret meeting under the moons' lights,
behind the shade trees. They had talked about these
things many times. But Rafe had only once mentioned
the thought that sometimes disturbed him: that he
wished these intimacies with Darrel might never lose
their charm—that perhaps it meant that he was one of
those odd, womanly creatures who feed on the minds
and souls of little boys, playing lovegames with them
long after the age when such things are commonly
done.

He had finally told himself firmly that a game was
exactly what this was with Darrel, no matter how special it seemed. It was all simply meant to be a fond
memory, to be locked away and perhaps be brought out
in old age to warm the feet.

Now, as Rafael lay close to his friend, wrapped in
comfort and security, he sighed. It was time to end the
game—surely Darrel was only prolonging this closeness out of love for him. To pretend he was still a child
for Rafe's benefit, when it was long past the time for
both of them to grow up. . . . It was a kind gesture, but
it would only hurt more, later, when the betrothal arrangements had finally been made, and the marriage
contracts legally signed. Certainly Darrel's family had
already arranged such things, even though the boy had

said nothing about it. Maybe he was staying quiet so as not to upset his friend. But then, he had asked Rafe to come here today just so he could tell him something important. What else could it be but the announcement of his engagement? Rafael closed his eyes tightly and prepared himself. He must be told. Best that it be now. . . .

Soft lips touched his cheek.

"Rafe, have you gone to sleep?"

Rafael smiled despite himself and shook his head, opening his eyes.

"I wanted to tell you," Darrel said. "I spoke with my father last night."

Inwardly Rafael nodded. Yes, here it was—

"I asked him to stop arranging meetings for me."

Rafael started, shocked to sudden awareness by the unexpected words.

"What?"

"I asked him if he would stop. I don't want to be married."

The younger boy sat up and looked at him curiously. "How can you say that? Ever since you were ten we've talked about your wedding." He smiled, remembering the precise and intricately laid plans which he, Darrel, and their mutual friend Margali had laboriously pieced together. "It would be in Midsummer, so that all the food would be fresh and the dancing could be outside. The best musicians, nothing but the best! We even settled out the communal table—we knew who should sit next to whom, so no one would fight. What happened to those plans?"

Darrel smiled and gazed warmly down with those beautiful dark blue eyes. He leaned over and hugged Rafael close to him, kissing him on the forehead. "You did."

Rafael's heart flipped over. No—this was too far,

now—had he dragged Darrel into the ravine with him? He pulled himself reluctantly, gently, from the older boy's embrace. No, man it was—at fifteen they had both been named adults, fit to do adult labor or marry, fit to—

Make their own choices. . . .

"No, Darrel," Rafael said softly, shaking his head. "You can't say that."

"Why?" Darrel's voice was suddenly uneasy, perhaps hearing pain in his friend's words. Slowly he moved his hand upward, stroking first the suntanned throat, and then the long brown hair which fell in thick waves to Rafe's shoulders. He caressed it gently, soothed by its softness, and smiled reassuringly. "We both know that it's true."

"No, it isn't," Rafael said firmly. "Not for you. Whatever happened to that beautiful girl you would finally choose, with black eyes and black hair, skin the color of gold-apples in cream? And the children you were going to have, with nut-brown hair like yours—" Rafael's voice broke.

Darrel shook his head, frowning. "I thought I wanted that, for a while." He paused and looked past the two of them, toward some distant place deep in the forest that surrounded the tiny village. "I thought about all those stories we told each other, and I don't want any of it. No nicely settled house with a wife, and children playing at my feet." He returned his gaze to Rafael, his smile warmer, more confident. "I want you."

Rafael turned away, shaking his head. This was *not* turning out the way he would've liked! Ruefully he heard the familiar proverb in his head: "The world will go as it will, not as you or I would have it." He smiled bitterly at the thought. What he *truly* wanted? To be a

child forever, to not have anyone stare at the two boys
who weren't yet married. . . .

"No!" he said sharply. "I won't let you ruin yourself! You've wanted all those things for so long, you
can't let me change all that. We're not children anymore, to lie together and laugh, and kiss in the dark! I
know what I am, and I can't change it. I'm—" Even
now he hesitated, unwilling to say the word aloud.

"Ombredin?" Darrel spoke it for him, wryly. "Yes,
I know you are. We both know that. But I've thought
about this, the way you say that being with women
makes you feel nothing." For of course Rafael had
tried, and found the experience unpleasant. Darrel nodded, thoughtfully, as if speaking his thoughts for the
first time. "I always laughed at you, thinking it was
such a funny joke. But I'm not laughing about this. I
understand what you mean, now. I realized it when I
was with Margali."

Rafael blinked. He had felt oddly torn when Darrel
had told him about the things he had done with her. It
had been so odd, to feel both happy and jealous at the
same time. "I thought you loved her. You said that."

"But I don't, not like you." Darrel gestured helplessly with his hands, searching for the proper words.
"It was nice with her, true. But when I was with you
it was *more,* it was wonderful. I can't really explain.
With you I can fly, I see with the eyes of a hawk. I feel
as powerful as the fires in autumn, or the snowstorms
in the months after that. . . ." He trailed off, self-
consciously.

Outside the memory, Rafe smiled. Darrel was warm,
caring, even when he made jokes, but he had always
voiced regrets that love poetry was not his strong suit.

Rafael flipped the shirt over and began a new seam.
The argument was so old, now. He nearly laughed to

think of it, the pain all but forgotten. *We were children then.*

It had taken Darrel days to convince Rafael that his feelings were genuine. And after that there had been arguments, misunderstandings among their friends and families—Rafael's great-uncle had been the worst. He had moaned and sighed for weeks, saying how grateful he was that Rafael's mother and father had both died when the boy was young. To Rafe's relief, his grandmother had been more accepting of his choice. But she had never been able to convince the old man to listen to their side of the dispute. He had died of a winter-fever soon afterward, leaving Rafael and his grandmother alone in the house, their argument forever unresolved. Darrel's family had been a little more understanding; they at least made the effort to be civil to their son's lover.

The stares and raised eyebrows had not yet abated even after so long, and there were still people who whispered of it. But of course there always would be. In small villages gossip was as common as snow, and by now, Rafael and Darrel had grown accustomed to being a popular topic of speculation. Neither of them minded so much anymore—just so long as the stories told were *reasonably* accurate.

With a gasp, Rafael suddenly remembered the soup which he had set over the fire to boil. Ah, that was good—it wasn't burned—he had not yet reconciled himself to the taste of burnt soup. He moved the pot carefully off the fire and set it on the edge of the hearth where it would stay warm. He had no time to stop for dinner just yet. There were several more rows of leaves to finish, and then he could eat.

He turned with a start, hearing a sound at the front door. Hurriedly he shoved his project back under the tough-leather wrappings, and pulled a thick blanket around his shoulders, rushing to answer the door. *Merciful Avarra! Darrel coming back now? He must be truly mad, to travel in this!* As if to underline his thoughts, the storm swirled outside with new intensity, the notes of an unraveled song beginning to scream out again. Rafe shivered and unlatched the front door.

A stranger stood there, stamping his feet and shaking the snow from his cloak. A lord, surely—his clothes were of a rich, heavy cloth and fine fur. He pushed the hood of his cloak back, revealing dark-red hair, dripping with melted snow. The man's features were delicate and fine. He *was* a lord, then—no poor villager would have a face like that, not reddened or roughened by the winter winds. Rafael faltered for a moment, but then stepped hastily away from the door and beckoned the stranger in. He bowed awkwardly, wrapped as he was in his blanket.

"*Z'par servu, vai dom.* Please come in."

The lord smiled. Rafe noticed then with surprise that he was the same age as Rafael himself, perhaps even a little younger. Bent with the burden of the weather, all men looked old at first. He returned the villager's bow with a word of thanks and stepped inside the warm house.

"Here, let me help you," Rafael said, quickly. He moved to help the young nobleman shrug out of his heavy cloak and wet wrappings, and handed him a towel to dry his hair. In minutes, Rafael had him sitting near the fire wrapped in a dry blanket, with his boots off.

Rafe had brewed some tea earlier in the evening and there was still some left, steaming on the hearth beside the pot of soup. He poured out a cup of it and handed it to his guest.

"This should thaw you out, *vai dom*," Rafael said softly.

"Thank you, again," the man said, turning to Rafe with a smile. "But please, I ask you, no more titles! My name is Erevan."

Rafael nodded, most of his stiffness gone as suddenly as icicles in the fire with the offering of a name. "Rafael," he said, by way of self-introduction. He was intensely curious to hear this noble's story. How had he come here, hours past dark? But of course he would never have dared ask a lord's business. That was another thing that Darrel teased him for—Rafael had always been painfully shy among lords, always so careful to use the proper respectful words. Darrel rarely bothered with such things, almost never worried about being too familiar or asking too many questions.

But Rafael shook himself. He was forgetting that he had a guest to attend to.

"Is your horse in our stable, Erevan?" He spoke the name carefully. Erevan nodded, swallowing a mouthful of tea.

"Yes, I found food and water for her inside. Thank you."

Rafael made a dismissing gesture, and looked out the window with an absent smile. *Lucky chervine—so you* won't *spend the night cold and alone, after all.* He sat down beside the lord, taking his usual place by the fire. He looked up as Erevan spoke with a hint of embarrassment.

"And I always thought that I would be able to find my way to my own cousin's house. But I seem to be a bit lost now, in the storm. Am I still on the right road to Armida?"

Rafael nodded. "Straight to the north of here is the path. Then you ride northeast, for nearly a day." He smiled. "Are you going there for the holidays, then?"

"For Midwinter's Day, yes," Erevan said. He turned his attention to his tea and soon drained the cup.

Politely, Rafael gestured to the pot of soup, only now aware of the rumbling in his stomach. He had eaten almost nothing all day. Erevan gratefully allowed his mug to be filled with the hot rabbit-horn broth. He sniffed it and smiled, then drank, nodding his approval.

"Very good! My compliments to your cook."

Rafael laughed softly. "You compliment me, then. I do the cooking here."

"You live here alone?" Erevan asked, with a slightly puzzled frown. He could sense another presence here, besides their own—it warmed the room fully as well as the fire did. And looking around the small cottage, it was easy to see that someone else lived here: there were two well-worn chairs at the small wooden table, the low bed in the corner was obviously slept in by two people.

Rafael shook his head. "No, I'm not alone. I live here with. . . ." He paused suddenly, horrified at the words which he had nearly spoken. He was no longer ashamed of who he was or angry at the names some people whispered behind their hands. Yet to simply *admit* such a shocking thing to a complete stranger! But he shrugged inwardly, looking over at his guest. Erevan's hair was completely dry now, copper streaks of it glinting brightly in the firelight. His guest was a lord, with red hair, and he had, certainly, all that magic which came with red hair. *Laran*, it was called, the power to feel other people's thoughts. . . . Of course, Erevan must know all his secrets already! But Rafael still used the words least likely to offend.

"I live here with . . . a friend." He half-smiled and turned away, focusing his gaze on his mending. He had made good progress tonight; there were only a few rows more before he would be done. The call to him was irresistible. Certainly his visitor knew Rafe's most important secret: it would not hurt to reveal a lesser one. He pulled the unfinished shirt into his lap and prepared to thread the needle and begin again.

Rafael smiled by way of polite apology as Erevan raised a curious eyebrow. But the lord only returned the smile kindly and watched as Rafael deftly began the pattern from where he had left it, swiftly pulling the thread up into tight, tiny stitches.

"Is this a gift for him, perhaps?"

Rafael nodded, not surprised at the accurate guess. "For Midwinter. It's nearly finished."

"Where is he now?"

Rafael gestured out the window. "He works in the great house at Armida. He is very skilled with horses."

Erevan nodded, curious. He knew most of the servants at his cousin's house; he wondered if he had met the man before. . . . But he changed subjects quickly. It would definitely not be polite for him to pry; perhaps a name would come later. He gestured instead at the complicated pattern Rafael was sewing on one of the shirt's sleeves.

"That's very beautiful work. I don't think my sisters could do better."

Rafe bowed his head graciously at the oddly-worded compliment. "My grandmother taught me when I was small. She always told me that it was a useful skill and that I might even make a trade of it some day. But I never fancied myself a tailor." He laughed softly. "She always used to tell me, 'You'd best pay attention to this I teach you—what would you do if stranded in a storm-shelter in the middle of a gale, and you tore your only pair of britches?' I used to tell her that I would sit with my backside *very* close to the fire."

Erevan laughed at that, and Rafael smiled shyly. "I always picked up my needle then, without fail." He turned his attention back to his sewing again—two more rows left. . . . "I'm very happy now that I did."

Erevan nodded his understanding, and the two fell silent for a time. The lord finished his soup and drank a second cup with relish, staring into the hearth's flames. He, too, had secrets, but he would never have given them up as easily as his host seemed to. He smiled to himself in amusement, thinking once again of the servants at Armida. He wondered what Rafael's lover would think of his *bredu* telling their story so freely.

But never have been able to speak of yourself *and smile, have you?* he said to himself. It was true that he had come to see his relatives at Midwinter, just as he had said. He was also coming to meet his betrothed-to-be, a distant cousin whom he loved well. But he would never have said the one thought on his mind— that he was not happily anticipating the coming wedding. Gabriella was a wonderful girl—he would never have argued that—but she deserved someone who could love her for herself and give her the children she had always wanted. He knew that he could never do this, not without feeling as though he were an actor in a play, forever in elaborate costume and painstakingly masked. And when the mask was finally lowered . . . how hurt Gabriella would be!

Yes, Erevan had understood his host's pause just now, the words which he had dared not say. Were they not the same words that he could never bear to use in describing himself? A lover of men, *ombredin*. . . . Yet here was such a man in front of him, normal enough. Certainly not a monstrous, leering thing, or a simpering, high-voiced woman wearing a skirt! He turned to face Rafael again, curious.

"Please, may I ask how long have you and—" he paused, with a gentle smile, "—your friend been living here?"

Rafael looked up with a slight shrug. "You may ask,

it's certainly no secret here." He smiled after a moment. "But I would rather you hear the truth from the source of the spring itself. So many here are eager to cling to every half-truth they can lay hands to, as if the truths themselves aren't interesting enough. And so few people actually bother to ask us. . . ." Rafael said softly. He paused and leaned over his sewing for another long moment—there, the pattern was complete now. Rafael tied off the end of the thread and held the finished shirt up in the lamplight, admiring it. He laughed suddenly.

"Darrel will not want to wear this! He will say it is too fine for anyone to see. But he always says that, and in the end I always manage to persuade him." He folded the garment carefully, and wrapped it up inside the leather coverings in which he had originally hidden it. He turned to Erevan, eyes warm in the light from the fire.

"We've lived here for six years, most of it whispered about." He shrugged. "There are still cold words, even after so long. But those things only hurt if you listen to them too seriously." He nearly smiled—he had said that so easily! Such a long time it had taken him, to learn to joke about all the gossip the way Darrel had always been able to. He took the packet and hid it carefully under the bed. "There," he said with a laugh. "Darrel would never poke about under there. He'd be afraid that I might ask him to sweep." He bent and picked up a small pile of mending, reasoning that he might as well do it now that he had thread all prepared. There always seemed to be mending to do. . . . Rafael began to mend a torn seam in a quilt and smiled absently. "But there's nothing that I would trade for life here, nothing! We have happiness, in exchange for a few whispers and stares. That's fair enough."

Erevan nodded. Somehow, his awareness seemed

stronger here. The undercurrent of emotion in the cottage was peaceful, oddly comforting. He sensed love here, security and warm contentment. Certainly there was none of the tension and distress that he could always feel when in a house full of arguments and fears.

The nobleman leaned back in his seat, allowing the warmths of both the fire and the house to envelop him. He closed his eyes, thoughtful and sleepy. Any minute now, he would be lost in dreams. . . .

"*Dom* Erevan?" Rafael asked softly. "I've made up the bed for you, if you want to sleep."

Erevan sat up slowly, blinking, and nodded. He frowned to see Rafael busily laying blankets out for himself on the floor.

"I don't want to push you from your bed—"

Rafael shook his head firmly. "No matter. It belongs to you tonight. You are my guest, after all." He resumed his spreading of blankets with a bemused smile. "For a while, my old grandmother lived here with Darrel and me. Surely you don't think we left *her* the floor?" Rafael pulled another blanket from a nearby box. Truly, that summer spent weaving had not been in vain! But there weren't quite enough sometimes for the coldest nights: Rafael had given thanks countless times that he had had Darrel to curl close to. But he said nothing of this, and watched to see that his visitor was securely tucked in. Then he blew out the lamp with a shiver and wrapped himself tightly in the blankets that were left. Tomorrow would be Midwinter's Eve. In this storm, Darrel would never be able to make it home before nightfall, but there would still be the festival the next day, and the gift. The thought warmed him, and he was soon asleep.

The next morning, Rafael woke early. The storm had nearly died now; thinking of its howling the previous night made him wonder how they'd ever been able to sleep. But now the wind only whispered, and the snow fell in large, soft flakes. Rising before his guest, Rafe shivered as he hurriedly restoked the fire and relit the lamps. He set water on to boil, along with the small bit of soup which had been left from the night before. He then moved quickly around the small cottage, tidying up. He smiled to think of the times that he and Darrel scolded each other for absentmindedly tracking snow or mud in or forgetting to pick up their clothes. After he finished scolding, Darrel sometimes made the joke that he would have to marry a woman, after all, if only to have her see that Rafe did his share of the house-work. If *Darrel* were the one to be scolded, of course, it was simply because his *bredu* was making too much fuss. . . .

Rafael had finished folding up his bedding and was running a comb through his disheveled hair when Ere-van sat up with a yawn.

"Good morning," Rafe said with a smile and a polite bow. "The tea should be hot soon."

The lord nodded, and crawled out of bed, soon thoroughly awake by the coldness of the floor under his feet and the chill of the house. He smiled to think of how similar everything was—everywhere he had stayed, from storm-shelter to the finest manor-house, it was always cold when one first woke up in the morning. He sat down by the hearth to warm his hands and was surprised to find a mug of tea suddenly pressed into them. He looked up to nod his thanks, but Rafael did not notice. He was sitting on the newly-made bed, pulling on his boots.

"I need to go out and see to my chervine. And to your horse, too, of course." He motioned for Erevan to stay where he was and smiled. Erevan could sense a hint of sadness in it. "You sit there and warm yourself.

It can be cold in the bed sometimes, when you sleep alone." He stood, stamped his feet down firmly into his boots, and jumped in surprise as the front-door latch rattled.

He hurried to open the door and stepped back in astonishment. Darrel leaned casually against the door-jamb, grinning to see his *bredu*'s suddenly flustered face. Rafael pulled him gently inside.

So early? Gods, he though in sudden dismay, *for him to be here now, he had to have ridden through the night*— "Are you all right?" Rafe asked, moving to shut the door. "Are you hurt, or frostbitten?"

The taller man smiled and shook his head. "I'm perfectly well. I left for home yesterday morning, but I got caught by the snow and blinded. I spent the night in the shelter, the one at the top of the pass." Darrel shrugged off his saddlebags and threw his cloak to the floor. "Whose horse is in our stable?"

Rafael ignored the question for the moment, glaring up at him. When he spoke his voice was dangerously soft. "I should have your head on my turnspit for doing something so stupid! To ride out into a storm like that . . ." He sighed, unable to hold back a half-smile. He had come to the conclusion more than once—that Darrel was mad—why should he be overly surprised to see him now?

"I'm perfectly well," Darrel repeated softly, returning the smile. He glanced over to see Rafael's guest, and his eyes widened.

"*Dom* Erevan? It's been some time since I've seen you."

Erevan bowed slightly, and spoke a greeting. So his curiosity was satisfied now: he *did* know this particular servant. "It has been a while. Since Cousin Lenorie's wedding."

Darrel grinned wickedly. "I remember that party. And a certain lord who drank a little too much. . . ."

Rafael gasped slightly and turned away. At times, his lover could be so disrespectful! But Erevan only laughed. "Gods above! Don't remind me! I could have danced with the Hastur himself, and not remembered it." He shook his head sheepishly. Darrel gestured toward Rafe.

"I do hope my housemate has treated you well?"

Erevan nodded. This was certainly true! He could not have asked for a more courteous host. Darrel returned the nod, pleased, and turned to Rafael, pulling him into a proper and formal kinsman's embrace.

But Erevan could not help but feel the special bond that was here. His undersenses blazed now with the warmth and affection which filled the room. Yet all that could be seen, by only the very observant, were the hands that secretly stroked Rafe's hair, just once, and Darrel's lips, which lingered on Rafael's cheek just a fraction of a second longer than necessary. Erevan saw and couldn't help but smile.

Rafael and Darrel broke apart, and Rafael stopped Darrel as the taller man turned to go outside again.

"Where are you going?"

"There wasn't enough food in the shelter for my chervine last night. I should go out and see to it."

"You sit," Rafael said firmly. "You've been out enough as it is. I was just going out myself."

Erevan watched, amused, as a replay of what had happened the previous night went on, and the other master of the house suddenly found himself sitting warm and dry in front of the fireplace with blankets wrapped around his shoulders and a cup of hot tea in his hands.

Darrel looked up with a bemused gesture at all his

lover's bustling. "You're fussing again," he teased softly.

Rafael smiled, pulling up his coat and hood. "We both know that I'm happiest when I'm fussing." He moved to the table, where Darrel had set the saddle-bags. *That one strap broke again, looks like. I'll just unload them, take them with me—*

"Don't touch those," Darrel said quickly. Rafael looked up, raising a questioning eyebrow. Darrel smiled, and shrugged.

"Something in there that I don't want you to see."

Rafe raised his hand carefully away—there, he was nowhere near them, see? He shook his head in amusement and left the cottage, shutting the door tightly behind himself. Darrel turned to the fire and gazed thoughtfully at his mug of tea.

"When Rafael mentioned you, I wasn't sure if it was the Darrel I knew. It's such a common name here." He looked at his second host and softly said, "He takes very good care of you, doesn't he?"

Darrel nodded. "Yes, he does." He shrugged, with a wry smile. "I can't be surprised that you know about us. Everyone else here does already. You seem to have taken it much better than most. Does it offend you?"

Erevan shook his head. Offend him? He might be *envious,* but offended? "No, it isn't all that strange a thing." He paused and reconsidered. "Well, yes, perhaps it is. I didn't realize that you could have peace, under all the scandal."

Darrel snorted derisively. "Scandal is the proper word. It was months before anyone would talk to us. And there are still those, though maybe they mean well, who congratulate me on what a fine *woman* I have." He pronounced the word with slight distaste; he found it ridiculous that Rafe could be considered anything other than the man he rightly was! "We laugh about it all now, at least when we have the time to talk. I'm not home very often."

Erevan nodded. "Rafael was telling me about Midwinter Festival, how you promised him that you would be here."

Darrel looked at him thoughtfully and nodded after a moment. He set down his mug, walked over to the table, and brought the saddlebags back over to his seat by the fire. He smiled as he untied the laces.

"Everyone will know about this soon enough, so I may as well tell you, too. I've always told Rafe that I would do my best to keep all my promises. To be here for Midwinter, even if I had to ride through a blizzard, that was an easy one. But this," Darrel reached inside the bag, pulling out a small wooden box. "This one I have always wished I could keep, and now I will." He removed the lid of the box, revealing a pair of thin silver bracelets, lightly inlaid with copper. "I always promised Rafe that someday I would get married. So I've been saving silver and copper coin for quite a while, and now Rafe will have the betrothal present he deserves. It isn't *di catenas,* of course, it couldn't be that, but it will be real enough."

Darrel lifted up one of the bracelets with a thoughtful smile. "I wanted to keep them a secret from everyone, something that no one could talk about. But I can't bear to keep them shut away." He clasped the silver band shut over his wrist and held it up to the lamplight, admiring the way the copper inlays glowed, fine lines of liquid fire. "I want everyone to see this, and see how proud I am of the man who wears the other one." He shrugged, with a mischievous smile. "It was high time everyone in the village had a new story to whisper about anyway."

Erevan nodded his head gravely, not daring to speak. His throat felt oddly tight. To be told such a thing, to be shown such love. . . . He touched the bracelet in the box with a gentle, almost reverent fingertip.

Mine and Gabriella's will look like this. . . .

His thoughts drifted to those of the *catenas*. He had not seen or signed any contracts yet, but of course the ceremony would be conducted *di catenas*. The bracelets did indeed resemble the ones Darrel held. But Erevan's would be shackles, locked with a key. For a moment Erevan pictured himself in a pair of the gold and copper things, with a fine but unbreakable chain connected to the bonds at his bride's wrists. No, he loved his cousin too much. He could never subject her to such imprisonment! She deserved to be free.

And so, he realized with a start, *did he. . . .*

He gestured quickly toward the box. "You should put those away, you know, before Rafael comes back."

Darrel nodded and reluctantly put the band back into its proper place. They would be seen again soon, tomorrow morning. He hid the box deep down in the saddlebag, even though he was secure in the knowledge that his *bredu* would never peek.

Rafael came in a few moments later, and stamped his feet, shaking snow off himself.

"The wind is definitely down. Merciful Avarra!" he said. "It might just stay a beautiful day today."

Erevan nodded and stood. "I think I'd better go, then, while it lasts. I have family to meet." He smiled secretly at his two hosts. "And you have a reunion of your own waiting for you."

Rafael blushed slightly, saying nothing, while Darrel moved to stand beside him, laying a warm hand on his shoulder. Inwardly, Rafael smiled. Of course, Darrel knew what had been said and had forgiven.

Darrel bowed respectfully to his guest. "If Rafael has your horse ready, shall I saddle him for you?"

Erevan shook his head. "No, it's all right. I've got-

ten used to doing it myself on the road." He bowed to
them and embraced them both in turn. "Thank you
both for your hospitality. I'll be sure to stop this way
again."

The two nodded, wishing Erevan well on his way.
With both good weather and good luck he would reach
Armida by nightfall. He left the cottage, closing the
door softly behind himself.

Erevan rode swiftly, blessing the Gods for putting
the wind at his back. As he cut a path through the new
snow, he thought about Midwinter. There would be so
many new things to discuss this New Year, plans to
change, new ones to be made. He smiled sadly to think
of it. There would be no wedding now—he was sure of
that. But though he knew that he would likely be
scorned and misunderstood, he would not necessarily
have to be lonely. There was an alternative path in
front of him now.

Erevan smiled to see the lights of Armida just ahead.
In the morning the Midwinter's Day festival would begin with the exchange of gifts. Darrel and Rafael
would be exchanging, too. Briefly, he wished that he
could be there to see it. But this was their moment. He
silently wished them a good holiday, and hoped that
they would be happy with what it would bring them.
Erevan had to laugh then, softly—the two of them had
not realized it, but they had given *him* a Midwinter's
gift, too.

The MacAran Legacy

by Toni Berry

Toni Berry says she has been "involved with mother-hood (six children), grandmotherhood (over a dozen), and great-grandmotherhood (one), you can see why I had little time for writing." Well, yes; I had little enough time for three kids. (Yet I firmly believe you can make time for what you want to do; I wrote over sixty books.) She adds that she "wrote this particular story for my daughter, Amanda, who never lets her copy of HAWKMISTRESS out of her sight." (Gee, that must be hard in the shower.) "She swears she uses laran *on her horses and they'd follow her anywhere."*

I believe you; I have a daughter like that.

Stephan MacAran tried to rid his mind of worry as he entered his only child's bedchamber at the end of a long and eventful day. "Hello, Lira," he smiled as he settled into the chair beside her bed.

She had been propped up, awaiting him. As she turned to him, her green eyes were wide and tearful. "Father," she sobbed, "will Kedric die, like Bryl did? I . . . I saw him today, when they carried him in, there was so much blood! And what will happen to our *verrin* hawks?"

Stephan gathered her into his arms, enveloping her in waves of comfort. "Hush, Lira," he murmured as he stroked her bronze-red curls. "Kedric will recover. It was not as bad as it looked. And, you are not to worry about our hawks, child, they will flourish as they always have."

He spent a few more moments soothing her and then he arranged her pillows and helped her to lie down.

"Now that you are comfortable, shall we have a bedtime story?"

She nodded and favored him with a limp little smile.

He could be found there in her bedside chair nearly every night, tucking her in and telling her a story. Even though she was ten years old now, it was a ritual they both enjoyed and refused to abandon.

As usual, Romillira begged for a story about her great aunt and partial namesake, Romilly MacAran. Romilly, legendary Hawkmistress to King Carolin, was Romillira's most beloved heroine.

He finished the story of Romilly's encounter with the banshees and realized she had fallen asleep.

He pulled the bedclothes snugly around her and gently kissed her cheek. He stood there a moment, then tip-toed from the room.

Closing her door, the tall, strongly-built Master of Falconsward went to seek his wife in their own bedchamber. He wore a worried frown that made him appear older than his thirty-one years. His thoughts were on the dead apprentice, Bryl. *Sometimes,* he thought as he traversed the hall, *being The MacAran is a heavy burden to carry.*

Mallira, blond and beautiful, smiled as he entered the room, "Come, my husband, 'tis cold in here without you and lonely, too." She patted the bed beside her, "Come, love."

He sighed, running his strong callused fingers through his wildly abundant auburn hair. *Malli, my love, my sorrow is great. It is I who sent them to that mountainside so early in the spring. I was blind to the dangers, and, as a result, Bryl is dead. It is my fault!*

These thought were transmitted to her with his *laran*, his telepathic powers.

Mallira answered him with her own *laran*. *Easy, dearest, do not punish yourself so. You could not know there would be an avalanche. You would never knowingly send anyone into unnecessary danger. Not on a whim or otherwise.*

Their rapport deepened and he allowed her warmth to wash over him as he climbed into the bed and into her arms.

Much later, as Mallira slept, Stephan relived the horrors of the day. He remembered with great sadness the way they had found Bryl's crushed and broken body. The Hawkmaster's promising young apprentice was wedged into a crevice where the force of the snow had driven him.

Kedric had been more fortunate. Only his legs had been injured and held fast by a fallen tree.

It was the hawk, hovering over the Hawkmaster, that had enabled the searchers to locate them so quickly the day after the avalanche.

The *leronis,* sent from the Tower, used her telepathy to examine and monitor the injured man.

She assured Stephan that Kedric should recover with little more than a slight limp. Exposure to the elements might have been his greatest enemy, but he had been rescued quickly and the very snow that had trapped him had helped to keep him warm.

For this, Stephan would be eternally grateful. But Kedric's recovery could take many weeks and the hawks needed daily care.

As soon as Bryl was properly buried, Stephan had sent a messenger to Scathfell. Now he lay awake, praying that his cousin, Scathfell's lord, would see fit to send aid.

Scathfell's Hawkmaster was a fine man and a very able teacher. To him was accredited the growing reputation of his apprentice, Vardome.

Vardome was the subject of much talk around the Kilghard Hills. It was said he was doing an excellent job with the training of the valuable *verrin* hawks used all over Darkover for their great hunting abilities.

It was this same Vardome that Stephan hoped to borrow until his own Hawkmaster could return to work.

Castle Falconsward had some of the finest *verrin* hawks in existence and their care must be assured.

Romillira crept toward the mews. She was curious to see the new Hawkmaster who had arrived several hours before. She wrinkled her lightly freckled nose at the unpleasant odor that always wafted from the hawkhouse and neared the entrance.

Peering in, she cringed from the aura of evil that seemed to emanate from the tall gaunt man inside.

At last! My chance! Fate has handed me my chance for vengeance. With no Hawkmaster to interfere, I can train these hawks to carry out my plan.

Suddenly, the Hawkmaster turned to see Romillira staring at him. He glared back at her with blazing green eyes.

He realized, by her stricken expression, that he had been carelessly broadcasting his thoughts, "Fool!" he muttered under his breath and closed off his thoughts.

Romillira trembled and began backing away from him, her eyes held, mesmerized, by the hatred in his.

In three long strides he was leaning over her, his dark umber brows gathered in an angry frown, his thinning red hair spiking away from his forehead like a multitude of horns.

"Stay away from here, *damisella!*" he growled, his voice an ugly rasp. "Stay well away from here!"

Tearing her eyes from his, she whimpered, turned and ran. Unknowingly, she plunged into her father's arms.

"Lira! What is it?" He tried to pull her away to get a good look at her. "Child, are you hurt?" Stephan demanded fearfully.

Sobbing, she shook her head and continued to cling to him, burying her face in his clothing, as Stephan renewed his efforts to loosen her grip.

Vardome stepped from the mews then, a sheepish grin on his elongated face, " 'Tis my fault, I fear. I must have frightened her, my Lord, when I told her to stay away from here. My apologies, of course. I did not mean to upset her."

Stephan nodded and chuckled. "Is that it, Lira? You were frightened by the new Hawkmaster?"

Romillira nodded. "He . . . he is evil, Father," she responded in a trembling whisper.

"Come, come, Lira. 'Tis no judgment to make of a total stranger," Stephan admonished as he led her away.

"But, Father, he is evil! He wishes to harm us, I felt it. Please, believe me!" She persisted, unable to accept the fact that her father would doubt her word.

"Nonsense. I admit Vardome is a bit strange looking, but I cannot allow your rudeness, Romillira. It is unbecoming and unfair."

Romillira fought back tears, "Father, it has nothing to do with . . ."

"Hush, Lira, we will speak to your mother about this," Stephan interrupted, his thoughts already on other problems.

Romillira trudged along beside him. Tears that

would not be stopped blurred her vision as her father's doubt blurred her world.

That night, as they sat down to their evening meal, she was rebuffed again. She tried to defend her distrust of the Hawkmaster, but her parents refused to listen.

Her father and mother were much puzzled by her uncharacteristic behavior and convinced themselves that it was a result of the tragedy to Kedric and Bryl.

In an attempt to alleviate the strain between them, Stephan held out his hand, palm up, and she saw a glowing blue orb resting there. "I think this would be a good time for a new toy, Lira," he said brightly, "It is called a Drynn Stone. I am sure you will enjoy it."

Later, in her own bedchamber, she stared at the stone defiantly. *How dare Father bribe me with this toy! As if I have not sense enough to know he thinks me daft and an infant that cannot tell evil when she confronts it!*

She glared a little longer at the strange blue stone that lay warmly in the palm of her hand. Curiosity, however, won out and she gave the stone a gentle toss in the direction of her door.

Curving in a graceful arc, the Drynn Stone returned to her. Somehow, warmed and attuned to her body's energy, the stone returned to her each time she threw it.

The next morning, Romillira resolved to learn all she could about the new Hawkmaster's plan for training their *verrin* hawks. *If I can go to Mother and Father with what I learn, maybe then, they will believe me,* she reasoned, *and they will apologize for thinking I am a silly child.*

That very next day, she took her Drynn Stone with her and played with it. Farther and farther she threw the stone. Unerringly, it returned to her, no matter how she tried to run from it. Purposely, she stayed clear of the hawkhouse, wanting her parents to think she had resolved her concerns.

The following day she played her innocent game again. Only now, she inched her way toward the mews, intent on a little undetected spying.

Within ten or so paces of the entrance, she stopped, appearing engrossed in her new toy. As she extended her *laran* she experienced a wavy of dizziness and she panicked. *Threshold sickness!* She was forcing a gift before its time and she understood the consequences fully. They were twofold and dangerous. Her awakening *laran* could run wild at any moment, causing serious harm or, possibly, death. Also, if Vardome were to pick up on her interference, the danger would be just as real.

Using a great deal of caution in her probing, she elected to stay clear of the Hawkmaster's mind and extend her *laran* toward the hawks themselves.

She felt a moment of exhilaration as she made contact. Several were dozing and she bypassed those. Her mind became entangled with a young fledgling whose frenzied mind sought only freedom. She broke that contact with a gesture of frustration and moved on.

At last, she located the hawk that Vardome held in thrall. The hawk trembled and bated in utter terror as Vardome bombarded its mind with the very essence of evil. He projected all of humanity's basest emotions: hate, rage, vengeance.

The force of the Hawkmaster's images pressed with unwelcome clarity into the hawk-mind and, thus, into Romillira's. The conceptual characteristics of these evils were laid out, step by step, like teachings on a lesson board.

Images began to appear in the frightened hawk's mind of himself attacking the MacAran family and in his confusion he cried out in protest, or, was that

...illira who cried out for release? She wrenched her mind free and fell to her knees, willing the last strand of contact to fall away.

Her mother found her there a few moments later. She was still trembling, still on her knees where she had fallen. Her face was pale, her eyes stared vacantly ahead.

Mallira hurried toward her, screaming her name. Sitting on the ground, she cradled Romillira's head in her lap. "Lira, snap back, Lira!" she sobbed, rocking back and forth.

Romillira stared at her mother, her mind a tumult, and she fought against the remembered horrors that threatened to rage back upon her.

"Poor infant," her mother soothed, "Why did we never think of threshold sickness? Oh, my poor baby. No wonder you were so confused. We must send to Hali Tower at once."

"But, Mother," Romillira sobbed, closing her eyes, "what about that poor tormented hawk? How can he withstand such sickness of mind?"

"Hush, child. 'Tis your sickness, not his. Will you not understand this?"

"No, Mother, 'tis the Hawkmaster who has the terrible sickness of the mind. Why am I the only one to see that? How can I save those hawks all by myself?"

"Not another word, Romillira," she helped Romillira to her feet. "Rudeness is never excused, threshold sickness or no, Although I know your father will be relieved when he understands what you have been going through."

Romillira cast her mother a weak look of exasperation but made no other response.

In her own room, after the evening meal, she tried to imagine a reason for the Hawkmaster's hatred for her family. What was his plan? And, why would anyone tamper with the minds of innocent hawks?

Laran, she knew, was a gift that carried with it grave responsibilities. She had been schooled in those responsibilities all her life. Do not invade the privacy of others, certainly never use your *laran* to harm anyone. Be especially considerate of the head-blind. Extra special care should be used on all wild creatures for they are the truly innocent.

Vardome is violating all of them! How dare he take advantage of the trusting rapport with those birds! And, for what purpose?

As they awaited the arrival of the *leronis,* she was kept well away from the mews. Someone was with her every waking moment and, though she did not know it, her parents checked often during the night to see that she was sleeping soundly.

The *leronis* came. Yes, Romillira seemed to be experiencing an early awakening *laran.* Very soon her parents should send her to the Tower to be properly trained.

Patting Lira's hand, she said she had every confidence in her parents' abilities to get her through the rough times.

The *leronis* departed early the next morning. Confident that Romillira would follow in the not too distant future, she waved a fond farewell.

Before Stephan went back to his work, her parents cautioned her to take care in exercising her *laran* and to call them if at any time it seemed to be activating on its own.

They presented her, then, with a puppy. Even though this was a gift that had been promised for a long time, Romillira felt certain that the timing was another attempt to channel her mind in safe directions.

Even so, she loved him at once and named him Sher.

Her rapport with him was instant and complete and she reveled in the warmth and love he returned to her.

She and Sher romped near the hawkhouse on several occasions. She knew Vardome continued his lessons in hatred and that his bitterness had something to do with his grandfather. Each time her *laran* reached out to the hawk-minds she would find one being subjected to Vardome's indoctrination.

Romillira was nearby on the day that one of the fledglings cried out in torment and died from his fears, his little heart bursting in a terrible agony of pain. Romillira, herself, had felt the constriction in her chest and had fallen to the ground, crying out in fear and in anger. Sher's moan of sympathy and his cold tongue on her cheek had served to pull her back into herself and she hugged him to her, allowing his love to soothe her.

Fools! The Hawkmaster flared at them all. *I try to give you power and you flap and bate and splutter. Where did the idea ever come from that* verrin *hawks were intelligent birds?* And yet, he did not stop. With gruesome determination, he began again.

Romillira shivered to her very soul a few moments later at the sound of his maniacal laughter. *That's it. They will all pay!* He shouted, "Mikhail's heirs will soon rue the day he dared to send his own *nedestro* son away as though he were nothing. Grandfather Loran was denied both his mother Nelda's care and his birthright when he was smuggled off to Scathfell. He would be so proud of me! This is a most fitting revenge!"

Romillira was stunned. The death of the hawk had left her weak and ill, but this revelation clutched at her in an even more sickening manner. Her family was honorable and proud and *cristoforo*. Such things should not be! She thought of her father and knew that he would never dishonor his family in that way. *Nor would Great grandfather Mikhail!* "Oh, Sher," she wailed, "What should I do? I know all about Festival-got children, but to send one away? When he would never have done such a thing in the first place?"

For days, she hugged the revelation to herself. What could she say that her parents would listen to? One night, as her father settled down beside her bed, she asked about Mikhail.

"I did not personally know him, Lira," her father answered, "He was already gone when I was born."

He leaned back comfortably and continued, "My father said he was a different man in his younger years. He was stern and unyielding before he thought he'd lost Romilly forever."

"And when Romilly came home to make her peace with him, he forgave her. Later, he forgave her brothers, too. Then, they were all happy together," Romillira finished with a rush, her eyes shining.

"Yes," Stephan smiled. "Exactly like that. Then, my father, Rael, eventually became The MacAran and now it is my turn."

"Father, could ... could Great grandfather have dishonored Luciella? I mean, could have fathered ..."

"Romillira! A thousand shames upon you!" Stephan leapt from his chair, his face the color of the Bloody Sun, his eyes wide with shock.

Romillira looked away uncomfortably, "I am sorry, Father. I meant not to ..."

Stephan held up his hand as if to guard himself from evil. "Not another word, Romillira. Not one!" He turned and left the room in swift, angry, strides.

"Oh, Father," she sobbed, "everything is going wrong. And you and Mother hate me! All because of that awful man."

She cried herself to sleep, her arms wrapped around

her only friend. Loving and sympathetic, Sher snuggled up to her, his adoring eyes filled with sadness.

Mallira approached her as soon as she completed her morning meal with a long list of passages from the Book of Burdens. She was not only to read them, she was to make faithful copies of them.

"And when you have finished them," her mother directed, "you and I shall have a long talk. Go, now, before I add more."

Romillira finished her task and entered her mother's sitting room with a staunch determination to have her say. In her hand were the copied passages. Passages that addressed childhood behavior, rudeness and respect. And, she felt, had nothing to do with her.

"Come, child, sit with me," her mother invited. "We will see what the Bearer of Burdens has to say about these things."

"First," Romillira stated defiantly, "we will see just what things we are speaking of! Mother, I must say some things to you, I must! When I am finished, if you still desire this lesson, than I will submit to it gladly." Romillira's voice, though it quavered, carried a conviction that gave Mallira pause.

While Mallira seemed caught off-guard, Romillira pressed her advantage. "The Hawkmaster thinks his grandfather is Great grandfather's son. A son that was hidden away so no shame would come to the family. He thinks this, Mother. I did not imagine this, how could I? Why would I? He believes it and he hates us for it!" She sat down then, folding her arms as if to say, there, I've said it, the rest is up to you.

Uncertainty held Mallira silent as she considered the possibility that Romillira might be speaking the truth.

As Romillira waited, the silence became too much for her and she began to pace nervously, her fingers fidgeting with the claspings of her gown.

Resolutely, Mallira took hold of her daughter's hand. "If your father is finished with his bookkeeping, we will get to the bottom of this!"

While her parents listened, Romillira recounted all her contacts with the Hawkmaster and with the hawks.

Stephan rose to his feet and paced the floor in the same fidgety manner as his daughter had done before. He made no immediate comment, but Romillira was certain that she saw belief in his worried eyes.

At last, he broke the silence, "I am not yet willing to grant total credence to all you say, Romillira. It is a fantastic tale, at best. However, I am convinced enough to do some investigating. What did you say his grandfather's name was?"

"I . . . I think he said Loran, or, maybe Doran. I was frightened, Father, I could have heard it wrong. I think his mother's name was Velda."

"The first thing I should do is go through the old records. But that may take some time, going back that far." Stephan pushed back his hair and turned a worried face to Romillira, "You must promise to leave this to me, Lira. If what you say is true, then this is a dangerous man. You are to stay away from him, do you understand?"

Gratefully, she nodded her agreement.

"Come, now, child," Mallira said gently, "We must not keep your father from his work."

Stephan patted her shoulder, "It may well be that we owe you a grave apology."

Tears streamed down her face as she followed her mother from the room.

For two days, she patiently waited, thankful to be, once again, in her parents' good graces.

"Mother, has Father finished holding court yet?" she asked. "Has he looked in the records for the Hawkmaster's grandfather yet?"

She played nervously with her hair ribbons and squirmed in her chair as her mother worked on her hair.

"No, Lira. He just sent word that he has several more disputes to settle and a poacher to try. He also wanted me to remind you of your promise."

"I know," Romillira responded, "I just wish that man was gone."

"Patience, child. Your father feels that the man could never succeed at any rate. You must show a little bit of faith in your father. Now, please stop wiggling and let me finish your hair."

"I do have faith in Father, he can do anything. I just know that Hawkmaster wants us all dead! And, I know the hawks are in unfair torment!"

"There," Mallira said as she gave Romillira a quick hug, "Your hair is finished. Now, I think you and Sher should go out and get some exercise. As long as you are mindful of your promise."

She watched for a while as Romillira and Sher tumbled in the grass and then she returned to her daily work.

Sher was a constant delight to Romillira. He was energetic, inquisitive, and very anxious to please his young mistress. As Lira tossed the Drynn Stone, Sher would run after it. When the stone changed directions, he would lose sight of it and run in circles until he saw it return to her. Then, he would bound back in her direction with yips and yelps of frustration.

Almost of its own volition, her *laran* cast out, trying to pick up thought impressions from the mews. The effort, from such a distance, was futile. She concentrated harder, her face wrinkling into a frown.

"Such a young, pretty face to be frowning like that," Stephan teased as he came up beside her. He sat down on a fallen tree trunk and sighed. "It was a very tiring day, Lira. Things that started out simple became complicated issues of law."

"Are you finished, then?" Romillira asked eagerly. "Are you going to see the Hawkmaster now and send him away?"

"Not just yet. I have had no time to study the records. I doubt very much that I shall confront the man today."

"Please, Father," Romillira begged. "Something terrible is going to happen, I just know it!"

"Lira, you must understand. I had better be well armed with facts before I even approach the man. After all, he belongs to Scathfell, not Falconsward, and I would certainly be held accountable for any false accusations. Even if I totally believe you, it is a matter of your word against his. You must consider this a lesson in patience."

He rose and smiled, "I think it would do us all good to take a nice leisurely walk. Come, we can find Mother. We have just enough time before our evening meal."

The three MacArans of Falconsward strolled about the grounds talking and laughing as they had done many times before the avalanche had changed their lives.

Sher scampered along behind them, investigating everything he passed, filling Romillira's mind with a jumble of puppy-sized sounds and smells.

The Red Sun was casting a fiery evening glow as a young *verrin* hawk swooped down toward them. Its wings took on the appearance of flaming destruction as it circled and dove at them again.

Romillira and her mother screamed in terror and threw their arms up to protect their heads as deadly talons raked the air above them. Sher ran to Romillira, yapping with fear. He cowered between her feet, his little paws covering his face.

Stephan looked wildly for a place of safety. At the same time, his *laran* reached out to the hawk. His senses pulled back in alarm. The hawk-mind was consumed with a frenzied fury. The familiar blood-lust had been replaced with a roiling, bubbling hatred for him and his family.

"Try to get to those rocks! They should give us some protection," he shouted as he began to shove them toward an outcropping of huge boulders that formed a sort of cavern beneath.

Romillira scooped Sher into her arms and scrambled for protection as the emboldened hawk closed in again.

His deadly claws ripped into Stephan's back and Romillira felt the force of her father's *laran* lash out in anger and revulsion.

Mallira, too, assaulted the hawk-mind with disgust and fury. *Go away,* her *laran* screamed, *you are horrible, grotesque!* Great pinions flapping malevolently, the hawk circled for another attack and Mallira raised her fist in anger, "Go! Leave us!"

Sher, too, became agitated and Romillira could feel the seedling fury in him, as his bark became vicious.

That's it! The hawk and Sher are picking up the anger from Mother and Father, just as the hawk learned it from the Hawkmaster. Anger is feeding on itself, like a raging wildfire. That poor bird, that poor beautiful bird! The thought flashed through her, a bolt of pure insight, and she began sending waves of comfort and calm.

Welcome, friend, her *laran* greeted the furious hawk. *Come in peace. Your kind has ever been friend to ours.*

"Father," she called, keeping the message to the hawk alive, "hold out your arm. Welcome him, he is our friend."

Instantly realizing her reasoning, both parents began sending warmth and welcome to the bird.

The hawk circled again and their *laran* sensed his first moment of indecision as he swerved away from them at the last moment.

Just as his fury seemed to abate, two more enraged hawks flew into view. Once again, he became embroiled in Vardome's bitter revenge.

Stephan did his best to shield his family and was bearing the brunt of the attacks, shielding his face and eyes as he maintained his aura of calm.

"Stephan!" Mallira screamed, "The Hawkmaster! He is urging them on, coming to join them."

I know. Disregard him for now. We must keep up our gentle welcome. It may be our only hope, right now.

"Yes. Yes!" Mallira responded, already extending her *laran* to the other *verrin* hawks.

Vardome appeared, screaming in rage. "See how it feels to suffer, MacAran! This is my grandfather's revenge, think on it as you die!"

He picked up a handful of rocks and started his own attack against them. Half-blind with fury, his dark brows drawn in an angry slash across his forehead, he inched closer, the wild hawks all around him. His aim, hampered by his anger, was bad and most of the rocks fell harmlessly short of their targets.

A few, however, made painful contact. Romillira cried out as a blow to her shin left an ugly red gash.

"Merciful Avarra! He will kill us all!" Mallira screamed as a fist-sized rock slammed against Stephan's temple and he slowly crumpled to the ground.

"Aha!" Vardome cackled, ducking his head as a *verrin* hawk swooped dangerously near.

Mallira stood frozen in horror, staring at the blood that trickled down Stephan's face.

"Keep it up, Mother," Romillira gasped, "Hawks do not kill for vengeance. Keep reassuring them. Mother, please!" She shrieked in terror as one of the hawks dug talons deep into Stephan's outstretched arm. "Mother!"

Dazed, Mallira stooped to pick a feather from the ground. Cooing softly, she used the feather to caress the bird who blinked hateful yellow eyes at her.

Romillira, stung by another rock, fell to her knees beside her father. She concentrated on the hawk that still gripped her father's arm, *No, my friend, no. This man would have you go against your very nature! You are a hawk, friend to man, not his enemy. Your rapport with us has always been one of trust, of mutual respect. Go in peace, all of you! And, please forgive us, we are not all evil.*

Suddenly, it was all over, the anger was gone. With a cry of pure joy, the three hawks swirled into the evening sky. As Romillira flew with them, she saw the terrain passing below, saw the small rustling creatures leap into the brush. She was stunned by the raging hunger, pure and sweet, that caused her mouth to water and her stomach to lurch with a frenzied desire for food.

Vardome's bellow of rage brought her back as he made a running dive and landed on Stephan's prone figure. "You will all die." He grabbed Stephan by the throat, buried his fingers deep in the skin, and shook him like an old rag.

Romillira and her mother attacked him together, fists pummeling. While Mallira grabbed a handful of his hair and pulled backward, Sher growled and bit into his ankle while Lira continued to pound him with her fists.

Stephan awoke and joined the melee. Flinging Vardome's hands from his throat, he took advantage of

Mallira's grip and rammed both fists under his attacker's chin.

Vardome flew backward and all three MacArans fell atop him, pinning him down amid grunts and growls from Sher.

At last, he was subdued, his hands tied behind him with Romillira's hair ribbons and a strap from Stephan's boots.

"We will take you to Scathfell in the morning, Vardome." Stephan sighed and pulled the man to his feet. "Your own Master can try you for your crimes against us, against those innocent hawks, and against nature itself."

"No," Vardome stated softly, staring with dead eyes at his enemy. "No MacAran shall judge me."

He died there, moments later, a victim of his own *laran*. He had simply caused his own heart to stop beating.

" 'Tis just as well," Stephan murmured, staring sadly at the lifeless body. "I pity him. Yet, if he had come to me with his story I would have done what I could to make things right. In his own twisted way, he was brilliant, you know."

A tear trickled down Mallira's cheek. "Such a waste of life. But there is no room on Darkover for evil such as his."

"Come," Stephan said, placing an arm around his wife and child, "We will send someone to carry him back. We are going home."

"What will you do about the hawks now?" Romillira asked quietly on their somber walk home.

Stephan's eyes twinkled and his smile was full of love and pride. "Kedric will be well soon, and a few more days away from the Tower will not hurt you over much, I think. I was thinking that perhaps you would consent to helping me with them for a short time. We could do it together, could we not?"

"Hawkmistress," Romillira whispered the revered word with a sense of awe.

The Word of a Hastur

by Marion Zimmer Bradley

One of the nice things about editing these anthologies is that I get to make the rules; and under my own operating rules, I get to include one of my own stories.

Several times, in the Darkover stories, I've quoted the proverb that the bare word of a Hastur is as good as the oath of any other man.

Here, then, is the story of how that proverb originated; about a young Hastur who kept his word under what must have been very difficult circumstances, to say the least.

As I require of every writer, here is an updating of my biography; I'm rapidly approaching senior-citizen status. As of June 1995, I will reach my sixty-fifth birthday. Big deal; but it means I get a discount pass on the Berkeley buses. I can say with confidence that I am one of the people who can prove that I am mentally competent, having had to establish it in court. (So much for all the people who think I'm slightly nuts.) "We're all mad here; you must be mad, too, or you wouldn't have come here." Anyway, "crazy" can mean "mentally unbalanced" or "wildly eccentric." And we're certainly all that, No?

No?

There was a good deal of comment all through the Domains when Valeria Ardais married the Heir to Hastur,

Jeremy. It was not only that he was two years younger
than she, but he was widely thought to be an intellec-
tual lightweight, and as everyone knew, the maiden
was a true scholar and thought by everyone to be destined for the Tower.

What very few knew was that it was one of the real
love matches of that unsentimental era. The reign of
Queen Sara was notorious for her devotion to King
Rafael the Third and gave her name to a whole era of
repression and firm parental control of the marriages of
young women. Nor did it become widely known that
Valeria had said to the Keeper of Arilinn itself—after
meeting with Jeremy and falling head-over-heels in
love with him—that if a marriage between them could
not be arranged, she would fling herself from the walls
of Arilinn to her death.

It was widely reported in the countryside that the
Keeper of Arilinn—also a Hastur, and an *emmasca*—
had said to old *Dom* Maurizio that if the girl was so
deaf to good sense and her duty to the Tower, she
should be not only allowed, but encouraged to commit
suicide, to avoid encouraging this kind of rebellion in
other dutiful daughters.

It was also well known abroad that most of the older
heads in clan and Council believed *Dom* Maurizio was
widely known to be chivvied about by his womenfolk;
which in those days was not widely admitted. Rather,
it was regretted as an offense to good order and decency. All girls were properly married off by parents
except a few madwomen who went off and joined the
Guild of Renunciates—who were well known for
shamelessly cutting their hair and defying their sensible fathers—were brought up to know that the first
duty of a Comyn daughter, no less than that of a
Comyn son, was to marry well and give her clan many
sons and daughters. There were those who still be-

lieved that if women were given any choice whatever, Chaos was come again.

But *Dom* Maurizio had lost three daughters in threshold sickness before they were fifteen years old, and his wife had given him three *emmasca* sons; and he greatly feared that Valeria would make good her threat to fling herself from the Tower. So he went to the old *Dom* Hastur, and made suit for Jeremy.

"This is not altogether wise," said old *Dom* Marco. "There are many *emmasca* sons in your line as well as mine; it is almost inevitable that if they marry, I can look for only an *emmasca* to call me Grandsire."

Old *Dom* Maurizio hung his head and said meekly that he was sure of it.

"But," he said, "if the girl should do herself harm, she will bear no grandson at all to either of us. And if she bears an *emmasca* she may later have a normal son; while it's for sure that the dead bear no sons for their clan."

"Why, there is a truth," admitted the old Hastur. "Better an *emmasca* grandchild than none—although there are many old fogies in the Council who would say that no grandchild at all would be better than an *emmasca*."

"No. There, I fear, I cannot agree with you, or rather, with them," said *Dom* Maurizio, who had half a dozen *emmasca* grandchildren and loved them all, and old Hastur sighed and admitted that there was much to be said for that point of view. And so, not without reluctance, the two grandfathers went to their sons and arranged for a wedding between Valeria and Jeremy.

Old *Domna* Camilla, it was well known in the countryside, never spoke again to either of them, and adamantly refused to show herself at the wedding; she was heard to say she had never thought that any son of Hastur would put his own personal happiness above the good of his clan; and until her death five years later, she never allowed Valeria to be received in her presence. And of course there were those—mostly among the more raffish members of the younger generation—to whom the two young people became almost the heroes of their generation and stood out against all that was stuffy and conservative.

But the two were wedded in all solemnity and ceremony by the heads of their clan with the Keeper of Arilinn, though reluctantly, to give the bride away; and from what happened in later years there began to be a tradition where the proverb grew up "as unlucky as an *emmasca* at a wedding." But though the Keeper of Arilinn—and most fair people—insisted that none of what happened was the Keeper's fault, there were enough to say that Armilla should not have lent presence to the wedding or even implied consent to it. Of course, the truth was that she had not, but no one bothered to find that out.

For the first three years all went well, though indeed, the first child born to the happy couple was *emmasca,* and folk looked grave and reminded the young couple, with much head shaking, that they had told them so. But neither Jeremy nor Valeria looked sufficiently chastened, and went on quite shamelessly enjoying one another's company, and ignoring everyone else.

In the next year war broke out in the hills, and Jeremy had to be away from home a good deal; and perhaps old Hastur hoped that in the confusion and calamity of war, Jeremy would forget himself and father a *nedestro* son somewhere.

But he did not, or at least if he did no one ever knew it. In the third year of the war, word did indeed go out that at last Valeria was pregnant again; they sent for a *leronis* to have the child monitored—a reasonable precaution for a woman who had borne one *emmasca* child who, however loved, could never be heir to either Ardais or Hastur. And the word went out—some people let it be known that the Royal midwife had gotten drunk and gossiped—that Valeria bore a normal son.

"But I want you to know," Jeremy said, seated by Valeria's side and holding her hand that evening, "that it is not for your ability to bear sons that I cherish you."

"Oh! Shocking," mocked Valeria. "Do you not know that many of that group of old ladies of either sex in the Council are offering up prayers that if I do not give you a healthy son, that this time I will die properly in childbirth and let you get on with the important business of any Hastur heir, which is to give his Domain a son."

Jeremy held her hand, repeating, "My beloved, it is not for your ability to bear me a son that I cherish you."

"Why, my lord, how dare you say so aloud! How the queen would disapprove!"

And Jeremy said quite vulgarly what the queen could go and do. Fortunately no one heard him except for Valeria, who secretly shared that viewpoint.

It was during that year while the war was still going on in the Domains that the Heir to Alton, who was well along in years, was killed; old Maurizio Hastur, being so well advanced in years, young Jeremy was sent to command the Guard and the Army raised that year in the Domain of Aillard. Since the son of the Heir to Alton was as yet a minor, hardly fourteen and not yet skilled in war, the command of the Guards and the Army was put under the command of Hastur. That year, Lady Valeria being near her time, Jeremy would not have left her alone; it was known that his major interests were not in fighting or military knowledge, but

no Hastur son could escape Army command in war-
time if he had sound limbs and his eyesight.

On the night when he was to leave, before the battle,
he knelt by Valeria's side to say farewell.

"I think you know that I care little for this war," he
said, "I would rather stay with you and our unborn
son."

"I know; that is the only reason I can bear to say
farewell," Valeria told him. "Yet swear to me that you
will return—no matter what may happen—when the
child is born."

He pressed her hand. "I will certainly return if I
can," he said. "But an oath is good only for those who
fear they may forswear themselves and need some extraordinary way to bind themselves. The word of a
Hastur is as good as an oath from any other man."

"So will you promise me on your word to come?"
and she sighed.

"I will, my darling; I promise you upon the word of
a Hastur, which I have never broken, that when our son
is born I will come to you.

And Valeria sighed again. "May all the Gods curse
this war!"

Jeremy shivered. "But not the men who go to fight
it? Surely you would not curse me, my precious?" For
upon the moment she spoke, it had seemed to him as
if a cold wind passed through the room.

"Never," she vowed, and so they parted, with many
kisses and words of love. And at dawn he rode forth to
join with the Army.

The war was long and bitterly fought; and in the
course of the greatest battle, Jeremy took a wound in
the thigh. At first it seemed to him not very serious,
but a few days later he took cold in his wound from lying on the bare ground, wrapped only in his military

cloak—for all the *leroni* who cared for the wounded had more than enough to do, and even for the Heir to Hastur there was little even of comfort to spare.

And so Jeremy died; alone and before dawn; and when the word came to Castle Hastur, there was no one who dared bring word to Valeria, since at dawn of the day before, she had fallen down in labor, and it went as ill with her as it could possibly go. Although, at dawn of the next day, she was still living, and the child had been born alive, but barely.

And while she lay in an upper chamber at Castle Hastur, alone—for old *Dom* Maurizio had ridden to fetch a *leronis* from the Tower, fearing that he should be left without even a child of Valeria's, there was a little stir in the room and Jeremy stood there.

"Jeremy!" she cried out, "you have come!"

"Why should that surprise you, my wife? Did I not promise you upon the word of a Hastur that I would come to you—and to him?" he asked, bending over the cradle where the child lay. "Soon I must go; and there will be ill news for you in the days to come; so you must be strong, and not rear him to be a warrior, but to keep war very far from him."

He bent and kissed her.

She begged, "Stay with me!"

He replied, "It is not lawful for the dead to mingle with the living. But I promised you to come when our son was born; and never have I broken my word. I cannot stay even to show myself to my father; so give him my greetings, and tell him that even now, I do not regret our marriage. I came to you, so that you might know that the word of a Hastur is as good as the oath of another man." So saying, he bent over the child's cradle, and kissed him, and kissed Valeria's brow. Then he said, "Know that one day you will be with me again, my Valeria. Meanwhile, care well for our son, and give my respect to all my kinfolk. Farewell for now." And so saying, he vanished away in the dim light of the room, leaving Valeria between tears and laughter.

Matrix Blue

by C. Frances

Every year, one thing I never get enough of is good short fiction. Usually what is good is not short, and what is short is not good.

This was one reason I was so delighted to get this; it's a little gem about a woman who fears she will have to leave her place in a Tower. This not very unusual theme has seldom been handled so well. When I bought this story, I knew nothing about C. Frances—not even if he were she, or vice versa. But I knew all I really needed to know; he or she writes a good story—and editors, like God, are no respecters of persons.

When the biographical information came in, I discovered that Ms. Frances is a student at SFSU working on a BA in Theater with a minor in Music. She has a cat, and lives with her "mother, sister, two dogs, another cat, and two birds. Whew!"

As Laria looked into the stream, she saw again the blue matrix stone and her eyes burned. She had followed every direction of the *tenerezu,* but the stone remained lifeless without even causing the nausea she had been told about. How could she not have *laran,* the precious gift of the Gods? She had grown up around *leroni* and had always had a rapport with them. She even experienced threshold sickness which comes with the development of *laran*. Maybe she shouldn't have waited so long to be tested, but she had just assumed. . . .

Laria's shoulders shifted under her sigh and her eyes almost teared up again when she realized that now she would go back to her father's people. To people she didn't know and, worse, people who didn't know her. Death seemed a better option, if she were brave enough. She couldn't remember many head-blind living at the Tower, certainly not in the Tower. Not even she had entered it and now she never would.

Laria splashed the water on her face to clear her eyes. There were bandits creeping out of the lowlands. Maybe, if she stayed out long enough, she'd be lucky and they would—Avron's voice came up behind her. He was her stability around the Tower and they had latched onto each other from the first. She had almost forgotten about him. He was already in a working circle. She was going to be handfasted to him, but now. . . .

"Laria, are you all right? I got worried when you didn't come by; especially when you spent such a long time with the *tenerezu*. They said you ran off." Avron's excitement at finding her melted when he saw her stained eyes, the red making her eyes bluer than water or matrix.

"What business is it of theirs?" She hadn't thought that the whole Tower would know!

"Laria, please, talk to me. We're nearly handfasted."

"Not any more, Avron. We can't be. Nothing can be."

"Give me one reason." *Please let the test be positive.*

"Find someone else, Avron." *I love you.* "I have no *laran*." *And I won't hold you back.* Laria felt trapped. She couldn't stay at the Tower, even if they asked, not with Avron around every corner. But she couldn't bear to leave her home.

Avron never expected this problem. It was too hard to believe with all they'd shared. She had to have some! Avron wanted to hold her, but her startling blue eyes held him back. Why did the *laran* have to mean so much? "Should it matter?"

"No, but it does. You know it does." By the cold pain in his heart he knew it was true and Laria's honest gaze told him she felt the same.

Laria bowed her head. "I don't belong here anymore. I can never give you the closeness any other Tower member could. I was hoping I had just a little." He held her and felt her small graceful form bending with sobs.

Avron was so upset he wished he could shake down the Tower. Why does *laran* have to change things? Couldn't she see how attracted everyone was to her. Talk inside his circle was often of her and her positive effect on the matrix workers. No one was pushing her out, not himself.

"I wish you had *laran*, too." He sighed. "But I love you, Laria, and all I want from you is your love and devotion. You have mine." He pulled away for a moment. What he was contemplating was near suicide, but he couldn't let Laria go. She had become the crux of his life. Carefully he began to disassociate himself from his matrix. There had to be a way to include her. When he turned back to her, he held out his matrix. He was not afraid. Laria's touch had never harmed him, but sent warmth and life throughout his being. "Take it."

Laria stared at his hand. This was his keyed matrix, a very live part of his mind and body. Removing it without training was dangerous and Avron was giving

it to her. She had come close to holding it only once
when they had clasped it between their hands in solemn promise to each other. "I can't." What have I to
offer him? "I love you, but I won't cripple you—in any
way." Not as a dysfunctional wife and not by diminish-
ing his *laran*.

So she ran, slipping, up the sloped embankment.
She wanted to escape, to run, to cease to exist, but she
stopped. Something called to her to stop. Later, she
thought maybe it had been the missing sound of
Avron's departure. Turning around in the brush she
saw the bandits who were already flocking toward her.
Her heart stopped when a dagger flew past her down
the streambed to shatter the matrix in Avron's hand.
Then Laria knew they hadn't seen her at all. Wildly
she ran down again toward Avron.

Laria didn't think or she would have known Avron
was dead. But she only reacted. As she slid into
Avron's crumpling form, her breathing slowed and her
mind cleared. Her soul matched resonances with Avron
and drew them both back together.

Avron didn't know what happened. He had been
watching Laria. Suddenly there was thunder in his ear
as lightning hit his hand. His tortured mind screamed,
"Why aren't I dead" and then—"I wish I were dead!"
His bones floated apart and his mind was tearing into
different parts of the overworld. But slowly he faded
back into his own mind and the familiar touch of a matrix keyed to his soul. And Laria was holding him.

All at once *laran* coursed through Laria, Avron's
laran, and she became his amplifier. Her blazing blue
eyes turned on the bandits and she knew that with
Avron's *laran* she could kill them and her anger boiled
up. But Avron's will was there with her, alive and caring, calming her. So a band of startled bandits were

lifted onto the main road, their minds muddled, but their bodies whole.

Inside the Tower, Avron couldn't stop looking into Laria's matrix blue eyes. Now there was no way they would cancel their handfasting.

Shards

by Nina Boal

Nina Boal, of course, is no stranger to these anthologies; and in addition to my anthologies, she's published fiction in PANDORA, and other small press magazines.

She is also, like my housemate Lisa, an avid figure skating fan and has been to many local (Baltimore) skating events. Just now (end of 1992), she's working only part time—courtesy of the economy—as a cab driver and teacher of adult literacy courses. She's about to take a course in electricity and mechanics to improve her job skills. Well, better her than me.

This story documents a strange use of laran, *and the duty of a prince.*

"Bring the Prince his dinner," Alaric Delleray, Regent of the tiny mountain kingdom of Serrano, snapped the order to his bodyservant. The white-haired man bowed, spinning away on his heels.

Alaric Delleray peered into a round mirror, also grasping his matrix crystal. A picture appeared—a lounge, part of a lush suite of rooms. A copper-haired boy of fourteen was dressed in Serrano green-and-white silks. He was playing a game of Castles with a blond opponent whose brown eyes betrayed nonhuman origins. Alaric let out his breath. Everything was as usual in this part of the castle; the mirror, functioning as a portable matrix screen, had shown him so.

Prince Dyan-Rakhal Gareth Serrano was the kingdom's Heir—and he had spent his entire life in his hermetically sealed suite of rooms. Never once had he been permitted to venture forth outside the suite's matrix-protected barriers—though Alaric could visit the young prince, and had done so regularly, giving lessons and parental guidance. Loyu, the prince's specially-manufactured *ri'chiyu* servant, was the only other living being who actually inhabited Dyan-Rakhal's quarters with him.

Alaric settled his head against the stuffed armchair's cushions. Gray-streaked chestnut hair tumbled over his forehead. *It's for his own good,* he reassured himself. The Serrano *laran,* which Dyan-Rakhal bore in full measure, was dangerously formidable. Alaric had to make sure that it was well-guarded and the knowledge of its workings kept secret. He had nursed the prince through threshold sickness, had given his pupil the necessary training in the Gift. The prince seemed content with his fate, as he always had been. How could he possibly long for an outside world he had never experienced? Alaric replaced the mirror in his pocket. *It's for the good of the realm as well.*

Alaric dug his fingers into the chair's springy arms as memories spun across his mind. He had been the late king's paxman, the brother of the late queen. Both of Prince Dyan-Rakhal's parents had been killed during a Scathfell raid on the castle. Alaric had managed to save the infant Heir as Serrano's armies had fought Scathfell to a stalemate, forcing their retreat.

Alaric had sworn himself to preserving the former king's son, as he had once sworn to his father. Dyan-Rakhal was the successful result of the realm's own *laran* breeding program. After the great battle with

Scathfell, Alaric had arranged for the child Heir to be placed in the shielded quarters, had arranged for the *ri'chiyu* to be a companion and bodyservant. Dyan-Rakhal depended entirely upon his uncle to raise him, and to teach him about the world and his enemies.

A panic raced across Alaric's mind. He swept his mirror out of his pocket, holding it next to his crystal. Pictures floated again on the screen's face, this time the purple, jutting peaks which rose above the estate. Flame-red tendrils from the setting sun reached past the mountains, bathing the castle in light.

A peaceful and tranquil scene, Alaric pondered, his moist hands clutching the mirror—deceivingly so. Enemies surrounded the realm, though there were less than before. From within the royal suite, the Heir's newly-awakened Gift had aided Alaric's own powers during the past months. With the Gift, armies were no longer needed; men need not throw their lives away in battle. Serrano had emerged victorious against Leynier and Rockraven, and these two realms had been forced to swear fealty. But Serrano still existed among hundreds of other contentious kingdoms which competed for sparse Darkovan resources.

Alaric's fears dissolved into a tight smile. Tonight and the next few days would be the culmination of long-sought goals. The *laran* weapon the prince bore would lay waste to Scathfell, as it had succeeded against Rockraven and Leynier during the winter. It would avenge the old king's death—would end the eternal warring once and for all. Dyan-Rakhal was one month shy of his fifteenth birthday, the day of his coronation as king. *On that day, he will be king, not only of Serrano, but of all the mountain realms around.* For the nephew on whom he concentrated his total devotion, Alaric Delleray would make sure of that.

Of course, the new king, in his innocence of the

world, would have to remain sealed in his chambers. Dyan-Rakhal would tend to the more spiritual and philosophical areas of rulership, while the Regent tended to more material areas. The Serrano Gift was strong—too strong, perhaps, for Dyan-Rakhal's own good. Alaric shuddered as he shut dangerous possibilities from his mind.

Dyan-Rakhal's head pounded. He strived to stem the shaking which crept through his body. His hands wrapped around the intricate carving of the chair's arms; he gazed into Loyu's wide, brown eyes, then at the chiseled pieces on the board. It *was* his move, wasn't it?

The memories of the last few months ripped into him. Quickly, he moved a pawn, then held himself rigidly as the tide claimed him.

Dyan-Rakhal stood by a glass table, in the tiny matrix chamber which adjoined his quarters. Uncle Alaric stood over him, blue eyes gleaming with encouragement. "It is your duty, my nephew. Use your strength, chiyu, your Gift. It is your greatest heritage."

Dyan-Rakhal nodded. His uncle had taught him everything he needed to know, had told him stories, sung legends to him. Even lullabies to sweep a young, restless child into the land of dreams. . . . Now he was older, almost a man. He was a prince, almost a king. He had to perform a prince's duty in a cruel world, against terrible enemies who would destroy him.

The Gift. He carefully extracted his crystal from its silken pouch. He focused his mind on the white lines of his power. The white lines curled upon the table, then sprang into a three-dimensional shape—Rockraven Castle, snow-laden in winter, its banners flapping in the bitter Hellers wind. Uncle Alaric handed Dyan-

Rakhal a thin, blue-white shard. He grasped the shard in his hands. He aimed it straight, then stabbed it into the model of Rockraven Castle. The shape collapsed on the table.

And through a wall-sized matrix screen, the prince saw the results of his handiwork. In Rockraven, past the mountain range, huge chunks of stone crumbled and fell down, ragged remnants of what had once been a castle. Screams echoed, then were silenced by toppling rocks and splintering wood. . . .

Dyan-Rakhal slammed his mind upon the swirling images. He swallowed against his churning stomach. The first time, when he had used his Gift upon Leynier—there had been falling buildings, people crying in terror. But it had seemed no more to him than pieces falling in a game of Castles. Just his enemies, his uncle had told him, like the green pieces facing his own red across the checkered game board.

They're real people, not game pieces, his own voice shouted inside him. Real deaths, caused by skirmishes whose reasonings he failed to grasp, no matter how many times Uncle Alaric explained them. The hammering in his head erupted again. He forced the white lines of his *laran* to form a shield which would protect his private thoughts from his uncle's prying.

"I think I've checkmated your king, Janu," Loyu's soft tenor voice intruded, chuckling. He pointed at the board, at Dyan-Rakhal's hopelessly scattered pieces.

Loyu never said "master" or *"vai dom"*, but used the intimate form of the prince's name. It had been a request the prince had asked of his servant long ago. Through the years, Loyu had become far more than a servant to Dyan-Rakhal. Loyu was the opposite of a Comyn Heir—head-blind, the product of artificial construction. Yet a tenday ago, shortly after the wrecking of Rockraven Castle, the two had sworn the oath of *bredin.*

It had been a secret ceremony—Uncle Alaric would have strictly forbidden a liaison between a *ri'chiyu* and the Heir to Serrano. Dyan-Rakhal gazed at his triumphant game partner, searched the depths of the alien, familiar brown eyes. *You cannot command the wind to stop blowing or the Golden Bell flowers not to bloom.*

Dyan-Rakhal gave an inner sigh. *Uncle Alaric forbids a lot of things.* His eyes floated toward a tiny window, the suite's solitary view of the outer world. Liriel's lavender moonlight lit the dusky sky. Visions spun inside Dyan-Rakhal's mind, thoughts he dare not think. At least, not *yet.*

A bell rang. "Our dinner, Janu," Loyu piped. He slipped easily back into the servant's role for which he had been manufactured, rising to answer the summons and fetch the meal. Dyan-Rakhal steadied the turmoil his lingering fears created in his stomach. He would need nourishment for the work he knew his uncle had planned for that night. Also for the work he knew *he* had planned.

Dyan-Rakhal put his hand on his crystal. Full-sized screens lined the walls of the matrix room, reflecting his own form as well as that of his uncle. "Scathfell," Uncle Alaric snapped his command. "Scathfell will belong to you on the day of your coronation, along with Rockraven and Leynier, perhaps all the mountain realms." The voice began wavering with its own eagerness. "All will be yours."

Dyan-Rakhal began drawing up the lines from his matrix, the lines of his power. He gazed into the glowing blue-white lights. More lines streaked out, strands invisible to his uncle—setting up an inner shield, masking his own intentions.

"Now build the castle," Uncle Alaric urged. The white curls which lay on the table began dancing into form. A gray, stone-hewn castle emerged, nestled within a mountain range. The high Hellers rose behind. "At last, we will deal with your parents' murderers. Now do your duty, the duty of a prince."

The stream of Dyan-Rakhal's own rage raced through his body. Smothered in the prison of confinement for far too long, his fury burst into the fires of his glittering matrix. His mind worked, drawing out more white tendrils. The stone castle's walls reshaped themselves into a familiar form. A banner flapped and yawed—the green-and-white of Serrano.

Dyan-Rakhal turned to face the Regent. He stared directly into the blue eyes of his uncle. "I will deal with my parents' murderers. It is the duty of a prince," he stated, echoing his uncle's words. He seized one of the blue shards which lay on the table. He plunged the needle into the modeled form of his own castle.

A creaking, tearing noise emanated, soon joined by a cacophony of others. Alaric Delleray stood stock-still, his face whitened with shock. His voice crawled out from between trembling lips. "Why?" A stone boulder plunged to the floor directly behind him.

"The murderers of my parents," Dyan-Rakhal whispered. "The lords who fight these *laran* wars as though moving pieces in a game of Castles. Alaric Delleray, Regent of Serrano, you are just as guilty as they. Use me, use my Gift to conquer? So that *you* can rule all of the mountain kingdoms?" The continuing rage spewed out, which had once been love for the one who had raised him. *Only for my Gift,* his bitter thoughts pondered. "Better that the kingdom be destroyed, that no one rules," he spat out. "Rather than a monster such as you."

Heavy oak beams crackled and groaned. Dust

whirled, glass shattered and flew. Dyan-Rakhal spun on his heels and fled the matrix chamber. A crumbling pile of wood and bricks muffled out the footsteps which strived to pursue him.

Loyu! Where are you, Dyan-Rakhal's desperate thoughts twirled out, forgetting that his *bredu* was head-blind and could not hear them. A slim hand grabbed his own, a face with anxious brown eyes now filled with utter relief. A gaping hole faced Dyan-Rakhal. Moving almost as one, he and Loyu leapt out into open space.

The stag-ponies clambered up the fir-lined slope. Dyan-Rakhal and Loyu clung to the saddles. Neither one had ever been taught to ride. By some miracle, the beats tired and drew to a halt when reins were tugged; Dyan-Rakhal had once read about it in a story book his uncle had given him.

They both slid off the stag-ponies. The two gazed down into the valley where red strands from the rising sun poked through the peaks. Shimmers illuminated a pile of rock and debris, where once a mighty castle had stood.

Dyan-Rakhal's head pounded. He had heard the screams of pain and terror while fleeing. His Gift had wrought its ugly destruction once again. He reached down into his boot. A single blue shard had been hidden, snatched and thrust inside his stocking. He extracted his matrix from its silk pouch. The ragged edges of wood, rock, and wounded flesh crawled through his mind, over and over. There was one final duty to be performed.

"Janu, are you sure that this is necessary?" was Loyu's concerned question.

Dyan-Rakhal nodded, then spoke. He had better get used to speech; it would be the only communication he

would have with all others from now on, not just with
Loyu. "What if another kingdom finds out and captures me?" Dyan-Rakhal posed his own set of questions. "What if my uncle's disease of conquest
suddenly seizes me, and I set out to do it? Who could
ever stop me?"

"I understand," Loyu answered. The brown eyes reflected his *bredu*'s lingering regret.

Dyan-Rakhal breathed deeply, letting his eyes scan
the river of stars which dusted the dawn sky. Then he
plunged the shard into the middle of his own crystal.
The crystal quavered, then exploded. A tearing agony
shredded his mind into thousands of pieces—then a
sudden shriveling. He staggered, his hands waving
wildly, struggling to hold on. Loyu offered his shoulder to steady him. It was as if he had lost a part of his
eyesight, as if he were *blind*.

The shadow across him seemed to lift. A peculiar
shroud persisted in clutching around his head. He
would have to compensate for it, learn to adjust. He
would wear this shroud for the rest of his life.

And yet, Loyu wore the cover on his mind. So did
the servants, farmers, and artisans who formed most of
the mountains' populations. Was it truly a blindness?
Or is it another Gift, another form of sight?

Dyan-Rakhal held Loyu's hand. He was no longer a
great Prince, he ruled over nothing. He and his *bredu*
were free to share the world with others, now his
equals. His eyes swept once more over the river of
dawn stars, the misted form of the far Hellers, the fir
trees which swayed in the wind as it whistled around
them.

Briana's Birthright

by Suzanne Hawkins Burke

Suzanne says about this story "I've always wanted to read more about Darkovan children, especially mixed-race ones who are more chieri than human."

She states that her husband nagged her daily to write a story for this anthology. "He has an unshakable faith that I can create wonderful stories."

That's a good place to start, anyhow. She has a couple of college degrees, has been happily married for 20 years (enviable in this day and age), has a 15-year-old son, and does 100% of her writing on the computer. She says, though, that honestly "I'd really rather read a good book than write one."

It's unfashionable to admit it; when I was teaching, I asked my class how many of them wanted to be writers. Every hand in the room shot up—including kids who could not write at all, and read only with difficulty. Flattering, but impractical, no?

Briana of the MacGregor Clan sat comfortably on her heels and glanced outside at the pre-dawn sky from her position near the rafters of the dairy barn. Perched on one of the support beams that crisscrossed the heights of the haymow, she looked down and across the shadowed loft to her small, neat chamber in the back corner. Briana had moved herself to the barn from the big house when she was eight years old, and that was

when the unseen *chieri* started monitoring her, sensing
a profound difference in this child.

She peered outside again. The storm seemed to
have passed, and there should soon be a beautiful,
Darkovan sunrise. She brushed back her long, silvery
hair which had never been trimmed, and it floated in
a shimmering curtain around her body, totally covering the skimpy shift she wore out of deference to anyone who might come into this part of the barn at
dawn. At age twelve, she was starting to bud tiny little breasts on her slender body, and the wrinkled old
granny who gathered straw for the chicken boxes said
the boys would bother her if she continued to walk
around naked.

Each morning in the rafters, Briana watched the red
dawn sky between louvered air vent boards that she
had angled open. The dark plum pre-dawn shadows
gradually gave way to a deep burgundy horizon with
faint scarlet and pink reflections on the bottoms of the
high clouds. Soon, a heavy red sun heaved itself over
the edge and sat there like a big, fat *cinnimelon.*

Far below her in the ground floor stalls, several of
the blunt-horned dairy animals were lowing mourn-
fully, anxious for their twice-daily milking. With a little sigh of pleasure for the start of a new day, Briana
effortlessly rose and walked fluidly across a narrow
girder to the knotted rope she had tied around the ridge
beam.

None of the other children were brave enough to
walk and climb so high, but she craved it like honey on
porridge. It bothered the others to see her up there,
however, and they never played in the loft anymore.
She descended the rope with an exotic technique that
made it appear she was just floating down its length.

In her little room, Briana tugged a simple woolen tunic from a wooden peg and tossed it over her shift. De-

fiantly, she accidentally-on-purpose did not don the thick socks and heavy shoes. They made her feet feel awful! She was taller and slimmer than any of the other children her age, and her skin had a smooth, translucent tone that defied freckles and sunburn. The boys didn't think she was buxom enough for their attention, but the older men sometimes gave her thoughtful glances.

Briana descended the loft ladder and walked to the end of the wide, raised aisle in the middle of the barn.

"Good morning, ladies." Briana walked the length and tossed hay into the long manger for the heavy, sad-eyed cows.

She turned when a small, bright-eyed boy squeezed through a trick board from outside and clambered up the midway steps.

"Hi, Briana," he declared cheerfully. "I got dressed all by myself. Can I give them their oats this morning?"

"All right, but just one scoop each." She gave an indulgent smile to five-year-old Nathan, her personal helper. He was an undersized boy with a ragged mop of sandy-red hair and a slightly toed-in foot. He had judged himself flawed and unimportant until he met Briana. Even at his tender age, Nathan wanted desperately to have a sense of purpose and service to the clan, but his frailness and awkward gait had left him miserable. Briana encouraged him and set him tasks without the dose of pity he felt from others, and he had found a sense of pride and self-esteem in working with her and the cows.

"Move over, Maggie. You, too, Bethany," grunted Briana as she slapped the flanks of each, shoved them into place with her shoulder, and tied the manger ropes around their necks.

"Nathan, I'm ready for the first pail." She snagged a

peg-leg stool from the wall and stepped over to the first cow in line. The little boy stood on the edge of the manger and proudly lifted the empty bucket over the top to her.

"Let's start with you, Eleanor." Briana deftly positioned the single-legged stool as she seated herself and put the bucket in place with the other hand.

She bowed her head and leaned the top of it into the side of the warm animal. As she rested it there, the girl instinctively projected feelings of calm and contentment to the cow, willing the udder to relax. Briana was innocently unaware of her own special abilities. She stroked the teats and lightly jostled the udder, unaware of lightly *pushing* with her immature *laran*. She firmly encircled one teat with her thumb and forefinger, her other four fingers squeezing out the first stream of warm milk into the waiting pink mouth of the old tom cat who sat under the belly of the cow.

"There you go, Tom. You're my poison taster." It was not totally a silly joke. Once in a while, a dairy animal managed to feed on a hidden patch of snakeroot grass, and it was better to lose a cat than a clansman.

Nathan couldn't contain a contagious giggle. "He's so funny! He looks like a clown at Midsummer Festival."

Tom licked his face and wiped his whiskers. The other cats nearby who weren't as brave as old Tom moved closer and settled impatiently with little cries and twitching tails. They knew she'd get around to them.

Briana settled into a comfortable rhythm, her fingers squeezing bursts of milk into the frothing bucket. It had been a long time since she had whimpered with the fierce, burning pain in her forearms that came from using hidden hand and arm muscles to milk the cows.

She was strong now, and the milking rhythm was second nature.

Nathan had joined her on the floor of the milking stall, but he stood far enough away to avoid the large cloven hooves. He waited warily with another bucket.

"Briana, how come you have to live in the barn?" he asked innocently in the high sing-song voice peculiar to precocious children.

"I don't *have to,* I *get to,*" she clarified as milk sprayed into the bucket with a steady pulse.

"Really?" he said in astonished awe. "Why?"

Briana smiled wryly to herself and wished she had a *jhizil-nut* for every time Nathan had asked *"Why?"* about things these past few weeks! Except for that favorite word, he didn't say much, and Briana had spoken more to Nathan than to anyone else in years.

"When I was your age, I slept in the kitchen helpers' room. At night, they kept the shutters tightly closed. I was always too warm, and I figured out how to unlatch the shutters and open them just a little bit after they were all asleep. I made sure to wake up first, and I closed them before the older girls got up. They were baffled at why it was often so cold, but no one caught me for a while.

"One night, there was a light snow. I only opened the shutters a very small crack, and I closed them before the girls woke up, but I couldn't do much about the snow drift on top of their shoe pile. They walloped me good, and one of their brothers cut a stout pole to bar the shutters after that."

"What did you do then?"

"Here, take this bucket and I'll continue my story when you get back."

Briana alternated the buckets by trading off when they were only half full. It was a subtle trick of hers

that Nathan hadn't picked up on yet, but he couldn't
have carried a full pail to the back cavern.

"Don't trip."

"I'll be real careful, Briana," he promised as he
started walking away. It was amazing how a little crea-
tivity and change in her routines had opened up this little boy who desperately wanted to feel needed.

"Bring it back and trade it for this next bucket as
soon as you can," she called as she squirted the cats
and began on another pair of teats.

She hummed a nonsensical tune as she worked, and
the cows contentedly chewed their cud. While Nathan
was gone, she thought about the early years of her
own life that the Lady MacGregor had talked to her
about when they had their little "moving to the barn"
talk.

Briana was an orphan, a not unusual status resulting
from the rugged conditions and unforgiving demands
of the inhospitable world of Darkover. Everyone had
forgotten that they were only a score of generations
away from their involuntary beginning on this planet
as shipwrecked colonists and space crew, but they had
clung to a level of civilization that would survive and
thrive in time. There hadn't been a functioning spaceport or an engineering crew preparing the world for
settlement, but there were farmers and scientists who
worked together in mutual cause after the original destination became unattainable.

She had no enduring memory of her mother. The
Lady MacGregor told Briana that her mother's name
had been Judith, and that she had been a gifted healer
who roamed alone among the hills of Kilghard to find
unique and important herbs and roots. People said that
Judith was a strange young woman who didn't talk

much and preferred to be alone unless someone needed her medicines or cures.

One winter Judith stunned everyone by quietly delivering herself of a baby girl. No one even knew she was pregnant. They said the heavy winter clothes must have disguised her condition. They said she must have met a lover in the hills. Maybe even a legendary *chieri*. Some remembered that Judith had been caught out alone during an early Ghost Wind the preceding spring.

The tiny infant was exquisite, and she had six perfect fingers on each hand, a trait considered by most to bring luck and prosperity to the entire household although no one could exactly explain why.

The Lady MacGregor assured Briana that Judith had loved her very much. She never took the baby with her into the mountains, but there were always willing hands to cuddle and rock the precious little girl while she was gone. There was even a wet nurse available when Judith's milk dried up unexpectedly early. Judith often brought her daughter little gifts from the forest: a snow owl's feather, a fist-sized acorn, a double-spiral horn shed by one of the wild goatlike animals.

When Briana was three years old, her mother went out alone to collect special night-blooming plants and was found dead the next day of scorpion-ant bites. Although Briana was *nedestro* with no acknowledged father, the Lady MacGregor immediately kept her as a fosterling to be loved and raised with the gaggle of other MacGregor cousins and supporting families in the extended household.

Young Briana was a solemn, quiet child. She was not unhappy, but the traditional household games and chores fitted her spirit no better than an ill-made tunic. However, it was necessary for everyone to contribute time and talent in their communal settlement, and tiny

Briana set herself to helping in the dairy as soon as she was old enough to carry a pail of oats. Girls were usually discouraged from manual tasks that they would have to forgo when they married and started bearing children, but she was so much happier there that no one bid her give it up.

Nathan rushed back and interrupted her reverie, trying to stand still and hide his keen impatience for the rest of her story. It had taken him forever to get up the nerve to ask her about herself. "The snow drift, Briana. What happened next?"

"Oh, I had to dry off all their shoes and was punished with no dessert for a week. It just wasn't fair. It was stupid for them to worry about a little snow. If it bothered them so much, I decided that maybe I should find another place to sleep."

"Weren't you scared?" he breathed.

"Oh, no. I'd been helping in the barn since I was your age, and I was a very stubborn eight-year-old who didn't have anyone that kept close track of me every day. The next week I took my things to the haymow, and the kitchen girls just thought I'd moved to another room. It was two weeks before one of the others tattled on me. By then, I'd proven that I was serious about sleeping out here. Everyone was horrified, but I put up quite a fuss.

"The Lady MacGregor talked to me for the longest time about a lot of things. Did you know she has a special 'sight' that can see into your very spirit? She told the others that I had to do things in my own way, that they had to remember I was not quite like them. The Lady finally said something about *fait accompli* and said she guessed it was all right to stay out here as long as I showed up clean for meals at the big house and came to talk to her whenever I had any more problems."

Briana traded milk buckets again, and Nathan dutifully supported the cycle as she moved to the next cow.

"After a few weeks, everyone took my new arrangements for granted, and some of the kitchen girls even brought out neat stuff to make it really nice. I think they felt a little guilty. I used to lie awake nights, wondering why I was different. No one will tell me anything about my father, and I dream about places and things that I've never seen. I get strange feelings, good feelings, like when my mother used to hug me, but no one is around! I don't get cold, and I can see the barn-owl and her nest in the rafters almost as well at midnight as I can in the morning. Last night there was a very strong wind, and I felt strange, like something is going to happen soon."

Nathan didn't really believe that part about the owl's nest. She was probably just pulling his leg. "What's it like up there? Can I go up sometime?" he asked daringly. He wasn't sure if it was decent for a boy to see a girl's private room.

"It's just a boxed corner of the haymow. I'll help you up the ladder later today, all right?"

Nathan sucked in his breath and nodded hopefully.

The barn door opened, and Rhoger shuffled inside, lank brown hair smashed flat under his woolen cap. He hawked and spat, squinting as a ray of garnet sunrise fell through a crack in the wall and speared his bloodshot eyes. The old man was supposed to feed the stock and do most of the milking, but he didn't like to get up early enough to help with the first set of cows anymore.

"G'morning, Briana," he said gruffly. It was obvious that he'd prefer the scent and taste of something stronger than fresh, warm milk. If only he could get fermented *firi* from the gentle cows, he might have been more interested.

"Good morning, Rhoger," said Briana evenly as she finished with the last glossy brown cow. "This group is all milked. I'll go make the butter."

Rhoger grunted, not displeased with the arrangement. Briana was all right. They had a working arrangement that suited them both pretty well. He just wished he could get over his shivers when he saw her milking with all those fingers. The kid with the limp and the puppy dog eyes who followed her everywhere also disturbed him, as though there was something special about Briana that the old man couldn't quite figure out.

Rhoger had always felt slightly unsettled in the presence of this girl-child who displayed such poise and self-reliance. She took care of herself and her chores without waiting for orders or approval from her elders. He also found it hard to look at her for very long. His eyes seemed to slide away before he could study her features very closely.

Briana toted the last milk bucket to the rear of the barn where a short tunnel led to a cool cavern inside the bluff. Poor Nathan always wore his coat in here, but Briana savored the chill.

The late Ian MacGregor had built the dairy barn of his small hillside holding against the entrance to a nice granite cavern in the Kilghard Hills. The cave was large, deep, and level on each of four different tiers. The ceiling was low, but there were vents that provided a constant flow of fresh air. A natural spring flowed noisily out of a narrow cut in the back corner and down into a deep hole not far away.

Pineknot torchlight disclosed a wide stone ledge where Briana poured the fresh milk through the strainer and set it aside to cool. She and Nathan rinsed and scrubbed the buckets under the small black waterfall. "When you've finished, go sweep the aisle where the hay got scattered. Then come back and we'll test the buttermilk."

Nathan obediently worked on the last bucket of his least favorite chore. The water was ice cold!

Briana pulled the milk vats from last night forward, carefully skimmed off the yellow cream, and filled the churn. The Lady of the house wanted fresh butter with her breakfast each morning, and making butter was one of Briana's favorite chores. She had a special hollowed-out stone seat where she could lean back and daydream while her arms moved the crank in the churn between her knees. Briana had wonderful daydreams.

"The buckets are done, Briana," Nathan said shortly with a quiver. His teeth were chattering and he had buried his small hands in his armpits.

"Oh, dear, come here, *chiyu*," cried Briana in genuine concern, pulling his pale, chapped hands into her own. She enveloped them and bent down to breathe on them. A tendril of warmth seemed to slither down her arms and into her palms. She was as yet unawakened to the powers of her *laran,* but it was working instinctively when presented with such a need. After a moment, there was almost too much warmth.

"How do you do that?" he cried in astonishment, jerking his toasted hands out of her hot ones.

"Do what? I'm just a little warmer than you, and it only seems like a lot." She looked at him and spread her hands as if to show there was no trickery. She didn't tell him she felt a strange tingling in her fingers.

Nathan frowned but didn't argue.

"Go finish the sweeping," Briana ordered gently. "That should warm you up some more."

As she leaned back and spun again the wooden gears that turned the inner butter paddle, Briana's mind began to slip into her favorite daydream. She glimpsed pale, slender faces and fine, long, silver-white hair. The beings in her dreams were very tall, but their six-fingered hands were rather tiny. They also had large, silver-gray eyes and delicate bones, just like herself. Their voices were sweet, and she imagined she could hear them thinking.

In her dreams, she was always in a wonderfully cold dwelling place, and everyone went barefoot, even in the bitter chill. She couldn't describe the persons or creatures in the room because her perception seemed to shift and alter whenever she tried to concentrate on the the details.

The rooms in her daydreams seemed to be built on platforms high in the trees. She often closed her eyes and relished the gentle, almost imperceptible swaying motion. She felt as if she could touch the green moss and tiny white flowers on the walls which seemed to give off an iridescent, silvery light.

When she wasn't inside a treetop room, her day-dreams delighted her with visions of intricate pathways across large branches high in the tops of the forest. She sometimes encountered funny little creatures much shorter than herself, with pale fur, flat noses, and red eyes. She tried not to startle them, but sometimes they gave shrill, birdlike cries and scrambled away into the mists. Something in her head told her they were *the small ones who are not wise.*

The magical daydreams of high, cool places were the best part of Briana's lonely life.

"Oh," gasped a tiny voice that was quickly muffled as Nathan covered his mouth and widened his vivid, blue eyes.

Briana abruptly opened and re-focused her own eyes, leaning forward with a jerk. "Goodness! You startled me, *chiyu!*" Her heart thudded for a moment, and it took her a second to realize she was back on the ground.

Nathan's eyes were on the butter churn, and he appeared terrified of something.

"What's the matter? You look like I'm holding the tail of a *kyor-snake*." She got a firmer grip on the crank and gave it a few good strokes.

Nathan's face was still white. "I finished the sweeping and came back. You were asleep and the handle wasn't moving, but I could hear the buttermilk inside swishing away," he blurted. He looked up at Briana, hoping to hear a logical explanation.

"Nonsense," she snorted in gentle disagreement. "Butter doesn't churn itself. I was just resting my eyes, but my arms were still cranking away."

"No. You weren't moving when I came in," he argued bravely. "I was going to sneak up and scare you until I got close enough to hear the churn making the butter all by itself."

"Well, let's see if we've got a monster in here," she said with a tolerate grin. "I assume you're still my assistant buttermilk tester, aren't you?"

Nathan quickly lowered his eyes and ducked his chin. It wasn't seemly for a boy to be so attached to buttermilk. He wasn't a baby anymore. At least Briana didn't seem to think anything strange about his secret craving. She never teased him in front of the other children, and she liked buttermilk, too.

Briana removed the heavy lid and wet paddle from the churn. She peered intently inside and inhaled the pungent odor.

"Nope, I don't think there is anything in here except butter and buttermilk." She looked at Nathan seriously as she rested on one knee to be at eye level with him.

He tightened his lips and shrugged his shoulders.

Briana poured the liquid into a large earthen pitcher and placed the hefty lump of butter on her shiny stone work slab.

"Here you go." She poured a generous cup for him and a small one for herself. "Tell me if it's good enough." She toasted his mug and downed her mouthful quickly, suddenly realizing that she was famished.

Nathan sipped the cool treat, goosebumps running down his back as Briana turned away to work on the butter. He adored her, but she scared him sometimes. The other women in the household called her *changeling* when she wasn't around. He didn't know what that meant, but maybe it had something to do with why she could do her work with her eyes closed. He didn't think anyone but himself had ever noticed, however, and this was the first time that he had been certain of what he had only previously suspected about the butter churn working on its own while she sat there asleep.

Briana kneaded salt into the butter and filled a small ceramic pot with a generous amount for the Lady's table. The rest of it was packed into less decorative jars for the rest of the household.

Turning to Nathan, she grinned and said, "Better wipe the milk ring from your upper lip before you go back. I'll not share our little secret toast else other greedy little boys start plaguing me during my chores. Will you help me carry these inside?"

She picked up the pitcher of buttermilk and the Lady's pot. Nathan swiped his sleeve across his mouth and took two of the others. He followed her out of the cavern and through the barn door into the side yard.

Briana looked across the frozen steppe to the dark forest and snow ridged mountains. The Lady MacGregor said her mother used to spend most of her time in that wilderness. The hunters and trappers re-

ported that there were forest-covered hills and valleys
for a ten-day journey before one reached the foot of
an awesome, impenetrable wall of huge snowy crags
and glaciers of ice that loomed up to cover half of the
sky.

Briana wondered if anyone would stop her if she just
started walking toward the forests one day. It didn't
cross her mind to think about supplies or weapons.
Whenever she thought about going, there was a funny
tingle behind her eyes, and her back teeth itched!
Maybe it was time for another talk with the Lady
MacGregor.

Snow was swirling in little tornadoes as the wind
swept between the barn and the big house. Nathan
hugged the butter jars tightly and shivered in his thick
winter breeches and coat. Briana merely laughed, lifted
her chin, and shook herself in pleasure. Her bare feet
and long, narrow toes made only faint tracks in the
snow as she executed a little step-dance.

Nathan rolled his little boy eyes in baffled bewilder-
ment and lurched ahead to the warm kitchen. He loved
her buttermilk, but the others were right. Briana was
weird!

In a lofty shelter some distance away, a pale white
chieri sat peacefully on a soft moss floor and focused
silver-gray *far-seeing* eyes on his/its first daughter in
the last hundred seasons. The frail body trembled with
a rush of intense emotion, knowing there would never
be another such joining of its body and soul. It was in-
spiring to observe the promising children of the infre-
quent unions between its long-lived kind and the
tenacious new settlers. An ancient kinship was enabling the telepathic *chieri* race to survive and infuse a
new generation with special abilities and hidden powers.

Nearly all mixed-blood children, regardless of their

birth mother, were raised in the human communities because they could not bear the cold of *chieri* life in high-summer, let alone winter. Most never knew their other parent.

Briana was unique. It was inevitable that someday the *chieri* would claim her as one of their own. *The first kireseth will bloom when all four moons are next together in the sky,* he thought. *After that, I will invite her here to collect the other half of her birthright.*

In the Eye of the Beholder

by Linda Anfuso

Linda says she's been reading Darkover stories since she was a teenager, and every time she read one of these anthologies, she'd say to herself "I can do that." So she did.

Linda is a Native American, Mohawk Nation, and is originally from upstate New York (my own old stamping ground) about two and a half miles north of Thendara—quite suitable for a Friend of Darkover. She received a Bachelor and a Master of Fine Arts, and is active in the struggle for Native American Rights.

By profession she is an artist (artist and musician are the only professions more difficult than writer in which to become independently established), and this is her first fiction sale, though she's written nonfiction and poetry, which she has read on public radio and television.

Since she's done a little of everything else, we're glad to see her here, too.

The sign over the door read "The Guild of Limners." It was beautifully painted and decorated with flourishes of copper gilt.

Eryn paused a moment before the door, straightening his tunic, then knocked. Holding his bundle under his arm, he tried not to look as nervous as he felt. He had rehearsed this moment a hundred times over in his mind during the long trip to Thendara. In his imagination he appeared confident and professional ... but now that moment had finally arrived, he wasn't as sure of himself as he would have hoped to have been. *What's done is done,* he reminded himself. *There's no turning back now.*

The door opened to reveal a large and airy hall. Holding the door was a young man, even younger than Eryn himself. His green tabard proclaimed his rank: apprentice. Eryn bowed and said in his most confident voice, "I am Eryn of Serrais. Journeyman Eryn of Serrais. I have an appointment with Master Therrold today."

The young man bowed in return. "We received your message in the relays, Journeyman Eryn. Master Therrold will see you in his office." The young man hesitated for just a second, then continued, "Uh, would you care to freshen up before you go in?"

Eryn flushed. So it was that obvious that he had just arrived in the city, was it? Well, the offer was welcome. He followed the apprentice through the hall to a small chamber, where he gratefully washed the grime of his journey from his face and hands. As for his clothes, well, his other change of clothing was in worse shape than what he was presently wearing, so he had little choice. The trip from Nevarsin to Thendara had taken its toll on his scanty wardrobe as well as on his meager savings. He would have liked to have purchased at least a new tunic for this meeting, but the truth of the matter was that he had not even enough money for lodgings tonight, if he would not be permitted to stay at the Guild House. Not that he thought there was a possibility of being rejected, no, he knew his work. It was good. Better than that which any of the monks of the Abbey could produce, Brother

Randolf had assured him of that. In fact, when it was apparent that Eryn had no calling to the monastic lifestyle, it was Brother Randolf who had suggested that he seek employment in Thendara with the Guild of Limners. He had already progressed to the level of Journeyman, and was possibly capable of Master level of painting as well. Of course, he couldn't achieve the rank of Master without the Guild's official approval, but even so, he thought, his work was that good. Let it be so, he prayed silently.

After drying his hands, Eryn brushed the dust from his breeches and boots with the damp towel. He ran his fingers through his hair to smooth it as much as possible. Sighing, he picked up his belongings and left the room. The apprentice glanced at him and grinned. Eryn returned the smile and followed him back through the hall. At the far end was a pair of double doors, intricately carved. The handles of the doors, and the hinges, like much of the decoration in the hall, were copper gilt. Eryn noticed this with approval. If the Guild was so affluent as that, perhaps they could afford to be generous with him.

The doors opened, and Eryn stepped inside. The office was, at first glance, more of a library than an office. Three of the four walls were lined with shelves of books, leather bindings gleaming warmly. Through the mullet glassed windows the afternoon sun streamed in, making the richly patterned carpet on the floor glow as if it was alive. On one wall was a fireplace, in which a small fire was burning. Above it hung a painting of an ancient battle. Next to the window was a writing stand; like the mantle of the fireplace, it was carved into patterns of oak leaves and acorns. At his desk sat a man of advanced years, who wore the robes and cap of a Master Limner.

Eryn bowed as the apprentice introduced him, "Here is Journeyman Eryn of Serrais."

The Master rose and nodded to the apprentice, who turned and left. The doors closed quietly behind him.

"So, Journeyman Eryn. I understand you have made a long trip. I trust it was a peaceful one for you?"

Eryn felt his hands go clammy. This had seemed all so easy in his imagination. He cleared his throat and replied, "Yes, sir. It was quiet enough. Longer than I expected, but uneventful. I'm glad to finally be here, though. . . ." his voice trailed off. Suddenly he didn't know what to say. All his fine words had left him.

Master Therrold sat, motioning for Eryn to do likewise.

"I have received several letters from Brother Randolf about you." He paused. Eryn nodded.

"He seems to think highly of your skill as an artist. In fact, he recommends that you be elevated to the rank of Master. Coming from him, I'd take that as high praise."

Eryn nodded again. This was more like what he had imagined. Therrold continued, "Brother Randolf mentioned that you were hoping to set up a shop here in the city. Is this still the case?"

Eryn cleared his throat, his carefully rehearsed words coming back to him. "Yes, Master. I paint portraits. Mostly miniatures, some panel paintings. I've been told they're good. I was hoping to sell my skills as a portrait painter."

"Ah. Well, then." The Master looked at him carefully. "Do you have a sample of your work with you, perhaps?"

Eryn brightened. This question was easily answered. He unfastened the clasp on his bag and withdrew a small packet of papers.

"Oh, yes, sir. I have several. I made some portraits

of the monks at the abbey, and a few of some of the women in the traveling party on my way here. They're not exactly my best, but they're good. They're pretty typical of the kind of work I do. I figure to display them in my window as samples."

The Master nodded as he took them from Eryn. "Your window. I see. Hmm," He examined the paintings, one at a time, holding them so the light could catch them. He pursed his lips.

"Well, they're passable. Not perhaps, Master quality . . ." He paused for a moment to let that sink in, "but passable nonetheless. Of course, I have no way of knowing if these resemble the sitters in any way, but they're reasonably done. Nice touches of highlights. Perhaps they *are* good portraits, eh?" He looked at Eryn with a smile. Eryn relaxed at that. Then came the dreaded question.

"So, you want to set up a shop. Well, as Journeyman, you have the right to do so. Brother Randolf's word is good with us here at the Guild. If he says you are a Journeyman, well, I won't dispute it. But as for Master, we'll have to see about that. It's for the Guild to decide. Perhaps in a year or so, when we've had a chance to see some of your best work, hmm? Well, if you want to set up a shop, how much are you prepared to spend? Guild dues are required of you, and you'll probably have to pay a tenday's rent advance."

Eryn groaned inwardly. So it had come to this after all. And he was so sure that they would make him a Master right off! If they had done so, they would have paid his first half year's rent and waived his Guild fees during that time as a courtesy. Now he was stranded in Thendara with hardly a coin to his name and no place to work, or sleep, for that matter.

In a rush, he explained all this to Master Therrold. He confessed how he planned to set up a shop, figuring the quality of his work high enough to win the rank of Master.

The Master frowned as he passed the packet of papers across the desk. "Did Brother Randolf suggest this plan?"

Eryn shook his head, "No. He said I ought to stay at the monastery and paint lives of the saints. But I really didn't feel any vocation for that, and I wanted to come to the city, so he sent me to you."

Master Therrold sighed. "I'm sorry, son, but there's not much that I can do for you. You can have a place to stay temporarily. We can postpone payment of your Guild fees by a tenday or so, but if you want to paint professionally, you must pay them. You can be a street painter to start with."

Seeing Eryn's crestfallen expression, he reassured him, "Really, now, it's not as bad as that. Some of the greatest artists began as street painters, you know. You can set up a stall in the marketplace, do quick sketches . . . you'll be surprised to learn how much you could earn on a good day. Save up, and you could rent a shop in no time at all, if you're good enough."

Eryn reached for the packet.

"I know, son, it's not what you expected. Well, have you any relatives who'd be willing to loan you some money? You're from Serrais . . .?"

"Yes, I'm a *nedestro* of Lord Alexi . . . but he already gave me money for my education at Nevarsin and for this trip. He said I deserved my chance, but he wouldn't give me money for a shop. He said I had to make my own way."

"And right he was," Master Therrold agreed. "It isn't so difficult to make a go of it if you're good."

"Oh I'm good enough, sir. It's just that I'd make a lot more if I had a shop. The nobility won't hire a *street artist* for their portraits."

"No, that's true, but you'll have a more interesting clientele in the marketplace than in the castle. You won't regret it."

Eryn was regretting it already. But there was nothing for him to do but make the best of it, as the Master suggested. He gathered up his paintings and replaced them in his bag. Bowing, he thanked the Master for his kindness and generosity. The words tasted bitter in his mouth.

The next two tendays passed quickly for Eryn. He left the Guild House early each morning for the marketplace. It took him a few days to determine where the optimum spot for him to set up might be. It had to be in good light so he could see clearly, and against a wall, so he could display his paintings easily. He borrowed a pair of stools from the Guild House, and drew his portraits using a board on his lap for support. It wasn't as elaborate or elegant as he would have liked, but it worked.

He drew first in charcoal, and when he earned enough money to afford it, he purchased some inexpensive pigments from the apothecary to replace his rapidly dwindling supply. He made up some ink, and thereafter sketched with a pen, which enabled him to get finer details.

Of customers he was never lacking. Word of his skill soon spread throughout the market. He kept his prices low enough for the most common person to afford them. Better to do many cheap portraits than only a few expensive ones, he reasoned. The more people who bought from him, the more quickly his fame would spread.

And spread it did. So much so, in fact, that his portraits became a topic of conversation at the Guild House. It was a mystery. People were flocking to his little makeshift stall in the marketplace, waiting in line in all kinds of weather to have their portrait done by this new young artist. Other limners began to complain, and mutterings of unfair practices began to be heard in the Guild House. It finally reached the ears of Master Therrold, who sent two of his finest portrait artists to the marketplace to observe this phenomenon. They returned late in the day, completely puzzled.

"I don't understand it. He paints well enough, but the portraits just aren't that good! Yet every single customer is absolutely happy with their purchase." The other nodded in agreement. "The work is good, but not *that* good. And it's strange, because always at some point early in the painting, he captures what I would consider an exact likeness. Anyone could see it. Then he paints some more, changing it ever so slightly, just a touch here and there. And hang me, but when the customer sees it, even if it clearly isn't as good a likeness as it was before, they love it!"

Master Therrold thought carefully. "Send for him. I want to see him tonight."

Eryn stood before the Master in eager anticipation. Perhaps they would now recognize his skill and accord him the rank he so deserved.

Master Therrold smiled and began, "So Journeyman, I hear wondrous things about your work. They say you're becoming a popular fellow."

"Oh, yes, Master. You were quite right about the marketplace. Perhaps by midsummer I'll have enough for a shop. It's going better than I hoped."

"So I've been told. They say your customers are quite pleased with your work. Is this true?"

Eryn nodded happily. Master Therrold continued, "They tell me that your portraits are, well, interesting. In fact, I've heard that they're popular even though they're not always so accurate. You never have a dissatisfied customer. What can you tell me about this?"

Puzzled, Eryn replied, "I'm not sure I know what you mean, sir. I think my portraits are quite accurate. So do my customers. Everyone says so."

"Is it only your sitters who say so, or do others as well?"

"I don't follow you, sir."

"Eryn, I've been told that your customers are *always* satisfied with your work, but the portraits are not always perfect likenesses. That's rather unusual, wouldn't you agree? Tell me, son, I will ask you right out, and if you answer honestly, I'll see that you are not punished if you swear not to do it again. Do you use *laran* to make your customers like their portraits?"

"Sir! I would *never* do a thing like that! It's against my oath!"

"So you do have *laran* ... you were trained at a Tower? Which one?"

"Neskaya, sir."

"And you swear you have never used your *laran* to make your customers happy with your work? Or to influence them in any way?"

"No, Master, never. That's illegal. I would never do anything like that!"

Master Therrold sat back thoughtfully. The boy seemed to be telling the truth. It was a strange situation. If he was lying, it wouldn't be the first time such a thing had occurred. Unscrupulous merchants as well as craftsmen who had more than a touch of *laran* occasionally used their psychic skills to persuade an unsuspecting customer that they were purchasing more than they had bargained for. One of the purposes of the Guild system was to eliminate such abuses. Of course, he *could* be telling the truth, as far as he knew it. It was possible that he was unconsciously using his abilities. It would bear further investigation.

"Eryn, I'd like you to paint *my* portrait, just as if I was another of your customers. Would you do that?"

"Well, certainly, sir. But if you think I'm using *laran* to cheat my customers you're mistaken. . . ."

Therrold cut him off with a wave of his hand. "Oh, I don't think you'd do it deliberately. At least I hope not. But I wonder, perhaps, if you're doing it without being aware of it."

Reluctantly, Eryn got his materials, and in the candlelight, began Master Therrold's portrait. He lightly sketched in the main features, and then, with his pen began to draw in the details. The only sounds in the room were the scratch of his pen on the paper and the occasional snap of a burning log in the fire.

From time to time, Therrold would take the picture from Eryn and examine it. Nothing unusual, nothing spectacular.

Eryn began to paint. His brush strokes were confident and neat, precisely portraying the face of the Master. At one point, Therrold bid him stop. He took the painting and looked at it.

"There—do you see? It is a perfect likeness. Splendid! I've had my picture done many times . . . this is as good as any master's work."

"But, sir!" Eryn exclaimed, "it's not finished! I still have more to do before it's done!"

"Not done? Nonsense! It couldn't be a finer portrait!"

"Here . . . let me work on it a bit more."

Therrold returned the painting, and sat back, struggling to compose his features. This was it, then, just as his men had reported. Well, he was ready. As Eryn continued to paint his portrait, Therrold extended all of his senses, seeking any possible psychic contact from the young artist.

There was none.

They sat like this for several more minutes—the painter concentrating on his work and the sitter concentrating on the painter. Finally, Eryn put down his brush and smiled. Therrold braced himself, but still no contact came as Eryn held up the portrait for him to see.

Therrold looked at the painting and suddenly burst into laughter.

"Of course! It's as plain as the nose on my face! You *did* use your *laran!*"

Eryn gasped. "No, I didn't!"

Smiling, Therrold explained, "You did! But not to influence *me* . . . you used it to influence yourself! The portrait was quite accurate a few minutes ago, before you changed it. See? Here you made my hair thicker, and my face looks younger. You have painted a portrait of me *not as I am, but as I see myself!* That's why everyone is satisfied with your work . . . you paint them as *they think* they really are!"

Eryn was stunned, his visions of greatness and hopes of glory rapidly disappearing.

"Is it wrong to do this, Master?"

"Wrong?" Therrold laughed, "there's nothing wrong with it at all! My son, you'll make your fortune!"

Eryn brightened at that.

"Does this mean you'll make me a Master now, sir?"

Therrold sat back in his chair, folding his hands in front of him.

"Well, now," he replied. "That's another story. . . ."

Transformation

by Alexandra Sarris

*Ms. Sarris says that she has been a science fiction/
fantasy fan since college, and "I rarely had the nerve
(or the discipline) or belief in myself to sit down and
write my own stories." She says that at this point she's
in transit; she's moving to Prague in the spring and is
pleased at the thought of finally getting around to using her college German and Russian.*

"Why won't this voice in my head stop?" Anelia
moaned. Like an itch behind her eyes that she couldn't
scratch, it had been tormenting her for two days, ever
since she had picked up that accursed Thing!

No one knew what to call it—Lady Marelie, who
was already Underkeeper while barely younger than
Anelia, had brought it to the Leynier estate on her slow
trek toward Neskaya. It had been found some months
before at the edge of the lake at Hali, when a hunter
spotted something glinting at the edge of the sands. He
unearthed a strange twisted coppery artifact which he
passed on to the local lord who, in turn, gave it to
Marelie. When she returned to Neskaya her matrix circle would study it to learn its purpose—it was clearly
laran-produced. Meanwhile, it served as a topic of
conversation wherever she stayed.

Anelia blamed herself. She was only fifteen, and she
had a healthy curiosity. But as a servant, she was sup-

posed to do her work and remain unobtrusive. She had no business being curious. That's what Lady Carissa Leynier always said just before having Rogel punish Anelia for "snooping." Anelia still smarted from her last caning. She wasn't snooping; she was just curious! Except this time something serious had happened to her.

Anelia knew that a Keeper's property was private and inviolate and definitely off limits to the likes of her. But she felt such a compulsion to touch the artifact that, while cleaning Lady Marelie's empty room, she just had to pick it up. As she turned it over and traced some of the intricate bluish swirls that seemed to interlace in a strange and hypnotic pattern, she began to feel slightly dizzy. After she put it back down, the voice started whispering in her head.

"Will you be quiet!" Anelia moaned, dropping her mop and shaking her head, as if to dislodge the voice. Almost instantly, there was silence. What had happened? Then the voice started up again. "Stop!" she said. It did. Somehow she had communicated with it! Perhaps because she felt more in control, when it began again, she could hear a very faint but distinct "Hello."

"Hello," she whispered back.

"Hello! Hello!" returned the voice, clearly delighted with the response.

"Who are you?" she asked tremulously.

"Vrrrrd" came back. She couldn't understand the word. The word was repeated. It still made no sense. More importantly, she realized with growing terror that someone was speaking to her from inside her head! "How can you be inside my head?" she quavered, straining to hear its response.

"I'm not!" it replied. "I'm in the overworld."

The overworld had to do with the Tower-trained.

Not a lowly servant that no one even bothered to test for *laran!* How could she be talking to someone in the overworld? The voice kept saying something until she understood. "Can you touch the matrix again?"

"What matrix?" she asked. The very word gave her the chills. She had seen the mistress use her starstone for small things around the house and even though it seemed beneficial, she distrusted its power.

"The copper matrix." That was a matrix? It didn't look like the starstones the Comyn wore. "Then you can hear me much better," it kept repeating until she heard all the words.

"But I don't dare go into Lady Marelie's box again." she argued. Look what happened last time. "What would she do to me if she caught me?"

"Nothing," the voice assured her, "if you ask her. Otherwise, you'll have this horrible noise inside your head that you can barely tolerate. Please!"

The more she thought about it, Anelia became convinced that she couldn't bear living with that voice inside her head. She would ask the Keeper for help. Lady Marelie had been nothing but nice to her, and her so weak and sick; her body was clearly not capable of sustaining long periods of matrix work. She'd already had two debilitating seizures on her journey toward Neskaya; and recuperation after every use of her matrix was long and painful.

That evening, as she brought Marelie her night-time tea tray, she tremulously asked if she could see the artifact. "Of course," Marelie smiled. "Bring me the box." Anelia gingerly lifted the box and placed it on Marelie's lap table. "Here it is," Marelie said, fishing out the coil and handing it to Anelia. "Strange, isn't it?" It was hard for Anelia to look at it as she fingered the intricate loops.

"Hurrah!" shouted the voice, sounding remarkably clear. Anelia flinched and nearly dropped the matrix.

"Oh, I'm sorry," she babbled. "Looking at it makes me dizzy." Frown lines wrinkled Marelie's brow as she retrieved the key and put it away.

"This made you dizzy?" she queried. Anelia nodded, but she could barely hear Marelie for the voice inside her whooping and crowing with joy. He—for it was clearly a young male voice, exulted, "I'm not alone any more!"

"I'd like to monitor you," Marelie said. Anelia goggled at her. "Perhaps you have a trace of *laran.*" As the Keeper reached out to touch Anelia's wrist, the servant girl recoiled and fled the room. Behind her, Marelie sighed with regret. Superstitious dread of *laran* was strong in the servants.

Partly to escape Marelie and partly for privacy, Anelia hurried to the root cellar—her special safe retreat. "Who are you?" she whispered.

"Vardin. My name is Vardin," the voice said with a yodel of joy. "I guess I got carried away." He had an infectious laugh, and Anelia found herself giggling with him. "You can't imagine how wonderful it is to talk to someone after such a long time! If I get overwhelming, please tell me to shut up."

"How do I do that?" she asked aloud with amusement.

"Just form thoughts. You don't have to speak them out loud. I can read you then."

"You have *laran.* And you're inside me."

"No, I'm not. I'm in the overworld. And, yes, I have *laran.* But I'm not Tower-trained." His thoughts radiated sharp distaste. "And you can hear me because you have *laran,* too."

"That's what Marelie said," Anelia responded with surprise. "But not very much."

"Enough for us," Vardin assured her.

"Then Lady Marelie could hear you, too. She's a Keeper—or will be soon, poor thing." Maybe she should tell Marelie about Vardin.

"No!" Vardin exclaimed vehemently. "Don't tell HER. I don't talk to Keepers." The bitterness in his voice washed over Anelia. "I can talk to you because I can trust you. I can't trust HER." Anelia felt confused yet flattered.

"Tell me about your life—what you do, what goes on, who's ruling, how you live?" Vardin demanded. "I feel as if I've been shut away for eons." He sounded so pathetically eager that her fear of his *laran* drained out of her. She could sum up her whole bland story in minutes—born on a poor farmhold, the fifth of eight children, never enough food. If it weren't for Lady Carissa, Anelia might be stuck like her mother, cold and half-starving, instead of being warm and dry, working and living at a great house.

"Tonight when you're in bed," he said, "I'll tell you about myself. My story is more complex." Anelia felt a fleeting sense of reluctance or perhaps shame from him.

In the meantime, she had to be content with his incessant questions about the family customs, the Domains, the Towers, and finally, the Ages of Chaos—which of course she knew very little about. Where had he come from that he knew some customs she'd never heard of and not others that she knew? Answering all of them, even though she needed only to form thoughts, left her hamfisted and fumblefingered as she helped serve dinner. Not a few times she received hard glares from Lady Carissa.

That night when she had blown out the light, he began at last. "My name is Vardin Leynier, and I was raised on this estate with my four brothers and sisters.

They all went to work in the Towers, except for me. When I was very young, my brother Armand always liked to use his *laran* to hurt me, and my other brother and sisters supported him. I think it was because he thought I was too weak to retaliate. I vowed to get him, but he was a *tenerézu*. . . ."

"What's that?" Anelia asked.

"A Keeper," Vardin replied.

"That's not true," she objected. "Everyone knows that only women can be Keepers."

"Maybe in your time," Vardin retorted, "but not in mine. Both men and women were Keepers. There were three of them in my family—and everyone spent several years at least in the Towers." He sighed. "My mother had five children—each one trained to be a Keeper except me. I was the weak one—I had a sickness very young, so I stayed with my mother, and missed out on going through the Tower training. I think she needed one of us to stay at home with her after all her other children had left. I didn't want to go into the Towers to be among people who were as arrogant and unpleasant as my brother Armand. I hated him and his kind, and all I wanted to do was destroy them and everyone else in the Towers for hurting me. So I damped down my *laran* so they thought I had very little, and even though I got a matrix, they expected little from me. But I couldn't help learning, just being in that household.

"I used to go into the overworld on my own, and I found that my thoughts could kill, so I tried to kill *laranzu'in* especially from Neskaya—where Armand was."

Anelia felt a chill wash over her at his dispassionate explanation. Well, everyone knew the stories about the monsters of the Age of Chaos. Then she realized he could read her thoughts.

"Yes, I was," he agreed solemnly. "A vicious, miserably unhappy child held by my mother's skirt strings, who had enormous uncontrolled power that no one knew about."

"Then my soul was captured in the overworld by *laranzu'in* from the Hali Tower," he continued. "They locked me in a room and left my body down in your world—neither dead nor alive. I was sixteen years old. Only when I repented of my deed did they promise to let me out. I hated them and cursed them for years until my hate burned away. Finally, I could understand the horrible things I had done, and why I was being punished. Then I waited for them to release me—but at last, I gave up. Zandru's nine hells—it's cold in the overworld."

"Hali Tower was destroyed at the time of Varzil the Good," Anelia commented.

Sadly, he said, "Obviously, along with any record of me. Now I see why no one remembered me. I want to leave the overworld, if I can. Barring that, I can at least talk to you."

Over the next few weeks, life transformed for Anelia. Never had she shared the intimacy, laughter, and fun with anyone as she did with Vardin, her disembodied friend. As she did her chores, he kept up a running commentary full of wit and sarcasm about her tasks, the other servants, the *coridom* Rogel, her master and mistress. She had a difficult time keeping her face straight as he mimicked Lord Damiano's pompous tone in delivering his latest pronouncement to family and staff. He ridiculed Lady Carissa's constant fussiness and whining, and contrasted that to Lady Marelie's quiet pain, unuttered and obviously unrelenting. "She shouldn't be a Keeper," he commented after Anelia had finished rubbing Marelie's feet one evening.

"She's too weak now—and on the relays, controlling all that matrix energy could kill her."

One day, Marelie decided to use her matrix to examine the intricate artifact. As she monitored it, Anelia suddenly felt a strange tingling in her head from Vardin. Finally, with a sigh, the Keeper came out of her trance to find Anelia laying down a tray laden with sweets and foodstuffs. The servant girl appeared calm, but inside, Vardin was shouting. "The key! That's the key!"

"Wait," Anelia cautioned, glancing at the Keeper. She was afraid that Marelie might overhear them, so she curtsied and left.

"When Marelie started activating the matrix, I suddenly realized how we can free my soul," Vardin babbled; his words could scarcely be understood in his excitement.

"How? What can I do?" Anelia still believed that Lady Marelie was far more capable of helping her friend than she was. "I can't go into the overworld to help you."

"That's not important," he declared. "Even though my soul is here, my body is still alive down there. I'm sure that using the key to free my body will also unlock my prison up here—and I'll be free!"

"What will prevent you from doing the same horrible things you did then?" Anelia challenged, though she could hardly imagine the kind of person he described himself to be those long ages past.

"I'm far different from the hateful young boy I was then," he assured her with a bitter chuckle. "I've had a lot of time to learn wisdom." Of that, Anelia was sure.

"But where is your body?"

"It's here; I can feel its presence on the estate. When Marelie activated the key, I could feel the vibration and see a cord connecting my soul to my body. I'm alive and attached to it. But if I've been here for so many hundred years, it has to have been put somewhere. We have to find it." Anelia had no idea where to look.

The next day he said, "What's that stone building out there behind the barns?" She looked out the window at a long low weathered edifice covered with vines that seemed to be built deep into a small hill.

"That? That's an old storage house; it hasn't been used for years," she said dismissively, "except for some of the servants who go there for lovemaking. Many a *nedestro* child has come out of nighttime revelry there."

"What's it like?" he asked.

She shrugged. "I don't know. I've never had any reason to go inside."

"I think that's where my body is. We need to get inside."

That night, Anelia took a covered lantern and slipped off to the storage building behind the barn. Because it was out of the sight of the main house, and it was so rarely visited, Anelia hoped that no one would notice her nocturnal exploration. But it ended abruptly because the hardwood door was locked. She trudged back to the main house wondering how to find the key to the building.

In the morning, she shyly asked the housekeeper about the building. The older woman smirked at Anelia knowingly as she indicated the key hung in the entrance to the pantry. The girl flushed. Later, unobtrusively, Anelia removed the key.

Before sunrise, while Liriel still hung pallid in the lower heavens, she wrestled with the lock on the building, accompanied by encouragement from Vardin. At some point, exasperated and frustrated, she wished he would just shut up—which he did. Moments later, the lock released, and she pulled open the door a crack—enough for her to slip inside. Lighting the lantern, she found herself amidst boxes, tools, stuff she couldn't even recognize.

"Not here," Vardin said. "Everything is too new." As far as Anelia was concerned, everything looked old and rotting. "Besides, I can feel my body pulling me back farther." Obediently, she trudged deeper into the structure, following its twisted aisles back into the darkest, dankest section. "It's here," he declared. "I can feel it!" She turned, letting the lantern shine in every box. Finally, she trained the light on a large oblong wooden box; surprisingly, it had a glass top. After rubbing off centuries of dust and dirt, she could see what it held—the body of a boy who looked younger than the age of sixteen, with a petulant mouth and bright auburn hair that flopped over his face. His body showed no decay or dessication; he could have been sleeping, although there was no perceptible rise and fall of his chest. Yet his limbs were twisted as though he had had an unquiet sleep. Vardin was indeed suspended in time.

"Look at the lock," Vardin said. She raised the lantern to get a better view in the light of one side of the box. Embedded in the wood was a starstone.

"What kind of lock is that?" It was all twisted and convoluted. Anelia rubbed her fingers over its strange surface and felt a tingling throughout her body.

"It's a matrix lock," he said. "It corresponds exactly to Marelie's matrix key. We need that key to open the coffin. I think that will release my prison door in the overworld at the same time."

Anelia moaned, "I can't get the key." Despair and fear washed over her.

"Yes, you can," Vardin asserted. "It's easy, and she won't notice."

"No, I won't!" The thought of touching anything in Marelie's box filled her with terror. Anelia ran down the aisles, bumping into boxes and bruising her legs. Finally she reached the entrance, doused the lantern, and slipped out of the building. What Vardin wanted her to do terrified her.

He tried to bring up the subject a number of times over the next two days, but she steadfastly cut it off, so great was her fear of her betters. "I'm not like you," she said bitterly. "I'm timid and afraid. I'm no one important."

"You are to me," he said quietly. "You're special to me."

"That's only because you're trying to persuade me to help you," she cried out. "You don't really care about me." The moment the words formed in her mind, she felt Vardin wince; and she herself knew that her accusation was unfair.

"That's not true," he whispered, but he didn't speak of the key again. A kind of strain had been created between them which made Anelia feel ashamed of doubting the motives of her friend. Under similar circumstances she would have asked for him to do the same thing. If only she weren't such a coward!

Then Marelie decided that she had enough of convalescence. She wanted to take a ride. Carissa Leynier suggested a picnic in the hills for the whole family. Anelia knew no better chance for getting the key would come. Marelie never left her box locked because NO ONE would touch the possessions of a Keeper. No matter how afraid Anelia was, without her making the attempt, Vardin might be trapped forever.

"Even if she detects it," Vardin assured her, "she will have to return, and by that time I'll be free and can protect you. You must prepare packs and clothing for our escape," he added. "Then we can leave as soon as you open the box. I'm good at hiding myself from the *laran*-gifted."

Not only did Anelia secrete enough food and clothing for their escape, but she also hid away two old but serviceable winter cloaks. With some guilt, she also decided to steal two ponies from the estate—older, sure-footed beasts. At some later time, she hoped to compensate the Leynier family for the theft. But they needed to put as much distance as possible between them and this estate.

Very early on the morning of the excursion, she took the ponies to the storage building and loaded them up. After having watched the riding party disappear into the fog-shrouded hills, she entered Marelie's room to begin her morning cleanup. While fixing the bed, filling the water jug, tidying the clothes, she glanced fearfully at the box. Finally, she could delay no longer. When she raised the lid, she just *knew* that Marelie would feel that alarm. She looked into the box. The key was not there! A thrill of shock bolted through her. All this for nothing! Frantically, she rummaged through the jewelry. There it was at the bottom. She snatched it up, slammed the box shut, and scuttled out of the room.

She prayed that what Vardin said about protecting her was true as she pried open the door to the old building. Once inside, it took several attempts before she could stop shaking long enough to light the lantern. As she stumbled down the aisles toward the coffin, every so often she flinched at the wavery shadows from her moving light.

"Don't worry; there's no one there," Vardin assured her. "I'd know."

At last she reached Vardin's coffin. She bent down and tried to aim the point of the matrix into the slot.

"No, no, don't stick it in," Vardin advised. "Lay it

flat. This is a kind of matrix lock. Normal rules do not apply here." Hesitantly, she did so. The key sparked and sizzled with blue light and melted into the lock. With a click, the coffin lid rose. Suddenly, Vardin's body gave a convulsive shudder and began to twist and arc. His legs and arms began spasming.

Anelia backed away in mute horror. "Blessed Avarra," she moaned. "It's all gone wrong!" Vardin had to be dying.

Gradually, the spasms stopped. Then he gasped and coughed, as he took in great heaving breaths. She realized then that his body needed time to adjust, to regain its strength, to function again. She crept closer, and as she reached out to touch the body, Vardin's eyes slowly opened. He gazed at her. Forcing his mouth into a pallid smile, he creaked, "Ane ... Ane ... li ... a." She grasped his right hand. "Th ... thank ... you." Those words took a great effort. Tears rolled down Anelia's face. He was back in his body after more than a thousand years.

Although he clearly needed to rest, Anelia knew they must flee. She practically dragged Vardin out of the coffin. Now he lay on the floor, panting. In her mind, she could hear him clearly, cursing the flesh that didn't obey his commands like his spirit body.

"This is harder than I thought," he gasped later as they leaned against some of the boxes. "I'm not used to this."

Anelia squeezed his hand in encouragement. "We have to get away from here soon. I'm sure Marelie knows that I've taken something from her box, and she'll send someone to look for me."

"I know," Vardin agreed. "But I'm far weaker than I imagined I would be." Over the next hour, they gradually tottered toward the door, resting shorter and shorter periods, as Anelia's fear grew like a choking smoke and Vardin's strength increased. As they approached the opening, a shadow fell across it. They looked up in surprise. Marelie stood framed in the doorway. They were too late!

"What's happening here?" she asked in puzzlement, her gaze moving from Anelia to Vardin. Their apprehension was palpable. She had obviously detected the use of *laran*, but didn't understand how. "Anelia, what's going on?"

"Ah, the *leronis*," Vardin purred, and he bent his gaze intently at her. She stepped back.

"Who are you?" she murmured, shaking her head. She groped for her starstone.

"No one," he said. "I'm no one." She looked down to her matrix. "Drop it!" he commanded silently, and the force of his *laran* caused her to slump down.

Anelia stared, open-mouthed. "Did you hurt her?" She was terrified of exacerbating Marelie's weakened state.

"No, I just put her to sleep—long enough for us to get far away."

"Are you sure she's all right?" Anelia bent down and inspected the *leronis*. Vardin chuckled bitterly. "I've used my mind to kill. I know the difference. When she wakes up, we'll be long gone."

The Leyniers were frantic. Where was Marelie? No one had seen her since her return to the house. She had felt weak at the picnic, and one of the Leynier sons, Andres, had escorted her home, where she vanished. They had spent much of the night searching for her. Suddenly she appeared, dazed and hungry.

"What happened?" Damiano demanded. "We've been hunting for you since yesterday." A hot stimulant and copious amounts of food helped clear her mind so that she could remember.

"I'm not sure," she responded. "I kept feeling very strange on the ride home, and realized a strange matrix was being activated. So I followed its traces to that building behind the barn, where I found Anelia with a strange young man." Her face clouded. "No one I have ever known before, but definitely Comyn; he had very strong *laran*." Her voice trailed off in confusion. "There was something about his mind. He did something to me that made me sleep. The sensation was not terrifying, just surprising. I didn't know anyone could do that to a Keeper." She looked up. "I need to look in my box." Rogel disappeared up the stairs.

"Where's Anelia?" she asked.

"She's gone," Carissa said. "A young man came from her mama asking her to come home—it was an emergency. She left yesterday morning. Andres talked to him."

"That was him," Marelie said. "I'm sure of it. But who is he? And what was going on?" Rogel laid the box in her lap. She opened it and rummaged through it. When she looked up again, her face was even more puzzled. "That matrix artifact is gone. What was its significance? And how did she know how to use it? Did she have any *laran?*" Carissa shook her head.

Marelie shrugged at this little mystery since it obviously had had no dangerous repercussions. When she got back to Neskaya, perhaps the circle would search through the rings for the artifact and even for Anelia and that odd powerful young man.

Meanwhile, Vardin and Anelia on their sturdy ponies were plodding slowly into the Hellers.

"I've always wanted to see Aldaran," she bubbled. "I've heard it's such a strange place."

He grinned at her. "Well, it will be really interesting

to compare what it's like now to my memories of it. Everything in this time is so different. I'm so thankful that I'm not alone and that you're with me." He leaned over and squeezed her hand. "And we've got the rest of our lives to learn to share it."

Amends

by Glenn R. Sixbury

Glenn Sixbury says he is a "Committed Kansan," an inhabitant of Manhattan, Kansas (the little apple) and that this story is a continuation of previous stories for my earlier Darkover anthologies. He adds that this story broke a writer's block for him. It is set in the time between DARKOVER LANDFALL and STORM QUEEN. "I have always pictured this Lord Aldaran as being the great-great-grandfather of the Mikhail Aldaran whose anger and stubborn nature provided many of the plot twists in STORMQUEEN."

Glenn says that "while waiting for my first six figure advance I'm working as the Assistant Director for Computing in the Department of Faculty Education and Development in the Division of Continuing Education at Kansas State University." He adds "If you think that's a struggle to read, you ought to try putting it on a business card." No, thanks.

He credits "providing constant moral fiber for my wispy dreams" to his wife, Brenda, his son Brian, and his daughter Amanda, not to mention the family cat, April, whose job seems to consist of "dusting most of my manuscripts with cat hair before they go in the mail."

He adds that his mother, Carolyn Sixbury, did her best to nurture his imagination when he was growing up and brought his brothers and him "through some

bad situations that most people never have to face."
He'd like to dedicate this story to her.
Certainly.

Mikhael felt older today than ever before in his
seventy-two winters. Gray hair dripped to his shoulders like a frozen waterfall and wrinkles tracked deep
across his face, heavy with the weight of departed decisions.

Today he would order a death, and as always, he
dreaded it more than his own end of time on Darkover.
With tired eyes of silvery-blue, he looked out on the
presence-chamber, its walls built in the same year he
had begun his reign as Lord of Aldaran. His citizens
had squeezed into the vast chamber like a herd of
chervine in a box canyon, driven there by the chilling
cry of a banshee.

Craven, the man who had brought the accusation,
stepped away from his fellow villagers. In his fifties,
he had lost most of his hair, and like the simplest
sheepsman, usually wore a hat—even when inside.
"The people of Aldaran ask for justice," Craven said,
and motioned to the side of the chamber. Two guards
pulled a young woman forward. Craven pointed a
knobby finger at her. "This woman, Lonira of
Ravensburg, murdered her own child."

Mikhael did not recognize the woman, although he
had met her mother on occasion. Lonira was the
daughter of Reney, the old midwife. No more than seventeen winters old with a body as slender as a winter
twig, she did not look capable of killing anyone.
Standing before him with her blonde hair uncombed
and her blue eyes dull and lifeless, she looked at her
feet and said nothing.

Mikhael did not need his *laran* to know that she was
feeling great sorrow and emotional pain. No guilt was

present in the lines that creased her face—only confusion and desperation. He waited, and finally, she raised her chin and gazed at him.

When he saw her face, his breath stopped short. For a moment, as she stared at him, it was if he were looking at Elline.

For Mikhael, that brief illusion recalled a late spring day, gone from the world for longer than he wanted to believe. Warm sunshine had bounced off his strong shoulders and had warmed his face as he and Elline had galloped their ponies through the meadows surrounding the Keep of Aldaran. The sticky, sweet hint of *kireseth* rode the breeze—not potent enough to be dangerous, but enough to make the world seem better than it was, without danger, filled only with the unbounding love revealed by their heightened *laran*. Married only since midwinter, he and Elline found a small glade. Beneath a clear sky filled with rare warmth from their red sun, they shared their passion to create a perfect afternoon. That day was the climax to a year that was the best of his life. Remembering that time now, it seemed as if only then had he truly been alive.

Craven's monotone voice drove the image away. "When I saw Lonira going into the woods by herself, Lord, I feared for her safety and her honor. I knew that her husband had died during the skirmish with the Ridenows this summer past. I followed her."

Mikhael barely stopped a smile before it tugged at his lips. Craven had the reputation of being honest, if unimaginative, but more than anything else, he was known best as a meddler, curious more about the affairs of others than his own.

"That's when I saw her gathering the calebain." Several members of the crowd gasped. Craven stepped forward and lowered his voice, as if sharing a secret.

"While most people do not know the uses of this root, my aunt belonged to the Sisterhood of Healers. On a rare visit when I was just a boy, I overheard her explain its use to my mother."

Mikhael waved his hand, acknowledging Craven's expertise. He had known his aunt, a good woman. She had been killed by Dry Towners many years ago—or so the rumors said.

"Lonira did not know I had come upon her," Craven continued. "Hidden by the trees, I watched, unbelieving as she dug the roots and sneaked away." Raising his voice and speaking more to the other people in the room than he did to Mikhael, he said, "I swear, I never dreamed she would use the roots for that purpose. I assumed they were for her mother, since she knows the healing arts. But when her mother came to tell me that the baby had died, I realized what had happened. Lonira had used the roots herself. She had used them to kill her own child."

Murmurs of agreement came from the crowd. Mikhael waited until they grew quiet. "Lonira, how do you defend yourself against this claim? Have you been wrongly accused?"

She shivered and stared at the floor. Hugging herself, she moved her lips, but no sound escaped. She tried again, and managed a quavering whisper. "No," she said and swallowed several times. Blinking against her tears, she added, "I deserve my punishment."

Mikhael shook his head. It was as he knew it would be. There was no choice to be made. He tried to sit up straight in his high seat, but he slumped, the weight of his responsibility pulling at his bony shoulders. He did not want to order her death—did not want another flame of life doused by his hand.

"Don't blame her, Lord. It's my fault. I'm the one who taught her about the root."

Mikhael recognized Lonira's mother as she stepped apart from the crowd. A large woman with graying blonde hair and powerful arms, she had wrestled more than one babe free of its mother's womb in order to save both.

But Mikhael was in no mood to lengthen this inquiry. He felt like dozing, and shook himself, an old owl ruffling its feathers at midday. "I know she is your daughter, Reney, and you wish to protect her, but I am only interested in what happened. I am too old and too hard to be swayed by pleas for mercy."

"You don't understand, Lord. There's more to the story."

"She is trying the same tricks that she tried in the village," Craven said. "She is simply stalling for her daughter's sake."

"I do no such thing. If you are to sentence my daughter to die, should you not at least hear why she acted so?"

Mikhael closed his eyes and rubbed his fingers across the stiff muscles in his neck. The joints in his fingers popped as he moved them, reminders of how very old he had become, of how long he had been judge over his people. *How many times have I been wrong?* he wondered. "I will hear what she has to say."

The midwife nodded, then curtsied nervously. "Life is not easy for a widowed woman in these hills, Lord. With so many available, no man wishes to marry a woman after she has belonged to another. But they wish other things. And for a woman who is unprotected by husband, brother, or father, a man is allowed to come and take what he wishes."

"Not in my realm," Mikhael said, and scooted forward in his chair, glaring at the people in the room. Had his authority slipped so much as he had aged? He remembered too clearly how Beltran had conquered the

Keep and then raped his baby sister, Lori; she had died giving birth to Domenic, the bandit's child. But that had been fifty-six years ago. "Who was it?"

"It's of no use to say now, Lord—and I won't." Reney glanced about the room, nervously, as if expecting a blow from behind. "I have my reasons."

Craven grunted, disgusted. "She won't say because it never happened, Lord. She's gone often. She cannot know for sure. I, myself, have seen Lonira outside in lewd breeches, working in the garden, swaying her body—" He paused, wetting his bottom lip and staring at Lonira. Suddenly angry, he said, "She invites men to come to her through her actions!"

"Enough. I've heard your story, Craven. It is Reney's turn."

Craven shrugged. Slowly, he walked past Lonira and Reney, pausing to stare at each of them. Lonira refused to look at him, staring at the stone floor of the presence-chamber instead. Reney stared back, her hands working nervously, as if she wished for a dagger. She waited until Craven had walked to the other side of the room before she spoke. "He's wrong, Lord. Lonira would never consent to having a man. She knows what that would mean."

Reney frowned and shifted from foot to foot. She began her story slowly, in a soft voice filled with memories. "Shortly after Lonira's marriage at last year's Midsummer Festival, we found that she was with child. We were all so happy. Then, before the first snows of last winter fell, her husband was dead." Reney paused, and her face hardened, revealing the grim expression of someone that has seen too much death. "Two tendays before Lonira's child was due, about the time of the first thaw, I delivered three babies in less than a day. That was in Remkraig. Summoned by the first father, I rode with him south to the village.

Once there, two other births took place, and all of these births were abnormally hard. It was when Liriel and Mormallor were full, Lord. Babies often come in batches at such times."

The phrase was like a dagger twisting between Mikhael's ribs. He shivered, remembering a scene from his bedroom. He saw both bright flames from the hearth and Elline's face mirrored in the new glass of the room's only small window. His wife was singing, a silly children's song, but one that she believed in, as all expectant mothers—tired of waiting—do:

> *When the purple and white rise at night,*
> *Take a stroll beneath the light,*
> *Your wait will end with their helpful pull,*
> *Babies come when moons are full.*

When she had watched the moons rise above the eastern mountains, she left the room and headed for the ramparts. Mikhael had tried to talk her out of it, but he had been captivated by her excitement. Together they had walked through the snow, bundled up against the chill of midwinter, their breaths forming dreams in the night air.

Mikhael shifted in the confines of his high seat, uncomfortable with the memory, and listened to Reney again.

"I was too late, Lord. When I arrived home, the labor was already far along, but not going as it should. Lonira was bleeding and still the baby would not come. I kept telling her it would be all right, but even then, I knew it wouldn't."

Mikhael gaped, his old jaw hanging slack. Reney was a clever woman seeking sympathy for her daughter, but she couldn't know the story—it had happened before she had been born. More important, no one knew everything, except for Mikhael himself; he was the only one there with Elline at the end. The midwife had left earlier in the day to deliver another baby. She had traveled a short distance—still within sight of the Keep. But when one of the many storms so common at midwinter had rolled across the Hellers, it had trapped her there as surely as if she'd been on the other side of the Wall Around the World.

Mikhael had done the best he could. He still remembered reaching out with his *laran,* touching his unborn baby's mind, and realizing, even before Elline, that the baby was dying, suffocating, as the body that had cared for it so long strangled it now as muscles spasmed trying to set it free. Mikhael knew before the baby came that it would be stillborn. He'd felt it die, and after the birth, as Lonira struggled for her own life, he sent the women away, raging at them like a man shouting from Zandru's coldest hell.

Using his *laran* in ways that he had done before, he tried to repair the torn flesh and stop the bleeding, tried to save the only woman he had ever loved, that he would ever love, and failed. There were no whispered phrases shared between him and Elline at the end, no encouragement, no sign that made him believe her struggle to give him a child had not been in vain. She had simply been taken from him, leaving him with nothing but unfulfilled dreams and an aching that he still felt forty-five years later.

Sudden silence brought Mikhael back.

Reney had finished her story, and using the back of her hand, she quickly wiped tears away from her cheeks. "I'm a good midwife, Lord, but I'm not sure I could have saved the baby even if I'd been there. But I was sure, as sure as I am of my own name, that Lonira would never be able to have children. She's just not built for it, Lord. Some women aren't."

She stepped closer to Mikhael, her eyes wide and watery. "We had a woman, gifted in knowing such things, check this baby. It would have been a boy—even bigger than her first. She would have died if she would've tried to have it, as surely as if she'd plunged a dagger into her throat."

Silent, with tears dripping from her cheeks, Reney hugged Lonira for the last time and then stepped away to wait for Mikhael's decision.

Mikhael hung his head, his eyes closed. His people might think he was dozing. It didn't matter. He was shaken, and he needed time to clear his head—to think. Unlike some simpler folk believed, the Lords of Darkover did not rule only because their ancestors had ruled; they ruled also because their *laran* gave them a wide variety of capabilities not available to the head-blind. It gave them the potential to be better leaders.

Slipping his fingers beneath his tunic, Mikhael touched his starstone. A sickening wave of rage and conviction swept over him. The crowd had not been moved by Reney's story the way he had. If he declared Lonira innocent and allowed her to go free, the citizens of Aldaran would kill her and their respect for him as a just and fair ruler would vanish. If he declared her guilty, there was no room for mercy in his sentence. Beliefs in this part of Darkover were strong. Children—born or not-yet-born—were sacred. To stop her pregnancy was the same to most of his people as poisoning the child's milk when it was three years old.

For Mikhael, it was not so clear. If he could have foreseen what would happen to Elline during delivery, he would have used the calebain root himself. Was he as guilty, then, as Lonira?

Hearing shuffling feet and more frequent whispers, he realized he could delay the decision no longer. Old joints popped loudly as he pushed himself to his feet.

Looking at his angry, expectant citizens, he knew there was only one judgment he could make. When he spoke, it was slowly, his voice filled with sadness. "I believe Lonira stopped the birth of her child." Sharp murmurs erupted from the crowd, but Mikhael stared his citizens down, silencing them without a word. "I, also, have killed. Sometimes it was in defense of myself or of Aldaran. Sometimes it was in defense of my family. At other times, it was as a punishment, such as the punishment I am expected to mete out today." Mikhael straightened himself, stiffening like an aged hawk surveying its realm, but too tired to fly. "I will not do it. Today there will be no killing."

Several people shouted. Angry, they pushed their way forward. Lonira was jostled as the guards of Aldaran rushed in to separate her from the angry mob.

"Listen to me!" Mikhael yelled, using his command voice. The crowd quieted immediately. "I also believe," he said, realizing that he was shaking, "in Reney's experience and knowledge." He stepped into the center of the room and grabbed Lonira. "Look at this woman! Even without a midwife, you can all see that she could not have borne the baby. She would have certainly died, and most likely, the child also. She knew this."

Releasing Lonira, he shuffled back to his chair. Lowering himself into his high seat, he surveyed the packed room for a moment, suddenly unsure of what he was doing, afraid of the words he was about to speak. "I rule that Lonira believed she was protecting her own life when she took the life of her child." Before his people could react, he added, "But I also rule the Lonira is not blameless. If she is allowed to go free, there is too great a chance that she will be put into the same circumstances again. Therefore, as her punishment, she shall become my personal servant, never again allowed to be with a man except one that has grown too old to father children."

Mikhael's shoulders slumped, his energy spent. Villagers in the crowd chattered excitedly, but none dared confront him here. He knew they thought he had gone witless with age, taken with the beauty of a young girl. For years, there would be whispers wherever he went—words spoken soft that they thought a man of his years could not hear.

It didn't matter.

Lust and selfishness, they could understand and even accept. Mercy and passion for the plight of a young woman would never be swallowed so easily.

Mikhael signaled to his guards. Lonira was taken away and his presence-chamber was cleared. Sitting alone, he stared at the lengthening shadows and wondered if he had made the right decision.

He remembered Elline—not as she had been at the end, but as she had been on that day in late spring, laughing and full of love beneath the skies of Darkover—and he smiled.

A Capella

by Elisabeth Waters

Always, from the beginning of these anthologies, I've tried to find either something short or something funny with which to wind up. Short not being possible, I settled for funny. Some people say I have no sense of humor; I don't laugh at Eddie Murphy comedies. But people who doubt my sense of humor can't have seen me laughing so hard I nearly fell out of my chair reading this.

Well, they say, "always leave them laughing when you say good-bye."

Elisabeth Waters has had a story in every one of the Darkover anthologies from their beginning. She has a novel, CHANGING FATE, at DAW, soon to be published, probably before this anthology. She has written short stories not only for me but for anthologies by Jane Yolen and Andre Norton, and this is certainly one of the funniest of her stories.

Domna Floria, newly returned to court to spend a time among Queen Antonella's ladies-in-waiting, walked slowly down the hall to the music room. Although the child she carried was not due for several months yet, she no longer felt inclined to skip down the polished marble corridor as she had as a child. Her father, Edric Elhalyn, had been Keeper of Thendara Tower as long as she could remember, so she had grown up in Thendara and spent a good deal of time at court.

Floria had worked at Thendara Tower as well, in the Keeper Renata's circle, until her marriage to Conn of Hammerfell and her subsequent pregnancy made her unable to do the work of a *leronis.* She planned to return when her children were old enough not to need her, for *leroni* were always needed for Tower work, but now she was enjoying the chance to spend time quietly with her husband—or rather she had been doing so until King Aidan had summoned her to court.

Queen Antonella was recovering from a stroke she had suffered the previous year, and the king doubtless thought that the presence of Floria, who had always been a favorite of the queen's, would cheer her. Conn, busy on the estates the king had recently granted him, had parted with his wife reluctantly, but he, too, was fond of King Aidan and Queen Antonella and wished them well.

And it isn't as if I had no friends here, Floria told herself, trying to cheer up. She seemed to feel blue all too frequently these days. The midwife said this feeling was normal and would go away after the baby's birth. *My mother-in-law and my father are both still working in the Tower here, my brothers are in town frequently, and Gavin Delleray is right here at court.*

At the thought of Gavin, she smiled. Gavin was unique. As the son of Queen Antonella's only sister, he doubtless would have been a favorite at court even had he been unremarkable, but nobody ever failed to notice Gavin. He was a talented composer, with a beautiful bass voice, and he had a flair for fashionable dress. But it was his custom of coloring his hair purple which people generally observed first. He and Conn's twin brother Alastair had been good friends since childhood, and they were all related, so he had formed one of Floria's circle of childhood playmates.

The best thing about being at court now, Floria thought, *is that I'll be able to hear the cantata he's written to celebrate Queen Antonella's recovery.* Floria loved music and thought quite highly of Gavin's talent, which was why she was heading toward the music room, hoping to catch at least part of his rehearsal.

The sounds she heard as she approached the room, however, bore no resemblance to any style she had ever heard Gavin use—or, for that matter, to any music she had ever heard *anyone* write, play, or sing. It sounded rather as though someone had made a viol using catgut strings without bothering to detach—or even sedate—the cat.

"No, *damisela.*" Gavin's voice sounded terribly weary, as if he had said the words at least fifty times that morning. "That's still not quite the effect we're trying for. Why don't we take a break?"

"But I'm sure I can get it," the voice was female, shrill and high-pitched, but it sounded slightly better speaking than it had attempting to sing.

At least I assume she was attempting to sing, Floria thought; *I hope she isn't playing a cat-viol.*

"I'm sure you can," Gavin sounded anything but sure, "but I'm ready for a rest now." Gavin wasn't a terribly strong telepath, but even so Floria could hear his thoughts now. *Badly overdue for a rest—maybe even a permanent one.*

Floria opened the door and stepped into the music room. "Gavin," she called lightly, "may I interrupt you for a bit?"

"Floria!" Gavin greeted her with the air of a man lost in a blizzard sighting a guide. "Come and meet Capella Ridenow." The woman standing next to him

smiled familiarly at Floria, although Floria was quite
sure that they had never met.

Floria crossed the room warily, pasting a social
smile on her face.

"So you're Floria," the woman chirped in an oddly
girlish voice, "I'm so glad to meet you. Uncle Aidan
and Aunt Antonella have so been looking forward to
your arrival. Oh, you're pregnant," she babbled on,
patting Floria's stomach. Floria recoiled, and Gavin
stepped between them to block any further physical
contact.

"Capella," he warned, "Floria is a telepath."

"That's nice," Capella babbled on heedlessly.
"When is the baby due? I was born at midwinter. Is it
a boy or a girl? I'd want a girl. Or is it twins, like your
husband and his brother? I think that's such a romantic
story, the twin dukes of Hammerfell, separated in
infancy—"

"Capella," Gavin interrupted her, "why don't you go
tell Queen Antonella that Floria has arrived."

"Of course," Capella gushed. "I'll be so happy to
tell her; Aunt Antonella will be so happy that you're
finally here." She dashed from the room, narrowly
avoiding a collision with the door, and clattered off
down the hall.

"Aunt Antonella?" Floria said to Gavin as he carefully placed a comfortable chair behind her and extended an arm in case she needed support. She rested
her fingertips lightly on his forearm as she sank gratefully into the armchair. "And the queen knows I'm
here; I've just come from seeing her."

Gavin sighed. "I had no intention of implying that
you had failed in your duty toward the queen; I just
wanted to get Capella out of here for a bit. She's driving me insane, Floria; I swear it!"

Even at first acquaintance, Floria didn't doubt him.

"Is she some kin of yours?" Floria tried to remember the women in the royal family. "Your mother was the queen's only sister and you are an only child. And the king has no brothers or sisters. What exactly *is* her relationship to them?"

"Zandru only knows," Gavin sighed. "Even Capella isn't stupid enough to call them aunt and uncle to their faces. She only does it behind their backs—she's an atrocious name-dropper."

"Quite," Floria agreed. "Is she married to one of the Ridenow sons? There must be at least six of them."

"Eight," Gavin corrected, "and five daughters. She's one of the daughters."

"You mean she isn't married?" Floria was surprised. "She must be at least thirty. But I can see how it might be difficult to find anyone willing to marry her. The Ridenow *donas* is empathy—but she doesn't even have the common courtesy to refrain from touching a telepath uninvited! To say nothing of her calling 'romantic' the fact that my husband and his brother were separated in infancy when their father was killed and their home burned over their heads, leaving each of them thinking the other dead."

"Actually, I have a theory about her," Gavin explained. "The Ridenow bred for empathy so that they could communicate with nonhuman species. I think Capella is the token nonhuman for the rest of the family to practice on."

Floria choked with laughter. "I really shouldn't laugh at her, and we shouldn't be making fun of her; I'm sure she's more to be pitied. She's obviously totally head-blind."

"*And* tone-deaf." Gavin groaned. "But she has a half-brother who is some sort of *nedestro* connection of the king's (the exact relationship changes each time she tells the story), and he got a place for her at court.

And somebody told the king she sang soprano, so she was assigned the soprano solo in my cantata."

He winced and collapsed into a chair next to Floria's. "How much did you hear as you came down the hall?"

"Enough to know she's not a baritone," Floria replied.

"I wish I had known you were going to be free of your Tower duties," Gavin sighed. "I'd have demanded *you* for the part instead." He looked at her hopefully. "Would you be willing to learn it? Please? Just so I can hear what it *ought* to sound like?"

"Of course," Floria said quickly. "I'd love to learn it. What are friends for?" They smiled at each other, sharing for a moment the perfect understanding that sometimes occurred between two telepaths. Then Gavin leapt to his feet, his energy and enthusiasm miraculously restored, thrust the score of the cantata into her hands and took up his *rryl*.

"Let's take it from the beginning," he said eagerly. "You don't have to sing full out, or even stand up if you don't want to; just mark it and see how much of it you can sight-read."

He played a few bars of introduction to indicate the tempo and nodded at Floria to indicate where the soprano solo began. Floria, whose sight-reading ability was quite good—especially when the composer was sitting next to her thinking hard about what the music ought to sound like—sang softly through the first section. She knew that her breath control was nowhere near what it ought to be—breathing was another thing that was more difficult when one was carrying a child—but her voice was clear and on pitch and she was managing the tempo quite well for a first run-through.

The clatter of hooves as a party of horsemen rode

into the courtyard outside the window masked the sound of Capella's footsteps in the hall, but Capella barely gave them a glance as she dashed to the window, threw it open, and hung out to stare avidly down at the courtyard. "Isn't he beautiful?" she asked rapturously.

Floria stared questioningly at Gavin, who rose and went to look out the window himself. "Are you referring to old Lord Alton?" he asked in surprise.

"No, silly," Capella giggled, "his horse—the white stallion—isn't he gorgeous? Someday I'm going to have a horse just like him."

Gavin was speechless, and Floria couldn't think of anything to say either. It wasn't the first time she had seen a female human go into raptures over a horse, but it was the first time she had seen the phenomenon in a grown woman. Usually this condition manifested itself in girls of eight or nine and was outgrown by their middle teens—or sooner if a girl actually had much contact with horses. It was difficult to romanticize something that tried to eat every passing plant while you were riding it, stepped on your foot, shed long stiff hairs on your riding habit, and either refused to move at all, tried to scrape you off on a low branch, or bolted with you. Floria was an indifferent horsewoman, to say the least.

But simple politeness demanded that she say something. "Are you fond of horses, *damisela?*"

"Oh, yes," Capella instantly replied. "I'm going to have to get Lord Alton to let me ride that one—he's such a beauty!" Then she saw the music score in Floria's lap. "What are you doing with that?" she asked suspiciously.

"Gavin was just letting me look at it," Floria replied calmly. "He's been one of my favorite composers since we were children."

Capella still looked suspicious, but all she said was, "Aunt Antonella wants to see you, right now." She reached for Floria, obviously intending to drag her to her feet, but Gavin blocked her and dragged her aside, while Floria hastily pulled herself out of the chair.

"Capella," Gavin said in an urgent undertone, "Floria is a strong telepath. It is considered rude to touch a telepath without her invitation; most telepaths find contact with strangers painful. And Floria is carrying a child, which makes her even more sensitive."

"I know that!" Capella said defensively.

"Very well," Gavin said. "I shall escort you ladies to the queen; I haven't seen her yet today." He extended an arm to each of them. Capella clung leechlike to his right arm, while Floria lightly rested her fingertips on his left sleeve, and they proceeded down the hall to the queen's rooms.

When they arrived, they found King Aidan there, along with Lord Alton, who was paying his respects to the queen and congratulating her on her recovery.

"Oh, Lord Alton," Capella said, barely managing to avoid interrupting his compliments to the queen, "you must let me ride that beautiful stallion of yours!"

Lord Alton started at her. *Obviously,* Floria thought, *he has not previously made her acquaintance either. Did the Ridenows keep her locked up in the attic until now?*

King Aidan tried to salvage the proprieties. "Lord Alton, permit me to present Capella Ridenow."

This should have been the Lord's cue to claim that it was a pleasure to meet the *damisela,* but this seemed to be beyond him at the moment. Floria wondered how often Capella had this effect on people.

"My stallion is a very dangerous animal, *damisela,*" he finally said with a fair assumption of courtesy. "I must request that no one but his groom go near him."

"Of course," King Aidan endorsed his words. "I have already given orders to my head groom to have him stabled at the far end of the long stable, away from the other animals. If you have any problems with his stabling or my servants, Lord Alton, feel free to come to me with them."

Lord Alton nodded. "I thank Your Grace," he said formally. He bowed over Queen Antonella's hand, King Aidan kissed her cheek, and the two men departed.

"But animals love me!" Capella protested as the door closed behind them. "I'm sure I can ride the stallion!"

"It would be most discourteous to do so without his owner's permission," Queen Antonella said slowly. Her speech was still a trifle slurred from the stroke. It was perfectly understandable to Floria, but she suspected that Capella might understand only what she wished to understand. Queen Antonella looked troubled, as if she shared Floria's suspicions.

"Floria," the queen continued, "since you and Capella are my two youngest ladies at present, you will share a bedchamber."

Oh, no! Floria thought. Aloud she said simply, "I fear, Your Grace, that I am far from an ideal companion at night. The child I carry tends to make my nights rather restless, and I should dislike depriving Capella of her rest."

"Oh, don't worry," Capella cut in, "you won't disturb me in the slightest—I'm a very deep sleeper."

The queen smiled faintly. "That's settled, then," she said. "You girls may leave; I wish to speak to Gavin now. I shall see you at dinner."

Perforce Floria curtsied over the queen's hand and withdrew, following Capella down the hall to the bedchamber allotted to them. Fortunately it was a fairly large room, and the two beds were on opposite sides of it. The maids had already unpacked Floria's things and put her favorite quilt, which she had brought with her, on her bed. She sank gratefully onto it and lay back against the pillows, feeling more tired than she would have believed possible. Capella was chattering away about something, but Floria fell asleep before she could figure out what it was.

Life at court quickly settled into a pattern. Floria got up early, while Capella still slept, ate breakfast with the court's few early risers, then sat with the queen in the mornings (which spared her both Capella's company and having to listen to Capella rehearse). Capella and Gavin would both appear at luncheon, and Capella would sit with the queen in the afternoons. Floria would take a nap after luncheon, enjoying the luxury of having their room to herself, and then go to the music room with Gavin, who insisted on teaching her his cantata "as an antidote to having to listen to Capella massacre it all morning."

"It is a shame," Floria agreed, making another notation in the copy of the score Gavin had made for her. "This is definitely the best thing you've done yet, Gavin. I hope that Conn will be able to come to court for the premiere; he'll want to hear this."

Gavin sighed. "If only I weren't stuck with Capella for the soprano. She's killing it, Floria, I swear it!"

"Surely she has improved at least a little since I last heard her," Floria said hopefully.

"No." Gavin shook his head. "It's incredible, but her performance hasn't changed a bit. Her consistency is amazing—she's convinced that she can sing and that she's doing it well, and she just does it the same way, over and over and over. . . ."

He paced restlessly about the room. "It's horrible of

me, I know, but I wish she would try to ride Lord Alton's stallion and get herself killed!"

Floria shuddered. "Don't remind me. She *is* trying; I've had to drag her back to our room three times this week."

Gavin stared at her. "What?"

"She sneaks out of our room, dressed for riding, in the middle of the night," Floria said grimly. "That's why the queen has us sharing a room, so I can keep an eye on her."

"Poor Floria! No wonder you look so tired. I hope you don't have to drag her back by force."

Floria shook her head. "When I catch her, she claims she must have been sleepwalking."

Gavin looked incredulous. "Does she really expect you to believe that?"

Floria shrugged. "I don't care. As long as she uses that story, she has no excuse not to go straight back to bed when she gets caught, so it has its uses."

"It's a stupid game," Gavin said flatly.

"True," Floria sighed. "Shall we try this section again?" She indicated her score. "I think I almost have that long phrase correct."

They worked steadily on the cantata for the next several hours. In fact, they lost track of time, so they were surprised when Capella entered the room. "What are you doing here, Floria?" she asked shrilly. "It's time to dress for dinner; we'll be late. What was that you were singing?" She looked at the score Floria held, and turned on Gavin. "Why are you letting Floria sing that instead of teaching it to me? *I'm* singing the soprano part."

It was unfortunate that Gavin lost his temper at that. Understandable, but unfortunate. "I have been trying to teach this to you for the past month!" he roared. "But you won't bother to listen to anything anyone says;

you insist that what you're doing—*I* wouldn't call it singing—is good; and then you don't even *recognize* your part when you hear it sung correctly!"

"That's not my part," Capella protested. "You haven't taught that section to me yet!"

"Oh, I've *taught* it," Gavin snarled. "You just haven't learned it. You're hopeless, and I'm going to the king and tell him so. I absolutely refuse to let you ruin my work—and I don't care whose bastard you *might* be distantly related to!" He stormed out of the room.

Capella stared after him with her mouth hanging open. "What's wrong with him?"

Floria sighed. She thought that Gavin had made his point fairly clear, probably to everyone in earshot—except Capella. "Shall we go dress for dinner, Capella?"

Capella regarded her through narrowed eyes. "*You're* doing this to me," she accused. "I'll stop you. I swear I'll stop you."

Life went on much as before, although Gavin had Floria working even harder on the cantata. He didn't speak of it, but Floria knew he hoped to persuade the king to let her substitute for Capella. Floria continued to keep an eye on Capella, especially in light of her threats, but Floria believed the threats to be empty ones until the afternoon she finished the solo and was startled by applause from the doorway.

"Brava!" Conn said, smiling at her.

"Conn!" Floria, moving faster than she had in weeks, ran into his arms. "What a wonderful surprise! Why didn't you tell me you were coming, and how long can you stay?"

Conn just held her for a moment, and Floria basked

in his embrace. It felt rather like warm sunshine only
better.

Gavin set aside his *rryl.* "Good to see you, Conn,"
he said, getting up. "I'll leave you two alone now; I'm
sure you have a lot to catch up on."

"No," Conn said, "I believe that we *three* have a lot
to catch up on. Sit down, Gavin." Gavin did, and
Conn, still holding Floria, sat down in the armchair
with her on his lap. "Tell me, who is Capella
Ridenow?"

Gavin groaned. "Words fail me; you'll have to meet
her yourself."

Floria sighed. "She's one of the Ridenow daughters,
currently serving as one of Queen Antonella's ladies.
She's head-blind and tone-deaf, and she's supposed to
be singing the soprano solo in Gavin's new cantata."

"My sympathies, Gavin," Conn said. "Is that what
Floria was singing just now?"

"Yes," Gavin said. "Floria has kindly agreed to learn
it so that I can hear what it should sound like. You
can't imagine what that woman does to it!"

"She would appear to be a very unhappy person,"
Conn said quietly.

Floria twisted to look up at his face. "Have you met
her?"

Conn shook his head. "She wrote me a letter."

Floria understood, but Conn had to explain to Gavin.
"I can sense things by handling physical objects.
Frequently-worn jewelry works best, but I can pick up
quite a bit from a letter, especially when the writer is
suffering from strong emotions at the time of writing."

"What did she write to you about?" Floria asked.

"She claimed," Conn said in a voice a bit unsteady
with laughter, "that you and Gavin were carrying on a
flagrant affair and making a scandal at court and that
she thought I ought to know about it."

Floria choked. "How kind of her," she said weakly.

Gavin was not amused. "That wretched, conniving, interfering, unscrupulous—"

"Calm down, Gavin," Floria said calmly. "You know as well as I do that Conn would never believe her nonsense."

"Certainly I trust my wife and my friends over some girl I've never heard of before," Conn said. "But it did provide me with an excuse to come to court and see you—and hear your new cantata, Gavin."

"If you want to hear it the way it should sound," Gavin snapped, "somebody will have to kill that stupid brat! It's bad enough that she thinks she can sing, but to try to slander Floria like this—it's outside of enough!"

"Has she been trying to sell this story to anyone but me?" Conn inquired.

"I don't think so," Floria replied. "I'm sure the queen would have said something to me if Capella were trying to make this common gossip." She twisted reluctantly out of her husband's hold. "And speaking of the queen, Conn, we had better go tell her you're here."

"True," Conn said. "I'm being horribly remiss in my manners; I ought to have paid my respects to her first—but I wanted to see you."

Floria smiled. "I think the queen—and the king— will understand."

"I'm sure they will," Gavin agreed as they went out into the hall together. "Love is not hard to understand for those who have experienced it."

They heard angry shouting as they approached the Queen's rooms. Gavin and Floria exchanged anxious glances.

"That's Lord Alton," Gavin said.

Floria nodded, "I hope Capella hasn't been bothering his horse again—but I'll bet she has."

"Is that idiot I saw in the stables as I arrived Capella?" Conn asked. "A woman in her mid-thirties with frizzy red hair?"

"Sounds like her," Gavin said. "What was she doing?"

"Heading toward the back part of the stables—the part that generally isn't used. She appeared to be going to an assignation with someone."

"Not someone," Floria sighed, "something. Lord Alton has a white stallion—"

"You don't mean—" Conn began carefully.

Floria laughed. "No, she just wants to ride the beast. Lord Alton says it's dangerous and forbade her, but. . . ." She shrugged. "Capella's not good at listening to anything she doesn't want to hear."

They entered the queen's rooms to discover that Capella was hearing it again.

"I told you that animal was dangerous," Lord Alton was shouting, "and I told you to stay away from him! And then I walk into the stable and find you in his stall!"

"You didn't have to hit him!" Capella screamed at him. "You're a brute and a bully!"

"I wouldn't have *had* to hit him if you hadn't gotten in the way. Don't you realize he was about to take a chunk out of your arm?"

"He was not!" Capella protested. "He *likes* me."

"That makes one of him," Gavin muttered *sotto voce*. Unfortunately, Capella heard him.

"You're all beastly and I hate you!" she screamed. "I wish I were dead!"

"Try to ride my horse again and you will be," Lord Alton said grimly.

Capella looked around for sympathy. Finding none, she burst into noisy tears and ran from the room.

There was silence for several minutes as the room's occupants regained their tempers, and pulse rates and breathing returned to normal.

Lord Alton turned to Queen Antonella. "Your Grace, I do apologize for this scene—"

The queen smiled faintly and shook her head.

"Nonsense," King Aidan said briskly. "Quite understandable reaction. That girl badly wants conduct." Then he looked at the group still frozen in the doorway. "Conn! Good to see you, dear boy! Come to see how your wife goes on, have you?"

Conn bowed over the king's hand, then the queen's. "I ask your pardon for coming uninvited, but," he smiled ruefully at Floria, "I missed my wife."

"Floria is a lucky woman to have a husband who loves her so," Queen Antonella said softly. She looked at Floria. "I suppose you want your room changed so you can be with him?"

"Yes, please, Your Grace," Floria said thankfully.

"Tell the servants to move your things while we're all at dinner," the queen ordered. "Capella's probably there crying right now; no need to disturb her."

Floria nodded. *I'm sure Capella didn't intend it that way, but she did me a real favor, sending that silly letter to Conn.*

"Such a shame she hasn't married," the queen went on. She looked at Gavin. "I don't suppose you'd consider it?"

Gavin shook his head firmly. "Not for anything in the world. She's tone-deaf."

The king chuckled. "That certainly wouldn't do in *your* wife, would it?" He frowned. "Still, she must have *some* good qualities."

"I'm sure she thinks she has," Lord Alton said. He was calmer now; his voice was down to a growl.

"Sounds like she thinks she can ride," Conn pointed out.

"She also thinks she can sing," Gavin sighed, "but believe me, she can't."

"If she were as good with horses as she thinks she is, I'd marry her myself," Lord Alton remarked. "Good trait to fix in the bloodline."

Floria bit hard on a quivering lip. "And if you gave her free run of the stables, you wouldn't see her in the house much."

Lord Alton laughed outright, and the remaining tension in the room eased.

Capella was quiet at dinner, but her look was obviously intended to convey the idea that she was plotting revenge. Floria, happy in the results of Capella's last attempt at revenge, didn't worry about it.

The next morning, Capella was missing—and so was Lord Alton's white stallion. Floria and Conn were sitting with the queen when Gavin came in with the news. He appeared to find it hilarious.

"No," he reassured Queen Antonella, "she's not hurt a bit. It seems she actually was correct when she said that animals like her. At least that stallion does. King Aidan tracked her with his starstone, and she was riding that beast with just a halter. She hadn't even bothered with a saddle! Lord Alton was quite impressed. He's gone after her, and he's going to take her home and get her father's consent to their marriage."

"What about her consent?" Floria asked. "Just yesterday she called him a brute and a bully."

"She'll consent," Gavin prophesied. "Her father will

see to that; he has too many children to indulge her whims when she actually gets a good offer."

Conn patted Floria's hand. "Don't worry about her, my dear. I'm sure she'll enjoy the prestige of being Lady Alton."

"You're right about *that*," Gavin agreed.

"Yes, I think you are," Floria said. "Anyway, I think she likes horses better than people, and Lord Alton has more horses than anyone else in the Domains. She should be happy enough."

"And I'm ecstatic!" Gavin said enthusiastically. "Now that Capella's gone, Floria can sing the soprano part in my cantata. I think this works out well for everyone."

DAW

MARION ZIMMER BRADLEY, Editor
THE DARKOVER ANTHOLOGIES

☐ **DOMAINS OF DARKOVER**   UE2407—$3.99

☐ **FOUR MOONS OF DARKOVER**   UE2305—$4.99

☐ **FREE AMAZONS OF DARKOVER**   UE2430—$3.95

☐ **THE KEEPER'S PRICE**   UE2236—$3.99

☐ **LERONI OF DARKOVER**   UE2494—$4.99

☐ **MARION ZIMMER BRADLEY'S DARKOVER**
                                      UE2593—$4.99

☐ **THE OTHER SIDE OF THE MIRROR**   UE2185—$4.50

☐ **RED SUN OF DARKOVER**   UE2230—$3.95

☐ **RENUNCIATES OF DARKOVER**   UE2469—$4.50

☐ **SNOWS OF DARKOVER**   UE2601—$4.99

☐ **SWORD OF CHAOS**   UE2172—$3.50

☐ **TOWERS OF DARKOVER**   UE2553—$4.99

DAW

MARION ZIMMER BRADLEY

THE DARKOVER NOVELS

The Founding

☐ DARKOVER LANDFALL   UE2234—$3.99

The Ages of Chaos

☐ HAWKMISTRESS!   UE2239—$4.99
☐ STORMQUEEN!   UE2310—$4.50

The Hundred Kingdoms

☐ TWO TO CONQUER   UE2174—$4.99
☐ THE HEIRS OF HAMMERFELL   UE2451—$4.99
☐ THE HEIRS OF HAMMERFELL (hardcover)   UE2395—$18.95

The Renunciates (Free Amazons)

☐ THE SHATTERED CHAIN   UE2308—$4.50
☐ THENDARA HOUSE   UE2240—$4.99
☐ CITY OF SORCERY   UE2332—$4.99

Against the Terrans: The First Age

☐ REDISCOVERY   UE2529—$4.99
☐ REDISCOVERY (hardcover)*   UE2561—$18.00
☐ THE SPELL SWORD   UE2237—$3.99
☐ THE FORBIDDEN TOWER   UE2373—$4.99
☐ STAR OF DANGER   UE2607—$4.99

Against the Terrans: The Second Age

☐ THE BLOODY SUN   UE2603—$4.99
☐ THE HERITAGE OF HASTUR   UE2413—$4.99
☐ SHARRA'S EXILE   UE2309—$4.99

*with Mercedes Lackey

Buy them at your local bookstore or use this convenient coupon for ordering.

PENGUIN USA   P.O. Box 999—Dept. #17109, Bergenfield, New Jersey 07621

Please send me the DAW BOOKS I have checked above, for which I am enclosing
$_____ (please add $2.00 per order to cover postage and handling). Send check
or money order (no cash or C.O.D.'s) or charge by Mastercard or Visa (with a
$15.00 minimum.) Prices and numbers are subject to change without notice.

Card #_____ Exp. Date _____
Signature_____
Name_____
Address_____
City _____ State _____ Zip _____

For faster service when ordering by credit card call **1-800-253-6476**

Please allow a minimum of 4 to 6 weeks for delivery.

A note concerning:

MARION ZIMMER BRADLEY'S
FANTASY MAGAZINE

Fans of Marion Zimmer Bradley will be pleased to hear that she is now publishing her own fantasy magazine. If you're interested in subscribing and/or would like to submit material to it, write her at:

P.O. Box 249
Berkeley, CA 94701

(If you're interested in writing for the magazine, please enclose a SASE for her free Writer's Guidelines *before* submitting material.)

THE FRIENDS OF DARKOVER

So popular have been the novels of the planet Darkover that an organization of readers and fans has come into being, virtually spontaneously. The Friends of Darkover is purely an amateur and voluntary group. It has no paid officers and has not established any formal membership dues. Thendara Council serves as a central point for information on Darkover-oriented newsletters ad maintains a chronological list of Marion Zimmer Bradley's books.   Contact may be made by writing to the Friends of Darkover, Thendara Council, PO Box 72, Berkeley, CA 94701 and enclosing a SASE (Self-Addressed Stamped Envelope) for information.

(These notices are inserted gratis as a service to readers. DAW Books is in no way connected with these organizations professionally or commercially.)

DAW

MARION ZIMMER BRADLEY
NON-DARKOVER NOVELS

- ☐ **HUNTERS OF THE RED MOON** UE1968—$3.99
- ☐ **THE SURVIVORS** UE1861—$3.99
- ☐ **WARRIOR WOMAN** UE2253—$3.50

NON-DARKOVER ANTHOLOGIES

- ☐ **SWORD AND SORCERESS I** UE2359—$4.50
- ☐ **SWORD AND SORCERESS II** UE2360—$3.95
- ☐ **SWORD AND SORCERESS III** UE2302—$4.50
- ☐ **SWORD AND SORCERESS IV** UE2412—$4.50
- ☐ **SWORD AND SORCERESS V** UE2288—$3.50
- ☐ **SWORD AND SORCERESS VI** UE2423—$3.95
- ☐ **SWORD AND SORCERESS VII** UE2457—$4.50
- ☐ **SWORD AND SORCERESS VIII** UE2486—$4.50
- ☐ **SWORD AND SORCERESS IX** UE2509—$4.50
- ☐ **SWORD AND SORCERESS X** UE2552—$4.99

COLLECTIONS

- ☐ **LYTHANDE** (with Vonda N. McIntyre) UE2291—$3.95
- ☐ **THE BEST OF MARION ZIMMER BRADLEY** edited
  by Martin H. Greenberg UE2268—$3.95

Buy them at your local bookstore or use this convenient coupon for ordering.

PENGUIN USA   P.O. Box 999, Dept. #17109, Bergenfield, New Jersey 07621

Please send me the DAW BOOKS I have checked above, for which I am enclosing
$_____ (please add $2.00 per order to cover postage and handling. Send check
or money order (no cash or C.O.D.'s) or charge by Mastercard or Visa (with a
$15.00 minimum.) Prices and numbers are subject to change without notice.

Card #_____ Exp. Date _____
Signature_____
Name_____
Address_____
City _____ State _____ Zip _____

For faster service when ordering by credit card call **1-800-253-6476**

Please allow a minimum of 4 to 6 weeks for delivery.

Jesse Hawk:
Brave Father

SHERI WHITEFEATHER

Silhouette®

Desire®

Published by Silhouette Books

America's Publisher of Contemporary Romance

Thanks to Shirl Thomas for being there whenever I need her,
Lisa Scaglione for adding a new voice to the critique group,
and Diana Rumm for talking me through a computer crisis.
Another thanks to Pet's Choice in Anaheim Hills
for helping me create Barney. And for Jesse's and Sky's
inspiration—a heartfelt hug to the Muscogee Nation,
a proud and beautiful people.

 SILHOUETTE BOOKS

ISBN 0-373-76278-X

JESSE HAWK: BRAVE FATHER

Printed in U.S.A.

Jesse Hawk Should Have Been Hers.

He should have come back, kept his promise. On the night he'd taken her virginity, he'd pledged his love forever. They had snuggled in each other's arms, tasted each other's skin, made secret vows. Young, romantic vows. And she'd kept hers, kept them locked in her heart until she'd cried herself to sleep at night.

No, Patricia hadn't agreed to move in with him when he'd asked, but she'd had her reasons—good reasons. The young man she'd loved needed a fair chance to pursue his career, and the baby in her womb needed some sort of financial stability. So she'd sent Jesse away, believing he'd return for her.

And more than a decade later he had returned. But not for her.

I'll never forgive you, she wanted to say. *But Dillon has the right to meet his father.*

Dear Reader,

In keeping with the celebration of Silhouette's 20th anniversary in 2000, what better way to enjoy the new century's first Valentine's Day than to read six passionate, powerful, provocative love stories from Silhouette Desire!

Beloved author Dixie Browning returns to Desire's MAN OF THE MONTH promotion with *A Bride for Jackson Powers,* also the launch title for the series THE PASSIONATE POWERS. Enjoy this gem about a single dad who becomes stranded with a beautiful widow who's his exact opposite.

Get ready to be seduced when Alexandra Sellers offers you another sheikh hero from her SONS OF THE DESERT miniseries with *Sheikh's Temptation.* Maureen Child's popular series BACHELOR BATTALION continues with *The Daddy Salute*—a marine turns helpless when he must take care of his baby, and he asks the heroine for help.

Kate Little brings you a keeper with *Husband for Keeps,* in which the heroine needs an in-name-only husband in order to hold on to her ranch. A fabulously sexy doctor returns to the woman he could never forget in *The Magnificent M.D.* by Carol Grace. And exciting newcomer Sheri WhiteFeather offers another irresistible Native American hero in *Jesse Hawk: Brave Father.*

We hope you will indulge yourself this Valentine's Day with all six of these passionate romances, only from Silhouette Desire!

Enjoy!

Joan Marlow Golan

Joan Marlow Golan
Senior Editor, Silhouette Desire

Please address questions and book requests to:
Silhouette Reader Service
U.S.: 3010 Walden Ave., P.O. Box 1325, Buffalo, NY 14269
Canadian: P.O. Box 609, Fort Erie, Ont. L2A 5X3

Books by Sheri WhiteFeather

Silhouette Desire

Warrior's Baby #1248
Skyler Hawk: Lone Brave #1272
Jesse Hawk: Brave Father #1278

SHERI WHITEFEATHER

lives in Southern California and enjoys ethnic dining, summer powwows and visiting art galleries and vintage clothing stores near the beach. Since her one true passion is writing, she is thrilled to be a part of the Silhouette Desire line. When she isn't writing, she often reads until the wee hours of the morning.

Sheri also works as a leather artisan with her Muscogee Creek husband. They have one son and a menagerie of pets, including a pampered English bulldog and four equally spoiled Bengal cats. She would love to hear from her readers. You may write to her at: P.O. Box 5130, Orange, California 92863-5130.

IT'S OUR 20th ANNIVERSARY!
We'll be celebrating all year,
continuing with these fabulous titles,
on sale in February 2000.

Special Edition

#1303 Man...Mercenary... Monarch
Joan Elliott Pickart

#1304 Dr. Mom and the Millionaire
Christine Flynn

#1305 Who's That Baby?
Diana Whitney

#1306 Cattleman's Courtship
Lois Faye Dyer

#1307 The Marriage Basket
Sharon De Vita

#1308 Falling for an Older Man
Trisha Alexander

Intimate Moments

#985 The Wildes of Wyoming—Chance
Ruth Langan

#986 Wild Ways
Naomi Horton

#987 Mistaken Identity
Merline Lovelace

#988 Family on the Run
Margaret Watson

#989 On Dangerous Ground
Maggie Price

#990 Catch Me If You Can
Nina Bruhns

Romance

VIRGIN BRIDES

#1426 Waiting for the Wedding
Carla Cassidy

BREWSTER BABY BOOM

#1427 Bringing Up Babies
Susan Meier

#1428 The Family Diamond
Moyra Tarling

The WEDDING AUCTION

#1429 Simon Says...Marry Me!
Myrna Mackenzie

#1430 The Double Heart Ranch
Leanna Wilson

#1431 If the Ring Fits...
Melissa McClone

Desire

MAN OF THE MONTH

#1273 A Bride for Jackson Powers
Dixie Browning

#1274 Sheikh's Temptation
Alexandra Sellers

#1275 The Daddy Salute
Maureen Child

#1276 Husband for Keeps
Kate Little

#1277 The Magnificent M.D.
Carol Grace

#1278 Jesse Hawk: Brave Father
Sheri WhiteFeather

One

Patricia Boyd loved him, more than life itself. She sat on the edge of his bed and brushed her fingers across his forehead, sweeping strands of dark brown hair away from his face. Eleven-year-old Dillon Hawk. Her son. Her heart and soul.

The morning sun shimmered through the blinds, illuminating the boy's room with slats of light. Patricia smiled. Dillon kept his room tidy. Each carefully constructed model car, battleship and airplane had its place, as did a favored pair of in-line skates.

"Hey, Mom." He grinned sleepily. "Are you leaving for work?"

"No. Today's Sunday."

"Oh, yeah," he said, pulling himself up against the oak headboard. "Breakfast at Grandpa's."

Sunday breakfast was a family tradition in the Boyd household. Omelets, hash browns and fresh-squeezed orange juice. "I have something else to do this morning, but Grandpa will fix your eggs."

"Cool. He always makes those spicy Spanish kind." Dillon pushed the covers away. "Where are you going today, Mom?"

To see your father, she thought nervously. Jesse was back, twelve years later. He'd bought the old Garrett farm, a piece of property between Arrow Hill and Hatcher. Of course, Jesse wasn't expecting her. He hadn't made an attempt to contact the woman he'd shunned.

"I'm going to visit an old friend," Patricia told her son. My first love. The man who gave me you. "I'll drop you off, then stop by Grandpa's later."

"Okay, but we might be at the hobby store by then."

Another family tradition, Patricia thought. Raymond Boyd purchased his grandson a new model every Sunday. He spoiled the boy, but then Dillon was easy to shower with affection and expensive gifts. Her son appreciated every heartfelt hug as much as every toy he'd ever received.

She kissed his forehead. "Wash up and get dressed."

"I'll hurry."

Twelve years had passed. Thirty more minutes wouldn't make a difference. If anything, it would give her a chance to check her appearance again, maybe sip a cup of herb tea. Anything to calm her nerves. "That's all right. There's no need to rush."

Patricia left his room and entered her own, a bedroom that was neither frilly nor bland. Antique wood furnishings, accented with winter-white and splashes of royal-blue, complemented the stained-glass windows. Every morning the sun reflected prisms of light across the bed.

She walked to the mirror and lingered over her reflection. She had chosen a straight white skirt, a pale-peach blouse and low heels—casual designer wear on a not-so-casual day.

Would Jesse recognize her right away? Or would he look twice to be sure? Her body was still slim, but her hips flared a bit more—a testimony to maturity and motherhood. Her hair hadn't changed much, she decided, aside from a slightly shorter cut and subtle caramel highlights framing her face.

Her face. She touched her skin, remembering how Jesse

marveled at what he called its "flawless texture." Would he find flaws now? The skin of a thirty-year-old?

What in God's name was she going to say to him? I was pregnant when you left. I waited year after lonely year for you to come back. You were supposed to prove to my disbelieving father that you really loved me.

"Mom?"

She turned to the sound of her son's voice, her heart leaping to her throat. "You're finished already?"

"Yep." He stood grinning at her, his damp hair slicked back with gel, his baggy khakis sporting a trendy label. "Ten minutes flat."

How could she forget Jesse's face when she saw a youthful replica of it every day? Dillon's straight white smile enhanced ethnic cheekbones, a stubborn jaw and sun-burnished skin. But it was his eyes, Patricia thought, that were the true gift from his father's mixed-blood heritage. Light-gray or a pale shade of blue, depending on the child's mood.

"I'm ready, too," she said, wondering if she'd ever be ready to face Jesse Hawk again.

The old Garrett farm came into view nearly thirty-five minutes later. It held an address in Hatcher, although the acreage spanned into Arrow Hill. How fitting, Patricia thought, that Jesse would choose a home located on the dividing line between dusty country living and opulent wealth.

Opulent wealth? Good Lord, her father was the most successful man in the county. He owned real estate—houses, apartment buildings, neighborhood shopping centers.

As Patricia steered her Mercedes down the graveled drive, she took note of the house and its condition. Habit, she decided, and a means to keep her mind on something other than her fluttering stomach. Although the wood structure had been neglected for some time, the splendor of the primitive architecture shone through. The house resembled a homesteader's cabin, small and rustic, and currently, it appeared, under renovation. She parked where the driveway forked, the other path leading to a newly constructed building behind the house, not nearly as rustic, but still charming.

She stepped onto the porch, fighting the urge to flee. Sooner or later she and Jesse would cross paths. It wouldn't be long before people realized her son and the new resident in town shared the same last name. And then there were those who knew the truth. Wasn't that how she'd learned he was back? A discreet female colleague had quietly mentioned that a man named Hawk was restoring the old Garrett place.

When she knocked on the door, the sound of barking dogs followed. She waited, waited some more, then headed toward her car. If Jesse was home, surely he would have responded to the yapping hounds.

"I'm sorry. I didn't know anyone was here," a deep voice said behind her. "I was working on the kennel out back. I've got a house full of strays." He chuckled. "But then I always do."

Patricia exhaled a shaky breath. She turned to see a tall, dark-skinned man squinting in the sun, his hand shielding his eyes, a dog—a sturdy rottweiler—at his side. When he moved closer and lowered his arm, her knees nearly gave way.

Jesse, in faded jeans and black construction-style boots, his bare chest a hard mass of sinew and muscle. The lean eighteen-year-old was gone. In his place stood a stranger.

"Oh, God," he said, and stopped dead in his tracks. "Tricia."

The nickname flowed through her like wine—a long-forgotten vintage. Sweet yet bitter. No one had ever called her Tricia but him. She lifted her chin, strode toward him, and extended her hand in a businesslike gesture. "It's nice to see you, Jesse."

Clearly caught off guard, he placed his hand in hers. "I hadn't expected you to come around here."

The handshake made them both uneasy, so she ended it quickly, choosing to adjust her purse strap instead. "Why not?"

"Just didn't."

"You could invite me in." *After all, damn you, I am the*

mother of your child. The innocent who waited for you all those years, believing like a fool, that you'd come back for me. Waited until hope turned to despair.

He slid his gaze over her in one slow sweep, reminding her of the day they had met. Only this time, there was no glimmer in his eye, no young, flirtatious smile. "The other dogs will just jump all over you."

"I like animals." She glanced at the loyal rottweiler beside him. It made no move toward her. It was an attractive dog, fit and muscular, its black coat gleaming in the sun. Jesse, too, had a gleaming mass of ebony hair. He still wore it long and flowing across his shoulders, but neatly trimmed sideburns added an air of maturity.

"What are you doing here, Tricia?"

"I thought it would be awkward if we ran into each other in town." She shifted her feet, stirring the gravel below. "I was hoping we could talk. Catch up a little." She needed to know what sort of man Dillon's father had become. Eventually she'd have to introduce them. Marlow County was too small for secrets.

Although Jesse frowned, he accommodated her. "We could sit on the porch a spell, I suppose." As he turned in the direction of the house, so did the dog. "Do you want a cold soda? I've got a cooler out back."

"No, thank you. I'm fine." She followed him up the stairs and sat beside him in a twig-style chair.

The rottweiler curled up at Jesse's feet, clearly content to be near its master. "What's his name?" she asked, assuming the massively built canine was a male.

"Cochise."

"That fits him. A warrior's name."

"In a sense, he is a warrior," Jesse said. "He's trained to know the difference between friend and foe. And he's been socialized since he was a pup."

Naturally, Jesse was a responsible pet owner. He wouldn't own a dog as powerful as a rottweiler without having it professionally trained. As for the strays he claimed to have, they made sense, too. Tricia remembered how he used to bring abandoned kittens into his apartment and feed them, even though he could barely afford food for himself.

"Are all the dogs inside the house strays?"

"Yeah." He tapped the windowpane and grinned. A curious mutt had its nose pressed against the glass. "I picked them up at the Humane Society just this week. I was in the process of building another kennel when you arrived."

He turned toward Patricia. She gripped the chair and steadied her breath. Dillon had flashed the same handsome smile earlier that morning. As their gazes met and held, Jesse's grin faded.

His eyes were guarded, she noticed, but still breathtaking. Most people would call them gray, yet Patricia knew they turned silver when he made love, glittered sensuously when he lowered his head to kiss a woman—touched his tongue to hers—filtered his fingers through her hair.

How many women had there been? she wondered. How many had watched those eyes change color, enjoyed that staggering touch?

Patricia smoothed her skirt. Jesse Hawk should have been hers. He should have come back, kept his promise. On the night he'd taken her virginity, he'd pledged his love forever. They had snuggled in each other's arms, tasted each other's skin, made secret vows. Young, romantic vows. And she'd kept hers, kept them locked in her heart until she'd cried herself to sleep at night. No, she hadn't agreed to move in with him when he'd asked, but she'd had her reasons—good reasons. The young man she'd loved needed a fair chance to pursue his career, and the baby in her womb needed some sort of financial stability. So she'd sent Jesse away, believing he'd return for her.

I'll never forgive you, she wanted to say. But Dillon has the right to meet you. She had told her son about his father, promising Jesse would be back someday. They just had to be patient and let him finish college.

"I'd heard this place sold a few months ago," she said, unaware then that Jesse had been the buyer. The property had been purchased under a corporate name.

"I've been coming back and forth from my rental in Tulsa, spending weekends out here, trying to get the renovations done. I hired a crew to build the clinic, but I'm doing most of the work on the house myself."

Immediately she thought about Dillon's interest in architecture. "I didn't know you had experience in carpentry."

He shrugged. "I did a little construction work during college. It put food on the table, paid the rent."

Patricia wanted to ask him about his education, if his studies had been difficult. She knew dyslexia made reading a struggle. Her son suffered from the same confusing disability. But asking Jesse about college would probably rehash their past and the part her father had played in it—a moot point after all these years. "So I can assume the building out back is a veterinary clinic."

He nodded. "I share a practice with three other doctors in Tulsa. We decided it was time to open a facility in the country."

That explained the company that had purchased his house. Apparently Jesse and his colleagues had formed a small corporation, the property serving as a tax deduction. "Looks like things worked out for you."

"Yeah."

They sat silent for a time, staring out at the dusty road. A butterfly winged by, and Patricia felt herself smile. As a toddler, Dillon used to chase the butterflies that graced his grandpa's abundant flower garden.

Jesse rocked his chair. "Are you sure you don't want a soda?"

"No, but if you're thirsty, go ahead."

His chair scraped the side of the house. "That's okay. I'm all right."

Think of something to say, she told herself, as they suffered through another bout of awkward silence. She tucked her hair behind her ears while he crossed one leg in male fashion, then uncrossed it, stretching both long limbs out instead. Physically, he'd changed. He'd put on weight, but the virile bulk suited his tall frame, considering it came in the form of muscle. And against the hard wall of his chest lay a small leather pouch, the medicine bag he'd always worn. She knew it contained items that were special to him. He had even placed a small lock of her hair within it. Surely he had discarded that romantic memento long ago.

"So, have you officially moved in?" she asked, not wanting to think about the past.

"Yeah, but I was in California not too long ago. My brother lives there, and his wife had a baby."

"Your brother? You mean you found him?" Patricia knew Jesse and his older brother, Sky, had been separated as children and taken to different foster homes when their parents died. Since Jesse was only two at the time, he hadn't known about Sky's existence until years later. At eighteen, Jesse had begun to search for his brother. But by then, Sky was long gone.

"Sky returned to Marlow County looking for me. So actually, we found each other." A warm smile touched his lips. "He's great. Everything a guy could want in a brother. And he has such a loving family. A sweet wife and an adorable baby daughter."

Hurt and envy pricked her skin. If you had come back for me, you could have had a loving family, too. "Sounds like you two got along well."

"Yeah. My brother and I talked about everything. Our heritage, our childhood, our work. He's been learning the Muskokee dialect." He rocked his chair again. "So what about you, Tricia. How's your life going?"

"Fine. I'm happy." I adore our son. He's my entire world. "I'm a real estate broker."

Jesse narrowed his eyes. "You buy and sell property for Daddy, right?"

Patricia lifted her chin. The sarcasm in his tone set her on edge. "Yes. I buy and sell property for my father's business." A highly successful company Dillon would inherit someday. "The income benefits the family trust."

"And what a tight little family it is," Jesse mocked. "Daddy and his precious daughter." He combed his fingers through his hair. "Or are you married, Tricia? Did you bring a suitable young man home for your father's approval?"

She waved her left hand. Apparently he hadn't noticed the absence of a wedding band. "I'm single," she snapped. "But I've matured, Jesse. Unlike you. Your childish grudge is most unbecoming."

"So sue me. Or better yet, try to run my life again."

She didn't want to have this conversation. Not now. Her father had been wrong all those years ago, but he'd made it up to her. He had loved her son from the moment the boy was born. And being a parent herself, she'd come to understand her father's motives, his overly protective nature.

"I didn't come here to dredge up the past."

He sighed. "You're right. I'm sorry. And I'm glad you're happy, Tricia."

Since the gentleness in Jesse's voice reminded her of the man he used to be, the youth she had loved so desperately, Patricia glanced up at the window for a diversion. Two dogs were perched there now, panting against the glass. She couldn't help but smile.

"You can let them out. I don't mind."

He grinned, flashing a set of straight white teeth. "Okay, but don't say I didn't warn you."

The dogs, three of them, barreled out the door in a whirl of fur and excited barks. Cochise sat, ears perked, watching the activity. Patricia was all but attacked, nuzzled and nudged with wet noses and hairy paws, so she tried to give each dog equal attention, petting them simultaneously. Jesse laughed as a small wiry brown-and-white mutt made its way onto her skirt.

Jesse knelt to stroke the dog on her lap while the other two lost interest and zoomed down the porch steps, Cochise staring longingly after them.

Jesse turned to his loyal companion. "Go on, boy."

The rottweiler instantly joined the strays.

While Patricia pretended to watch the dogs, she scanned Jesse's profile—features familiar yet changed—a man she no longer knew. A man, unfortunately, still capable of capturing her eye. The thought disturbed her. Patricia liked to think of herself as immune to tall, dark and rugged.

When he turned suddenly toward her, she focused her attention on the wiggling canine on her lap, hating that she'd been caught staring. "This one's cute," she said, scratching the dog's ears. "He looks like one of those movie dogs. You know, the sweet, scruffy stray."

His expression turned almost wistful. "You used to love those kinds of movies. They always made you cry."

She nodded, hoping she appeared less affected than she felt. "I remember. The happy-ending tearjerkers. My goodness, how many of those did we watch?"

Too many, Jesse thought, his heart clenching. Cuddling in front of the TV with Tricia was an image that still haunted him. How many times over the years had he thought about her, missed her, ached for her?

Tricia had changed, grown even more beautiful than in his memories. She wore her silky brown hair a tad more stylishly these days, a professional chin-length streaked softly with golden lights. Her body had blossomed into a womanly blend of cleavage and curves, and those legs, those long trim gams looked as though they had the strength and agility to wrap themselves around a man for hours. And they had, he remembered, as his groin tightened. Those were the most painful images of all. The youthful passion, the sensuality of shyness, the tender, inexperienced lovemaking.

Fresh out of high school, Jesse had moved to Marlow County in search of his roots, but found Tricia instead. Nervous about college, he'd gone to the public library where he'd debated signing up for a free literacy program. When he'd walked away without joining, she had approached him—a sleek brunette in shorts and sandals claiming she had volunteered as a tutor. He'd lingered over her in one slow torturous gaze and fell instantly in love. And then three months later his world fell apart.

As Jesse gazed up at the porch roof, his mind drifted back to the day Tricia had betrayed him. She had come to his apartment that August afternoon, looking tired and pale.

"I shouldn't have told my father about your scholarship," she said, her voice shaky.

Jesse shook his head, dismissing her guilt. He'd just had a life-altering confrontation with her father—a man who despised him. "You didn't know he'd be able to use it against me." A cruel twist of fate had dealt that card, it wasn't Tricia's fault.

Her voice continued to quiver. "What did you say to him?"

"Nothing." Pride had kept him silent, masking the rage. Jesse knew Raymond Boyd had been trying to destroy his relationship with Tricia since it started, but despite her father's wishes, she had continued to date him. That thought gave him hope. After all, it was modern-day Oklahoma, and they were both adults—strong-willed eighteen-year-olds. A poor Indian boy loving a rich white girl was no longer a crime. "Don't worry, I'm going to fight back."

Immediately her eyes filled with tears. "How? There's nothing you can do that will change any of this."

Jesse took a deep breath. He could go to a different college, one Raymond Boyd didn't have an affiliation with. It wouldn't be easy, but with Tricia by his side, he could accomplish anything. She was part of his strength, his soul.

"I want you to move in with me, Tricia."

The tears collecting in her eyes began to fall. "If I do that, how will you be able to go to college? You know my father meant what he said. He'll have your scholarship taken away."

Jesse's scholarship was from Winston College of Veterinary Medicine, a privately funded institution providing an education in conventional veterinary medicine as well as extended studies in holistic remedies, acupuncture and homeopathy. In spite of Jesse's reading difficulties, his advanced knowledge of herbal healing had earned him the rare scholarship. But now, Raymond Boyd had the power to take it away.

As it turned out, Tricia's father and George Winston, the founder of the college, were fraternity brothers. So if Jesse didn't end his relationship with Tricia, he'd lose his scholarship. Fraternity blood, as Raymond had put it, was thicker than water.

Jesse dried Tricia's tears, then took her in his arms, the fragrance of her hair, silk of her skin, creating an ache. Being that much in love scared the hell out of him, as did the fear of living without her.

"I know that if you move in with me, I won't be able to go to Winston," he said, explaining his frantic plan. "But I'll find another school that will accept me. And I'll apply for financial aid. There must be government grants available."

"Oh, Jesse." She blinked back another stream of tears. "You know how important the holistic care program is to the dean at Winston. So far, it's the only veterinary school in the nation that offers extended studies in alternative medicine. It's where you're meant to go."

Deep down he knew what she said was true. The ancient practice of herbal healing had been passed on to him by Tall Bear, a Creek medicine man, and it was Tall Bear who had introduced Jesse to the dean at Winston, offering a trade. Jesse would assist the director of the holistic care program in exchange for an education in conventional veterinary medicine. The dean had agreed to the unusual scholarship proposal, but if George Winston, the man who held the purse strings, suddenly changed his mind about funding it, the deal would crumble.

Jesse trapped her gaze. "I don't want to lose you, Tricia." Healing animals was his destiny. But so was Tricia. Choosing between them wasn't possible. He was willing to make sacrifices to have them both, work himself to the bone if he had to. And he knew Tall Bear would understand. The wise old medicine man would tell him to follow his heart. What Raymond Boyd proposed to do might not be illegal, but it was unethical. Morally wrong.

Jesse took Tricia's hand and squeezed it. "Somehow I'll find a way to make this right. Maybe the dean at Winston will help. Maybe he'll recommend me to another school." Jesse swallowed back his nervousness, his fear. "Please, Tricia, move in with me."

"Oh, God. I can't. Not now." She paused, inhaled a deep breath. "First of all, I would never expect you to prolong your education for me. You deserve that scholarship. Think about it, Jesse. We can be together after you finish college. You can come back for me.'' She closed her eyes, then opened them, blinking away her tears once again. ''If we moved in together now, we'd never make it financially. We'd never earn enough money to survive, let alone get you through college.''

Jesse pulled away. *Money*. The word alone clenched his gut. Once, Tricia had convinced him there was no dishonor in being born poor, orphaned or learning disabled. But suddenly the shame, the humiliation of being poor ripped through him like a knife, slicing his heart in two.

When Tricia lifted her hand to his cheek, her gentle touch made his skin burn—a sickening combination of love, hate, confusion and pain. She had just chosen her father's money over him. She wasn't willing to live in a tiny apartment or ride around town in a battered pickup. She wanted the luxury her father could provide, the fancy car and designer clothes.

''Come back after you finish college,'' she said, skimming her fingers over his jaw. ''Come back for me, Jesse. Prove to Daddy that—''

''Damn it, Tricia,'' he interrupted, still hurting from her touch. ''You should hate your father for this, but instead you expect me to prove myself to him.''

She dropped her hand. ''Daddy's wrong, but I could never hate him. He's raised me all by himself...and I...'' She glanced away and clutched her stomach. ''Please try to understand.''

He did understand. Tricia didn't love him the way he loved her. They had no future. All he'd be to her in a few years was the guy who had taught her how to please other men. Rich men Daddy wouldn't scorn. Fine, he thought. He'd take advantage of that scholarship, go on with his life and leave Tricia to her daddy's money.

''You'll come back, won't you, Jesse?''

''Damn right, I will,'' he told her, deciding then and there that he'd return to Marlow County someday, but not for the girl who had chosen her wealthy father over him. Jesse Hawk would come back to find his roots, make his home in the town where his parents had lived and died.

And that's what he'd done. Of course now, twelve years later, Tricia was here stirring all those painful memories.

Jesse sighed. He knew he should be a proper host and invite her into his home, but he wouldn't dare. He couldn't bear to see her among his belongings and then watch her leave. His house would seem far too empty afterward, and damn it, he'd suffered through enough loneliness.

All because of Tricia. And her father.

"Look," he said, "I know you didn't stop by to talk about the past, but there's something I need to say."

When he paused, she gazed up at him, her hair catching a soft breeze.

He focused on his next words, hating that she looked so beautiful. So ladylike. "I wasn't really in love all those years ago, and neither were you. I mean, we were only kids. Teenagers experimenting."

Her skin, that flawless complexion, paled a little, and Jesse felt a pang of regret from his perverse need for revenge. But he'd be damned if he'd ever admit that he had pined for her, missed her so badly he'd actually unmanned himself with tears.

"So," he said, finishing his speech, "I never should have asked you to live with me. What we had wasn't anything more than puppy love. A strong infatuation. It never would have worked."

"I'm well aware of that," she responded, her voice tight.

"That's just my point. I don't blame you for not moving in with me." And he didn't. Not now that he was older and wiser. The blame was in her loyalty to Raymond Boyd, in her expecting Jesse to come back to town and grovel at her old man's feet—worship the real estate tycoon as though he were some powerful pagan god. It still stung that Tricia had valued her daddy's money over Jesse's love. If she had asked him to come back to sweep her off her feet and tell Raymond Boyd to go to hell, Jesse would have been there with bells on. War paint and feathers, too.

"I should go." She placed the dog gently on its feet, stood and brushed off her skirt.

Jesse remained seated a moment longer, looking up at her. If he'd rattled her, she was doing her best not to show it. Aside from the loss of color in her cheeks, she appeared cool and professional. Aloof.

He rose slowly. "I'll walk you to your car."

"That's not necessary."

"I insist."

The gravel crunched beneath their feet. Her steps were light, his heavy, just like the ache in his chest. The strays circled Jesse and Tricia as they walked, barking playfully. Cochise took his place at Jesse's side, and he patted the dog's head for comfort. Cochise had been his companion for longer than he chose to remember, and more loyal than any woman could ever be.

They stopped at Tricia's car, an expensive white model. She'd graduated from a sporty convertible to four-door luxury. As she searched the interior of a leather handbag for her keys, Jesse caught a whiff of her perfume. The scent was unfamiliar, but it sparked a weakness in him he couldn't deny.

Damn her. Unable to stop himself, he cupped her face.

Her eyes flashed. "Don't touch—"

He silenced the rest of her protest with his lips, crushing them brutally against hers. The kiss was demanding, hard, hungry and lustful—filled with years of pain. He pressed her against the car and felt a shiver slide from his body to hers. She responded to his blatant tongue thrusts and melted like warm, scented wax, her hands gliding down his arms.

Satisfied that he'd made her as weak as he, Jesse tore his mouth away. "Don't come back, Tricia," he said, forcing air back into his lungs. "I don't want to see you again."

He turned and left her standing at the car, hating that a part of him still missed her—a flaw he intended to keep buried. Forever.

Two

After a long, shaky drive, Patricia parked her car in the circular driveway on her father's estate and willed herself to take control. Jesse's kiss had left her skin tingling and her heart pumping, conjuring needs and feelings that were best to ignore. She twisted the end of a lipstick tube, leaned toward the rearview mirror and attempted to camouflage his aftertaste with an icy-mauve hue.

The feminine maneuver failed. Jesse was still there, hard, sexy and demanding. Patricia sighed and checked her appearance. Hopefully no one would know. She looked cool and polished, as always. She'd learned long ago how to keep her nerves inside where they belonged. She was, after all, Patricia Boyd, the daughter of the most prestigious man in the county. She had an image to uphold. And she'd fought to preserve that image even when she'd become the object of raised eyebrows and none-too-subtle whispers. Giving birth to an illegitimate child wasn't what the citizens of Marlow County had expected from Patricia Anne Boyd. Attending Princeton and marrying a Harvard man was more her style, but she'd done neither. Instead she'd stayed in Arrow Hill, become an active member of Boyd Enterprises and raised Jesse Hawk's son.

Patricia made her way to the front door and opened it, grateful her father's domestic staff didn't work on Sundays. Because she'd been raised with cooks, housekeepers, chauffeurs and nannies, she'd always wondered what being part of a "normal" family would feel like. Patricia's mother had died before Patricia's second birthday, and as far as she was concerned, there wasn't a nanny alive who could replace what she'd lost. Raymond Boyd had done his best, though. And Sundays were special in his house—no staff, just family—a union that now included Dillon.

The Boyd mansion was stereotypical of old money and power: fresh flowers at every turn, a marble foyer, a winding staircase with a slick wood banister. The white-tiled kitchen was a cook's delight with its industrial-size refrigerator, abundant counter space and center isle. Copper pots and pans dangled above the stove—a kitchen cliché that lent the massive room a homey appeal.

Patricia found her father in his office, a room rife with masculine furnishings. Since he rarely worked at home, the ornate antique desk seemed like a rich man's prop, decked with brass ornaments and a humidor filled with imported cigars. The French doors that led to an impressive flower garden were open, inviting a blend of summer fragrances.

He glanced up and smiled. He sat at the desk with impeccable posture, a handsome man nearing the age of retirement, trim and fit with manicured hands and neatly styled graying hair. He looked like what he was, Patricia thought, domineering and headstrong, yet, below the surface, capable of immense kindness. And from what she remembered, Jesse had similar personality traits, only the younger man's were packaged in a more rugged appearance with long, windblown hair and large, callused hands. Neither would appreciate the comparison, she knew, although under different circumstances, Jesse Hawk and Raymond Boyd might have found each other admirable.

"I took Dillon into town for a new model, then dropped him off at the Harrison estate," her father said. "They called and invited him for a swim."

Mark Harrison was Dillon's best friend. He was a nice, enthusiastic boy, and her father approved of the family. The Harrisons, too, came from old money. It sounded snooty, but things like that mattered in Raymond Boyd's world. Patricia also knew her father overlooked Dillon's illegitimacy, something the Harrison family had done.

"That's fine." She sat in a tuck-and-rolled leather chair and absently ran her fingers over the brass tacks. Not having to face Dillon immediately after facing Jesse seemed like a small blessing. At times, her eleven-year-old son appeared capable of reading her emotions, no matter how well hidden. No one but Dillon could do that.

"Did you eat?" Raymond asked. "It's past the lunch hour."

Patricia glanced at her watch. Food was the furthest thing from her mind. This was, she decided, a perfect opportunity to tell her father who and what occupied her thoughts. Dillon was gone, and the household staff wouldn't be poking about, dusting furniture or offering entrées from a carefully-selected luncheon menu.

She scooted forward. "Dad, Jesse's back."

He turned his chair slowly, although she imagined his heart had taken a quick, unexpected leap. "For good?" he asked.

Patricia nodded. "He bought the old Garrett place. I went by there this morning."

"So you've seen him, then?"

"Yes."

"Did he come back for you?"

She kept her eyes steady and her expression blank. The question hurt almost as much as the answer. She had insisted years before that Jesse would do right by her, and her father had called her young and naive for believing so. Jesse would forget about her. Eighteen-year-old boys often confused lust for love. For Patricia the lesson had been a difficult one. Jesse had seemed so sincere. He had even offered to sacrifice his scholarship to be with her. That alone had convinced her it was true love.

"No. He's opening a veterinary clinic behind his house."

Raymond squared his shoulders as though preparing for an emotional battle. "Did you tell him about Dillon?"

"No. Not yet." She held up her hand in a failed attempt to confront her father's disapproval. "Jesse and Dillon have the right to know each other."

"Oh, Patricia." He let out a long sigh. "Do you honestly think someone like Hawk is going to make a suitable father?"

"But Jesse was raised in foster care. Establishing roots was important to him. He wanted children more than anything." For Dillon's sake, she prayed that was still true.

"Really? So is he married with a family now?"

She dropped her gaze. "No." A happily married man wouldn't have kissed her like that. And as far as children went, the strays he took in were as close as he got, of that she felt certain.

Raymond drummed his fingers on the desk.

Tricia looked up. "What am I supposed to do? Keep my son a secret? His name is Dillon *Hawk*, Dad."

"Giving the boy that name was a mistake. Dillon should be a Boyd."

Patricia rubbed her temples. That useless argument always resulted in a headache. "It's too late to turn back the clock. And somehow I've got to get Jesse to agree to see me again."

Her father's eyes hardened. "What happened? Did he toss you off his property?"

"Not exactly, no." She pressed her temples again. Worse than having been told not to come back, was Jesse's admission that he'd never really loved her. After all these years, hearing it out loud had been like a blow to the heart. "He told me he didn't want to see me again."

"Mom? Grandpa?"

Patricia and Raymond turned simultaneously toward the open doorway to find Dillon staring into the room, his hair still wet from an afternoon swim.

Patricia slanted her father a nervous glance. How much had

Dillon heard? "You're back early," she commented casually to her son.

"Mark ate too much candy and got sick, so his mom brought me back."

"Did you eat a lot of candy, too?" Raymond asked, smoothing his sideburns in what Patricia recognized as an anxious habit.

"Not as much as Mark." The boy moved a step closer, his ever-changing eyes a steely shade of gray. He turned to Patricia. "How come my dad doesn't want to see you again?"

Oh, God. So he had been eavesdropping. "Dillon, come sit down. We need to talk. Dad?" She looked at her father, dismissing him politely. Raymond Boyd didn't know how to be objective when it came to discussing Jesse.

"I'll take a walk." The older man stood, then squeezed his grandson's shoulder as the child took a seat next to Patricia. "I'll be in the garden if you need me." He exited through the French doors, his loafers silent as they touched the stone walkway.

Patricia reached for Dillon's hand and found it cold. She rubbed it between her palms. He shouldn't have heard what he did. She should have been more careful. "Just because your father and I parted ways doesn't mean that you shouldn't get to know him."

The boy's voice quavered. "But it's not fair that he doesn't like you anymore."

She sighed. Apparently Dillon had only overheard the tail end of the conversation. For that she was relieved. And she couldn't help but admire his attempt at chivalry. "Life isn't always fair, sweetheart."

"But he shouldn't have been mean to you." Dillon tugged his hand away, stood and paced in front of the desk, appearing suddenly older than his eleven years. "I don't want you to tell my dad about me. I don't care if I ever meet him."

Patricia drew a deep breath. "He lives here now, and one way or another, he's going to find out he has a son. He'll come looking for you, Dillon."

"Then let him." The boy stopped pacing and pushed his

hair out of eyes that were clearly his father's. "Just promise
that you won't go back to his house. Please, Mom. Promise."

"Okay." If Dillon needed time to deal with his feelings,
then Jesse Hawk would have to wait.

"Yoo-hoo!"

Now what? Jesse rolled his shoulders and strode from the
examining room into the reception area of the clinic. Half the
supplies he'd ordered hadn't arrived, and the brand-spanking-
new air-conditioning unit had decided to quit on the muggiest
day of the decade. So what if it was under warranty? The
inconvenience irked the hell out of him. He was not in the
mood for visitors.

"The clinic isn't open yet," he said, then broke into a grin
when he saw his guest cooling herself with an ornate fan. No
one but Fiona Lee Beaumont wore rhinestoned glasses and
carried jeweled fans. The woman's hair was still a gaudy shade
of red, he noticed, and whipped around her head like a bee-
hive. And she had to be pushing seventy these days.

"Jesse Hawk, as I live and breathe." She lowered the fan.
"You grew into one hunk of a man. You look just like your
daddy."

He hugged her frail frame, touched by the reference to his
father. Fiona lived in the same trailer park where Jesse had
spent the first two years of his life. She remembered his parents. Not well, but she knew their names and what they had
looked like. Jesse didn't even have a photograph of his parents. "And you, dear lady, are still the love of my life. I've
missed you."

She patted his cheek. "So you're an animal doctor, with
your own practice and everything."

He shrugged. "Yeah. It's a step up from working at the pet
store." How many pounds of kitty chow had he packed into
Fiona's ancient Oldsmobile? She was what the town of
Hatcher called "The Cat Lady," an eccentric old woman who
shared her worn-out trailer with at least two dozen pampered
felines, some that slept there, others that just came to visit.

"I have a brood of my own now, Fiona."

"Yes, I noticed. You've got six dogs in the yard, and that gelding back there's a real looker. Big, handsome paint."

"I've got a bird, an iguana and three ferrets, too." He sent her a playful wink. "Hell, I might even have a cat or two around here somewhere."

She smiled. "Your old boss told me you moved back. Also said he'd be sending business your way."

He leaned against the front counter. "Larry's a good man." Larry Milbrook of Larry's Pets and Feed had given Jesse a job twelve years before, when Jesse had drifted into town wearing holey jeans, time-worn boots and a tattered backpack with more of the same.

She peered past his shoulder. "So have you hired someone to run the reception office?"

"No, not yet. I'll probably only have the clinic open three, maybe four days a week. The rest of the time I'll be out on ranch calls. Horses like me." And he liked them. Horses, it seemed, ran in the blood. Jesse's brother, Sky, made his living as a stunt rider, and their father had worked as a ranch hand and trainer most of his life.

Fiona walked around the counter, allowing herself access to the computer. She tapped the keys with bony fingers flaunting rings as bold as Texas. "So are you going to hire some pretty young thing?"

"No," he responded quickly, thinking about Tricia. Young and pretty still felt like heartache. Because he tried to avoid the Daddy's-girl type, he'd picked up the habit of dating women slightly older than himself, ladies who looked nothing like the long-legged, fine-boned Patricia Boyd. And even then, dating was rare. He'd become a bit of a recluse; he and his animals. There were times he'd considered building an ark, loading his pets and sailing to the ends of the earth to numb the pain associated with his lost love.

"So you're going to hire someone more mature, then?" Fiona pressed on, pulling Jesse back into conversation.

He eyed the old woman. Apparently she needed a job. Feeding dozens of cats and living on a fixed income couldn't be easy. He imagined the rent had increased in that trailer park she called home. Some thief owned the place, some slimeball slumlord from Tulsa.

"I could use a mature lady around here. Someone who has a way with animals. Say, you wouldn't be interested, would you?"

"Me?" Her eyes widened beneath the pointy-framed glasses. "Hmm." She played the drama out, patting the side of her bouffant and gazing up at the ceiling as though the offer needed consideration.

"Oh, why not?" she said finally. "I did take some computer classes at the Senior Citizens' Center, and quite frankly this place could use a little jazzing up."

Jesse looked around. The room was simple and sterile, mostly white with touches of gray. Well, he thought, if anyone could add color, it would be Fiona Lee Beaumont in her fake baubles, dyed hair and god-awful pantsuits. Lord help him.

"How about a cold drink to celebrate," he suggested. There was no turning back now. Fiona was already arranging the reception desk to her liking, her bracelets clanking in the process.

He brought her a canned iced tea and chose a soda for himself. She whipped out her fan again and drank the tea from a paper cup, fanning and sipping like an aging Southern Belle.

"So," she said, "have you been keeping in touch with the Boyd girl? She was so lovely. Always wanted legs like that."

He raised an eyebrow. "You know damn well her daddy hated me."

"Doesn't mean the two of you haven't been carrying on a secret rendezvous."

Jesse finished his drink. "Tricia came by last week, but nothing happened." Nothing but a kiss that had made him hungry for a thousand more. "That romance is history."

"Well, in any case, you must be proud that she gave the boy your name. It was gossip for a long while. This county flourishes on gossip, especially tidbits concerning the rich."

Jesse's heart nearly stopped. "What are you talking about? What boy?"

"Oh, my." Fiona chewed her fading lipstick line. "Oh my,

oh my." She reached for his quaking hand. "You mean after all these years, she never told you about your son?"

"Miss Boyd," the receptionist said over the intercom, "there's a Mr. Hawk here to see you. He—" the young woman paused and lowered her voice "—seems quite upset. He threatened to find your office himself if I don't accommodate him. Should I call Security?"

Patricia straightened her spine, preparing for a battle Jesse would surely force her to wage. He knows, she told herself, taking a deep breath. He found out about Dillon.

"I'll see Mr. Hawk, Susan. There's no need for Security."

Within seconds Patricia's door opened, and Jesse shouldered by the receptionist. Petite and pale, Susan looked like a quivering mouse next to him, eager to escape something even more dangerous than a surly tomcat. A grizzly, Patricia decided. A grizzly with long black hair and gunmetal eyes. When in God's name had Jesse gotten so big?

Avoiding his glare, Patricia rose and nodded to the receptionist. "Thank you, Susan. Please hold my calls." She glanced at her watch, determined to keep her manner professional. "I'll let you know when this meeting ends."

The woman cast a wary glance at Jesse, who kept his stare focused on Patricia. "Yes, Miss Boyd." She darted out the door and closed it soundly.

"Well…" Patricia smoothed her jacket. Did she look as nervous as she felt, or did her red suit boast confidence? She lifted her chin. If her designer apparel didn't, then certainly the plush office should.

"Can I get you some coffee?" she asked, sweeping her hand toward a wet bar. "Or would you prefer something cold?" Like the frost glazing your eyes.

"Cut the crap, Tricia."

He strode toward her, his faded denims and casual T-shirt mocking the decor. Suddenly the hours of labor spent perfecting the office seemed insignificant. He dwarfed the room and all of its high-powered pretense.

"Do you have a child?" he asked. "An eleven-year-old boy?"

She resisted the urge to remove the scarf draped around her neck. Deep, calming breaths were difficult as it was, and the flowing strip of silk felt like a noose. "Yes."

He stepped closer. Dangerously close. "And am I his father?"

"Yes."

"And tell me," he said, moving closer still, "did you know you were pregnant when I left town? Did you know then that you were carrying my child?"

"Yes," she stated once again, refusing to offer an explanation. She had begged him to come back for her. The fault was his.

He stood dead still, his metallic eyes boring into hers. "Do you know how hard it is not to hate you right now?"

"No harder than it is for me," she shot back. Love and hate were only a fine line apart. And she had loved him once. Loved him beyond comprehension.

She wanted to scream, claw his skin and make him bleed. But instead she stood facing him as years of pain stretched between them. God help her. Jesse was back, making her insides ache all over again. Everything hurt: her lungs as they battled for air, her heart as it pumped erratic beats. Yes, she struggled not to hate him. How could she not?

"By the way," she said, angry that he hadn't asked, "your son's name is Dillon."

He flinched, and those eyes, those slate-gray eyes lightened, softening his stare. He repeated the name in a near whisper, his voice cracking. "Dillon."

Patricia glanced away. She didn't want to see that side of Jesse, the vulnerable, gentle side she had loved. In that moment he could have been eighteen again—the teenage boy who had pledged "forever." The man she'd almost come to hate. The thought made her sad and sick inside.

Jesse raised his voice to a commanding level once again. "I want to see Dillon. As soon as possible. I have a right to see my son."

She reached toward the edge of her desk, felt for the ridge and leaned against it. "I'm sorry, but Dillon isn't ready to meet you." That truth intensified the sickness, especially when Jesse jerked as though he'd been struck.

"What?" He pulled his hands through his hair. "Oh, God, what are you saying? Does he know about me? Does he know I'm his father?"

"Yes, he knows, he's just confused right now." She gestured for Jesse to sit, and surprisingly he did, lowering himself onto a contemporary leather sofa. She seated herself beside him. "This isn't easy for Dillon." She thought about her son, about his sensitive, protective nature. "He used to ask about you, but now that so many years have passed, I think he's gotten used to the idea of not having a father."

Jesse scrubbed his hand across his jaw. "Did he tell you he didn't want to meet me, or are you just assuming—"

"He told me," she answered honestly. "And he asked me not to go back to your house. Made me promise I wouldn't."

Jesse's breath hitched. Big, strong and vulnerable, she thought. He looked as though he wanted to cry, bury his head in his hands and let the tears flow. Patricia touched his shoulder and felt it shake. He was, she realized, as hurt and confused as Dillon. He leaned toward her, reached up and skimmed his fingers across her cheek. She wanted to cry, too. Cry for their youth and what should have been.

Patricia closed her eyes as images of Dillon flashed through her mind—birthday parties, skinned knees, warm hugs, toothless grins, fevers, chicken pox. Years of motherhood. A sweet, loving little boy who had waited for his father to return.

She opened her eyes and pushed Jesse's hand away. "Damn you. Why didn't you come back?"

He clenched the hand that had touched her, his face still except for a twitching muscle in his cheek. "Because I didn't know I had a child," he hissed. "You stole him from me. Dillon is my flesh and blood as much as yours, but you kept him for yourself. You didn't want me involved in his life."

"Stole him?" She moved to the edge of her seat. "I gave birth to him. Loved him, rocked him, fed him from my breast.

And I told him about his father. Good things. But you didn't come back and prove me right. So I'd say Dillon has the right to decide if you're worth meeting."

He rose and began to pace the room, the restless movement reminding her of Dillon. How alike yet different they were. Father and son. Strangers.

"Oh, God," he said, anguish vibrating his voice. "What if Dillon never wants to meet me?"

She took a deep breath, composing herself. Watching Jesse hurt didn't seem to ease her own pain, the ache he'd renewed. "Dillon will come around. He's just angry...upset that—" She paused, exhaled again. "He knows that you and I—that our reunion hasn't been a friendly one."

Jesse stopped pacing and turned to face her. "That's what's wrong? You and me?"

"Dillon's a sensitive child. It bothers him that we're not friends," she said, grateful she hadn't been forced to reveal the conversation Dillon had stumbled upon. She hadn't forgiven herself for that act of irresponsibility. Her son's emotional well-being had been jeopardized simply because she hadn't thought to close a door.

Jesse trapped her gaze. "I'm taking you to dinner tonight."

Patricia startled. "What?"

"Our son wants us to be friends."

Just like that? Sit down for a cozy dinner and wipe away years of pain? Two people who not more than ten minutes before had admitted they were battling hatred? She stood to face him. "You're crazy."

"Damn it, Tricia. Don't you dare fight me on this." He took one of her business cards off the desk and handed her a pen. "Write your address down. I'll pick you up at seven."

She did as he asked and shoved the card back at him. For Dillon, she told herself. She'd do it for Dillon. Deep down she knew the boy wanted a father.

"We'll go to The Captain's Inn." Scowling, he grabbed the pen and tossed it back onto her desk; it rolled off and landed on the floor. ''But remember, this isn't a date. We're making peace with each other for the sake of our son.''

Well, she thought as he left her office and shut the door with a smart bang, we're off to one hell of a start.

Three

Jesse came home to find Sally, a six-foot iguana, speculatively eyeing Barney, an animated African gray parrot. Apparently in the mood to show off, the chatty bird sat atop the lizard's terrarium reciting gibberish he'd picked up from the television. Since Barney had figured out the buttons on the remote control, he spent his days switching channels. He adored the clatter of game shows and cartoons, but occasionally Jesse caught the bird tuned in to a soap opera, his head cocked curiously.

"Hi, guys," Jesse said, as he passed. Barney and Sally didn't know that in the real world, lizards and birds weren't supposed to be friends. Although Jesse's woodsy home boasted plenty of greenery and primitive artifacts, it was hardly a jungle. Barney and Sally had been hand raised in captivity.

Turning the corner, he strode into the kitchen. Uneven stacks of dirty dishes cluttered the chopping-block counters. He blew a windy sigh and filled the sink with warm water, adding a fair amount of soap. Dissolving dried pancake syrup and crusty chili would take some elbow grease. He wasn't the sort to ignore chores, household or otherwise, but his organized existence had gone to hell and back since he'd set eyes on Tricia again.

Keeping busy was important, he decided, and pacing the floor with cigars in his pocket wouldn't do. He might be a new father, but his son wasn't an infant. Dillon Hawk was eleven years old. And although it wrenched his heart, he couldn't blame the boy for being apprehensive about meeting him. Apparently Dillon respected his mother enough to stand up for her honor, something a young brave had the right to do.

He dunked another set of dishes and wondered how he and Tricia were going to tackle friendship. It was, of course, Jesse's only option if he wanted a healthy relationship with his son.

What was the boy like? he wondered. Was he tall for his age? Dark or fair in coloring? Shy? Outgoing? Did he wear his baseball caps reversed, or did he avoid hats altogether? What television shows did he watch? Was there a girl in the neighborhood he had a painful crush on, or was Tricia the only female who had yet to influence his life?

As Jesse scoured a frying pan, he tried to envision the items on Tricia's shiny black desk. Had there been a framed photograph he'd missed—a snapshot of his son? He'd been too keyed up to even think about searching for a picture, much less grill Tricia for sentimental facts.

Her secret had blinded him from anything but rage. Damn her for not telling him about their baby—for making him miss the first eleven years of his son's life. She knew how badly he had wanted children, how he longed for a family of his own. But Jesse had given up on that dream soon after Tricia's betrayal. Children meant a wife, and a wife meant falling in love—something he never intended to do again. Sure, maybe the weak part of him had never quit missing Tricia, but the other side, the proud, willful side, had suffered from her disloyalty—almost to the point of hating her for it. And now, God help him, he had no choice but to befriend her.

A deafening sound drew Jesse's attention. He dried his hands and went back into the living room where Barney had decided to blast the volume on the TV.

Having abandoned the iguana, the African gray patrolled the coffee table, protecting the remote control like an armed guard.

"Come on, pal, that's too loud." Jesse reached for the remote, then scolded Barney when the parrot went for his hand. "Don't even think about."

Barney ducked his head in what looked like shame. Jesse set the volume on mute and grinned at his feathered friend. "Want to learn a new word?"

The bird stepped closer, inching its beak toward the remote in Jesse's hand. He hid the device behind his back. "No TV. A new word."

"Cochise," Barney squawked.

"Cochise is outside with the other dogs." Although some would disagree, Jesse believed parrots did more than mimic. They were extremely intelligent birds, and Barney knew that Cochise was the dog that shared their home.

"Dill-on," Jesse said, emphasizing each syllable.

He wanted Barney to learn his son's name, as he intended to introduce Dillon to all of his pets—hopefully soon. While the bird listened, Jesse sat on the edge of the coffee table and continued to repeat the name in a slow, patient tone.

A short time later, the African gray fluffed his feathers. "Hello, Jesse."

Jesse smiled. Was Barney's parrot-voice spiced with an Oklahoma twang, or was that his imagination? "Dillon," Jesse coaxed once again. "Hello, Dillon."

"Hello, Jesse," came the quick reply.

No. No. No. "Hello, Dillon."

Barney bobbed his head. "Hello, Jesse. Hello."

Jesse set the remote down. "We'll try later, okay?"

"Okay." The bird repeated the familiar word, then pecked at the buttons until he discovered sound once again.

Jesse's mind drifted back to his son. Would he meet Dillon
tonight, or would the child refuse an introduction until he felt
certain his parents had worked through their differences? He
removed Tricia's business card from his pocket and gazed at
the address she'd written. What would Dillon think of him?
Jesse wondered as he studied the card. Would he fit the boy's
image of a father? Or would Dillon be expecting someone
suave and sophisticated, like the kind of men Tricia probably
dated?

Jesse combed his fingers through his hair. He couldn't enter
his son's home for the first time empty-handed. He should
bring the boy a gift. But what? He had no idea what would
interest an eleven-year-old, especially one born into wealth.
Dillon probably had every video game and computer software
available, not to mention sports equipment. The thought
nagged him. How was he going to compete with Tricia's
money?

You're not even going to try, a sensible voice in his head
said. Parents shouldn't compete for their child's affection.
Love comes from the heart, not the wallet.

Even so, he still intended to take his son a present. He felt
for the leather strap around his neck and reached under his
shirt for the medicine bag he'd worn since his own youth. Yes,
he'd take Dillon a gift.

And what about Tricia? Should he offer her something as
well? Flowers perhaps? She used to love sunflowers. Their
bright yellow heads always made her smile.

Jesse went back into the kitchen and began scanning the
phone book. He'd make dinner reservations first, then locate
a florist for the biggest, brightest sunflower arrangement he
could find. Tricia had given birth to his child, and for that he
should thank her.

"Hi, Elda." Patricia set her briefcase on the kitchen counter
and greeted her friend. She preferred to think of the nurturing
woman as a friend rather than an employee. Raymond Boyd
had hired Elda Yacabucci as a nanny for Dillon while Patricia
suffered the stigma of being an unwed mother in an affluent,

but narrow-minded, community. Patricia had protested at first, not wanting her son raised by nannies. But she'd given in soon enough when she'd realized Dillon needed care while she furthered her education.

The year Patricia and Dillon moved out of the Boyd mansion and into their own home, they'd taken Elda along, offering her accommodations in a guest house located on the property. These days, Elda did more cooking and cleaning than baby-sitting, but the older woman didn't seem to mind.

"Dillon's having a snack in the den," Elda offered, as she headed toward the laundry room, basket tucked against an ample hip. "I made lasagna for lunch, and now that boy's hungry again." Elda, a nonjudgmental woman who attended mass every Sunday and routinely wore her salt-and-pepper hair in a tidy bun, glanced back and sent Patricia a pleased smile. "I fixed him another plate."

Patricia returned the smile. For most kids a snack would consist of crackers and cheese or a piece of fruit, but then, Dillon wasn't most kids. He thrived on Elda's leftovers.

Patricia poured herself a cup of decaf and went to the room they referred to as the den. Dillon watched TV from the sofa, a tray of half-eaten food on a glass-topped coffee table. He appeared relaxed in the brightly lit surroundings, his feet tucked under him. Patricia didn't think dens should be dark and brooding, so she'd decorated the room with printed fabrics and blond woods. The pale decor suited the rest of the house with its high ceilings and whitewashed walls.

"Hi, honey."

He turned away from the TV. "Oh, hi, Mom. You're home kinda early."

Patricia sat in a recliner and placed her coffee on a nearby end table. No point in wasting time, she thought. "I came home to talk to you. I saw your father today. He stopped by the office." Barged in was more like it, but she'd have to withhold the more colorful details from Dillon.

The boy picked up a decorative pillow and twisted the end. "What did he want?"

"We talked about you, and then he invited me to dinner."

That, she decided, was certainly a simplified version of the emotional meeting.

Dillon's gray-blue eyes widened. "Dinner? Really? Are you going to go?"

"I thought it might be a good idea." She sipped the mocha-flavored drink and tried to appear calmer than she felt. "He's trying to make an effort to be friends."

"Then I suppose you should go. Be kinda rude not to."

She nodded. Apparently that was Dillon's way of giving his permission. The thought relaxed her somewhat. "Do you think you'd like to meet your dad tonight? Maybe just say a quick hello?"

Fear crept into his eyes. "He's coming here? To our house?"

Clearly Dillon wasn't ready to face the man, the stranger, who had fathered him. "That's all right, honey. There's no hurry for you to meet him. You could stay at Elda's while he's here."

The boy had a different suggestion, one that said he wanted to hide out—avoid even the slightest chance of running into Jesse just yet. Apparently Elda's guest house was still too close. "Why don't I go to Grandpa's instead? I could spend the night there. Grandpa won't mind."

"Sure. That's fine." She could hardly blame Dillon for his panic. He'd been surrounded by a loving, familiar support group. And now, as he neared the beginning of adolescence, his missing father had returned, stirring raw emotion.

Patricia rolled her shoulders. "I guess I'll go up and take a shower." Or turn on the jets in her tub and soothe the ache in her muscles and the edge in her nerves. She, too, was panicked about spending time with Jesse.

Jesse straightened his jacket and eyed the outside of Tricia's house with mounting anxiety. He'd never been completely comfortable in Arrow Hill, with its overly manicured yards and custom-built homes. The farther he'd traveled up the hill, the more uncomfortable he'd become. Maybe because the houses kept getting bigger, more extravagant. Jesse had always been a country boy at heart. A small ranch dwelling suited him fine.

Tricia's sprawling two-story home was modern in design, with large bay windows and plenty of shrubbery illuminated by torchlights. He rang the bell, hoping his appearance would meet with Dillon's approval. Jesse had banded his hair into a ponytail and wore dark jeans, a tan shirt and black jacket. He wasn't a fancy man and never would be, but he had a frame that well suited the cut of Western-style clothing.

"Hi." Tricia opened the door. "Come in."

He stepped into the tiled entryway, feeling suddenly foolish. A man as tall and dark as he, carrying a bright yellow bouquet, probably looked a bit odd. He offered the sunflowers to Tricia quickly.

"I remembered that you used to like these," he said. "Hope you still do."

"They're wonderful. Thank you."

The familiarity in her smile made his heartbeat skip. And when she hugged the bouquet to her chest, she could have passed for a teenager again. But she wasn't, Jesse reminded himself. Tricia was a woman now. He devoured her long, lean form in one slow, agonizing sweep. An incredibly sexy woman. A white knit dress, laced with tiny silver threads, shimmied down her curves, then stopped to expose those endless legs and a pair of wicked pumps.

"You look terrific," he heard himself say.

"Thanks. So do you."

He followed her past a cream-colored living room and into a kitchen that sparkled with white counters and slick black appliances. Beside a tall window, four black chairs circled a contemporary white table. She arranged the sunflowers in an ebony vase and placed it on the table.

"Can I get you a drink?" she asked.

"No, thanks. Is Dillon here?"

"I'm sorry, no. He decided to spend the evening with his grandpa."

Immediately a rage of red-hot envy shot through Jesse's gut, turning his stomach inside out. "You mean your father?"

Tricia flashed a challenging look. "That's right. My father."

He wanted to turn and walk away, then hire a sharp, city attorney to legally pry his son from Raymond Boyd's child-stealing clutches. But that, he knew, would only end up hurting Dillon. Jesse would have to win the boy over with love and patience. Something he doubted Raymond Boyd was capable of offering. Boyd may have tainted Tricia with all that money, but Jesse would be damned if he'd lose his son to that cocky old bastard's checkbook.

"Why don't you give me a tour of the house," he suggested, in an attempt to redirect his focus. For Dillon's sake, he had to befriend Tricia, and arguing about her father would only cause a bigger rift between them.

Her expression softened. "All right."

The house was too modern for Jesse's taste, with too much glass and not enough wood. It was well crafted, he supposed, but it lacked the charm of older homes—the history and warmth. Tricia had chosen pale colors throughout, so when they stepped into her bedroom the shock of royal blue pleased him, as did the stained-glass window. Jesse scanned the room and noticed traces of the slightly careless Tricia he remembered: an open book, facedown on a nightstand, a coffee cup with lipstick stains, a discarded silk robe on the bed.

The rest of the house was proper, he realized, decorated to entertain those in her father's staid circle. But Tricia's bedroom rebelled from that mold—mixing bright colors and slightly scuffed antiques. She had even tossed in a trio of Western relics including a small wooden chair upholstered in calfskin, an ancient clay pot and a leather-covered trunk.

"This is nice," he said, trying hard not to picture her slipping into that big bed at night, French lingerie barely covering smooth, creamy flesh.

"Thanks. It's my sanctuary. The bathroom, too. Sometimes I work incredibly long hours so soaking in a whirlpool tub really takes the edge off."

Great. Now he imagined her completely naked, immersed in a tub of bubbling water, eyes closed, legs slightly parted.

Get a grip, he told himself. She's not your lover anymore.

Jesse turned away from the bathroom, struggling to ignore the hunger, the curiosity that had surfaced. What sort of lover had Tricia become? Was she still a sexually shy girl playing the sophisticate? Would she blush if he whispered his fantasies in her ear, or would she flash a siren's smile and rake her nails across his back? Maybe a little of both, he decided, watching the graceful way she moved. Tricia was a lady through and through. But ladies, even the most properly bred, could be naughty at night.

He caught Tricia's eye. She stood beside an antique dresser, head tilted, silky brown hair brushing her cheek. An almost-shy siren, he concluded, the kind of woman who could make a man beg.

"Jesse," she said impatiently. "You're not listening. I asked you a question."

He swallowed. "What? I'm sorry, were you talking to me?"

She held out a square object. "Do you want to see a picture of Dillon?"

Immediately his heartbeat doubled. "Oh, God, yes." Their son. The child they had created.

He strode toward her and took the framed photograph from her hands.

"It's fairly recent," she told him. "Last year's school picture. He'll be in sixth grade next semester."

Jesse traced the boy's face—a face, he noticed, that looked remarkably like his own. Younger, softer, but his just the same: deep-set eyes, high, slanted cheekbones, a jaw that would grow more square with age. And there was Tricia in him, too: the regal tilt of his head, silky hair a rich shade of brown, nostrils that flared with a smile.

"He's perfect," Jesse said. "He's us, both of us."

She nodded, her eyes a bit glazed. Watery. A mother's pride, Jesse assumed, pleased by Tricia's outward emotion for their child.

"Come on. I'll show you Dillon's room. I'm sure he won't mind. He keeps it spotless." She smiled and blinked away the glaze. "Unlike me. If I didn't have a housekeeper, my room would be a disaster."

"Yeah. You always were a little messy." Just enough to mar that charm-school image, he thought. He used to like how she'd leave her sweater on a chair or kick her shoes into a corner.

"And your son is just like you," she said, as he followed her down the hall. "Everything in its place."

"Oh, yeah? You should have seen my kitchen today. It…" They stepped into Dillon's room and Jesse forgot his last thought, letting his words drift.

The first thing he noticed were the models—airplanes, cars, ships—each one displayed on a wooden shelf and angled just so. A desk, a computer, a small television and a stereo system dominated one side of the spacious room, a bed and oak dresser the other. The double bed was framed with a sturdy headboard and covered with a quilt reminiscent of an Indian blanket. Jesse touched the colorful fabric, suddenly feeling closer to the child he'd yet to meet.

"He picked out that bedspread," Tricia said. "And all the oak furniture, too."

Jesse reached under his shirt and removed his medicine bag. "I want Dillon to have this." He slipped the worn leather pouch over a post on his son's headboard.

Tricia moved closer. "But that's your protection."

"And now it will be his." A person rarely offered his personal medicine to another, but Jesse wanted to give his son a spiritual piece of himself. "He doesn't have to wear it if he doesn't want to." Just knowing the bag and its contents would be in the child's room were enough. Modern-day spirit bags were often kept in homes, cars, purses, backpacks. "And tell him it's okay to touch the objects inside and add his own special items. He can even remove things if he wants to." He ran his fingers over the leather. Jesse had made the bag when he was about Dillon's age; stitched the buckskin and cut the fringe.

"Are you going to start another bag for yourself?" Tricia asked, as though tuned in to his thoughts.

"I don't think so." An inner awareness told him that that pouch had the power to benefit him still; protect him and his son.

"Thank you," she whispered. "For giving Dillon such a special gift."

Jesse released the leather and watched the fringe dance. He looked up at Tricia. She stood silent, her gaze following his every move. He glanced away. The moment felt too intimate, he realized. Much too tender between him and the woman who had broken his heart. Jesse squared his shoulders. He would keep his vow to befriend Tricia, but nothing more.

"We should leave for the restaurant," he said in a polite yet unemotional tone.

She turned away, her voice equally detached. "I'll get my jacket."

The Captain's Inn sat on a hilltop, presenting a view of Marlow County. Jesse had never eaten there before, but knew Tricia was accustomed to its fine linen tablecloths and nautical decor. She nibbled on a hearts-of-romaine salad while he spooned into a bowl of clam chowder.

Jesse preferred casual dining, since things like choosing the correct fork to use still managed to elude him. But proper fork or not, lobster tail, he remembered, was one of Tricia's favorite meals, and The Captain's Inn was the only restaurant in Marlow County that served lobster. A sense of masculine satisfaction washed over him. This time around, he could afford to take Tricia out for a pricey dinner that included a bottle of good wine. Jesse couldn't tell by the taste, but since the waiter had suggested it, he assumed the chardonnay was a decent vintage.

"Does Dillon like school?" he asked. So far they'd kept the conversation centered on their son.

She tilted her head as though mentally forming an answer. "He does now. But he didn't always." She raised the napkin from her lap and dabbed her lips. "By the second grade, Dillon wasn't keeping up with his peers anymore. He could barely read."

A knot of guilt formed in Jesse's chest. "Is he like me? Did he inherit my—"

Tricia interrupted gently. "Learning disabilities aren't always hereditary, but yes, Dillon has been diagnosed as dyslexic."

Jesse pushed his soup away. He knew how painful elementary school could be for a child who couldn't read. For a while Jesse had slipped through the cracks, pouring all of his youthful energy into finding ways to hide his disability. And being a foster child who'd gone from home to home and school to school, he'd played the game well. But anonymity hadn't lasted forever. Eventually the other students poked fun and called him "dumb," while teachers began complaining to his foster parents that he wasn't trying hard enough. By the time he'd been diagnosed with dyslexia, he was a quiet, somewhat brooding loner.

"So how did you handle it with Dillon?" Jesse asked, still feeling responsible for his child's disability. Why, damn it, did that gene have to surface?

"At first I looked into enrolling him in a special school," Tricia responded. "There are a few private schools that specialize in educating dyslexic children. None are particularly close by, but I was willing to commute." She sipped her water and continued, "But I ended up hiring tutors instead. Dillon wanted to go to school with his friends, with the kids he'd known since kindergarten."

For once Jesse was grateful for Tricia's money. Hiring tutors was a luxury most families couldn't afford, and he was certain Tricia had found the most qualified educators available. "So he's doing okay now?"

"Much better." She smiled. "And Dillon and I are both involved in a nonprofit organization that educates parents and schools about learning disabilities. We've organized quite a few fund-raisers." Her smile faded. "I remember how difficult it was for you, Jesse. I never forgot the things you told me."

He wanted to change the subject, but knew that would seem disrespectful to Dillon—the child burdened with his father's disability. Jesse knew firsthand how being dyslexic would affect Dillon for the rest of his life.

"I joined a dyslexic support group in college. It really helped to know there were others out there."

Her eyes brightened. "Our chapter has been talking about organizing adult support groups. Maybe you could get involved."

"Yeah, maybe." He toyed with his spoon. Should he admit that Tricia had been instrumental in his decision to join a support group? That he'd missed her encouragement, her early-morning tutoring sessions?

Their waiter came by, removed their plates and offered another basket of warm bread. Grateful for the interruption, Jesse decided to skip the admission, choosing to comment on the view instead.

"Pretty out, isn't it?" Their table faced a large window. Lights twinkled in the dark, making the dusty flats of Hatcher and the rolling green of Arrow Hill seem like equals.

She gazed out the window and nodded, but when she turned back, a trio of men being seated at the table across from them captured her attention. Jesse tightened his upper lip. One of the men, a trim, executive type, eyed Tricia as he passed.

"Do you know him?" Jesse asked under his breath when she had the audacity to show her discomfort. Tricia, who rarely revealed her emotions.

"Peter is a business associate. An attorney."

Jesse glanced over at Peter and caught a quick, hard stare in return. A territorial stare. Clearly the young, impeccably dressed lawyer had designs on Tricia. Business associate my foot, Jesse thought. Any fool could see Tricia was dating the guy. Why else would she be so damn edgy? She'd been caught in what seemed like a compromising situation—a candlelit dinner with another man, a roughneck, no less.

Great. Just what he needed, some suave boyfriend of hers giving him the evil eye all night. Jesse had the sudden urge to rearrange the guy's snooty face. Peter looked to be the country club sort—proper, well-bred—a man who knew which wine to order and which fork to use.

Jesse clenched his fists as the waiter brought their entrées. Was Tricia sleeping with Peter? Had that jerk touched her with those manicured hands? Jesse unclenched his fists and gazed at his own hands, at their crude texture. Had Tricia compared them as lovers? Weighed them against each other in her mind?

Jesse cut into his halibut and decided he didn't give a rat's ass if he was using the proper utensil. And Mr. Country Club in the pinstripe suit could take his silk tie and shove it where the sun refused to shine.

Tricia could tear up the sheets with whoever the hell she wanted. Jesse had no intention of resuming their love affair. None whatsoever. So what if she still made his heart hurt? That didn't mean a damn thing. He stole another bitter glance at Peter. Not a damn thing.

Four

——

Patricia and Jesse stood beneath an archway outside the restaurant and waited for the valet to bring Jesse's truck. He drove one of those huge four-wheelers decked out with a shiny black paint job, enormous tires and flashy rims. A masculine vehicle, Patricia thought, one that suited his rugged appeal.

"Looks like it may be a while," he said. "There are quite a few people ahead of us."

She nodded. "It's a popular restaurant." And tonight they appeared to be short a valet.

He moved closer as an elderly couple brushed by en route to their BMW. "I guess the wait won't kill us."

Patricia caught a woodsy note of Jesse's cologne. She thought their "friendship" dinner had gone fairly well, aside from Jesse's quiet mood swings and intermittent scowls. But then he had always been sullen, a manner that matched his dark, dangerous appearance. Even as a lean, catlike youth, he still had that hard, feral charm—an edge that made women hungry and other men wary.

"Your boyfriend and his buddies just came out."

"What?" Patricia glanced over her shoulder. Peter Crandall sent her a practiced smile. She turned back quickly. "He's not my boyfriend."

"Bull."

Agitated, she straightened her spine. "Don't you dare pair me with that gold digger." She'd had the misfortune of being seated next to Peter Crandall at two long, dull charity dinners, and now the man phoned her office and sent roses. Roses. How unimaginative.

"Gold digger?" Jesse's mouth twitched into a smile.

"This isn't funny. I'm tired of men pursuing me for my father's money."

Jesse kept his voice low. "Hell, I figured you were sleeping with the guy."

Offended now, Patricia turned to face her ex-love and hissed beneath her breath. "How dare you think such a thing? I don't fall into bed with every man who looks my way. What kind of woman do you take me for?"

She hadn't fallen into bed with anyone since Jesse left town, but he didn't need to know the details about her nonexistent sex life. Like a fool, she'd remained faithful for years after his departure. The thought irked her. While she'd tucked their child into bed at night and waited for Jesse's return, he was probably rolling around with some bouncy, big-busted coed. Patricia cursed her stupidity. By the time she'd accepted the fact that he wasn't coming back, she'd become accustomed to sleeping alone.

He slipped a strand of her hair behind her ear. "Sorry, okay? How was I supposed to know? Peter looks like your type."

She sighed. Since when did she like fair-haired men with country-club tans? "It just seems like he's everywhere I go."

Jesse's eyes darkened. "Do you think he's stalking you?"

"No. We just run in the same circle. He comes from old money, only his playboy father lost most of their fortune in gambling debts. So now Peter intends to marry and rebuild the family dynasty."

"With his wife's inheritance," Jesse added.

Patricia nodded. And Peter had made subtle references to her past, as though her having an illegitimate child meant she was easy pickings. "I wish he would set his sights on someone else."

"So you want to get rid of him?"

"Of course I do."

"Then put your arms around me."

She glanced back at Peter. He was watching. "We're going to make him think we're lovers?"

"That's right. Lovers."

Suddenly she felt decadent, but then why wouldn't she? Jesse Hawk had that immoral effect on women. She stepped closer, lifted her arms and drew them around his neck, telling herself this was all for show.

"Now what?" she whispered, as her heart skipped an unsteady beat.

"Brush your lips over mine," he coaxed. "Kind of slow and sexylike."

She slid her fingers through his ponytail, through that thick, gorgeous mass of dark hair. He had hair on his chest, too. Just enough to play with, she recalled. "What about all these people?" Couples and small groups waiting, some impatiently, for their vehicles.

"What about them?"

"They'll watch."

Jesse shook his head. "They might glance our way, but they're too proper to stare. Peter, on the other hand, has a stake in this."

She cupped the back of Jesse's head and drew his face closer at the same moment he slid his hands under her jacket, chasing chills up her spine. Their lips met in a soft, sensual tease. Patricia closed her eyes, felt his mouth move against hers.

Were they kissing? she wondered. Or was this a prelude to a kiss? An erotic taunt of man, woman and warm aroused breaths?

He tested the seam of her lips with his tongue as images

from the past clouded her mind. He used to do wicked things to her with that tongue—things that made her body quiver and her skin tingle. Things that embarrassed her afterward.

She wouldn't be shy now. Patricia was no longer a gullible, inexperienced teenager. No, she realized ironically, she was a grown woman who'd barely survived a broken heart—an inexperienced thirty-year-old.

Damn him, she thought, moving closer, wanting to feel the ridge in his jeans. Maybe she would still blush. Or maybe she'd run her hands all over that hard, virile body and make Jesse Hawk beg for mercy. Make him miss her the way she'd missed him.

Angry, Patricia plunged her tongue into his mouth and tugged a little viciously on his hair. He kissed her back, meeting her defiant strokes lustily. But much too quickly he pulled back and caught his breath. For Patricia the kiss ended the way it had begun, like unprotected sex—exciting and risky. She wanted more.

While she struggled to rein in her hormones, Jesse leaned forward again and pressed his lips to her ear. "You did well," he whispered, his voice tinged with arousal. "Now Peter will think we're headed to some cheap motel to tear each other's clothes off."

Patricia sobered immediately. Somehow she'd forgotten all about Peter Crandall. Forgotten why she had agreed to kiss Jesse.

Mortified, she tugged her jacket closed, hiding her distended nipples. How could she have gotten so carried away? In public, no less, standing in front of one of the most prestigious establishments in Arrow Hill.

She dared a quick glance around. The crowd had lessened, but not enough to her liking. She felt like a first-class slut. Her. The woman who hadn't had sex in twelve years.

Jesse reached for her hand. "Perfect timing. The truck's here."

Perfect timing for whom? She had to climb into that enormous beast. Last time there hadn't been a curious army watching.

The valet opened her door, but Jesse gave the young man a tip and sent him on his way. "I'll help her up."

He held Patricia's waist while she attempted to keep her balance and her hemline down at the same time. She failed. Miserably. Her dress hiked just as her bottom hit the seat.

Jesse stood staring at the tops of her thigh-high hose. She pulled the dress down and glared at him. "Shut the door."

He blinked and lifted his gaze. "Huh?"

"The door. Close it."

"Oh. Sorry."

He hopped into the driver's seat with ease, but he wasn't wearing a short skirt and high heels. If she were in a better mood, that ridiculous visual would have made her laugh. But as it was, she'd checked her humor at the curb.

He turned toward her. "How do those things stay up like that?"

She snapped the seat belt into place. "What things?"

"Your nylons."

Good God. "They just do. Now will you drive?" She wanted to put as much distance between The Captain's Inn and herself as possible.

He kicked the truck into gear and pulled out of the parking lot. "Are they uncomfortable?"

Patricia rolled her eyes. Men and their weird obsessions. "Why? Are you in the market for a pair of hose?"

"Yeah, if they've got legs like yours attached." He stopped at a red light and flashed a naughty country-boy smile, his gaze melting over her like a pad of honey-flavored butter.

An unwelcome heat settled between her thighs. That sexy smile had probably seduced half the women in Tulsa. She'd be damned if she'd let it work on her. "Don't act like a stallion in the process of mounting a mare, Jesse. It's ungentlemanly."

His smile faded. "Hey, you're the one who wore that skimpy dress."

Did he have any idea how much designer fashions cost these days? "This is a perfectly respectable garment."

"It's short," he challenged. "And tight."

Patricia stared straight ahead. "Is that why you thought you had the right to make that crack about cheap motels?"

He pulled the truck over, cut the engine and killed the lights in one angry motion. They were in the residential area of Arrow Hill, parked in front of a large limestone house that belonged to a doctor her father golfed with occasionally.

"As I recall," he said in a low, seething tone. "You were the one who jammed your tongue down my throat."

She raised her hand to slap him, but he caught her wrist and cuffed it with a deadly grip. "You're a spoiled brat, Tricia. How the hell I'm ever going to be friends with you, I'll never know."

"You're just acting like this because you want to sleep with me," she blurted out, jerking her arm free.

Her words managed to silence them both. Too late to bite them back, she thought, as Jesse turned away. He knew she'd spoken the truth. And she was certain he knew she craved him, too. Somehow, they'd rekindled an unwanted sexual attraction—a need they couldn't fill.

He drove her home, without a response. Patricia refused his offer to help her exit his truck, so, to avoid breaking her neck, she removed her shoes before climbing out. She walked to the front door in her stocking feet, and upon entering the house, heard his truck roll out of the driveway.

They would have to see each other again, she realized with an emotional sigh. They had a child to consider and twelve years of pain that could never be forgotten.

The following evening Patricia sat across from Dillon in the kitchen, watching her son study the leather pouch Jesse had left behind. Dillon had returned from his grandfather's house not more than twenty minutes before. He'd found the gift and brought it downstairs.

"So the stuff inside is medicine?" he asked, handling the worn buckskin carefully.

She nodded. Although she had a limited knowledge of Jesse's culture, she knew enough for a simple explanation. "Yes, but it's not drugstore medicine. People place items in a spirit bag that are special to them, objects they feel will protect them in some way. Everyone's bag contains something different.''

"So what's in this one?"

"I don't know, but your father said it was okay for you to open it. He also said you could remove anything you wanted to, and put your own special items inside."

"I don't think I want to open it." He placed the bag on the table, fingering the beaded pattern in the center. "It looks kind of old. Like my dad's had it a long time."

A swell of pride warmed her heart. Clearly Dillon respected the gift he'd been given, honored it in his own youthful way. Most kids would have dumped the contents onto the table without the slightest regard for their sentimental value. "Your dad made that bag when he was about your age."

And Jesse had worn it always, Patricia recalled, even when they'd made love. Although the pouch served as a spiritual totem, it had also been like an extension of Jesse's physical being. She was glad Dillon had it now. It seemed right somehow.

Patricia tried not to think about how her dinner with Jesse had ended, or what a distraction he'd become. She'd had the most unproductive day of her life. She'd gone into work and stared at the office walls, returning only a few mandatory calls. Luckily her father hadn't witnessed her slump, since he'd taken the day off to be with Dillon. In the last few years Raymond Boyd spent most of his time engaging in recreational activities. Patricia assumed that was his way of gearing up for retirement, as well as preparing her to take his place.

"Are my dad's feelings hurt?" Dillon asked, jarring Patricia from her thoughts.

"You mean because you don't want to meet him?"

"Uh-huh."

She studied her son's serious expression. "Your father was orphaned when he was only two. Besides a brother in California, you're his only family. So I would imagine he's hurting. But he's also willing to give you the time you need."

"I think I should meet him," the boy said. "As long as

you'll be there, Mom. I don't want to hang out with him all by myself.''

"Of course I'll be there." Patricia smiled. It seemed as though Jesse's medicine had touched Dillon already, opened a small door between father and son. Yesterday Dillon had panicked, but tonight he'd made a mature decision, even if he was still afraid. "When do you think we should have this meeting?" she asked him.

"I don't know. This weekend, maybe. Does he have weekends off?"

She had no idea what Jesse's schedule was like. "I could stop by his house before work tomorrow and find out." She could call, of course, but that would be the coward's way. And Patricia had never been a coward. "Maybe I could invite him to a picnic. We could meet at the park." A neutral place surrounded by tall trees, fuzzy squirrels and ducks gliding across a man-made pond.

"Okay." Dillon picked up the medicine bag. "Elda could fry some chicken and make potato salad."

"Sure, I'll talk to her after I see your dad." Dillon's former nanny prepared all of their meals, so it was only natural for him to suggest Elda's fried chicken. Patricia had never learned to cook. Scrambling eggs and boiling hot dogs, she could handle. Beyond that, she didn't have a clue.

Dillon put the leather pouch in his pocket and went to the refrigerator. He poured a glass of milk and looked back at his mom. "Did my dad give you those flowers?"

Patricia reached for the sunflower arrangement. "Yes, he did."

"So you're friends now, right?"

Friends? No. They were ex-lovers caught between hunger and hatred. "We're working on it," she answered, then changed the subject hastily. "Do you want to go into town for a hot-fudge sundae? I'm dying for dessert." She needed to sink her mouth into something rich and creamy, something that would curb her craving for Jesse.

"Sure." Dillon abandoned his milk. "But I have to get my shoes."

"No problem. I need my purse." She followed her son upstairs, her mind straying once again to Jesse—the man she'd never really gotten over.

The next morning Jesse stared at the reception area in his clinic. Good Lord. He'd attempted to unlock the door, only to find Fiona had beat him to it. And now he could do nothing but gape, his jaw feeling as though it were inches from the floor.

She smiled, her red bouffant higher than usual this bright summer day.

He closed his mouth. "You redecorated?" Stupid question, he thought. The clinic looked as though a litter of dalmatians had befriended a jungle cat.

A tiger-print valance decorated the top of each window, and the vinyl chairs, formerly all white, wore black doggy spots. Framed pictures of well-known cartoon animals littered the walls.

Fiona began arranging a tall display stocked with rawhide chews and squeaky toys. "It looks great, doesn't it?"

The wall display looked just fine, but he knew she meant her other handiwork. "It's...colorful," he managed to say, forcing a smile. She looked so pleased with herself, he couldn't bear to burst her bubble. Maybe his clients would appreciate her efforts. The place did have charm—in an animated sort of way.

"I'll have to bring Barney in," Jesse said. "He'll feel right at home."

Fiona adjusted her glasses. "Barney?"

"My parrot. He loves cartoons. Watches TV all day."

She beamed. "He sounds delightful. Just delightful."

As the front door opened, they both turned to see a sleek brunette walk into the room, black heels clicking on the sterile white floor.

Jesse's heart took a sudden leap. Tricia.

He couldn't think of anything to say. Last night Tricia had accused him of wanting to sleep with her, and this morning there she stood—his living, breathing, walking fantasy. Of course he wanted to sleep with her. What man wouldn't? Especially a guy like himself, he decided, who had already known her touch. Unfortunately, twelve years didn't seem all that long to his libido.

"Oh, my." Fiona's Southern drawl interrupted the silence. "Don't you look lovely, Patricia." The older lady turned toward Jesse. "Doesn't she look lovely?"

His gaze locked with Tricia's. "Yeah. Lovely."

Sexy would have been his word choice—long-legged Tricia decked out in another of her classy business suits. This one, a striking emerald-green, sported simple gold buttons. The jacket hugged her waist, and the skirt rode several inches above her knees. Jesse's blood warmed. Was she wearing those thigh-high nylons underneath?

Tricia broke their riveting stare. "You look lovely yourself," she said, turning to Fiona with a smile. "It's been ages since we've seen each other."

Of course it had, Jesse thought. Fiona Lee Beaumont and Patricia Ann Boyd didn't dine at the same restaurants or shop in the same stores. The eccentric Cat Lady and the richest girl in Arrow Hill came from different worlds.

"I work for Jesse now," Fiona responded, her smile equally friendly. "And I'd offer you a seat, but the paint's not dry."

Tricia glanced at the spotted chairs. "That's all right. I don't intend to stay long. I just stopped by to talk to Jesse for a few minutes." She continued to study the chairs. "I assume he put you in charge of decorating."

"Fiona surprised me," Jesse offered before the elderly woman could respond.

Tricia met his gaze once again, only this time with a spark of amusement in her eye. "You did a wonderful job," she told Fiona. "Very clever, painting the chairs."

"Why, thank you." The older lady patted her starched bouffant. "Always had a flair for the arts."

Jesse stole a glance at the chairs, hoping that shiny black paint wouldn't eventually rub off on people's behinds. Spotted butts weren't exactly the rage.

After the women exchanged a few more pleasantries, Jesse

excused himself and Tricia, then escorted her to the break room for some privacy.

Playing the proper host, he poured two cups of coffee, offered her cream and sugar, and watched while she sweetened her drink. She took a sip and placed the cup on the card table that dominated the small room.

He wondered if she'd come by to address their strange relationship—enforce some rules for future "friendship" dinners, like keeping their hands and their mouths off each other. Would he be able to follow those rules? Sexual spontaneity wasn't Jesse's usual style, but with Tricia he found himself acting on impulse and not liking it one damn bit. That's why he hadn't responded to her accusation last night. She'd damaged his heart, yet he still wanted to sleep with her. What did that say about his character?

Tricia seated herself in a fold-out chair and crossed her legs, her voice as feminine as the silky blouse beneath her jacket. "Fiona is a gem, isn't she? I always liked her."

Jesse lifted his cup and sipped the hot brew in an attempt to act casual. He hadn't expected small talk, but he'd play it Tricia's way. She didn't need to know those legs of hers had become his obsession, that visualizing them wrapped around his waist was a fantasy he couldn't seem to shake.

Besides, he had to agree, Fiona was a gem. The nutty old lady was fast becoming his dearest friend. "Yeah, she's a doll, but I nearly had a heart attack this morning when I came in and saw the waiting room."

"I'll bet."

A smile brightened Tricia's face. God, she was pretty, he thought. A classic beauty who wore her sensuality with style and grace. Jesse scrubbed his hand across his jaw. Damn her. Why didn't she just get to the point?

"So is the clinic officially open yet?" she asked.

More small talk? Jesse struggled to keep his cool. Offering her coffee had been a mistake. People tended to linger over coffee. Her legs and his libido weren't good company over a steaming cup of Java. "No. I had to reorder some supplies that never arrived. And besides that, I've been busy on ranch calls. I picked up some new accounts since I came to town. Nothing major, just some recreational riders, but every little bit helps.''

"You always did love horses. I should have known you'd specialize in equine care.''

"Yeah.'' And last night she'd accused him of acting like a stallion in the process of mounting a mare. "What's on your mind, Tricia? Why did you stop by?''

"I was getting to that,'' she said, rising to stand on those gorgeous limbs. "I was hoping you had time for a picnic this weekend.''

"A picnic?''

"Dillon wants to meet you.''

Immediately Jesse's heart soared into parental heaven as a smile spilt across his face. "A picnic sounds great.'' He reached out to touch to her hand. "I promise I'll be a good dad.''

She brushed his knuckles. "I'm sure you will, Jesse. But you have to remember how much time has passed. You can't expect a relationship to develop overnight.''

He nodded. Jesse knew how much time had passed, and he also knew it was Tricia who had kept him from being a father to his son. Forgiving her, even for Dillon's sake, might not be possible. So wanting to make love to her again, he decided, was sheer insanity. Tackling friendship would be challenge enough. He turned his back and rinsed his coffee cup. More than enough.

Five

On Saturday afternoon Jesse sat beneath a shady tree in Arrow Pond Park, Cochise lolling at his side.

"I'm nervous," he told the dog. More nervous than he'd ever been in his life.

Cochise lifted his head, then nudged Jesse's knee as though offering comfort. Jesse stroked the rottweiler's coat. He'd brought the dog along for moral support. Waiting by himself would have been far too lonely.

Cochise was attached to a leash, although the rotty was much too well behaved to run off. The park did seem a bit lax about the animals-on-leashes rule. Jesse noticed a few mutts were loose, trotting playfully after their families. But Cochise didn't look like most mutts. The rottweiler was built like a prizefighter, his head the size of a basketball. Jesse chuckled. Most folks cleared the sidewalk when they saw Cochise coming. Little did they know the big dog would have whined at their feet if given half the chance.

Jesse gazed at Cochise. The rotty perked up his ears in response. Did they look alike? Supposedly dog owners were notorious for choosing breeds that resembled their own appearance.

"Tricia probably thinks I'm a dog," Jesse said. He knew she was as hurt and angry over their past as he. Supposedly she had expected him to return after college to prove his worth to Raymond Boyd, yet she had kept their baby a secret. That made no sense.

He turned his attention to the pond, to the ripple of sunlight shooting across the water. This was not the time to dwell on his dispute with Tricia. This perfect summer day belonged to Dillon.

As though his mind had conjured their images, Jesse turned to see a slim brunette in the distance, a young boy at her side. "Oh, God, they're here."

When Jesse hopped up, so did Cochise. The rotty waited patiently as Jesse took a deep, cleansing breath and tried his damnedest to look dadlike.

He gripped the dog's leash and strode in their direction, his focus on Dillon, on the boy's straight posture and somewhat baggy, casual clothes. He looked healthy, his hair longer and his skin darker than in the photograph Jesse had seen. Summer seemed to suit Dillon Hawk.

"Hi." Tricia spoke first as they came face-to-face. And although she made the introductions in a warm voice, they sounded odd. "Dillon, this is your dad. Jesse, this is Dillon."

Jesse dropped Cochise's leash and stepped forward a little as Dillon placed the basket he carried onto the ground. "It's nice to meet you," the child said, automatically extending his hand.

"I've been looking forward to today," Jesse responded, thinking how proper Dillon suddenly seemed. He shook the boy's hand and searched Dillon's face. The eleven-year-old glanced at him briefly, took his hand back, then lowered his gaze to the rottweiler. "That's Cochise," Jesse offered quickly. "He loves kids."

The rottweiler parked his butt in the grass and wiggled more than a professionally trained dog should. Jesse figured the dog had spotted the Frisbee poking out of the tote bag on Tricia's arm.

"He's pretty cool. Can I pet him?" Dillon asked.

"Sure." Jesse watched his son move toward the rotty. At least the boy liked his dog. So far Dillon still hadn't made direct eye contact with him.

"I saved us a shady spot," he told Tricia, relieving her of the oversize bag. "That's my blanket and ice chest over there."

"We brought a blanket, too."

"Oh."

Small talk, Jesse thought. He'd never been good at it. Naturally, Tricia was. She filled the awkward silence easily, taking charge in a non-intrusive manner.

"Why don't you take Cochise's leash," she suggested to their son, "and I'll carry the basket."

"Okay," Dillon answered, the rotty sniffing him happily.

The boy looked up at Tricia and sent her a smile Jesse wished had been for him. *You can't expect a relationship to develop overnight.* Although Tricia had warned him with those words, Jesse had hoped to bond instantly with his son.

They used both blankets to make their picnic area bigger. Tricia suggested lunch, but Dillon said he wasn't hungry yet, so they drank lemonade and talked about the weather, the ducks in the pond, the possible age of the trees. The forced conversation made Jesse uneasy since his son seemed to be avoiding him. The park buzzed with family activity, but Jesse doubted any was quite as uncomfortable as theirs. Then again, Tricia and Dillon were family. He was a stranger looking in. Would he always be the wayward father, an outsider struggling to find a place in his son's heart?

Cochise whined at the tote bag, then wagged his bobbed tail. "He wants to play Frisbee," Jesse said. "He already spotted it in the bag."

"I'll play with him," Dillon offered.

"Sure. Okay." Apparently dog and child wanted to escape. At this point, Jesse wasn't about to mention the park rule about dogs being leashed. He unhooked the leather strap from the rottweiler's collar.

Dillon turned to his mom. "It's okay with you, right?"

She smiled. "Of course."

"Cool." Dillon searched for the Frisbee that had fallen deeper into the bag. Cochise whined again, only louder this time.

"Go on," Jesse told the dog as Dillon stood, yellow disc in hand.

They tore off together, within sight but far enough away to have room to play.

Tricia drew her knees up and watched the activity. "Cochise sure is excited."

"Yeah. He's a Frisbee fanatic." Jesse watched, too, marveling at his son, at the sudden laughter spilling from the child as Cochise dived for the neon disc. "Dillon won't even look at me, Tricia."

She turned to face him. "Oh, Jesse. He's nervous. Scared to death, in fact. Here you are, this big, brawny man he's supposed to impress. And you do seem a little uptight. I'm sure he senses that."

"I'm not uptight. I'm—" he blew a frustrated breath "—just trying to act like a dad." Which was crazy since he'd never had a dad and didn't know how one should act. The death of his parents had left him alone from an early age. Being withdrawn was second nature, feeling like a stranger in other people's homes, with other people's families. He didn't know anything else. "I'm nervous, too. I want Dillon to like me."

She scooted closer. "He will if you relax. Just be yourself, Jesse."

Yeah, right. Easy for her to say. She'd always known who she was and where she'd come from. Roots, he thought. Tricia had established roots. Jesse's had yet to take hold.

"You look cute today," he told her. She rarely wore such casual clothes. The denim shorts and flowery cotton top gave her a girl-next-door appeal. Well, sort of. Those long, bare legs didn't quite fit that wholesome image.

For an instant she leaned against his shoulder. Half-tempted to keep her close, Jesse almost put his arm around her. But realizing he wasn't her husband, lover or boyfriend, he stopped himself. Their time together had ended years ago.

"Look at those two," Tricia said, gesturing toward Dillon and Cochise.

Jesse smiled. Dillon had invented a new game. Rather than throw the Frisbee toward Cochise, he would fling it in the opposite direction, then race the dog for it. The rotty never looked happier. The boy looked happy, too, his brown hair shining in the Oklahoma sunshine.

"He's a handsome kid," Jesse said.

"Of course he is." Tricia bumped his shoulder again. "He looks just like you."

A short while later, Dillon and Cochise returned. The child fell onto the blanket, the dog panting beside him. "A drink, Mom," Dillon said dramatically. "Hurry before I die."

Automatically Jesse filled a plastic cup with lemonade and handed it to Tricia. She passed it to Dillon. He leaned forward and guzzled the cold liquid while Tricia cautioned him to slow down. Jesse grinned. At that moment Tricia sounded like a typical mom. Dillon ignored her warning and drained the cup in record time.

Following suit, Cochise went to the water bowl Jesse had placed on the grass and lapped greedily. Afterward the exhausted rotty curled up at his master's feet.

"Do you think Cochise looks like me?" Jesse asked out loud. Tricia had called him big and brawny. The black-and-tan dog was big and brawny, too.

Tricia laughed. "Actually, Jesse, there is a resemblance." She turned to their son, moving so the boy would have an unobstructed view of his father. "Don't you think so?"

Dillon gazed at Jesse and their eyes met and held. Gray eyes, the same yet different. Dillon's were edged with blue. Oh, God, Jesse thought. He's looking at me, not through me, but at me.

Remembering what Tricia had said about Dillon being nervous, Jesse flashed his warmest smile. "You know, if Cochise resembles me, then he favors you, too. Your mom seems to think that you and I look alike.''

"Oh." Rather than return the smile, Dillon glanced down at his hands, openly uncomfortable.

Jesse swallowed. Damn. Apparently Dillon didn't want to compare his features with a man he'd just met. A stranger.

A stream of silence ensued, but this time Tricia didn't intervene. She sat quietly as well. Unsure of where to look, Jesse glanced up at the tree and caught sight of a squirrel scurrying up the bark. "Look! That little *eró* was spying on us."

Dillon and Tricia followed his gaze. Bright smiles lit their faces. Thank God for animals, Jesse thought. They'd always been his salvation.

"Why did you call it that funny name?" Dillon asked, watching the furry critter peer through the branches.

"*Eró?*" Jesse said, pronouncing the *r* with an *hl* sound. "That means squirrel in Muskokee. The *eró* teaches us about preparing ourselves for the future. They gather and store nuts the way we store information."

Appearing genuinely interested in the lesson, Dillon turned his attention to Cochise. "How do you say dog in Muskokee?"

"*Éfv.*" Jesse glanced at Cochise and grinned. The rotty was snoring. "And aside from teaching us how to sleep at a picnic, dogs carry the gift of loyalty. There's no creature more loyal than a dog."

"You're a veterinarian, huh?"

The question pleased Jesse. That Dillon cared enough to ask mattered. "Yeah. I just opened a clinic behind my house." Should he extend an invitation for his son to visit him at home, or was it too soon? Should he let Tricia talk to Dillon about it first?

As Jesse contemplated the answers, Dillon inched closer, then reached into his pocket and removed a familiar object.

Oh, God. Jesse's heart raced to keep up with his pulse. The medicine bag.

The eleven-year-old held out the bag. "I haven't opened it yet. I um…wasn't sure…"

"We can open it now," Jesse suggested, reaching for the pouch, his hand a little shaky. "Together."

Together. Patricia swallowed the lump in her throat. Jesse and Dillon were together at last. How many times had she dreamed of this moment, hoped for it? But reality, it seemed, never lived up to one's dreams. In Patricia's dreams, this meeting would have happened years ago. She knew Jesse had been angry when he'd left town, but regardless, he had promised to come back. Or that was how it had seemed to her.

You'll come back, won't you, Jesse?

Damn right, I will.

How pathetically naive she'd been. She had waited for Jesse, far longer than necessary, always making excuses: he was dyslexic so college would take him longer than most; he wouldn't return unless he was successful; he was waiting for the right moment.

As all the hurt and anger came rushing back, Patricia lifted her drink and sipped, telling herself now wasn't the time to rehash the past. Jesse was back, and more than willing to be a father. So what if he had never really loved her, that didn't mean he wouldn't love their son.

Patricia sat quietly while Jesse explained the meaning behind the objects in his medicine bag. Jesse had placed a bear claw in the bag because he believed his father's people were from the Bear Clan. His brother, Sky, however, preferred to think they had descended from the Wind Clan.

"But Sky is biased," Jesse told Dillon. "His wife's name is Windy. So he seems to think that's some sort of sign."

"Where did you get this?" Dillon asked, studying the claw.

"I found it in the woods, embedded in a tree. So that was like my sign. But I don't know if we'll ever find out what clan we're really from. No one around here seemed to know my parents very well. I guess they pretty much kept to themselves."

Sadness seeped into Jesse's tone, but Patricia noticed he brushed it away quickly. Clearly this moment with Dillon was too important for him to mar it with heartache.

She watched as Dillon examined his father's medicine: the tip of a hawk feather, a sprig of sage, a small collection of gemstones, a wallet-size picture. A newborn baby, Patricia noticed.

"This is Shawna," Jesse said, fingering the photograph. "She's my brother's daughter."

Dillon took the picture. "So Shawna's my cousin."

She heard the awe in her son's voice, understanding it well. She, too, had suffered the loneliness of being an only child, wishing for brothers, sisters, cousins and wild, wacky family reunions.

Patricia sighed. Jesse had called her spoiled, but she didn't view herself that way. Being raised on a private street had its drawbacks. So when her father had offered her and Dillon a permanent home in his mansion, she'd politely refused. She couldn't bear to have her son rattling around in that house the way she'd done, longing for companionship or a friendly neighbor, kids playing out front. Beautiful as the mansion was, it seemed hollow at times. Haunted. Not by ghosts, but by seclusion.

"What's in here?" Dillon asked Jesse, lifting a small square of waxed paper.

"That's...um—" Jesse reached for the object, then dropped his hand, as though the tiny package had the power to singe his fingers "—a lock of your mom's hair."

Patricia's heart soared to her throat. Jesse lifted his head and their eyes met.

All at once, a flood of conflicting emotions rushed through her. She had offered that small clipping because Jesse had held her close one afternoon, wishing he could keep a part of her with him forever. "I miss you when we're not together," he'd whispered. "God, Tricia, I love you so much."

When did you realize that you didn't really love me? she wanted to ask. That I was just an infatuation, a means to sate your youthful lust? And why on earth had he kept a lock of her hair tucked away in his medicine bag all these years? Surely he considered that bag much too sacred to house tro-

phies from his sexual conquests, so there had to be another
reason.

She held his stare. His uneasy stare. He'd forgotten about
it, she decided. Forgotten he had it until this awkward moment.

"That's yours now," Patricia told Dillon while she continued to hold Jesse's gaze.

Dillon slipped each item back into the pouch. "This is like
a time capsule or something. It's pretty rad."

Neither Jesse nor Tricia spoke. Dillon's words were all too
true. A time capsule. Pieces of their past. Painful mementos.
Jesse looked away, and Patricia wanted to scratch and scream,
push him to the ground and fight for her honor—win back
what he had taken from her. Not the lock of hair, but the love
it represented. She had given herself freely to him: heart, body
and soul. And now damn it, she wanted to destroy it all, every
glorious, painful memory.

Dillon stuffed the medicine bag back into his pocket. "Can
we eat now, Mom?"

"Of course, honey." She feigned a calm voice and proceeded to unpack lunch.

They ate fried chicken, potato salad and strawberry parfait
while Cochise gnawed on a barbecue-flavored rib bone Jesse
had brought along.

"Are you okay?" Dillon asked his mother as she picked at
her food.

Trust Dillon to sense her uneasiness. "I'm fine. I'm just not
all that hungry."

"The chicken's great," Jesse remarked. "You're quite a
cook."

Patricia balanced her plate on her lap. "I didn't make it.
Elda did. She's our housekeeper."

"Elda used to be my nanny," Dillon added. "But I don't
need one anymore."

"Yeah, I guess you're too old for that sort of thing." Jesse
smiled at his son, but when he turned toward Patricia, the
smile faded, telling her what he thought about Dillon being
raised with a nanny.

She sent him a defiant stare. ''Elda has become a very dear friend.''

He held her gaze. ''Well, she's a good cook. I'll say that much for her.''

''My mom's too busy to cook,'' Dillon said, as he took another helping of the strawberry parfait. ''She works really hard.''

Patricia's stomach clenched. Was Dillon making excuses for her or offering a show of support? Suddenly, not knowing how to fry chicken made her feel inadequate.

''She'd probably be a great cook if she had more time to learn how,'' Dillon offered, making Patricia aware of his motives.

Her son wasn't condemning her. He was building her up for his father's benefit, trying to prove her worth to Jesse. Jesse, who had an I told-you-so look in his eye. A look that clearly said, ''I knew you were a spoiled brat, Patricia. A pampered rich girl. You don't know how to cook because there's always been someone available to do it for you.''

She wanted to throttle every gorgeous inch of him. She did work hard. Extremely hard.

And so do millions of other single mothers, her guilty conscience said. Women who came home from a hard day at the office and made their children dinner rather than head for a luxuriously scented bath. Women who washed their own clothes, cleaned their own houses.

So I'll learn to cook, she decided. And when she did, she'd jam the best damn meal Jesse Hawk had ever tasted right down his throat. How dare he come to town after the fact and criticize her life-style. Where was he when his son was cutting his first painful teeth? Off bumping hips with some college bimbo?

The day wound down quietly, and when they parted ways, Patricia watched Dillon and Jesse shake hands, even though she could tell Jesse had hoped for a hug. Too bad, she thought. He'd have to earn his son's affection. Become the father he should have been all those years ago.

Six

On Monday morning Patricia sat across from her father in his office at Boyd Enterprises waiting for him to speak. An "emergency meeting" usually meant an important deal was in danger of collapsing.

Raymond cleared his throat. He looked discomposed, Patricia thought. Although his suit was impeccably pressed, his tie had been loosened, which meant he'd been tugging at it. He rarely resorted to that nervous habit. She scooted to the edge of her seat. Something was definitely wrong.

"I received a disturbing phone call this morning, Patricia." His words sounded uncharacteristically personal, as though the phone call had been her fault.

Patricia held her breath. "And?"

"And I'm appalled," he spouted. "How could you behave like that in a public place? And with *him?*"

The air she'd been holding whooshed out. *Him.* Undoubtedly that bitter-sounding reference meant Jesse. And her behavior clearly meant that lusty kiss in front of The Captain's

Inn. She straightened her posture defensively, a mix of shame and anger building inside her chest. "Peter Crandall called, didn't he? God, I hate that man."

"Is that all you have to say for yourself, young lady?"

"Don't speak to me as though I'm a child. I have the right to have dinner with whomever I choose," she retorted.

"Dinner?" Her father drummed his fingers on the desktop. "Is that what it's called these days?"

Patricia glanced away. She had practically devoured Jesse that evening, struggled to sate an appetite that raged blindly out of control—a sexual starvation of sorts. "I kissed him. So what? I haven't been out with a man in months." And the business associates she attended charity functions with didn't inspire her libido.

"We're not talking about just any man." Raymond pulled at his tie. Patricia recognized it as the one Dillon had given him last Christmas. "I can't believe you've taken up with Jesse Hawk again."

She blew another anxious breath, feeling like a chastised teenager, a girl who didn't have enough sense to come in out of the rain. Or in this case, stay out of Jesse's arms. "I haven't 'taken up' with him. The only reason we kissed that night was to make Peter think I had a lover so he'd quit pestering me."

Raymond slanted one graying eyebrow. "And whose ridiculous idea was that?"

Jesse's, of course, but she wasn't about to admit it. "I'm not a naive young girl anymore. I know what I'm doing this time." Nothing but befriending her son's father, she told herself.

Raymond shook his head, blatant disapproval sending creases across his forehead—deep, hard creases. "You're asking for trouble, that's what you're doing. And apparently where *that* man is concerned, you're as naive as before."

I am not, Patricia chanted as she left Boyd Enterprises seven hours later and proceeded to Jesse's house. She had promised Dillon she and Jesse would try to be friends, and that was all she intended to do. No more hungry kisses or spine-tingling caresses. Her father was wrong. Dead wrong. She could handle herself just fine around Jesse Hawk. Eleven years as a single mother had taught her plenty. She didn't need a man in her life, especially the one who had left Marlow County without a backward glance.

Then why, she wondered, had she just parked in Jesse's graveled driveway?

To invite him to a charity function, she told herself a moment later, to fulfill her obligation to Dillon. And maybe, just maybe, to thumb her nose at her father for sticking his where it didn't belong. A grown woman shouldn't have to defend herself for one measly, out-of-control kiss.

Patricia knocked, and Jesse answered the door wearing faded jeans and a pale-gray shirt, untucked and unbuttoned. The color of the fabric made his eyes appear silver, a metallic shade she used to love.

"Hi," he said, peering around her, apparently hoping to see Dillon.

"I just got off work," she offered, explaining their son's absence.

"Yeah, me, too."

He didn't need to say that he'd been out on ranch calls. She could tell he'd spent his day around horses. He had that cowboy-veterinarian look about him: scuffed Western boots covered his feet, and hard-earned sweat trickled down the center of his chest.

He followed her gaze. "Sorry. I haven't showered yet."

No apology necessary, Patricia thought. She couldn't help but appreciate his rugged appearance. A man who tended horses on a hot summer day had the right to sweat. She'd always believed doctors were a noble breed, especially the ones who cared for sick children and ailing animals.

"I won't keep you long," she said.

He stepped away from the door. "That's okay. Come on in."

Much like the man, his house exhibited a primitive charm: hardwood floors had been polished to perfection; chinked log walls and hand-crafted tables displayed a collection of tribal artifacts. A long headdress hung on one wall trailing brightly

colored feathers, while weavings, baskets and pottery empha-
sized American Indian traditions.

"Your home is beautiful, Jesse." She knew he had been
responsible for a good portion of its restored beauty, refinish-
ing tables and stripping ancient floors.

"Thanks." He motioned toward the hallway. "The addition
is almost done. I plan on using it as a guest room. This place
has two bedrooms, but one of them is pretty tiny."

Patricia glanced down the hallway, then startled as a
squawking noise sounded behind her. She turned to see a gray
parrot perched atop a tall, wire cage, its feathered head cocked
at a curious angle. Below the cage sat a large glass terrarium
inhabited by a bright-green iguana. The top of the lizard's cage
was open, offering the reptile the same freedom the bird had,
only the iguana chose to remain within the security of its
home, nibbling on a platter of fruits and vegetables.

Jesse grinned. "That's Barney and Sally. Barney, say hello
to Tricia."

The parrot ruffled his feathers, then whistled like a construction worker checking out a babe on the corner.

Patricia burst into a girlish giggle. Barney had puffed himself up, pretty and proud, like a peacock. "I'm flattered, Barney. Thank you."

Jesse shook his head. "That bird watches way too much
TV. I swear I didn't teach him that."

She almost laughed again. Jesse looked embarrassed by the
parrot's flirtatious behavior. But then, Jesse had never been
overly flirtatious. He wouldn't think of whistling at a woman.
His methods were much more subtle. And effective, she decided, remembering the first time she had allowed him to slip
his hands under her blouse. He had actually asked for permission to touch her, his voice low and alluring. Refusing hadn't
seemed like an option. She had wanted to feel his hands on
her breasts.

"Tricia?"

She snapped to attention, jerking her shoulders in the process. "What?"

"Do you want to sit down?"

"Oh, yes. Thank you." She lowered herself onto a tan-colored sofa and told her memories to behave. They had just been teenagers experimenting. Or he had been, anyway. She had been a girl in love. A foolish girl, too young to know better.

Patricia gazed at Jesse's naked chest. How dare her father accuse her of being naive now. Hadn't she told Jesse off after that kiss? She lifted her gaze to Jesse's sun-bronzed face. They both knew Dillon was their only bond, their reason for socializing. Their romance had ended long ago.

"I came here to invite you to a charity ball this Friday," Patricia said. "I have an extra ticket and thought you might like to go." She hadn't actually planned on attending, at least not until today. She had only purchased the tickets because the money was being donated to an important cause. She was tired of attending charity functions with business associates, men who idolized her father's money.

Jesse sat across from her in a leather chair. "A ball?"

"Dinner, dancing, that sort of thing," she explained. "The chief of staff at the hospital arranges it every year. The proceeds are used for cancer research." Patricia's mother had died of a cancer that had gone undetected until it was too late. The thought made her sad, homesick for a woman she didn't remember. "I only bought the tickets to help out with the charity," she admitted, to let Jesse know he hadn't been invited because a previous escort had bowed out. "But truthfully, I could use a night out."

"Sure. Okay. But a ball sounds kind of fancy. Am I supposed to wear a tux?"

She nodded. "It's a black tie event. You don't mind taking me on a friendship date, do you?"

"No, not at all."

She stood to leave. "Thanks. I'll let you go." He was probably anxious to shower and change. Patricia knew she was. Her feet ached from a new pair of pointed-toe pumps.

He walked her onto the porch. "I'm still going to get to see Dillon on Sunday, right?"

"Of course." After she and Dillon had their customary breakfast with her father. "I'll bring him here, okay?"

He smiled. "That'd be great. He can meet Barney and Sally."

Patricia watched as a warm wind stirred Jesse's hair, and tried to picture him in a tuxedo. Would he look more handsome than most? "Will you pick me up at seven on Friday?" she asked.

He nodded, and she thought for a moment to ask him if they could take her car, but immediately decided against the suggestion. It would probably sound uppity to a man like Jesse. Besides, she could handle riding in Jesse's enormous truck, just the way she could handle being near him. He'd look like any other man in a tuxedo, only taller and broader, with eyes the color of lightning.

Jesse had never worn a tux, been to a charity ball, nor stepped foot in a mansion, but tonight he was doing all three.

He offered Tricia his arm as they entered the Milford estate, then waited while she checked her wrap. Tricia could have been a goddess, he thought, a creature as perfectly formed as the hothouse orchid he'd attached to her wrist. A beaded gown flowed over her curves like a lavender waterfall, each iridescent ornament reflecting tiny rays of light. The fabric draped in back, exposing the top of her spine in an enchanting display of delicate bones and creamy flesh. She belonged in this environment, was born to grace its overwhelming finery. She had grown up in a house like this, been raised by nannies and had eaten meals prepared by French cooks. For her, charity balls came as naturally as breathing.

Jesse, on the other hand, felt as though he was choking. Drowning in fear. He had been a ward of the state, a dyslexic foster child struggling to read—a boy who'd lived in modest homes with families that weren't really his. And since he had pretty much avoided social functions, his high school prom included, he'd never envisioned himself at a charity ball with a wealthy socialite on his arm. A woman who could point out original works of art as easily as reciting the alphabet.

As Tricia led Jesse toward the staircase, she told him about the Milford Estate. The Dutch Colonial structure, built in 1928, was the oldest mansion in Arrow Hill. The original owner, an elderly oil heiress, had willed her home to the Arrow Hill Historical Society, an organization she had founded. She had also left a sizable trust with instructions that the money be used to maintain the mansion for private tours and charity functions. Just like this little soiree, Jesse thought, anxiety mounting.

The entire third floor housed the ballroom. It was grand, historic and scary as hell. Sparkling chandeliers winked from the ceiling. Intricately carved moldings boasted 1920s craftsmanship, and leaded-glass doors accessed twin terraces laden with statues, wishing wells and potted greenery.

An old-fashioned bandstand awaited the arrival of an orchestra, and linen-draped tables displayed floral arrangements, silverware and crystal goblets. But most intimidating were the people—women in glittering gowns being escorted by men who probably owned their tuxedos. Jesse had rented his.

Tricia accepted a glass of champagne from a waiter carrying a small tray. Jesse took one, as well, even though beer was more to his liking. Of course, he knew better than to expect frosty mugs of domestic ale.

"Most of these people live in Arrow Hill," Tricia said as she scanned the room. "I've known a lot of them since I was a child."

It was a diverse crowd, some younger than Jesse, others old enough to be grandparents. Since there were no other Indians present, Jesse knew he would not go unnoticed. His height alone set him apart as did his ponytail and a tiny silver hoop that pierced his left ear.

Tricia guided him through the ballroom, introducing him to doctors and lawyers, local politicians and women sporting diamond necklaces as big as squash blossoms. He shook hands with the men and smiled at the ladies, then chatted with a trio of board members from the Historical Society. They questioned him politely, inquiring about the purchase of his home. It appeared as though they appreciated his efforts to renovate

the nineteenth-century farmhouse. Of course they did, Jesse
thought with a wry smile as he dutifully answered their questions. The old Garrett homestead wasn't exactly a historical
mansion, but some of its acreage bordered the green peaks of
Arrow Hill.

After the board members moved on to mingle, Jesse caught
sight of Peter Crandall strolling past in a high-and-mighty
manner. Rather than ignore Peter's condescending stare, Jesse
raised his glass at the fair-haired attorney, then brought the
champagne to his lips. Pleasure followed the bubbling liquid
down his throat. The mocking toast had felt nearly as good as
socking Peter's snobbish jaw and watching it bruise. Jesse
smiled as Tricia led him toward their assigned table. Maybe
he could handle this society stuff after all.

Then again, maybe not, he decided fifteen minutes later.
Dinner started with a watercress salad seasoned with a tangy
vinaigrette dressing. Jesse would have preferred lettuce and
tomatoes smothered in ranch. He almost felt silly eating delicate greens from a cut-glass platter. Suddenly his hands
seemed big and clumsy. But hopefully no one would notice,
especially since he was sandwiched between two beautiful
women. Tricia graced his right while a stunning blonde sipped
champagne on his left.

When the soup arrived, Jesse breathed a sigh of relief. It
appeared to be a down-home broth, a cream of something-or-
other. Potato, maybe, with chives sprinkled on top. He could
handle that. He grew chives in his garden.

He dipped into his soup, swallowed a spoonful, then
flinched. It was cold. Ice cold. Good God. He'd already suffered through that frilly salad.

He waited until Tricia tasted her soup, then leaned toward
her and pressed his mouth to her ear. "Mine's cold," he whispered. "Is yours all right?"

"Yes," she whispered back. "It's supposed to be served
chilled."

Mortified, he felt his face sting with the heat of embarrassment. "Oh. Sorry."

"That's okay. It grows on you."

But fancy balls never would, he decided. Jesse Hawk didn't belong in Tricia Boyd's world. Hell, she was probably thinking she should have left him back at the farm.

He was incredible, Patricia thought. Real and refreshing. She didn't care if he didn't know what vichyssoise was. Over half the population in America had probably never eaten chilled potato-and-leek soup.

Jesse squared his shoulders, and Patricia's heart gave a little lurch. The fact that he'd successfully paired a ponytail with a tuxedo proved his sense of unpretentious style. The women at their table kept stealing admiring glances, and since Jesse had never been prone to small talk, the few words he'd offered held meaning—profound depth. He was, by far, the most intriguing man at the party.

Maybe too intriguing. By the time their waiter served dessert, Michelle Page, the blonde on Jesse's left, stared blatantly at his profile, drinking in those gorgeous features: the hollowed cheekbones, chiseled jaw, slightly aquiline nose.

Don't you dare, Patricia wanted to say. Michelle had already taken enough that should have belonged to her, including the homecoming queen crown during their senior year at Arrow Hill High. To continue a teenage rivalry seemed a bit petty, but Michelle had kept it alive all these years, flaunting her accomplishments and treating Patricia badly in the process.

Michelle licked the whipped cream from her cappuccino, her tongue darting daintily. She'd always used those full, overly glossed lips to her best advantage, pouting prettily when she didn't get her way. Patricia cringed inwardly. Men, no matter their age or level of intelligence, usually panted at her feet.

"You're the new veterinarian, aren't you?" Michelle cooed to Jesse's profile.

He turned, and Patricia wondered if he was smiling. Or drooling. She couldn't see his face.

"Yes. Jesse Hawk. Nice to meet you."

She extended her hand, then tilted her head, spilling golden waves over her shoulder. "Michelle Page. You don't happen to have a business card available, do you?"

Witch, Patricia thought. She'd recited her name and asked for Jesse's number all in the same breath.

"Sure." He removed a card from his jacket and handed it to her.

Michelle tucked it into an evening bag that matched her dress, white satin and silver sequins showcasing every curve she owned. "I have an Afghan named Sasha, and I have the feeling she would adore you."

"Afghans are wonderful dogs," Jesse said. "Naturally well mannered and elegant."

The blonde smiled as though the compliment had been meant for her, then cut into a strawberry lime tart. "This is my favorite dessert." She tasted it and moaned. "I think it's all that spun sugar."

A sugarcoated tart, Patricia thought, how fitting.

Michelle lifted a forkful toward Jesse. "Do you want a bite?"

He didn't answer, but he didn't move, either. Was he stunned? Aroused? Opening his mouth to be fed? Patricia wanted to kill them both. Murder them with her bare hands. Mavis Delinsky, the chair of the Arrow Hill Arts Council, watched from the other side of the table, her faced pinched in disapproval. Was it Michelle's abominable manners that bothered Mrs. Delinsky, or Jesse's typically male reaction?

Finally he spoke, lowering his head to the dessert in front of him. "No, thank you. I have my own." He turned toward Patricia then, lifting his gaze. "Would you like to dance?"

Since her heart had suddenly stuck quite happily in her throat, she nodded, rather than choke out a response. She'd been too busy with jealous thoughts to notice the band had begun to play.

He rose and asked the other guests to excuse them as he scooted Patricia's chair away from the table. Mrs. Delinsky smiled and nodded. Michelle huffed like an insolent child.

Jesse and Patricia joined the other couples on the dance floor. The romantic music, reminiscent of the era of the house, lulled Patricia into a trance. Or was it Jesse's arms? The gentle way in which he held her, his hand sliding down her back, teasing her spine?

They fit perfectly, the length of their bodies a sensual match. Men were rarely tall enough to suit her, but then she had compared every man to him, to his commanding height.

"We always felt right," he said, as though reading her mind. "Like we were meant to dance together."

She closed her eyes as his fingertips sparked an electrical charge down her spine. The first time he'd touched her, she'd known he was the one. "I remember."

He dipped his head, his breath brushing her ear. "Did you wear this dress for me?"

Did she? Maybe subconsciously. Her bare back used to be a fascination of his, a place to nip and kiss and nuzzle. She opened her eyes, forced herself to remember her surroundings: the other couples, the orchestra, the guests who sipped international coffee and watched the dance floor.

"Is it warm in here?" she asked.

"Your skin is warm."

He drew her closer and she realized he danced the way he made love—slowly and provocatively, a motion as smooth as a river current, as alluring and dangerous. She could feel his muscles beneath his jacket, a body she knew, yet didn't. The change in him aroused as much as frightened her. He could still hypnotize her, make her believe she belonged exclusively to him. She knew everyone in the room must have thought so, too. They probably looked like lovers who'd rekindled their long-ago-but-not-forgotten affair. By now their past was public knowledge. Patricia Boyd was dancing with the father of her child, melting bonelessly in his arms.

As the orchestra began another song, Jesse swept her into the rhythm. Patricia danced regularly at these functions, and other men customarily cut in on her partners. But that wasn't going to happen this time, she realized. Jesse had staked his claim, his hold gentle but unmistakably possessive.

"What are you thinking about?" he asked.

"You," she answered automatically. Her eyes locked on

his, and beneath the ballroom lights his gleamed like polished silver—the lining on the cloud she found herself floating upon. Lying wasn't possible, not when she bordered the gates of Heaven. "You're an incredible dancer."

A fleeting smile teased his lips. She resisted the urge to capture it with a kiss. "Only because of you. You taught me, remember?"

"Yes." She remembered, all too well.

She could see them in his tiny apartment swaying to the radio. A dance step, a caress. A twirl. An affectionate nibble. She'd taught him to dance, and later that night, he'd schooled her in the art of lovemaking. It hadn't been the first time they'd made love, but it was one of the most erotic. He'd undressed her in front of the mirror, then trailed kisses down her body while she'd watched their reflections. Watched until her heart pounded and her vision blurred, his mouth and hands driving her beyond the brink of sanity.

Struggling to clear her mind, Patricia gripped Jesse's shoulders. "Could we go outside, please? I think I need some air."

They found a secluded bench on the nearest terrace, a corner shielded by potted ferns and indigenous flowers. Patricia took a deep, cleansing breath. Stars dazzled a velvet sky and sweet, exotic scents thrived in the night air. A few feet away water spilled from a fountain of dancing cherubs.

"This is perfect," she said.

"Are you sure you're okay? You looked a bit dizzy back there."

"The dance floor was too crowded." And her memories too close. Too real.

"Are you cold? I can get your wrap or you can wear my jacket."

"No, thank you. I'm fine." The breeze felt good. Life sustaining. Freedom from the heat that came with Jesse. "Did you enjoy the meal?" she asked, steering the conversation toward idle chitchat.

"The salmon was good." He glanced down at his hands then back up. "But I didn't like the soup."

And he didn't like not knowing what it was. His body language told her so, during dinner and now. "Truthfully it's not one of my favorites, either. Next time I can find out what's on the menu."

"You mean there's going to be a next time?"

"There is if you'll agree to escort me."

When he tilted his head, moonlight gleamed upon his hair. "Will you wear another backless dress?"

The night air tickled her spine. "I suppose that could be arranged." She had a closet full of ball gowns, gauntlet gloves and satin pumps. She'd wear whatever pleased him. "I have to warn you, though. Sometimes they serve chilled pumpkin soup."

He made a face, and they both laughed. "I guess chicken noodle is out, huh?"

"Afraid so."

"Pot roast, too?"

Pot roast. Patricia moved closer and took his hand. Jesse was such a country boy, always finding pleasure in the simplest of things. "You've been a wonderful escort, Jesse."

"Adapting to the environment, am I?" He chuckled and squeezed her hand. "If we were on my turf, I would have punched Peter Crandall's lights out. He kept giving us dirty looks."

She sent him an amused smile. If they'd been on his turf, maybe she could have dragged Michelle into a cat fight. Ripped the blonde's hair out by its hidden dark roots.

As Jesse urged her head to his shoulder, Patricia willed the image away. The evening was too beautiful to waste on disruptive thoughts.

Apparently Jesse agreed. They sat quietly for a time, listening to the notes of old-fashioned music flutter through the breeze like melodious butterflies. Suddenly they were the only two people on earth, sharing the sky, absorbing the elements.

Jesse lifted his hand to her cheek, and she realized how much he belonged to those elements. She could feel beauty in his touch, the glow of the moon, lull of the wind. He was a part of something wondrous, and so was she.

"Tricia?" he whispered, his unspoken question clear.

He wanted to kiss her, was asking for permission.

Patricia closed her eyes, her answer rising like a tide, a warm, inviting wave. "Yes."

His mouth took hers, swept her into the taste of his lips, his tongue. She inhaled the faint scent of his cologne and shifted in his arms, giving those big, callused hands access to the dip in her dress, her naked back and tingling spine.

Need, not naiveté, drove her. She knew what she wanted, recognized the hunger. The danger. The overwhelming thrill.

He caressed her skin and sipped from her lips, making love to her mouth with slow, sexy strokes. She could almost recall what it felt like to have him inside her, thrusting rhythmically, his flesh hot and hard beneath her fingers.

He came up for air, his breath raspy and aroused. "We shouldn't be doing this."

"I know." Dizzy, she blinked to bring him into focus. "Do you want to stop?"

His short laugh came out broken—rough and sexy. "No. Do you?"

Not now, she thought, as she pulled him closer. On this seductive summer evening he tasted like the Jesse she remembered. The young, passionate man she had loved.

She slid her tongue into his mouth and sighed. Tomorrow she would probably suffer the consequences of her actions, but tonight she simply didn't care.

Seven

Today was awkward. First Patricia had struggled through breakfast with her father, knowing he disapproved of her most recent "friendship date" with Jesse. And now she was at Jesse's house, seated on his sofa, pretending they hadn't kissed each other senseless the other night.

"Isn't Barney great, Mom?" Dillon asked.

She nodded and smiled. The parrot bounced across the coffee table, dancing to country music coming from the stereo. "He's adorable."

She looked up and caught Jesse's eye. His lips were curved into a smile, too—those moist, sexy lips she had all but devoured. God help her, but she could still taste him.

"How did you teach Barney to do all this stuff?" Dillon asked his father.

"African grays are extremely intelligent birds. And given half the chance, most parrots will do more than just mimic." Jesse opened a small wooden box above the stereo and removed a stack of flash cards. "Okay, Barney," he said, holding up a yellow square. "Tell Dillon what color this is."

The parrot waddled over to the edge of the table and eyed the sunny paper, then looked at Dillon as if to make sure the child was watching. Apparently the bird enjoyed having an enthusiastic eleven-year-old as his captive audience.

"Yellow," Barney squawked, bobbing his head proudly.

Both Jesse and Dillon praised the spirited parrot. "Good boy," they said in unison, then laughed.

Patricia's heart warmed. Father and son had just shared their first spontaneous moment—a burst of casual laughter.

Fifteen minutes later Patricia and Dillon followed Jesse on a tour of his house, Dillon's newfound friend in tow. "This is my room," Jesse said, as they entered his woodsy domain.

Dillon moved forward, Barney perched quietly upon his shoulder. "Wow, look at the bed."

Yes, Patricia thought, look at the bed—the place where Jesse slept each night. The four-poster bed was handmade from pine logs, crafted to rugged perfection. A thick, homey quilt displayed a native print, while sage burned from a clay pot, purifying the air.

Patricia's throat constricted. The room was much too inviting, a natural setting for lovers to share during warm summer nights and chilled winter dreams. A place to cuddle and raise a brood of happy, healthy children.

"Did you build the bed yourself?" Dillon asked his father.

Jesse nodded and stroked the wood. Patricia followed the movement of his hand, the masculine caress.

"It's beautiful," she offered.

"Thank you." He looked up and their eyes met. And for a moment they held. And remembered.

Everything, she realized: the first time they had shared a bed; their disciplined tutoring sessions; the afternoon he'd left town; the charity ball two days ago. Their lips meeting, tasting, hungering for more. She could still hear the music blending with the spray from the fountain, the cherubs dancing on water.

Patricia glanced away. No more romantic evenings. Being alone with Jesse was much too dangerous now. He was off-limits, she decided, unless their son was present. She'd have to forfeit that offer to have him escort her to another charity ball. Next time they'd probably end up kissing on the dance floor, and then her father would be privy to the gossip it would cause. The last thing she wanted was to be accused of being naive again.

The tour of Jesse's house ended in a country-style kitchen, a large room with a scarred wooden table, an old-fashioned stove and chopping-block counters. Just like the rest of the simple homestead, the kitchen whispered of the past. Patricia thought Jesse had done a beautiful job of transforming the farmhouse into a modern haven for his animals and a well-tended herb garden.

"My mom's learning to cook," Dillon announced as Jesse prepared sandwiches for lunch. "Aren't you, Mom?"

Patricia nearly dropped the soda Jesse had given her. Dillon's words boomed in the air, a sudden reminder of who she was—a thirty-year-old woman who had never done a day's worth of domestic work in her life.

"Elda's teaching me to make a few things." A lopsided cake, chicken that tasted dry, overly browned biscuits, lumpy gravy. Of course none of the disasters were Elda's fault. Patricia had managed the mistakes all on her own. But allowing Elda to take over would have been cheating.

Jesse turned toward her, an amused smirk alight on his handsome face. Damn him, she thought. He moved with ease, making sandwiches from a meat loaf he'd cooked the night before. He could build a bed, vet a horse, wash his own clothes and bake a meat loaf. It wasn't fair that he never failed at anything. Whatever Jesse Hawk did, he did well. Including kiss, she added, staring at his mouth once again.

"Hey, Mom," Dillon said, tapping the table. Her son sat across from her, hand-feeding Barney from a bowl of diced fruit. "Why don't you cook dinner for me and Dad next week? Show us what you learned."

Patricia fought the urge to panic. What was she supposed to make? Burned biscuits and lumpy gravy? A lopsided lemon cake for dessert? "Your dad might be busy next week."

Jesse brought the sandwiches to the table and shooed Bar-

ney away when the bird got nosy. "Are you kidding? I
wouldn't miss the opportunity for a home-cooked meal. Any
night you say is fine."

"That's great," Dillon chimed.

Wonderful. How could she refuse now? Jesse and Dillon
were smiling at each other. Dillon had just referred to Jesse
as Dad for the first time in his father's presence, something
Patricia knew Jesse had been waiting for. A family bond had
just taken place, making her dilemma that much harder. And
Dillon looked so proud, so eager to show off his culinary
skills. He hadn't been home to sample the disastrous effects
of her cooking lessons.

Patricia nibbled her thumbnail. Should she admit she wasn't
ready? She glanced up at Jesse. Now, he stood beside the table
watching her, those provocative lips twitching into a grin. Apparently the image of the richest girl in Arrow Hill slaving
over a hot stove amused him.

"How about Friday evening?" she heard herself say. "I'll
make a pot roast." A wholesome American meal, Patricia decided, with all the trimmings. So what if she had less than a
week to refine her culinary skills. She dealt with multimillion-
dollar deals on a daily basis. How difficult could tossing a
roast into a pot be? She straightened her spine and reached for
a sandwich, determined to ignore Jesse's amused grin. She
would do this for Dillon.

Late Friday afternoon Patricia studied the salad and com-
mended herself on a job well done. It looked festive, she
thought, a variety of lettuce with cherry tomatoes, carrot shav-
ings and cucumber slices. She'd skipped the mushrooms since
she'd decided to sauté them in wine. Okay. She took a calming
breath. All she had to do was refrigerate the salad and move
on.

According to Elda's instructions, the roast would take about
an hour and thirty minutes to bake, which would give her
plenty of time to peel, boil and mash potatoes.

She checked the microwave clock. Jesse was scheduled to
arrive at seven. Oh, goodness, should they eat in the dining

room or the kitchen? The kitchen table didn't seem like more than a breakfast nook to her, but Jesse might think differently. She wanted this dinner to go off without a hitch. Maybe she'd ask Dillon what to do.

"Mom!"

Patricia smiled as she snagged a tomato from the salad. Speak of the young devil.

He came rushing down the stairs in a flurry of cotton and loose-fitting denim. "Mom, you're never going to believe what happened."

"What?" She was used to Dillon's drama, his boyish theatrics. He looked too excited to be announcing bad news. She knew enough not to panic.

"Mark's cousin broke his leg."

She covered the salad and placed it in the refrigerator, then rechecked her supply of bottled dressings. "Oh, that's too bad. I'm sorry to hear it." She had met Mark Harrison's cousin a few times. He seemed like a nice kid. "I'm sure he'll be fine."

"Yeah, but now he can't go water-skiing with Mark this weekend. Mark's family is leaving for the river tonight." Dillon rocked on his heels. "They asked if I could go instead."

"Tonight?" Now she felt a panic coming on. "They're leaving tonight?"

He gave a quick, anxious nod. "I know it's short notice, but Mrs. Harrison said you could call her. They don't mind me going. They were planning on having an extra kid, anyway." He shuffled his feet, pleading his case. "I've been on vacations with them before. Plenty of times. And I know how to water-ski. I went last summer." Before Patricia could respond, Dillon continued, "Mrs. Harrison is like you, Mom. She nags us about wearing sunblock and everything. I'll be in good hands."

Patricia couldn't help but smile. A nagging mom. In a sense that did make her feel better. And the Harrisons were like family to Dillon. He'd been friends with Mark since kindergarten. She studied Dillon's wide, gray eyes. She could see how badly he wanted to go.

Dillon persisted. "Their summer home is really nice. It's

right near the river. I was there for two weeks last year, remember?''

She remembered. Mrs. Harrison had called Dillon an angel,
a pleasure to have around. But he's my angel. My baby. Regardless, it didn't seem fair to keep an active eleven-year-old
boy home for pot roast when he could go water-skiing. "I'll
phone Mrs. Harrison.''

Dillon rushed into her arms for a swift, strong hug.
"Thanks, Mom. I love you.''

She combed her fingers through his hair. "I love you, too.''

A moment later he flew up the stairs, and Patricia called
Mrs. Harrison. When she had been assured by the other
woman that they'd take good care of Dillon, Patricia helped
her son pack. He'd be gone before Jesse arrived.

Jesse. Oh, Lord. "I wonder if I should call your dad and
cancel.''

Dillon jammed a second pair of swim trunks into a canvas
suitcase. "Don't do that. You already started cooking. And
Dad said he was looking forward to a homemade meal.'' He
paused and looked up at her. "You're not mad about me leaving, are you?''

"No, sweetheart. I'm not mad.'' Just a little scared, she
supposed, about being alone with Jesse again. She glanced at
the clock beside Dillon's bed and admonished herself. It was
only dinner. One short evening. What could possibly go
wrong?

A hundred things, Patricia realized frantically after Dillon
was gone. Timing a meal was impossible. The roast was nearly
cooked, but the potatoes weren't even done boiling, let alone
mashed and seasoned. The mushrooms hadn't been cleaned
yet, and the table wasn't set. She'd decided on the dining room
because the kitchen was a mess. But worse than the kitchen
was her own appearance. Her hair felt limp, her lipstick worn,
her summer dress speckled with red dots from a dessert Elda
had referred to as strawberry-cream surprise. The surprise was
that it took longer to make than anticipated and still needed
time to chill.

Patricia checked on the potatoes again, poking several with

a fork. How soft did they have to be before they would mash properly? Now she couldn't remember a thing Elda had told her. And like an idiot, she'd given the older woman the entire weekend off. Elda was fifty miles away visiting her grand-children.

When the doorbell rang, Patricia accidentally dropped the fork into the scalding water, then tore off to answer the sum-mons with a silent curse.

Jesse was early, tall and handsome in a white Western shirt and blue jeans, his clean scent suggesting freshly showered skin and a splash of aftershave.

He smiled. "Hi, Tricia."

She blew a nervous puff of air from her lungs. He had no right to look so crisp while her hair and makeup wilted. Rather than say hello, she began to ramble. "Dillon's not here. His friend Mark invited him to go water-skiing this weekend. They left about an hour ago with Mark's parents." Patricia chewed her bottom lip, picturing the kitchen fiasco. "It's just you and me," she added, hoping Jesse might decide to go back home.

No such luck. Although his smile had faded, he stepped inside. "That's okay, I guess. So Dillon water-skis, huh?"

She nodded. "Snowboards, too. He promised to call when they got to the river. The Harrisons have a summer home there." She fingered the strawberry stains on her dress. "I didn't have the heart to tell him he couldn't go. It was a last-minute invitation, and he was so excited."

"I understand. Maybe I can see him midweek sometime. I'd really like to get past this weekend-dad thing."

Midweek meant her time, too, she realized. Dillon still wasn't willing to visit with Jesse by himself. "We'll figure that out when the time comes." How could she think clearly knowing a piece of silverware was boiling with the potatoes? She pointed to a wet bar in the living room. "Feel free to fix yourself a drink. There's soda and beer, or something harder if you prefer. I have to check on dinner." She darted into the kitchen and left Jesse staring after her.

Jesse poured himself a soft drink and sat on the edge of the sofa. He'd never seen Tricia so distracted and flighty. Well, hell, he was a bit nervous himself. He had expected this to be a family dinner with Dillon present. But now it was just Tricia and him. A dangerously lusty combination. They'd practically swallowed each other whole last Friday night, kissing for hours on end. And not only at the ball, but in his truck and on her doorstep, too.

He took a swig of the cola. Okay, so they'd gotten a little carried away on that "friendship date." That was no reason to hide out in the living room while Tricia barricaded herself in the kitchen. He could be alone with her without fantasizing about tearing her clothes off. Their attraction wasn't lethal. He'd survive this dinner and so would she.

He followed a pleasant aroma to the kitchen, then paused in the doorway. The normally cool, calm, sophisticated Tricia moved about the room like a wind-up toy gone awry, blowing bits of hair out of her eyes and mumbling frantic curses. And no wonder, he thought with an amused grin. Her kitchen resembled the aftermath of a war, food casualties strewn everywhere. Cucumber and potato peelings battled strawberry stems and lettuce cores for the sink while spills of undetected origins splotched the counters.

"Do you need some help?" he asked, biting the inside of his cheeks to keep his grin in check. She looked too adorable for words, flour dusting her chin, two oversize oven mitts competing with the allure of a soft, summer dress.

When she spun around, one of the mitts flew off and landed on the floor like a deceased puppet. "I can't find the beaters for the mixer. How can I mash potatoes without them?"

She was in a state of panic, he realized, bordering hysteria and quite possibly tears. He came forward and removed her other mitt. "Just relax, honey. I'll help you find them, okay?" Was she actually rummaging through cabinets and drawers with those silly things on?

"Thank you," she said in a choppy breath.

He found the metal beaters on the counter beneath a haphazardly tossed hand towel while Tricia sipped ice water in an apparent attempt to regain her composure.

Within minutes she was back on her feet, graceful as ever, and determined, Jesse supposed, to make up for her uncharacteristic breakdown. He withheld an animated chuckle. Buying into the lady-of-the-manor act was a bit tough since she still wore a spot of flour on her pert little chin.

They worked side by side in companionable silence. She mashed the potatoes, he sliced the meat and thickened the gravy. She set the table, he sautéed the mushrooms. Together they brought platters and bowls into the dining room, and right before they sat down to share dinner, Jesse reached forward and brushed the flour from her chin.

Clearly embarrassed, she shook her head. "I must look a mess."

No, he thought. She looked beautiful. Sexy and tousled. Good enough to carry to bed and cover with kisses. He swallowed. A home-cooked meal and a gorgeous brunette. Suddenly jasmine perfume and the aroma of pot roast were a strangely enticing combination.

"Messy suits you."

"Right." She laughed. "I doubt the designer of this dress would appreciate the strawberry stains."

He stood beside her at the table, scanning the length of her dress. It flowed over her curves like a stream of lilacs, a side slit exposing one long bare leg. On her feet she wore high-heeled sandals. He didn't see any strawberry stains. Only flowers, sheer cotton and woman.

"We better eat before it gets cold," he said, scooting back her chair. Gaping at her wasn't doing either one of them any good. This was a friendly dinner, not an orgy for misbehaving hormones.

After dousing his salad with bottled ranch, he served himself a mound of potatoes and several thick chunks of roast, then poured gravy over both. "So Dillon's quite the little sportsman, huh?"

She nibbled on her salad, taking proper, ladylike bites. "Yes, but he's a lot like you. He excels at lone sports. He's never really been a team player."

It was the dyslexia, Jesse thought. Focusing on too much

activity at once was difficult for most dyslexics, making team
sports frustrating and confusing. "So he's going to call tonight, right?"

She nodded. "Soon. Probably."

"Good." Jesse missed his son, even though he understood
the boy's enthusiasm for a weekend at the river. Jesse enjoyed
the allure of water, too. The cool, refreshing feel of it. "I'm
sure Dillon will have a great time."

"He felt so guilty about skipping out on dinner. He must
have apologized a hundred times before he left."

His kid had heart, Jesse thought. A tender boy with a warrior's soul. He was as proud as a man could be. "Well, he
missed a good meal. I'll say that much."

"It is good, isn't it?" She dipped her spoon into the potatoes, her eyes twinkling as she smiled. "I don't think I could
have managed without you, though. We make a wonderful
team."

"Yeah. Great food and beautiful babies."

Instantly they both froze. There was no soft music, no candlelight, no flowers but the ones sprinkled upon her dress, yet
his simple words spilled sensual images into the air. Young,
hungry lovers making a beautiful, gray-eyed baby.

He tried to look away but couldn't. Now he wanted her,
smooth and silky and naked beneath him.

Tricia, it seemed, couldn't turn away, either. Her gaze was
locked on his, sloe-eyed with a sweep of dark, curling lashes.
Was she thinking that she wanted him, too? Wanted to drag
his head to her breasts and watch him flick his tongue across
her nipples? Feel them peak to his touch?

Silence ensued, intensifying his senses—the allure of her
perfume, color of her hair, length of her fingers, shape of her
nails—those blush-pink nails, long and wickedly feminine. He
could almost feel them clawing his skin.

"Jesse?"

He blinked, then shivered, struggling to respond to the
sound of Tricia's voice. In his mind's eye, her legs were
wrapped around his waist, her head reared back, her—

"What?"

"Do you want dessert?" she asked, her tone a tad too husky. "It should be ready by now."

He smiled. Was that her answer to sexual tension? A bowl of something sweet and frothy? "Sure. Why not?" At this point he was willing to indulge in whatever she offered. Tricia Boyd was, and probably always would be, his fantasy.

She bumped the table as she stood, and his heart gave a boyish lurch. His living, breathing, walking fantasy. His one true obsession. The lover from his youth.

Eight

Patricia breathed a sigh of relief. The kitchen was almost clean. Jesse had offered to help, and between the two of them, they'd run the garbage disposal, wiped the counters and loaded the dishwasher. Now they were hand-washing pots and pans.

They made a wonderful team.

Great food and beautiful babies.

A shiver tiptoed up her spine, those tiny fingers of electricity that surfaced whenever Jesse was near. Patricia remembered that he'd sparked a current on the night she'd conceived their son, the one and only time they had neglected protection. The condom box had turned up empty, but by then they had been too needy for each other to stop.

Jesse bumped her shoulder as he took the frying pan from her hands to dry it. "Sorry," he said, his voice quiet but not quite controlled.

"That's okay." She wouldn't look at him. Couldn't, she realized. Not without sinking into those gunmetal eyes.

He walked away to place the pan in the cabinet below the

stove. She began washing the mixing bowl, scrubbing it clean of dried potatoes. He returned to stand beside her again, finish the chore they'd agreed to share.

Patricia handed him the mixing bowl, the last dish of the evening.

"Where does it go?" he asked.

"Up there." She pointed to the cabinet above her head.

Suddenly they were no longer side by side. He moved behind her, his breath tickling her nape.

She reached up to open the cabinet, and he leaned forward. Oh God, she thought, what are we doing? Jesse was pressed against her, and she could feel every virile motion, every hard-earned muscle bunch and flex.

The mixing bowl clanked against a glass casserole dish. She tried to focus on the sound rather than the sensation shooting up her spine. The front of his jeans had bumped her bottom, the ridge beneath his zipper hard and aroused.

"Tricia," he whispered her name, his lips brushing her ear.

She locked her knees to keep herself from falling to the floor. His mouth teased her neck. Little nibbles. Sweet tender bites.

Don't moan, she told herself. Don't give him that much power. Don't...

But she did. She moaned—a low orgasmic whimper that had him growling behind her. She had power, too, she realized. He wanted her as badly as she wanted him.

She glanced down to see his cowboy boots and her sling-back heels. Even their shoes looked sexual. Lord help her, she was losing her mind. And it felt incredible.

She turned slowly, shifting in his arms until they stood face-to-face. Their eyes met. His glimmered like shards of silver, smooth and shiny—a long lingering stare. Those eyes could steal her breath, she knew, strike her like lightning.

He lowered his head; she offered him her lips. The moment, the very instant, they made contact, they slammed into each other with an urgent, openmouthed kiss. He caught her rear and pulled her tight against him, rocked his hips so she could feel his erection. She thrust her tongue into his mouth over and over, mimicking the motion of his body. The carnal dance they both craved.

The kiss ended in a desperate pant for air. They sucked life into their lungs and stared at each other again, their chests heaving.

A moment later Jesse placed his finger against her lips and traced their shape, marveling, it seemed, at the pleasure she'd given him. Patricia smiled, took his hand and led him from the kitchen in a silent invitation.

He paused at the foot of the stairs. "Are you sure?"

She stroked his face, the features that formed his ethnic beauty. She understood the question, the deep implication. If they made love, it would not *be* love. Was she willing to accept an affair?

"Yes, I'm sure." Patricia knew what she wanted. She was not a naive young girl, but a grown woman hungering for completion, sexual gratification with the only man who stirred her blood.

He nodded and smiled, allowing her to take him where they both chose to go.

They entered her bedroom, stopped to kiss, then slowly undressed each other. She released the buttons on his shirt; he helped her step out of her dress. When they were naked, he turned her toward the mirror so she could see their reflections.

He looked almost mystical beside her. The stained-glass window glowed from a light shining in from the balcony, spilling a rainbow over his skin. His chest was wide and powerful, his belly corrugated, his sex full and aroused. Patricia caught her breath. Tonight all that male perfection was hers.

"You're beautiful," Jesse said, causing her to meet his gaze in the mirror and study her own reflection. She, too, stood bathed in a rainbow of color, her lips swollen from his kisses, her hair slightly mussed. She glanced down at her protruding nipples and prayed she wouldn't blush. He was pressing his mouth to her shoulder, taking little nibbles, sending chills up and down her spine.

She knew what he intended to do.

He flicked his tongue over her skin. "Do you remember, Tricia?"

"Yes. I thought about it at the ball when we danced."

"Me, too." He pulled at her earlobe with his teeth. "I thought about how much I wanted to do it again. How much I've missed you."

He moved to stand in front of her, and she realized he wasn't asking for permission. He was taking what he wanted, and God help her, she had no choice but to let him.

"Watch, Tricia. And feel."

He nuzzled her breasts, then teased one aching nipple with his tongue. His touch was the same, yet different—stronger, experienced, self-assured. He rooted at her nipple and she held him there, encouraging him to suckle. The sensation flowed through her veins like molten wax, so she let herself melt. And purr.

He dropped to his knees, slid his tongue to her belly and laved her navel. "Watch," he whispered again. "Let me make new memories."

A pulse pounded between her legs, a throbbing, uncontrollable heat.

Patricia fisted his hair. "Jesse." His name was a plea, an urgent prayer.

He caressed her legs, her inner thighs, the part of her craving more. She rotated her hips and caught sight of her own reflection, the flush on her cheeks, the wanton look in her eyes. The blatant, hungry need. He must have seen it, too. Felt it. Because before she could plead his name once again, he loved her with his mouth, his tongue making tender swirls, then deep moist strokes.

Should she tell him that he was still the only one? That she hadn't let another man...

No, she couldn't. Not now. Not while the room spun, the kaleidoscope from the stained glass twirling around her. He grasped her hips as if to steady her, hold her while she bucked and made throaty little sounds. Pleasure lifted her higher. Pleasure and need and emotions she couldn't begin to describe. The spray of color, the ruthless thrust of his tongue swept through her like a tornado, a whirlwind of greedy aches and hungry urges.

Was that her scream? Her cry of release? Patricia wasn't sure. All she knew was that she'd soared into oblivion, into that warm, sensual place only he could take her, and when she came back down, she was wrapped in his arms, panting his name.

Flesh against flesh. Fair against dark. Jesse savored the feeling, the image. Tricia clung to his neck, shuddering with sexy little aftershocks.

The reflection of her bed shone in the mirror. It was tousled, unmade. His next breath nearly clogged his lungs. Knowing that they would make love on the same sheets she'd slept on the night before aroused him. Made him hotter. Harder.

He tongued her ear and slid his hands down her back and over the curve of her bottom. The impulse to track her scent made him feel primal, animalistic—a male searching for his mate. Tricia's fragrance had the power to seduce—a sea of jasmine, a swirling vine of exotic white flowers. He wanted to dive in. And swim.

Jesse swept her up and placed her on the edge of the bed. She smiled, so he kissed her, daring her to taste herself, that sweet, womanly flavor that had nearly driven him mad. The fact that she'd watched had driven him mad, too. He knew she wouldn't be able to walk into her bedroom and stand before the mirror without recalling what he'd done to her, the decadent thrill, the orgasm that had left her quivering in his arms.

Tricia gripped his shoulders and pulled him down. They rolled onto the bed. Blood leaped to his fingers, making them itch to touch. She had changed, grown and matured. Her breasts were fuller, hips rounder, tummy marked with pale, faint lines.

He traced one of those delicate lines and felt her body, that smooth liquid body, tense.

She turned away. "They're ugly."

"No." He caught her chin and brought her face back to

his. "They're from my child, Tricia. My flesh and blood. The baby you carried in your womb for nine months." He didn't understand why women didn't take pride in the marks left by pregnancy. "Giving birth is part of your medicine now. It makes you even more beautiful than before."

Her expression softened, and he tried to picture how her tummy must have looked swollen with his child. He would have made love to her then, too. Thanked *Esaugetuh Emissee*, the Master of Breath, for the miracle bestowed upon them.

They lay side by side gazing at each other, their hands drifting over warm flesh and emotional need. This wasn't love, Jesse thought, but it wasn't just sex, either.

She shifted onto her knees and leaned forward, exploring the physical change in him. He had matured, as well. The years, he knew, had made a man out of him. Bitter and angry sometimes, but a man just the same.

She roamed his chest first, the wall of muscle he'd inherited from his father.

"Your body's different. Stronger." She placed her head against his heart, let it thud in her ear. His heartbeat was strong, too, he supposed. Excited. Eager.

"Your nipples are hiding," she teased, twining her fingers around his chest hair.

Jesse fisted the sheet. He wanted to spring forward, cuff her wrists and slam into her, devour all that femininity. Instead he remained still and allowed her to play. This would be a new memory, he told himself, a moment to think back on while he was alone in his own bed, craving her touch.

She scraped his stomach with her nails, abrading gently. His heartbeat stumbled; her hand slipped lower.

Tricia was sliding into dangerous territory now, making this memory too damn real. She had lowered her head, her mouth barely brushing his—

"You can't do that," he warned in a voice that sounded remarkably like a growl. "Not this time. I won't...I can't..."

She dropped her lashes, and his strong, steady heart threatened to kick its way out of his chest. A coquettish smile tilted her lips. Somewhere along the line that sexually shy eighteen-year-old had turned vixen.

Tricia flicked her tongue, and he nearly flew off the bed. "But you did it to me, Jesse."

"Yeah, but women can…you know…more than once, and…"

She kissed his belly, lingered there, then brought her face next to his. "I want a rain check."

He drew a deep, ragged breath. It was all he could do not to push her back down and let her have her wicked way with him. His body throbbed, cried out for relief. He couldn't wait. Couldn't play this teasing game anymore.

He had to have her.

Now.

This thundering instant.

"My jeans," he groaned, lifting Tricia off the bed with him. He had to find his jeans, his wallet, the condoms he prayed were still intact. God only knew how long he'd been carrying the damn things around.

They rummaged through his wallet like a couple of frenzied teenagers, dumping the contents onto the floor.

"Here!" Tricia located a foil packet and dragged him back onto the bed.

Feeling her roll that thin veil of latex over him was suddenly the most seductive act he'd ever experienced. They kissed while she did it, made wild love with their mouths. She nibbled his bottom lip, pulled and tugged and drove him half-crazy.

He pushed her down and straddled her. She arched her back, thrusting those gorgeous breasts, those taut rose-tinged nipples. Desperate for her, he took one in his mouth and fed.

The outside light still burned, shooting streaks of color from the window over her skin, over that smooth, feminine body, those sleek grown-up curves. He took her other nipple, captured it with a slash of blue, a beam of red. She moaned and raked her nails over his back—lightly, ever so lightly.

Blood raged in his head, roared through his veins, throbbed

in his groin. He lifted her bottom, sank into her, then felt her wrap those endless legs around him.

Warm, wet, tight heat. Almost like the first time.

I'm home, he thought, as she lifted a hand to his cheek and caressed his skin, exploring his features with the tips of her fingers.

He moved. She moved with him. He groaned. She gasped. He nibbled and kissed. She bit her nails into his back and made his eyes go blind with fresh heat. She was Tricia, old and new. The same, yet changed. A touch of innocence remained, wrapped in the woman she'd become, the sensual siren, the well-bred lady with a naughty smile and blush-pink claws.

They went a little mad, crazed for each other. They took and took, releasing all the want that had been building, the desire, the need. It was a marathon, he thought, as she battled for control, then rode him, her naked body painted in light. She looked surreal—living, breathing art—the woman he'd missed, cried for, nearly hated, once loved.

Still wanted.

He caught her in his arms and rolled, pinning her beneath him again. Increasing the tempo, he lifted her hands above her head, locked them with his. She was close, so close. He could see her losing the battle, giving in, gasping.

He lowered his mouth and kissed her—hard—so hard it nearly took his breath away. She began to shudder then, shudder and chant his name. He watched her, watched until a growl, an animalistic sound, rose in his chest and ripped from his throat. She hugged his hips with her legs, tighter and tighter, and together they climaxed—man and woman—spilling into each other, spinning inside a rainbow.

"Don't move," she whispered, a long, quiet moment later. "Don't go away."

"I won't." Probably couldn't, he thought. All the blood had drained from his body, stealing his bones with it. "Are you asking me to spend the night?"

She nodded. He could feel the movement against his chin. "I want to sleep in your arms."

He had to smile, even though it took every ounce of energy he owned. "Then I'd better move, or else I'll be sleeping in your arms. And since I weigh a hell of a lot more than you do, you'll hate me in the morning. Either that, or you'll need traction."

She laughed. "I'm already numb."

He shifted until she lay in the crook of his arm, warm and comfortable. He couldn't bear her hating him, not even as a joke. "Close your eyes, Tricia."

She slept just like an angel, he thought. He kept a light on so he could watch her, watch and wonder if she would sprout wings, dust the bed with fluffy white feathers. Tomorrow, they would talk, he decided, no matter how difficult that conversation would be, or how much he dreaded delving into old aches. They had to confront the past, come to terms with it somehow. No, he didn't want to fall in love again, wasn't sure if he actually could, but he wanted to keep making love to Tricia—find a place in her life, be her lover and her friend.

He slipped out of bed to wash, careful not to disturb her. A man couldn't sleep with a condom on, he thought, as he walked past the spilled contents of his wallet. Strange Tricia wasn't on the Pill. She was thirty now, a woman who had probably enjoyed a variety of lovers.

He cleaned hastily, anxious to climb back into bed, hold her close. It was time to sleep, not dwell on the other men who had felt Tricia's touch, known her as a lover. He'd been her first, damn it. Nothing could ever take that away.

Patricia woke with the sun, blinked sleepily, then smiled. Beside her was the most incredible creature on earth, all dark and male, muscle and sinew. Night-tousled hair fell upon his shoulders, framing that perfect jaw, those strong features. Even in sleep, he emitted power.

She trailed a finger over his chest and around his nipples. She followed the hair that grew there, followed it down to the thin line that marked his belly. The sheets blocked her view. They were tangled around his legs, his hips.

She discovered a pocket of air and slipped her hand inside.

The sheets were soft and cool, his flesh warm. A giggle threatened to bubble. She felt wicked. Wonderful. She brushed his thigh, found his—

Oh, heavens. He was aroused.

"I wasn't asleep."

The sound of his voice nearly stopped her heart. She lifted her gaze and collided with lightning.

"Hi," she said. The greeting sounded foolish, even to her own ears. Hi wasn't what a woman said to man when she had her hand between his legs. Was it? Patricia wasn't quite sure.

His mouth curved into a roguish grin. "You were all over me. Did you really think I'd sleep through that?"

She had barely touched him, she thought. Barely had time to play. And now, damn it, her skin felt flushed. It was the light of day, and she was blushing like a schoolgirl.

He reached beneath the sheet, took her hand and closed her fingers around him. "Do it some more. Make me hard, Tricia."

She bit her bottom lip. Was the stain on her face growing deeper? "You already are." He felt like iron, a rod of steel. And she felt embarrassed for having been caught. She wasn't used to waking up beside a man, wanting him so early. Even Jesse. He'd been gone for twelve years.

"I can get harder."

"Jesse!" She giggled when he moved her hand, melted when he kissed her.

They tumbled over the bed, landed in each other's arms and smiled, the moment suddenly gentle, romantic.

"I've always liked your hair," he said, combing his fingers through it. "You're so sophisticated. So ladylike." His fingers trailed lower, down her neck, over her breasts. "I couldn't believe you smiled at me that day."

A tingle shivered up her spine. They were naked, recalling the day they had met. It seemed right somehow. Sexy. "You were the most handsome man I'd ever seen."

He circled her nipple, lowered his mouth to taste. "I was barely a man. More of a boy, really." He moved to her other breast, teased the peak with his tongue. "Just out of high school."

"Me, too." She nearly melted into the bed. Bittersweet memories and foreplay. Her head swam with it. "We were both kids."

"But I wasn't used to proper girls." He rose above her, steadied himself. "It made me want you even more."

She remembered how much he had wanted her, how much she had wanted him. "You taught me how to feel."

Was teaching her still, she realized as his mouth took hers.

They made love again. Slower than before, lazier. She slipped into the rhythm, the easy flow.

They danced on water, she thought, a warm quiet wave, a sensual current. The hunger that had made them crazy last night kept them sane this morning. She held him close, felt his muscles come alive beneath her fingers. He sipped her like wine, drank until he was full, then came back for more.

The pulse at her throat fluttered. She wanted him to keep drinking. Tasting. Coming back for more. He moved inside her, his hair falling over his forehead, his cheekbones high, lips full and sensual.

Patricia caught her breath on a sigh. Jesse Hawk was still the most handsome man she had ever seen. And for one dreamy, dizzy instant, she was eighteen all over again, losing her virginity and her heart.

Nine

Patricia snuggled in Jesse's arms, then glanced at the clock. "It's still morning."

He smoothed her hair. "Yeah, we were up early. Hey, do you have anything here for breakfast?"

She smiled. He could switch gears so easily. Lovemaking one minute, food the next. Men, she assumed, were like that. She wasn't an authority on after-sex practices, but she'd heard plenty of other women talk and compare notes. "The fridge is stocked. What are you in the mood for?"

"Hmm. First off I could use a strong dose of caffeine. Then maybe some bacon and eggs."

She shifted to look up at him. "Do you trust me to cook for you?"

He chuckled and kissed the tip of her nose. "Maybe we should do it together."

Patricia elbowed his rib. "Thanks a lot. Afraid I'll burn the kitchen down?"

He sank his teeth into her shoulder in a playful bite. "No,

it's just that cooking with you is so much fun." He bit down a little harder. "Come to think of it, everything I've been doing with you lately has been kinda fun."

She nudged him again, and they both laughed.

"Typical male," she said, humor suddenly failing her. Did he joke around with his other lovers? Nibble their skin? Cook breakfast with them?

She still ached to think of him with other women, it still made her raw inside. She placed her hand against her heart, grateful for the beats. She hadn't lost it, nor did she intend to. She'd had a moment of weakness during their lovemaking, but she'd recovered. Of course, not being in love anymore didn't seem to keep her jealousies under control. It bothered her that he kept condoms in his wallet. Mostly because she knew they hadn't been placed there with her in mind. Last night had just happened; neither of them had planned it.

Don't, Patricia. Don't ruin what's happening. Accept it for what it is. "I think I need a shower before we tackle breakfast."

"Yeah, me, too."

"You're welcome to use the guest bathroom down the hall." She knew he'd already used her bathroom this morning, but only to dispose of the condom. He wouldn't shower in someone else's house without asking or rummage through drawers for toiletries. Jesse had a proper, respectful side. She kissed his stubbled cheek. "Feel free to help yourself to a razor or whatever else you need." Out of habit and decorum, Patricia kept the extra bathrooms well stocked for overnight guests: disposable razors, unopened toothbrushes, mouthwash, shampoo.

"Thanks." He nuzzled her neck. "Guess I could use a shave."

A cluster of goose bumps raced up her arms. She didn't remember his beard being that heavy, but then, most of those massively formed muscles were new, too.

She was learning about him all over again, and about herself, as well. Being naked with him felt strange. Not between the sheets, but afterward. It was an effort not to dash for a robe and cover herself. But she would seem inexperienced if she put on a robe just to walk to the bathroom. And Patricia didn't want him to know just how inexperienced she was. She glanced down at the contents of his wallet still strewn across the carpet. The corner of a foil packet winked beneath a credit card. Apparently sex happened often in his world.

He grabbed his jeans. "I'll meet you downstairs, okay?"

"Okay. How about whoever gets there first starts a pot of coffee?"

"Deal." He tipped her chin for a quick kiss, then headed down the hall.

Patricia watched him. He moved like a man comfortable in his own skin, a fluid male animal, big but athletically graceful. She damned the other women who had sampled that gorgeous body, then entered her bathroom and jerked a towel from the linen closet.

The water invigorated, washed away the jealousy, the snips of hurt and anger threatening to ruin the day. She needed this quiet time, this moment to reflect. And Jesse had sensed it. Rather than tease her about doubling up in the shower, he'd respected her privacy, her morning routine.

Of course, he probably had a morning routine, too. He was a single man, used to going his own way. Freshly scrubbed and meeting in the kitchen for breakfast seemed to suit them both. Patricia smiled and lathered her hair. Maybe next time they would shower together. She stepped under the spray of water and let it sluice down her body. And maybe next time she would redeem that rain check. Drive Jesse Hawk crazy with her hands.

Her mouth.

She stumbled, then laughed. Good heavens. She was fantasizing. Alone. In the shower. A thirty-year-old woman suddenly alive with the afterglow of incredible sex.

Patricia towel dried her hair and studied her reflection. She looked different. Reborn. Sensual. She sprayed her favorite perfume, stepped into the cooling mist, then slipped on a pair of lace panties and matching bra—provocative lingerie for Jesse to peel away later.

Now what? A cotton dress? A satin slip? No, she thought. A floral silk robe, slim-fitting but not overly sexy, a garment that zipped rather than tied. If he wanted her again, he'd have to uncover her inch by willing inch.

Patricia passed the guest bathroom. The door was closed. She smiled and proceeded down the stairs. Looked as though she would be the one making coffee.

She entered the kitchen, then stopped dead in her tracks.

"Well, good morning, sunshine."

Panic rose in her throat, restricting her next breath. Her father sat at her kitchen table, a pot of coffee brewing behind him, his demeanor relaxed.

She reached for the front zipper on her robe, her hand shaky. How could this be happening? *How?* Her father had an "emergency" key to her house, but he didn't look caught up in an emergency. She could see that he'd brought a box of pastries with him. Her kitchen smelled like French-roasted coffee and cinnamon rolls, but at the moment, the aroma was anything but inviting.

She forced out a breath. "What are you doing here?"

He cocked his head. "Now is that any way to greet your dad? After all, you scheduled this meeting, remember?"

Meeting? She took a step forward, nearly tripped. No, that couldn't be. Couldn't.

"My goodness, Patricia, what's wrong with you?" He reached down and lifted a small file box. "Financial statements. We agreed to handle them here this morning instead of at the office on Monday."

"Oh, my God, Dad, I forgot." Any minute now, she thought, the room was going to spin. She couldn't see straight. Think straight. Her father sat at her table while Jesse showered in one of her bathrooms, and it was all her fault.

"No harm done. Just relax. I've got all day." He walked over to the counter and opened the pastry box. "When you didn't answer the door, I figured you must have overslept. I thought about calling on the cell phone, but decided to come in and start a pot of coffee instead." He held up a cinnamon roll oozing with glaze. "I brought Dillon his favorite treat. Where is the little rascal, anyway?"

"Dillon's at the river with the Harrisons." And her lover was upstairs, probably half-naked, shaving that sexy beard stubble. Her lover. The man her father despised. "Dad, I don't really think I'm up to working on the financial statements this morning. I—"

Patricia's lame excuse about not feeling well faltered. Her dad wasn't looking at her. He stared beyond her, his shoulders tense, his gaze stone cold.

She didn't have to turn to know Jesse stood behind her. Her father's expression said it all.

The air grew thick, the coffee-and-dessert aroma cloying. Patricia heard Jesse step further into the kitchen, felt his hand on her back. A light, possessive touch. A masculine claim.

Her father's expression turned harder, his gaze following Jesse's every move. Oh, God. What should she do? She didn't want to hostess this soul-piercing reunion. The past swirled around them like an evil poltergeist.

She exhaled a ragged breath and turned toward Jesse. "Last week I scheduled a meeting for this morning with my father, but I forgot."

Jesse gave a short nod without looking at her. He watched her father instead. And her father watched him. Both wary. Eyes filled with hate.

Jesse hadn't dressed, not completely. He wore jeans and nothing else, no shirt, no shoes. His hair, damp from the shower, had been combed straight back. His face, taut with anger, appeared stronger, sharper, more raw-boned. There would be no question in her father's mind that Jesse had spent the night. Jesse's appearance, and hers as well, announced this was "the morning after."

Coffee, her brain said inanely. Should she offer them coffee, ask them to sit? "Maybe we—"

Too late. Too slow. Too timid. Her father's voice canceled hers, his words slipping past a clenched jaw. "I see you're back, Mr. Hawk. Taking advantage of my daughter again."

Jesse rose to the challenge before Patricia could stop him.

He removed his hand from her spine, then jerked his head as a stray lock of hair dared to cover his face. He strode closer to Raymond, his steps precise, calculated. Patricia feared he intended to count coup: circle the enemy, strike, gain honor in battle. When he stopped just short of physical contact, the air in her lungs whooshed out.

"Your daughter is a grown woman, *Mr.* Boyd," he said, emphasizing the title with bitterness. "And if she wants a relationship with me, you can't stop her. Not this time."

"When it concerns my daughter's welfare, I can do whatever the hell I please," the older man said sharply, his face coloring with rage.

Patricia couldn't find her voice, so she hugged herself for comfort, her gaze darting nervously between her father and her lover. As Jesse spoke, she glanced his way and realized she'd never seen him look so sinister. A muscle ticked in his cheek as a mocking smile curled one corner of his lips. His rage was cooler, more controlled. Taunting.

"Tricia knows her own mind," he said. "Her body, too."

Her dad fisted his hands, and Patricia's knees threatened to give way. "Why, you arrogant young pup. It's all about sex to you, isn't it?"

Jesse's seething control didn't falter. He had schooled himself well, Patricia thought, as she groped the counter for support. He stood tall, a warrior in his own right.

"Don't you dare judge me. Or my intentions. You don't know a thing about me. Not a damn thing."

"I know exactly who and what you are," Raymond retorted. "You used my daughter twelve years ago, took advantage of her innocence." He paused, exhaled a slow breath. "You told her that you loved her so she'd go to bed with you. That's the oldest male trick in the book, and you played it to perfection."

Another wave of dizziness swept over Patricia. She didn't want Jesse to answer. They had closed that door last night by agreeing to have an affair. No pretenses. No false promises. She didn't want to hear about the past, think about it.

"Well, let me tell you something, Boyd," Jesse said, his

voice rough. "I was in love with Tricia all those years ago. What I felt for her had nothing to do with sex."

Stunned, Patricia steadied herself. How could he say that? How could he stand there and lie to make himself look noble? Cheat to win this vengeful war with her father?

Devastation rushed through her hard and quick. Just weeks ago he had stated the cold, humiliating facts. *I wasn't really in love. We were only kids. Teenagers experimenting. I should have never asked you to live with me. What we had was nothing more than puppy love. A strong infatuation.*

He hadn't come back for her. Hadn't loved her. Damn him for saying otherwise, for not being man enough to admit the truth to her father. Shamed by her naiveté, Patricia summoned the strength to square her shoulders. How could she have slept with him again? Sex would never be simple, not with Jesse. Their past would never go away.

Raymond shook his head. "You're a liar, Hawk."

Yes, she thought. He is.

"Dad, please." She turned to Jesse, her legs remarkably steady. "We need to talk. Privately."

Jesse and Tricia went into the den and closed the door while her father remained in the kitchen. That old bastard didn't even have the decency to leave, Jesse thought. Raymond Boyd parked his ass at the table as if he owned the joint. Jesse almost laughed, a sick, exhausted laugh. Hell, Boyd probably did own the place.

"I can't believe that happened." He slumped onto the sofa, his hands suddenly shaky. "How the hell did your dad get in, anyway?"

"He has a key."

Of course he did. Boyd owned the house, or that corporation of his probably did. How could Tricia stand to work for her father, live in one of his homes?

Jesse studied Tricia. She stood with her arms crossed, masking her emotions as usual. "Come on, honey," he coaxed, "sit down before you fall down. You don't have to act brave for me. That had to be awful for you."

She continued to stand. "Yes, it was."

He dragged a hand through his hair. "I'm sorry. It was just such a shock to see him there, and then when he—"

"I'm not going to sleep with you again, Jesse. That was a mistake."

His hand nearly caught in his hair. Suddenly he couldn't breathe. Couldn't move. "You're choosing your father over me? He disapproves, so you're telling me to go to hell?"

"Think what you want," she said, her voice cool. Typically aloof.

He pushed himself off the couch and strode toward her. Did she have any idea how difficult it had been for him to bare his soul? To admit that he had once loved her? He'd just defended her honor, but she didn't care. She hadn't changed a bit. Nothing mattered to Tricia but her father's money.

Their gazes locked, and a knot of revenge formed in his gut. It moved swiftly, painfully, coiling around his intestines like a snake. He felt it poison his thoughts, his next words. His heart.

"What the matter, little rich girl?" he asked with a deliberate sneer. "Are you afraid you'll lose your inheritance? Will Daddy take away all those millions if you continue to sleep with the enemy?"

Tricia's immediate response came in the form of a quick, hard slap. Jesse didn't flinch. Instead he stood dead still while her palm cracked across his cheek. He didn't feel it. Not even the slightest sting. The ache from their past had already crashed over him like a vicious tidal wave, dragging him under, spewing and splashing hurtful memories.

How many times had he sat alone and cried? Thrown books across his apartment because the words made no sense? Worried that he couldn't get through college without Tricia by his side? Felt stupid? Poor? Not good enough?

For years he had attended classes at a school owned by her father's fraternity brother, fearing at any given moment that the rug would be pulled out from under him. And all the while, Raymond Boyd was playing Grandpa to his son, stealing the child who was rightfully his.

Jesse turned away from Tricia and headed for the French door that led to the backyard. He needed fresh air. Trees. The sky. The world that wasn't owned by Boyd Enterprises.

The sun radiated warmth, so he lifted his face, let it wash over him. He felt the patio tiles beneath his feet and realized he wore no shoes. His boots, his shirt, even his wallet was still in Tricia's room. Something glinted near the door. He turned. A pair of Dillon's in-line skates.

He moved toward them, knelt, then picked one up and spun the wheels. Damn, he missed his son.

"Jesse, what are you doing?"

Trying to breathe, he thought, glancing up at Tricia. Trying to survive another bout of emotional warfare. Anguish.

He stood, skate in hand. Tricia's skin glowed in the morning light, that flawless complexion never seeming to fail her. How could she look pretty to him now? After what she'd done? God help him, but that robe she wore only added to her femininity, reminding him of their recent lovemaking. The silky texture, smooth lines, seductive curves.

Jesse withheld a sarcastic laugh. Suddenly he felt used. Men weren't supposed to feel used after sex, but he did. What an idiot, letting himself care for her again.

The skate wheels quit spinning, intensifying the quiet. The ache. "You're not going to stop me from seeing Dillon," he said, fearing an upcoming battle for his parental rights. He didn't intend to be just a weekend dad. Eventually he wanted joint custody. He'd already begun turning his guest room into a bedroom for Dillon by adding shelves for the boy's models, a desk for homework.

Tricia pushed her hair away from her cheek, a chestnut sweep that never misbehaved. It had dried to perfection. "How can you say something like that to me? I would never use our son as a pawn." She crossed her arms, narrowed her eyes. "If I didn't want you to be Dillon's father, why would I have given him your last name?"

Good question, he supposed. He hadn't quite figured that one out yet. She'd kept Dillon a secret from him, but told the

rest of the world that he had fathered the boy. It made no
sense. Absolutely none.

"Fine. I'll make arrangements to see him later in the week.
Alone. I don't want you there, Tricia."

"Well, you don't have a choice." She lifted her chin, apparently intent on looking him straight in the eye. "Dillon
doesn't want to spend time alone with you. He's not ready
yet. Good God, Jesse, he barely knows you."

His heart constricted, then bled, gushed with even more
pain. Did his son consider him a nuisance? An obligation? He
placed the skate back onto the ground next to its mate. "Okay.
But we're going to have to be civil. At least pretend we like
each other."

She sighed, and he noticed how tired she looked. How emotionally weary. "I know." She reached for the door handle.
"Go inside and get your things. My father is still here, and
we have work to do. I'll have Dillon call you when he gets
back on Sunday."

"That's fine. If he wants to." Forcing Dillon into a relationship wouldn't work. Jesse remembered how aggressive his
second foster parents had been, how they had expected him to
accept them overnight, as if he was a robot rather than a kid.

Jesse went upstairs while Tricia headed for the kitchen. He
knelt on her floor and gathered the contents of his wallet,
jamming items inside hastily. Ignoring the unmade bed, he
grabbed his shirt and shoved on his boots. The faint scent of
jasmine still drifted through the air. He left the room without
glancing back. Now the exotic fragrance was painful as hell.

She paced the kitchen like a nervous feline, caged, trapped
within the past. No way out.

"Patricia, sweetheart. He's gone. Please sit down before
you fall down."

Her head snapped up. She stared at her father. *Sit down
before you fall down.* Jesse had said the same thing to her just
minutes ago. Or was it hours? She'd lost all sense of time,
reason.

She walked over to the file box beside the table and picked

up a stack of the financial reports. "You're right. We have work to do."

He took them from her hands. Her dad sat at the table, a mug of coffee in front of him. "You're in no condition to work, young lady. Why don't you let me fix you some breakfast?"

Patricia shook her head. She and Jesse were going to make breakfast together, and then she was going to let him seduce her. Watch him peel off her robe, unzip the stupid thing one inch at a time. "I'm not hungry."

"A cup of tea, then?" Her dad dropped the reports back into the file box and got to his feet. "Chamomile, with two spoonfuls of honey. That's your favorite, isn't it?"

Patricia only stared. Chamomile reminded her of Jesse. "I haven't drunk that in years, Dad." Not since she'd accepted the fact that Jesse would never return for her. "I used to drink it because he told me that it soothed restlessness." She felt a flood of tears collect in her eyes. "So you see, whenever I was restless for him, I'd…"

"Oh, Patricia." Her father placed the canister of tea bags onto the counter. "I'm sorry."

She wiped her eyes. "I'm being silly. Acting like I'm eighteen again."

He took her hand and guided her to the table. "I know it hurts, baby, but he's not worth it. He lied about loving you, you know that, don't you? He said that because I trapped him."

She glanced up at the ceiling, willing her eyes to remain dry. "I know. If it had been the truth, I wouldn't have told him to leave." She fingered the zipper on her robe. Love was a strange emotion. Confusing. Impossible to understand. Even though she wasn't in love with Jesse anymore, his betrayal still hurt.

Her dad squeezed her hand, making Patricia grateful for his presence. He was a hard man at times, stern and overly protective, but he loved her the way she loved Dillon. Parental love never went away. If anything, it grew with each passing day.

"You'll be okay," he said. "You're strong, Patricia. You'll weather this."

She studied her father's features, his aristocratic look. He resembled a politician, she thought, a distinguished man, subtle streaks of gray in his hair, a trim physique. She'd inherited his mannerism, his stubborn nature and take-charge attitude. Their wills clashed often. But not today. She wouldn't be defending Jesse Hawk today.

"Did you love my mom?" she asked, suddenly missing the arms of a mother. The comfort only another woman could offer.

He furrowed his brow, picked up his coffee. "Now what kind of question is that?"

An honest one, she thought. "You never talk about her, Dad."

"You know I'm not a talker. What good would it do? She's been gone a long time."

And he didn't love her, Patricia realized. Not as much as he should have. Not the way she had loved Jesse. Her mother hadn't been the love of her father's life.

He glanced up from the rim of his cup, and when he placed the coffee back onto the table, she could see that she'd unnerved him. His hand seemed unsteady.

"I cared for your mother deeply," he said.

Patricia nodded, unable to respond. He'd cared for her mother, but he'd loved someone else. A long time ago, she decided, before he'd married her mom. Did that woman die, too? Had everyone her father ever cared about died? Is that what made him so protective? She sighed, knowing it wouldn't pay to ask. He would never discuss his personal life with her, past or present. Raymond Boyd, the prestigious real estate tycoon, guarded his emotions like a treasure.

"I could really use some food," he said. "Are you hungry yet?"

No, but she'd eat to appease him. Breakfast, he'd always told her, was the most important meal of the day. She pushed her chair back and rose. "I'll scramble us some eggs." It was the one thing she knew how to cook.

"How about eggs Benedict from the country club bistro instead?"

Patricia turned back toward her father. He was trying to get her out of the house, she realized. Trying to help her forget. "Okay, Dad, you're on."

At least she wouldn't run into Jesse at the country club. She wouldn't have to see him until after Dillon returned. "I'll get dressed," she said, praying her bedroom wouldn't trigger an onslaught of tears. The lovemaking that had occurred there still seemed fresh.

No, *raw,* she decided, as she tackled the stairs. An open wound that would probably never heal.

Ten

___

Jesse watched the white Mercedes roll onto the graveled driveway. It looked out of place on his property, he thought. It probably cost more than he made in an entire year.

He reached down to pet Cochise's head. "Dillon's here," he told the rottweiler. "Tricia, too," he added under his breath, his stomach clenching. He hadn't seen her since that kitchen confrontation with Boyd.

Dillon hopped out of the car, said hi, then grinned at the dog.

Cochise whined and wiggled.

"Go say hello," Jesse urged, knowing Cochise would receive the hug he longed for.

As Dillon knelt to embrace the dog, Jesse spotted a strip of leather beneath his son's shirt. The sight evoked an inner hug, a warm fuzzy feeling. Dillon was wearing Jesse's former medicine bag, the spiritual connection they shared.

He moved forward, then crouched beside the boy. "I was wondering if maybe you'd like to help with some chores," he said. The idea had stemmed from Jesse's own childhood, a fantasy of standing beside his father, doing ranch work. He used to conjure images of the father he'd never met, create his face, his mannerisms. "I haven't had the chance to feed the animals yet, and I've still got plants to water, a fence to mend."

"I can feed the animals," Dillon volunteered quickly. "Even clean up after the horse if you want. Muck the stall. That's what it's called, right?"

Jesse's heart did a big, floppy somersault. Dillon Hawk was his kid all right. Not too many eleven-year-olds would offer to shovel manure. He grinned. "Yeah, that's what it's called."

Dillon turned impatiently toward the car. "What's taking Mom so long?"

Good question. Jesse rose to his feet. Tricia sat behind the wheel, fumbling through a leather briefcase. "Guess she's looking for something." Or avoiding me for as long as possible.

"Mom, come on! I have to help Dad with some chores."

Tricia exited the car and placed her briefcase on the hood. "You two go ahead. I'll catch up."

Chicken, Jesse thought. She wouldn't even look at him. Wouldn't lift her eyes from the case. Instead she continued to dig through the damn thing as if her life depended on it.

"You lose something?" he asked, forcing a tone of normalcy into his voice.

She glanced up, and Jesse could have kicked himself. He would have been better off ignoring her. Her skin had that flawless appeal, the creamy glow that always made him itch to touch it. Sunlight suited her. The streaks in her hair sparkled like polished brass.

She stepped away from the car. "I brought some reports with me to go over, but it looks like some pages are missing."

He lifted an eyebrow. So she'd decided to flaunt her role today. Patricia Boyd, busy young executive. Beautiful, rich, important. Even her clothes emitted power. She'd paired sleek leather boots with a summer pantsuit, a classy beige number that probably sported a designer label. Her jewelry consisted of a delicate gold watch and tiny pearl earrings. The proper heiress, elegant, not too showy.

"Do you have a fax machine?" she asked.

I'm not a country bumpkin, he wanted say. I do run a business. "Yeah. It's in the clinic."

"Could I trouble you to use it?" She spoke in a professional tone. Although there was no bite, there was no genuine warmth, either. A voice that would neither alarm nor offend their son. A voice the child had probably heard her use a thousand times before. "I'd like to call my father and have him fax the missing pages."

Her dad. The last person on earth Jesse wanted dialing his fax line. He glanced back at Dillon. The boy still knelt beside Cochise, ruffling the dog's ears. "Sure, Tricia." He reached into his pocket and tossed her his keys rather than chance a touch. The gentle sweep of fingertips would be too familiar. Too painful. "The fax machine is in the front office. Help yourself."

She caught the keys, then closed her briefcase. "Is there an alarm?"

"No." In his opinion, alarm systems were for city dwellers. Or millionaires. He didn't fall into either category. "The light switches are in the break room."

Her overly polite smile struck him as feigned. "Thanks. I'll drive around back. Dillon, honey, I'll catch up. Okay?"

"Sure, Mom. Say hello to Grandpa from me."

Her gaze locked with Jesse's before she turned away. He watched her get behind the wheel, start the engine, pull forward.

"You ready, son?"

The boy popped up, dusted his jeans. "Yep. Ready and able."

Ready and able he was. Dillon smiled, listened, took direction, then squealed in delight when he entered the kennel area to feed Jesse's ever-changing array of four-legged friends.

"This one's new." Dillon squatted to cuddle a poodle-terrier mix that wiggled at his feet. "I don't remember seeing him last time."

Jesse smiled. "Yeah, except that little one happens to be a she."

"Oh. Where'd you get her?"

"The pound."

The boy looked up, cuddled the dog a little closer. "You saved her."

Jesse swallowed. The awe in the child's voice made him proud, a little misty-eyed. He used to imagine gazing up at his own dad like that. Imagine his dad smiling back at him. His mom, too. He pictured her as being the prettiest lady on earth. "I guess so, yeah. She'll stay with me until I can find her another home."

Dillon's voiced cracked a little. "They were gonna put her down, huh?"

"Yeah, but they don't like doing that." Jesse regarded the animals he rescued as orphans, and he knew firsthand what being orphaned had felt like. "I just couldn't leave her there. She's such a sweet little thing." He remembered children in foster care who were just as sweet, kids whose chances of being adopted were slim to none.

He ruffled the top of Dillon's head. "We better get these dogs fed. We've still got a horse to tend to."

The boy grinned and lunged to his feet. "Yes, sir."

Thirty minutes later Dillon stood inside the gelding's stall, stroking the animal's nose like an old friend. The equine bonding, much to Jesse's delight, happened instantly.

"Does Hunter like sugar cubes?" Dillon asked.

"Yep. Carrots, too." Jesse had given the horse his mother's maiden name since the gelding wasn't registered and didn't have a family history of his own. He thought the powerful name suited the sturdy paint. But then, Hunter hadn't always been packed with muscle. Five years before, Jesse had rescued the neglected gelding from a rental stable that had been charged with animal abuse.

Dillon climbed onto a pipe rail and let Hunter nuzzle him. "I've always wanted a horse. It's sort of my secret wish."

Surprised by Dillon's admission, Jesse joined his son on the rail. The boy came from millions. Why would he secretly long for something his mother could certainly afford to buy? "Do you know how to ride?"

"No." Dillon shook his head. "But my grandpa does. I saw pictures of him with his horses. The pictures were from a long time ago, before my mom was born." He gave a sad smile as Hunter nudged him for more attention. "Grandpa hates horses now."

Jesse smelled a rat. A big, rich one. "How do you know that?"

"'Cause he said so when I asked him about those pictures. He seemed real upset that I found them. He said I wasn't supposed to go snooping through his stuff. That was a few years ago, but he told me never to talk to him about horses again, that he hated them." Dillon hugged Hunter's beefy neck. "Grandpa threw those pictures away, but when he wasn't looking, I took them out of the trash."

And the boy probably had them hidden in his room somewhere, Jesse thought, hoping someday Boyd would change his mind. Damn that old man. "You know, Dillon, I can teach you to ride. You can learn on Hunter." The gelding was as gentle as a rocking horse and just as smooth. "I'll talk to your mom about it and then she can tell your grandpa so everybody knows what's going on." He reached over to touch a lock of his son's hair. Dillon deserved the right to explore his dream.

"Really?" The child's eyes lit up, suddenly more blue than gray. "That would be so cool. Can we start today? Right now?"

Jesse smiled, pleased by Dillon's youthful enthusiasm. "We can start with ground rules today. You've got to know how to handle a horse on the ground before you can climb on his back."

"But Hunter likes me."

"Yeah, he does, but he's a lot bigger than you, and he can take advantage if you let him." Jesse hopped off the rail. "Why don't you go into the house and get some carrots for Hunter, and I'll go talk to your mom."

Tricia was sure as hell going to get a piece of his mind. How could she allow her father to dictate Dillon's life because of his own selfish problems? In Jesse's opinion, a man who had owned horses, then hated them later, was no kind of man at all.

Patricia felt like a coward—a disorganized one. She'd misplaced more things that week than she cared to admit. She rolled her shoulders. She hadn't planned on hiding out in Jesse's clinic, but now that she was there, she dreaded leaving. It hurt to look at him, see him looking back at her.

She closed her eyes. She'd barely been eating, sleeping. And checking her reflection in the mirror in her bedroom was the worst kind of torture. Jesse still lingered there, on his knees, making love to her.

"Tricia?"

Startled, she opened her eyes and righted her posture. She sat at the reception desk in Jesse's clinic, and he stood on the other side staring down at her. She lifted her papers and shuffled them. "I was just getting ready to leave."

"Well, you might as well stay put, because I need to talk to you."

Not now, she thought. His voice had that confrontational edge. "This isn't a good time. We agreed to behave in a civil manner when we were with Dillon."

"I am being civil, damn it. And what I have to say is important."

She rose from the desk and walked around to the other side. If he was going to persist, then she didn't intend to give him the advantage of peering down his nose at her. She removed her jacket and placed it on the counter. She'd changed her clothes three times that morning. Three times in front of that mirror. "All right. What's on your mind?"

"Your dad has no right to squelch Dillon's dreams."

Patricia blinked. "What are you talking about?"

"Dillon wants a horse, Tricia. He's wanted one for years."

She leaned against the counter, silently stunned. "He told you that?"

"Yeah, just now."

"But he's never said anything to me." And since she hadn't

been raised with horses, she'd never thought to offer her son
riding lessons. Arrow Hill had an equestrian center, but she'd
never been part of the horsy set. Most of the Arrow Hill eques-
trians were the polo type, a little too showy for her taste. The
struggling ranchers and cowboys lived down below, in
Hatcher, but she'd steered clear of them, as well, knowing she
didn't fit into their world, either.

"What does this have to do with my dad?"

Jesse's voice took on a bite. "He's the reason Dillon never
said anything. Apparently your old man hates horses."

"Oh, goodness. I never knew that he and Dillon had talked
about that." She was aware that her father had owned horses
at one time, but that had been before he'd married her mother.
"I don't think he hates them exactly. I think something happened, like maybe he took a bad fall." Fear, she thought,
would make a man like Raymond Boyd testy. "I never pursued the subject because I wasn't interested in riding."

"Well, Dillon is, and your dad should have been more considerate."

"You're right, of course. I'll—"

Jesse interrupted briskly. "You'll tell your father that I'm
going to teach my son to ride. That Dillon will come here
twice a week for a lesson." He softened his expression, then
blew a tired-sounding breath. "I'm not doing this to spite your
old man, Tricia. I'm doing this for Dillon."

"I know." She didn't doubt that Jesse loved their son, that
Dillon was the number-one priority in his life.

"Come on." He headed toward the break room. "If you're
done, let's lock up. I promised Dillon he could start his lessons
today."

After Jesse turned out the lights and secured the door, Patricia started toward her car.

"What's the matter? Afraid to walk with me?"

She stopped and turned. Yes, she thought, she was. Strolling
next to him on a beautiful summer day held too many memories. Sunshine, shady trees and moist kisses used to be a
favored combination. "Of course not. I was just going to put

my briefcase away. My jacket, too.'' The morning chill, she noted, was gone. At least in the air.

His gaze swept over her, and suddenly she felt naked. Exposed and raw.

"You better get yourself a pair of jeans and Western boots if Dillon wants you to stay for his lessons in the future. Either that or keep clear of the barn. Suits and spiky boots don't cut it around here."

She ignored the sarcasm in his tone. Apparently he thought she'd overdressed for the day. He hadn't, she noticed. He wore a country uniform of faded denim and tanned leather. His hair, dark as a moonless night and free as the wind, fell about his shoulders. He looked rooted to the land, the rugged surroundings.

The old Garrett farm was certainly a charming place, she thought, as they continued toward the barn. Although it was no longer a working farm, the soil still seemed rich and fertile. Jesse's garden bloomed with tall, flowering plants and herbal aromas.

When they neared a small red building, Patricia smiled. Dillon sat outside on a pipe corral that extended from the barn, babying a huge brown-and-white horse. She'd never seen her son look so happy, so relaxed.

"He needs this," she said.

"Yeah." Jesse stared straight ahead. "He's a terrific kid. You did a good job with him, Tricia."

"Thank you."

They moved forward in silence. Patricia knew this was as civil as things were going to get. Forgetting or forgiving didn't seem possible. The welfare of eleven-year-old Dillon Hawk was their only tie.

Four days later Patricia sat in Jesse's truck, jammed against the door. She could feel his animosity toward her, knowing he resented her presence. Jesse had called and invited Dillon out for a casual dinner, apparently hoping for some time alone with his son, but the plan had backfired. Dillon had insisted she come along.

He pulled into a parking stall and cut the engine. "Hope this place is okay," he said, not quite masking the strain in his voice.

Patricia opened her door. "It's fine." She knew his comment had been directed toward her. Did he think she was too snooty for cheeseburgers and a milk shake? Or was that his hurt talking? His disappointment that Dillon had refused to be alone with him?

They entered the restaurant, a family-type diner in Hatcher with red vinyl booths and waitresses darting by in crepe-soled shoes. The atmosphere was too friendly for Tricia's mood, too lively to ease the tension between old lovers. The lights were bright, the crowd noisy. While elderly couples ate pie and drank coffee, young parents studied their menus in haste, their children either chattering mindlessly or banging on metal high chairs.

Tricia scooted into the corner booth first. She used to imagine places like this, wondered what it would feel like to be a part of a middle-class family who shared household chores and dined on a budget. She'd tried to give Dillon and herself a sense of normalcy in their lives, but, looking around, she knew their lives had never been this normal, this lovingly chaotic.

"Go on, son," Jesse said, directing Dillon into the circular booth.

Dillon shook his head. "I want to be on the end. You can sit next to Mom. I hate being squeezed in the middle."

"Come on, Dillon. I'm bigger than you. I don't want to be squeezed in the middle, either."

The boy refused to budge. "I had to sit in the middle in the truck."

"Yeah, well, I was driving so that doesn't count."

Patricia narrowed her eyes. Jesse and Dillon had the same stubborn scowl etched upon their faces, the same brooding expression. Dillon's stemmed from youth, but Jesse's was a clear indication that he didn't want to sit next to her. At least clear to her, anyway.

"Will you both please sit down. You're causing a scene."

They weren't, of course. No one in the noisy restaurant paid them any mind, but Jesse's childish reaction intensified her displaced sense of belonging. The lonely rich girl on the hill, wondering how the other half lived.

"Fine." Jesse scooted in and bumped her arm, as Dillon took his place. "Sorry," he muttered.

She stiffened. "That's all right." But it wasn't. Not any of it. Not the faint woodsy note of his cologne or the broad feel of his shoulder pressing hers.

Things couldn't get much worse, Patricia thought, until their waitress turned out to be a client of Jesse's—an overly talkative lady who chatted about her truck driver husband, their three rambunctious kids and a pug named Bruno that Jesse had treated for kennel cough.

"Doctor Hawk," she beamed, "I'm so glad you brought your family." She smiled at Patricia next. "You've done a wonderful job fixing up the old Garrett place. Those gorgeous flower beds and that garden. You must love it there."

Patricia's heart rammed against her chest. The flower beds. The herb garden. Warm touches that weren't hers. "I—" She cleared her throat. *Think,* she told herself. Think of a proper way to tell this woman that you're not Jesse's wife. "It is a lovely home, but—"

Dillon jumped in before she could complete her answer. "We don't live there. My mom and dad aren't married. Now can we just order? Please."

A moment of stunned silence ensued but, much to Patricia's chagrin, the waitress recovered first. The friendly lady forced a smile, an overly polite gesture meant to ease the discomfort of everyone involved.

"Looks to me like you've got a hungry one there."

"Yes," Patricia responded as Jesse remained silent beside her. Apparently Dillon's blunt response had upset him even more than the waitress's misconception. She could see a slight tremor in his hands, hear a hitch in his breath. He looked hurt, confused, angry. All the same emotions stirring inside her.

Their dinner arrived twenty minutes later. Patricia's food hit her stomach like a rock, even though she had only taken a few bites. She glanced at her son. Rather than meet her gaze, Dillon stared at his plate, painting ketchup swirls with his fries. She had already warned him in a tight but quiet voice to expect a parental talk after dinner. Correcting her child in a public setting wasn't her style, but then Dillon had never embarrassed her in public before. This experience was new. Painfully new.

After Jesse paid the bill, he tipped the waitress personally. Patricia assumed he must have offered a simple apology, as well, because the woman squeezed his arm before he turned back toward her and Dillon.

"What did you tell that lady?" Dillon challenged his father the moment they stepped outside. "What did you say to her?"

Jesse continued toward the truck. "I told her that we were having some family problems," he answered in a quiet voice. "She's a client of mine, and I felt I owed her the courtesy of an explanation."

"Family problems." Dillon snorted. "Yeah, right. You and my mom aren't family."

Jesse stopped dead in his tracks as Patricia reached for her son's arm. Suddenly she knew exactly what troubled the boy. No one but Dillon could read her emotions and, tonight he'd read them well—every last awful one. If she hadn't been so self-absorbed, she would have recognized his pain sooner.

Dillon jerked free of her hold, then faced his father. "Do you think I'm stupid? I can tell that you don't like my mom. You didn't even want to sit by her." He turned to look at Patricia, his steely gaze boring into hers. "You're no better, Mom. You're a liar, too. You've only been pretending to be friends with my dad. You hate him as much as he hates you."

Dillon's accusation hit her like a head-on collision. They stood in the middle of the parking lot, emotions racing by like drunk drivers on a single-lane highway. Dangerous and out of control. And wrong, so very wrong. "I don't hate your father," she said, "but there are times that I don't like him. And you're right, we're not friends, not in the way we led you to believe. But we tried, honey. Honestly we did."

Jesse moved forward, his voice shaky, his stare humble but focused. The shamed warrior. "I'm sorry, son. I guess I haven't been a very good father, but I'd sure like a second chance. And as for your mom and me...well, we've got a lot of past between us. Things I can't explain. Things that just go wrong between a man and a woman.''

Dillon held his dad's gaze. ''Do you hate her?''

''No.'' The response came quickly, gently. Sadly.

''Then how come you can't be friends?''

Jesse reached over to touch Patricia. His hand brushed her shoulder, then fell. ''I'm not sure. I think maybe it's because we haven't talked. I mean really talked. You know, about important stuff.''

Like why he didn't come back, Patricia thought. And why she had kept her pregnancy a secret. ''We could do that now,'' she suggested, searching Jesse's gaze.

''Yeah, we could.'' He managed a small smile. ''If that's okay with Dillon.''

''It's okay with me,'' the boy replied, ''but I think you should go someplace by yourselves. I don't want to be around in case you start arguing.''

''We won't.'' Patricia placed her arms around her son and hugged him tight, praying those words wouldn't come back to haunt her. There was a lot to rectify, possibly too much for one night.

Eleven

———

Jesse unlocked his front door and ushered Tricia inside. He had taken Dillon home where the boy would spend the evening with his former nanny, watching a rented movie and snacking on popcorn.

"Can I get you some hot tea or something?" he asked, unsure of how to start this talk they'd decided to have.

Tricia twisted a leather tassel on her handbag. "Yes, thank you. Tea sounds nice."

Peppermint, he decided, heading for the kitchen. Peppermint soothed nervousness, something both he and Tricia appeared to suffer from at the moment. Poor digestion, too. The burger he'd eaten had pummeled his stomach like an angry fist. He imagined Tricia's dinner had upset her, too. Stressful situations and food didn't usually mix well.

He set the water to boil while Tricia took a seat at the kitchen table.

Jesse turned away from the kettle and leaned against the counter. "I deserved that lashing Dillon gave me tonight. He was right, you know. I didn't want to sit next to you. I guess I was the one behaving like an eleven-year-old.''

She angled her chin. "Don't most boys that age like girls? I know Dillon does. He's over that cooties stage.''

Jesse felt a boyish tug pull one corner of his lips, a kid smile, chock-full of admiration and anxiety. Tricia Boyd still made his heartbeat skip. "I never thought that you had cooties. That wasn't the problem.''

Her return smile was fleeting. "I know.''

The tug moved from his lips to his belly, causing it to clench. The problem, he decided, was their past, the subject neither of them knew quite how to broach.

He turned back to the stove, grateful for something to do. The water wasn't boiling, but it was nearly there, hot enough. He pinched a handful of leaves from a windowsill plant and dropped them into an old-fashioned teapot he'd found at a flea market. It wasn't a delicate piece of china. It looked sturdy and weathered, like the house, like himself.

He poured the water and brought the teapot to the table, along with two cups, two spoons and a jar of fresh honey he'd purchased from a local supplier.

They sat for a short while and let the brew steep. He didn't have to explain the purpose to Tricia. He had schooled her about some of the more common herbs, taught her how to extract their healing properties. He had shared himself with Tricia during that ill-fated summer, offered her everything he'd had to give.

She poured the tea and added honey to hers. "Peppermint,'' she said, upon tasting it. She took another sip, then tilted her head, her hair brushing her cheek. "It's supposed to be an aphrodisiac, isn't it?''

That damned boyish pull returned, tugging his groin this time. "In large quantities, yeah. But that's not why I chose it.'' The idea of seducing her had merit, though. Sex was easier than talking. Tumble onto the sheets, sink into that temporary high, feel and forget.

"Where should we start?'' he asked, lifting his drink. "I'm not very good at this sort of thing.''

She watched him through eyes that had turned suddenly wary. "You're not good at the truth?"

The accusation stung, a bite the warm brew couldn't ease. He placed his cup back onto the table. "What's that supposed to mean?" He'd been honest all along. She sure as hell couldn't make that claim.

Tricia tucked her hair behind her ears. "It means you lied. Years ago and just recently."

He leaned back in his chair, consciously distancing himself from her. "Maybe you'd better fill me in."

"All right." She sat a little straighter, spoke a little sharper. "You lied to my father in the kitchen. You told him that you used to be in love with me. That wasn't the truth, not by a long shot."

He brought his body forward, his heart pounding in his head. "That wasn't a lie. I loved you, Tricia. So damned much." It still hurt, hurt to admit, talk about. "You were my life. Why do you think I asked you to live with me? I was willing to postpone my education for you." Sweep her off her feet, he added mentally, tell her dad to go to hell. "You refused. You sent me on my way."

She shook her head. "You thought you loved me, but it was only lust. You figured that out soon enough. You even admitted it the day I came to see you, the week before you found out about Dillon. You told me that we were just kids experimenting. That what you had felt for me was nothing more than a strong infatuation."

She was right. He had lied to her, and she'd believed that lie even after he'd retracted it. "What I told your father was the truth, I swear it. It wasn't about sex. I loved you." He took a deep breath. "I said those awful things to you that day on my porch because it was just so hard seeing you again."

Her eyes glazed with unshed tears. He wanted to go to her, hold her, but he knew she wouldn't welcome his touch. There were more issues. He could see them in her eyes, as she battled her tears. He placed his hands around his cup and held on to that warmth instead. He had issues, too.

She bit down on her bottom lip as though it could stop the

tears, keep her in control. Cool, sophisticated Tricia, he thought. She didn't like to cry.

"If you loved me, Jesse, why didn't you come back before now?" Her voice broke a little. "I asked you to come back for me. And you promised you would."

He gripped the cup, white-knuckled it. She'd just raised some of his issues, twisted them into hers. "You asked me to come back to prove my worth to your father. That's not the same thing as coming back for you."

She glanced up at the ceiling. "Your worth?" She brought her gaze back down, blinked. "What does that mean? I wanted you to prove to my father that you loved me. Show him that what we'd had was real, that it was the kind of love that would withstand the test of time." She exhaled a ragged breath. "I argued with Dad over it. I insisted he was wrong about you, that you weren't just using me for sex. And I made him promise that when you came back for me—" she paused for another shaky breath "—he'd have to make things right somehow."

Make things right. Jesse pushed back his chair and got to his feet. He needed to move, pace, release his own pent-up breath. "I thought it was about power and money. I'd go to college and come back a better man. Educated, but not too independent. The kind of man your dad could order around. The puppet son-in-law. I honestly thought that's what you wanted."

He stopped pacing and caught her wounded look. "What was I supposed to think? You refused to move in with me. You told me that we didn't have enough money to make it on our own." She'd hurt his pride, his stupid male pride. "You were rich and beautiful, with a flashy convertible and fancy clothes. I figured you weren't willing to give all that up."

"I was in love with you," she said softly. "More than life itself."

Jesse walked over to her and knelt at her feet, his emotions riding his body like a roller coaster. "Then why didn't you tell me about Dillon? Why did you send me away knowing you were carrying my child?"

* * *

Tricia touched Jesse's face. Would he understand her decision to keep Dillon a secret? Could she make him understand? "I didn't tell my father about the baby, either. Not at first. On the day that I discovered I was pregnant, I told him about your scholarship instead." She had taken a home-pregnancy test in the morning, then spoken to her father just hours later, certain everything would be all right. "I thought that if my dad knew about your scholarship, he'd see you in a different light. I wanted so badly for him to accept you. Even more so since I was pregnant."

She lowered her hand to Jesse's shoulder and clutched his shirt. The devastation from her father's reaction had changed her life, altered her decision. "I had intended to tell you about the baby, but when my dad threatened to have your scholarship taken away, I knew I couldn't."

"But why?" Jesse placed his palm against her stomach, as though reliving that awful day, changing it in his mind. "I would have married you, Tricia. You knew how much I wanted a family."

"And my father would have destroyed your scholarship, your future, what you'd worked so hard for. I couldn't live with that on my conscience."

"But you could live with me not knowing about my son?"

She covered his hand with hers, held it tight against her tummy. "I lived with it because I felt I had to. But a day didn't go by that I didn't hurt over my decision."

"You could have contacted me at school, Tricia. You knew where I was."

She had thought about it, so many times. She had considered doing just that. "Even after Dillon was born, my father's opinion of you didn't change. So I knew that if I contacted you, he'd make good on that threat, and you'd lose your scholarship." Surviving the degree of her father's hatred toward Jesse hadn't been easy. In the beginning, he'd seemed obsessive, beyond protective. "I was so certain you'd come back for me." And then her father would have been proved wrong. "I was so young, so inexperienced in life." Sheltered by an overpowering parent. "In my mind everything would be all right once you came back."

Jesse met her gaze, his eyes suddenly clouded with dismay. "You asked me to return after college. You knew how long it would take for me to become a vet. Are you saying that you waited for me all those years?"

She nodded. "In my heart, you were my husband. The man who gave me a son, my soul mate, the person I was destined to spend the rest of my life with." She caught her breath as the pain of all those years welled up inside of her. "I was faithful, Jesse. You're still the only man I've ever made love with."

"Oh, my God, Tricia." He dropped his head onto her lap. "I had no idea. I'm so sorry."

She stroked his hair, gave comfort even though his response made her ache. He was apologizing for his sudden guilt, for having been with other women while she'd remained faithful. "You promised you'd come back for me," she said finally, her voice broken. "You promised."

He lifted his head, skimmed her cheek with his fingertips, a painful, familiar touch. "I didn't. Not in the way you thought. I never said that I was coming back for us to make a life together, not after you refused to move in with me. You misunderstood. We both did."

A misunderstanding. Could it be that simple? That horribly simple. "I made promises to Dillon based on what I believed. He waited for you, too. We included you in our prayers every night." Patricia willed the tears burning her eyes not to fall. Crying would only shatter what was left of her emotional stability. "But eventually we both gave up. Too much time had passed." Too much heartache, she thought. But now she understood why Jesse had stayed away for so long. He had felt as if she had made her choice by refusing to share a life with him then—a decision she had to live with now.

"Will we ever be able to get past this?" he asked. "Be the kind of friends Dillon wants us to be?"

"I hope so."

"I'd like to try."

Patricia's heart clenched. He meant it this time, truly meant it. She could see the sorrow in his expression. "We can't change what we've been through."

He remained at her feet, on his knees as though pleading for forgiveness. "No, we can't. But we can start over. Are you willing to be my friend, Tricia?"

She nodded. "I think I'd like to get to know you. Not who you were, but who you are now." She didn't want to recapture their youth. She couldn't bear reliving all that pain, all those memories.

"I'd like to get to know you, too." He stood, then stepped back a bit awkwardly as though unsure of what to do next. He looked manly yet boyish, almost shy. "I think our tea's cold," he said, glancing at the table.

"That's all right." Because her heart was warm, she realized. Still a little sad, but warm. She smiled and got to her feet. "Can I have a hug, Jesse?"

His answer came in the form of a gentle embrace, a sweet rocking motion that sent those dreaded tears down her cheeks. She let them fall, let them soak his shoulder like a cleansing rain.

She had never cried in his arms, never experienced the comfort that came with being coddled, thoroughly comforted by a man. He was whispering, words she didn't recognize, Creek words, guttural but soft. They rose like a song, then drifted over her like a native balm, an ancient healing.

"Jesse." She lifted her head and kissed him, tasted him, ran her hands over his face, his hair.

Their tongues met and then mated. But not in lust, she thought. The feeling, the warm, moist sensation was something more. Something she couldn't name. "It can't be love," she whispered. "Not anymore."

"It's need," Jesse told her simply.

"Yes, need." A condition requiring relief, substance. She reached for the buttons on his shirt, undid them one by one. She needed to feel his heartbeat beneath her fingers, the heat of his skin, strength of his muscles. "Your bed," she told him. She wanted him there, on the pine bed he had crafted. She wanted him to caress her body the way he'd stroked the wood, shaped it with his hands.

He nuzzled her neck, buried his face in her hair. "No regrets, Tricia. We take what we need with no regrets."

"No, not take. Give," she said, as he swept her up and carried her to his room. "New friends giving." Everything but their hearts, she thought. They would protect their hearts.

He placed her on the bed and covered her with his body. His chest was bare, his pants unfastened. He looked sexy, tousled and hungry, a man she was anxious to know.

Feel.

She slipped her hand into his jeans, smiled as he grew harder. Hungrier. He shifted his hips, rocked against her touch. A sense of newness washed over her, a sense of discovery. He kicked off his boots and tumbled her across the bed, undressing her as she freed his erection. Her blouse fell to the floor, her bra flew across the room. He tugged her skirt down, groaned in masculine appreciation when he unveiled her nylons, the thigh-high stockings she often wore.

Rather than remove them, he stroked the length of her legs, thigh to ankle, kissing as he went. "I've had fantasies about you," he said, pulling her panties down and plunging a finger deep inside her. "Fantasies just like this."

She reared and bucked, her back arching, her limbs quivering. He gave her pleasure, she thought. Pure primal pleasure. And wicked desire. She lay naked, her silk hose still in place—the naughty fixation of his fantasy.

They rolled over the bed, again and again, their hands hot and greedy on each other's skin. All the wrongful anger, the old hurts, the past aches gushed into a geyser of passion. Patricia could feel it rising in her blood, threatening to burst.

He sucked her nipples, licked and nibbled while she fisted his hair, then pulled his face back up to hers. They kissed, the kiss of lovers—man and woman on the brink of sexual ecstasy. He slipped on protection, then rose above her.

Yes, this was need, she thought, as he lifted her hips and pushed himself deep inside her. She grabbed hold of the wood, clutched the post while he stroked harder, filling her completely.

"Give me more, Tricia," he said, his hair dipping over his forehead, sweat glistening his skin. "More."

She gave him her release, her wild, soul-shattering orgasm. And when she went slack in his arms, he gave her his.

A week later Jesse and Patricia relaxed in Jesse's backyard on a stretch of grass that framed the abundant herb garden. Patricia decided she preferred Jesse's house to her own. She could feel the warmth, the care, the history that dwelled there. She supposed it would always be referred to as the old Garrett farm. The Garretts were the original owners, the nineteenth-century family who had first worked the land. They'd be proud of Jesse, she thought, pleased with his connection to their soil.

"Have I told you how great you look in jeans?" he asked, slanting her a smile.

She laughed. "Yes, but you can tell me again." Her denims actually felt good, the prewashed fabric smooth but rugged. Jesse had insisted that they recline directly on the freshly mowed lawn rather than "fuss with a blanket." Apparently he thought grass stains suited a pair of Levi's, broke them in correctly.

He leaned over and kissed her. "You look great," he said again. "Sexy."

Sexy. She supposed she did, at least to a man like Jesse. A woman in a trim-fitting blouse, jeans and Western boots fit the environment. And the environment had its own brand of sex appeal: a carpet of grass and flowering plants beneath a clear blue sky.

Patricia reached into a canvas bag and removed a leather-bound photo album. "I made this for you."

"Pictures?" He opened the cover and gazed at the first photograph. Immediately a smile lit his face. "This is Dillon, isn't it?"

She nodded. "It was taken at the hospital soon after he was born." Patricia had collected photos from some of her other albums and placed them in this one, hoping to present Jesse with a treasured gift. "He had lots of hair, didn't he?"

Jesse looked up. "He was beautiful. I wish I'd been there."

Her eyes misted. Crying, for some reason, came easier now. "I know. I'm sorry."

He leaned against her shoulder and turned the page. "Me, too."

"First birthday party," Patricia pointed out. "We let him dive into the cake. Well, actually we had two cakes. One for the guests and one for Dillon." "We" meant herself and her father, but she'd decided to omit his name. Her dad was still a subject of rage with Jesse. Patricia sighed. Deep down her goal was to bring the two men together, convince them to embrace the present, release the bitterness of the past.

She brushed Jesse's shoulder and continued to narrate events in Dillon's life, pleased with Jesse's laughter, his easy smile. She had even included photos of herself, the young woman he had loved. Knowing that he had once loved her made their budding friendship seem right somehow. It also made the nights they spent in each other's arms feel right, too. Lovemaking—wild, wicked sex with roving hands and whispered fantasies. She couldn't get enough.

Patricia caught her breath as Jesse turned his face toward hers. He was beautiful. A male animal in his prime.

"Did you take pictures when you were pregnant?" he asked.

She wrinkled her nose. "Yes, but I looked awful." Her father was a camera buff, a shutterbug. He snapped pictures at every turn. The Boyd mansion was filled with framed photographs.

Jesse tapped her nose. "I'll bet you looked gorgeous. All legs and tummy."

"I couldn't see my feet toward the end. I was huge."

"I want one of those pictures."

Oh, Lord. She glanced away. "You're kidding, right?"

He lifted her chin, bringing her eyes to his. "Why are you so uncomfortable about your pregnancy?"

She struggled to hold his gaze. "I gained so much weight—"

He interrupted gently. "That's what pregnant women are supposed to do. It's natural and healthy." He skimmed his fingers over her cheek, then slid them through her hair. "I know it's more than that, Tricia."

"I missed you," she admitted quietly. "It was such a difficult time, carrying your baby and not having you there. I know it was my choice, but it was still hard." She reached into the grass, hoping to draw strength from the land. "This community pretty much ostracized me." She looked around, remembering Jesse's home was in Hatcher. "Well, not this community. The one I live in, the proper citizens of Arrow Hill."

Her father had been her saving grace, but she decided to keep that thought private, at least for now. "Society girls in Arrow Hill aren't supposed to have illegitimate babies." She imagined there had been a few secret abortions, parents scurrying their daughters off to the city, places where no one knew their prestigious names. Her father had never suggested such a thing, not once. He'd stood beside her, insisting she hold her head high. It was, after all, his grandchild she carried—a Boyd. Needless to say, her decision to give Dillon Jesse's last name had devastated her father.

"I would have married you, Tricia."

"I know." But her father would have ruined Jesse's future, something that would have probably destroyed their marriage in time. Young marriages often failed, even without the stress of disapproving in-laws. "It's over now. I got through it, and no one treats Dillon badly. He's well accepted." And those who didn't approve of her son's birthright knew enough to keep their opinions to themselves. Patricia wouldn't stand for Dillon being the subject of hurtful gossip.

"I still want a picture." Jesse linked his fingers through hers. "I want to be a part of your pregnancy somehow. Imagine being there. See how you looked."

She brought their joined hands to her lips and kissed his knuckles. "You're a special man, Jesse Hawk."

"And we made a special child." He turned his attention back to the photo album and studied Dillon's kindergarten picture. "A very special child."

Twelve

The following Saturday Jesse answered his door, Cochise at his side.

"Hi, Dad."

"Hey, there." He reached out and squeezed his son's shoulder.

Dillon smiled and stepped into the house, then patted the dog's head. "Mom will be coming in a minute. She's fixing her lipstick. I'm gonna go say hi to Barney, okay?"

"Sure." Jesse remained at the doorway and waited for Tricia, amused by her decision to "fix" her lipstick. He'd only end up kissing most of it off, anyway. They didn't maul each other in front of Dillon, but they nuzzled and kissed, natural forms of affection that appeared to please the boy.

Tricia stepped onto the graveled driveway, and Jesse frowned. Instead of jeans and boots, she wore a tailored suit, her hips swaying under a slim-fitting skirt, shapely legs ending in a pair of low-heeled pumps. Why the professional attire? Today was family day: Dillon's fifth horseback riding lesson, fresh-squeezed lemonade, a picnic lunch on the grass.

She made her way up the porch steps, a perfectly coiffed woman. "Hello," she said, before pecking his frown with a chaste kiss.

Jesse's lips moved into a smile, the scent of jasmine enticing him like a floral cloud. He opened his mouth and guided her into a deeper kiss. She raised her arms and circled his neck while he slid his hands down the curve of her spine. He couldn't get enough of Tricia Boyd. Not nearly enough, he thought, as she teased him with her tongue.

She leaned back, then dabbed at his chin, removing what he assumed was a smear of her freshly applied lipstick. "I'm sorry. I can't stay," she said. "Last-minute meeting. One of those things that can't be helped."

He furrowed his brow. "What about Dillon?" He enjoyed these casual days with his son, longed for them.

"Don't worry. He's staying."

Jesse's pulse quickened. "By himself?"

She nodded, her voice quiet. "He's the one who suggested it when I told him about my meeting."

Jesse tried to contain his excitement in case Dillon walked onto the porch. He didn't want to come on too strong and scare the boy away. This would be their first solitary visit, their first father-son experience without Tricia present. A bonding Jesse desperately needed.

Tricia left five minutes later, her luxury car spitting gravel beneath its tires as it rounded the driveway in one sleek turn. Both Jesse and Dillon stood on the porch and watched her go.

"How about a walk?" Jesse asked, before the moment turned awkward. Suddenly Dillon looked lost—like a kid on the first day at a new school. Jesse understood the feeling. Fear edged his excitement, the kind of fear that came with being an inexperienced parent.

"Can Cochise come?"

"Sure." Jesse knew the dog would ease Dillon. And himself as well. Cochise had become their shared companion, much like the medicine bag Dillon wore.

Hopefully they'd be able to walk off their anxiety, Jesse thought, as they headed toward the back of the property. Dillon's lesson would go easier once they became accustomed to being alone. Although Dillon was a natural horseman, he rode the corral fence with a distracted eye, often searching for Tricia's approval. Jesse sensed the boy suffered from a mixture of sorrow and guilt over his grandfather's aversion to horses and assumed Dillon felt like less of a traitor whenever he spotted his mother's smile.

"Let's walk through the garden," Jesse suggested, refusing to allow Raymond Boyd to intrude on this beautiful summer day.

They cut across the grass and laughed as Cochise forgot his manners and loped ahead of them. Although Cochise wouldn't dream of digging up all of Jesse's hard work, the dog had no qualms about sniffing his way through the plants.

As soon as they entered the garden, Dillon knelt to touch a sprig of parsley. "Mom told me that you're going to build a greenhouse before winter comes."

"Yeah. I've always wanted one." Jesse inhaled the herbal scents, the sweet earthly aroma. "But this is the first land I've ever owned." He knelt beside Dillon as the boy fingered another plant. "That's chicory. It'll bear flowers until the fall."

"A medicine man taught you all this stuff, huh?"

Jesse nodded. "His name was Tall Bear. I met him when I was fifteen. The lady who was my foster mother at the time had scheduled a spiritual healing with him, and she invited me to go along." It had been the first moment in his life that he'd actually felt like a part of something truly important.

Dillon settled onto a stepping stone. "Was Tall Bear nice?"

"Yeah, but he was powerful, too." Tall Bear had knowing eyes, Jesse thought. Ebony eyes that could see into a person's soul. "He was gentle but strong. Everything a healer should be."

Dillon drew his knees up. "He died, didn't he? You're talking about him like he's gone."

Jesse felt a familiar sting behind his eyes. He missed his mentor, missed the man's gentle guidance. "He died during my first year at college." A lonely time, a time of sadness and growth. He had mourned Tall Bear the way he had mourned

Tricia, aching and alone, praying for the strength to go on without them.

Dillon got to his feet, so Jesse rose from his knees. They walked through the garden in silence for a while, breathing soothing aromas, taking in the sights and sounds of Mother Earth. Tall Bear would have liked Dillon, Jesse thought.

When the boy's grumbling stomach interrupted the quiet, Jesse chuckled. "How about some grub before we saddle Hunter?"

Dillon grinned and patted his misbehaving belly. "That's okay by me."

They turned in the direction of the house, Cochise taking his place beside them. "Fiona made those cookies you like. She left them with me yesterday." When Dillon didn't respond, Jesse glanced over at his son and noticed the child's smile had faded. "You don't have to eat them right now. You can take them home if you want, share them with your mom."

"Is Fiona poor, Dad?"

Since the question caught him off guard, Jesse stopped walking, halting Dillon and the rottweiler as well. "She can afford to bake cookies for you, son."

"Yeah, but she lives in the trailer park. My friend said that it was really yucky there."

Yucky. The description stung. Jesse's parents had lived in that trailer park. Hell, he'd lived there for the first two years of his life. And he'd return to that "yucky" place if it would bring his parents back. He'd take poor over the loss of a family any day.

"It's a little run-down," he said, drawing a deep, steady breath. "But it's not the people's fault who live there. The man who owns the park doesn't take good care of it. He doesn't fix things when they're broken."

Dillon cocked his head. "Too bad it's not for sale. If it was, I'd ask my grandpa to buy it. My grandpa would fix that place up."

Jesse bit back his resentment and reached out to hug Dillon instead. He held the boy tight against him, felt his eyes water as the child returned the embrace. Would they always have

Raymond Boyd between them? Would Dillon continue to see his grandfather in a false light? The man who had threatened to destroy Jesse's future, the evil mogul who had taken Tricia away?

"Would you feel better about Fiona baking cookies for you if I gave her a raise?"

The child gazed up at him and nodded, and Jesse's heart constricted.

Raymond Boyd didn't deserve Dillon Hawk. Not one bit.

Later that evening Tricia stood at Jesse's door, moonlight shimmering behind her. "Dillon's spending the night with a friend," she said. "So I thought maybe I could, too."

Jesse blinked. She could have been a goddess, a forest nymph with long bare legs and a siren's smile. A mythological maiden who had just invited herself to share his bed. What a fantasy. He had the sudden urge to take her where she stood, on his ancient porch with the moon and the stars peeking down from the sky. He could all but feel her mouth on his, hear the mewling sound that would purr from her throat.

"Jesse, can I come in?"

Incense burned in a clay pot, a CD played on his stereo—native music, drums, ancient chants—scents and songs from the earth. Primal elements to make love by.

"Huh? Oh, yeah. Sure." He grinned a little sheepishly and stepped away from the door.

She glided into his living room, an alluring creature with rubies winking at her ears. She lifted a velvet bag, an embroidered satchel a nymph might carry. "I came prepared," she said. "You know, pajamas, toothbrush, a change of clothes." She placed the bag on his coffee table. "So, can I stay? Or are you going to send me home?"

"Very funny." He lifted his hand to her breast and skimmed one of her nipples; it peaked at his touch. "You're not wearing a bra." He grazed her other nipple and watched it bloom.

She made that sexy little mewling sound, and he shivered. "That's not all I'm not wearing."

He stepped back to look. Really look. Feast his eyes and drink her in. The dress could have been a slip, a designer's dream of antique lace and new silk, the color of fresh cream. And beneath the fabric, he saw a hint of female nakedness.

Arousal hissed in his breath.

She moistened her lips, then scanned the length of his body. "I'm here to collect on my rain check."

Her blatant stare made him feel nearly as bare as she, his skin freshly showered, a pair of sweatpants riding below the waistband of his briefs. He swallowed. "Rain check?"

She moved closer, the glow from an amber lamp illuminating the tips of her breasts, the shadow of curls between her legs. "Don't you remember, Jesse?" She stepped closer still, close enough to graze his cheek with hers. "I'm going to do to you what you did to me." She pressed her mouth to his ear and nibbled. "After all, you are the one who taught me how."

Seduction. The word pounded in his head, his chest, his groin. "You're seducing me," he said, as scented smoke rose and curled in the air.

Suddenly he felt inexperienced as hell, all hot and nervous and excited. Ready to explode. Tricia was the only woman he had ever allowed to touch him with that degree of intimacy. Twelve years, he thought, as she toyed with the waistband on his briefs. Twelve years of missing the feel of her mouth, the silk of her hair against his thighs.

She untied the drawstring on his sweats and pushed them down, then knelt to remove his shorts. He watched and waited, barely able to breathe. She stood, stepped back and slipped off her dress, let it pool at her feet. They were both naked, and he couldn't move, couldn't take what he wanted.

This was her seduction. Her bad-girl fantasy.

She kissed his neck, pressed her lips to a throbbing vein. He closed his eyes and let the carnal sensation drift over him, the vibration of pulse against pulse, woman against man.

She ran her hands over his chest, traced the pattern of hair, took one flat nipple into her mouth and sucked. Jesse opened his eyes, aroused by the scrape of teeth against his other nipple. Wild Tricia. Wicked and sweet.

"You're so beautiful," he said. She looked vibrant in the dim light, bloodred gems glinting at her ears.

She smiled and dropped to her knees, gazed up at him and nipped his belly. The muscles in his stomach jumped, anticipating her next move. He slid his fingers into her hair.

Waiting. Wanting.

She loved him thoroughly. With her hands, her tongue, her mouth. He watched as she took him shaft to tip. Over and over. Teasing, tasting.

Faster. Deeper.

He fisted her hair as a low growl rumbled in his chest. Pressure built upon need. A soul-shattering ache, an uncontrollable throb—hunger too close to the edge.

He rasped her name and yanked her to her feet, covered her mouth with his and fed. Fed while he pushed her against the wall, knocked into a shelf and sent a collection of baskets tumbling.

He entered her there, against the wall, his heart pounding to the beat of native drums. She went as mad as he, locking her legs around him while he lifted her hips, pulling his hair, scratching, clawing, devouring him with frantic openmouthed kisses.

It was raw, primal. He felt her climax rip through him, felt his own rise and then crash into a feverish swell—a thundering, staggering scream of pure sex.

She gasped, her breath warm upon his neck. He turned his head and whispered her name, held her while she shuddered with tiny aftershocks. His limbs turned weak, his vision hazy, but he knew who was in his arms and how she affected his world.

They slid to the cool hardwood floor. He stroked her cheek and wondered inanely if his callused fingertips were too rough. Too hard. Too brutal. It mattered now. Tenderness after the storm, he thought. The peaceful lull of Tricia. He wanted to hold her forever.

"I didn't hurt you, did I?" he asked.

"No." She looked up at him. "Why, did I hurt you?"

He chuckled and kissed the top of her head. Equal-opportunity sex. She'd been just as rough, he supposed. Just as brutal. Sweet, wild, inexperienced Tricia. "No, baby, you didn't hurt me. I'm a big, tough guy. I can take it."

She nudged his rib for the barb, then snuggled closer. He shifted their positions so his back was to the wall, so she could rest against him. The incense had burned out, but the CD kept playing. And like their mood, the music had softened, drums giving way to flutes. He traced lazy circles on her stomach, content to be with his lover.

His lover. The mother of his child. "Are we going to go to another charity ball?" Jesse asked.

"If you want to," she answered.

"I do." He wrapped his arms around her. He wanted the society of Arrow Hill to see them together again. He wanted all those snooty jerks who had snubbed Tricia during her pregnancy to know that the man who had placed that baby in her womb hadn't abandoned her purposely. He still cared about her.

Patricia could almost see his heart. Tonight Jesse wore it on his sleeve, or his bare shoulder, she thought, leaning into his nakedness, the mass of muscle that formed his chest.

Something was happening between them, something more than friendship. She gazed around, studied the wood furnishings, the masculine warmth that dominated the room. Jesse was everywhere. She could feel him in the ancient weapons, the Native regalia, the traditional pottery, the contemporary art. She stared at a painting across the wall and wondered why she hadn't noticed it before. It was a sensual study, a man and a woman in each other's arms. *Lovers.* She knew the title, had seen it advertised in a Southwest magazine. Jesse didn't own the original. His framed copy was a print, but no less beautiful, she thought.

"It's new," he said, as though reading her thoughts. "I bought it yesterday."

Warmth spread through her like a balm, tears misted her

eyes. *Lovers.* The picture could have been them. Not their looks, but their emotions. She understood the woman's need to touch her lover, keep him close. "It's us."

"Yeah." His response came out rough. Raspy.

Patricia slid her fingers through his and brought their joined hands to her lips. It scared him, she realized, what was happening between them. He knew it was there, but he didn't want to think too deeply about it. He had bought the picture, placed it in his home, but he was still protecting his heart.

"Want some dessert?" he asked. "I've got ice cream. Or sherbet, I guess."

He'd just switched gears, she thought. And he'd done it purposely. "That sounds good," she responded, taking care to keep her voice light.

She stood and watched him dress, watched him pull up his sweatpants and knot the drawstring tie. No, they wouldn't speak of it, but it was there, haunting them like a ghost.

Love.

Patricia Boyd and Jesse Hawk had fallen back in love. And in their state of denial, they clawed each other during sex, locked their hips and swept away the tenderness their hearts wanted so desperately to feel.

While Jesse went into the kitchen, Patricia slipped on her dress and opened her bag for the lace panties she'd brought along. They had a made a conscious decision to become lovers, spent one evening discussing birth control like responsible adults. He had been willing to keep a fresh supply of condoms handy, but she'd opted for the Pill instead. She didn't want anything between them, not even a lubricated film of latex.

He returned with two glass bowls. "Wanna sit on the porch?"

She nodded and accepted the orange sherbet offering.

The evening was warm, a clear summer night. A three-quarter moon shone in the sky, competing for brilliancy, it seemed, with a vast number of glittering stars.

Patricia tasted the sherbet, let it melt on her tongue. "Where are all the animals tonight?" she asked, realizing they were alone.

"Cochise is visiting with the other dogs, and Barney fell asleep in my room. Sally was in her cage, but I guess you didn't notice her. She's the quiet one of the bunch." He lifted his spoon and grinned. "And those sneaky little ferrets were probably hiding somewhere, watching us make love."

She returned his smile. Those sneaky little ferrets were an adorable trio of furry mischief makers with big, round eyes and pointy noses. "I'll bet they're making off with my bra as we speak."

He lowered his gaze to her breasts, sucked the sherbet from his spoon. "What bra?"

She felt her nipples harden. "I brought one with me, in my overnight bag."

"Panties, too?"

A familiar heat settled between her thighs. "I'm wearing them."

He cocked his head, so she crossed her legs. She was still damp from his seed. The thought embarrassed and excited her. She knew they would make love again before morning.

She glanced away, her chest suddenly tight. Making love wasn't the same as admitting to being in love. When, she wondered, had it happened? At what precise moment had she fallen back under his spell?

"What's the matter, Tricia?" Before she could answer, he left his seat and crouched before her. "You look sad."

"I'm fine. Just feeling melodramatic."

"We still have some past between us," he said. "Everything hasn't gone away."

"I know." They still had her father to contend with, the bitterness both men still harbored. "We could talk about it."

"No." He shook his head. "I want to talk about happy things. Things we can share. I want to know what your favorite movie is. If you have a hobby. What it felt like to breastfeed our baby." He gazed up at the sky. "And I want to know if you'll sleep under the stars with me tonight."

God, she loved him. Loved the catch in his voice, the expectation in his eyes as he turned back to her for an answer. Those ever-changing eyes. "Yes," she said. She wanted to cuddle in his arms, search for the Little Dipper, tell him how extraordinary it had felt to hold his son to her breast.

But most of all, she longed to share the rest of her life with him. Longed for the moment he would admit that he loved her, too.

Life was good, Jesse thought. Passion and friendship with Tricia and meaningful hours spent with his son. On this bright weekend afternoon, he sat on the corral fence with Dillon, sharing the day.

Hunter poked his head over the fence and nuzzled Dillon. The boy reached back to pet the horse. Jesse chuckled. Rather than pester his new riding partner, Hunter was supposed to be enjoying the freedom the corral provided, rolling around like horses did after a healthy workout. Dillon had taken the gelding through his gaits with a God-given talent, making Jesse beam like a new moon. Within three short weeks, Dillon Hawk had proved he was born to ride.

"Hey, Dad, when am I gonna get to meet Uncle Sky?"

"Soon, I hope. He mentioned coming for a visit in September." Jesse and Sky made weekly phone calls to each other. They were as close as two newly acquainted, long-distance brothers could be.

Dillon grinned. "I can't believe he's a trick rider. That's so cool."

Jesse ruffled his son's hair. "I'm sure Sky would be glad to give you a few pointers. He's looking forward to meeting you."

The boy took a swig of water from one of the canteens they kept on hand to combat the heat. Dillon's skin had continued to tan to a rich, golden-brown, his hair a little lighter from the sun. "Does Sky speak Muskokee, too?"

"Yeah, but he learned it by himself, from a dictionary. Tall Bear taught me." And Jesse thanked the Master of Breath every day for the guidance Tall Bear had given him.

"Are you going to teach me?" Dillon asked.

"You bet I am. That language is part of your heritage." Jesse had already been schooling Dillon about the Creeks, passing on songs and stories Tall Bear had shared with him. Just days ago they'd spent hours discussing the early culture of their tribe, including religious practices, the names and backgrounds of chiefs who had ruled, the acceptance of mixed-blood marriages.

Dillon had exhibited a special interest in the *busk:* the Green Corn Dance, a four-day event where Creek men would fast, then dance in the spirit of moral renewal. The *busk* signified a time of forgiveness, where old grudges were exonerated and brotherhood reigned supreme. The boy had asked numerous questions about the festival, anxious to hear every spiritual detail.

Dillon studied his father with a serious expression, a look Jesse had come to recognize. "Uncle Sky must be a good reader if he learned the Muskokee language from a dictionary. That seems like it would be hard to do."

"Yeah." Sky's ability to absorb the ancient dialect on his own had impressed Jesse, as well. "My brother likes to read. It's one of his favorite pastimes." He shifted his feet, hooking his boot heels onto the fence rail. "But, you know, just because you and I are dyslexic doesn't mean that we're not as smart as everybody else. I used to think that about myself, but I know better now."

Dillon placed the cap back on his canteen. "Mom says that all the time—about people like us being smart. She tells everybody who will listen that Einstein was dyslexic."

"Well, he was. And it's good that she spreads the word." Tricia's devotion to literacy made Jesse proud. "I plan on getting involved with the dyslexic society your mom organizes fund-raisers for." He took a drink of water, then glanced up to catch Dillon's approving smile. "She said they need someone to head up an adult support group."

Dillon scooted closer. "I help out with the younger kids at the charity picnics. We're thinking of having pony rides for them this time. That'd be cool, huh?"

"Yeah. Cool," Jesse agreed, enjoying his son's youthful enthusiasm. He could see Dillon leading bright-eyed four-year-olds around on stubby little ponies.

They sat quietly for the next few minutes, enjoying the Oklahoma sunshine, the country smells permeating the air. Hunter still had his head over the top rail, begging Dillon for attention. The boy complied, stroking the gelding like a favored pet. Jesse smiled. Those ponies were going to adore his son, follow him around like overgrown puppies.

"Dad?"

"Hmm?"

"I wish my grandpa still liked horses."

Immediately Jesse's blood ran cold. Raymond Boyd was a name he'd just as soon forget. He couldn't think of an appropriate response so he lifted the canteen to his lips instead. Although Dillon knew Jesse and his grandpa weren't friends, the boy had been spared the brunt of their hatred.

Dillon reached into his shirt pocket and retrieved a small white envelope. "I brought those pictures with me. The ones of Grandpa from a long time ago." He opened the envelope. "Grandpa looks so happy in them. I don't understand what could have happened to make him hate horses." The child glanced at the top photo. "Mom says that maybe he took a bad fall or something. But I don't think that's it, 'cause he doesn't seem scared for me, now that I'm riding."

"How does he seem?" Jesse managed to ask.

The boy shrugged. "I don't know. Okay, I guess. We don't really talk about it." He held the pictures out in an innocent offering. "What do you think, Dad?"

Jesse drew a deep breath and accepted the small stack of photos, unsure of what else to do. He couldn't very well refuse to look at them, not with his son waiting anxiously for his opinion.

He lowered his gaze to the first snapshot. It depicted Boyd striding a well-groomed mount, a muscular quarter horse. Jesse flipped to the next picture. Boyd again, this time with a different mount, an equally impressive palomino. Boyd did look happy—a man in his twenties, full of life and vitality. A contradictory image, Jesse decided, recalling the older man's bitter demeanor in Tricia's kitchen during that awful confrontation.

He continued to look through the photos hastily until one in particular caught his attention, made him stop and stare. Boyd stood beside a striking young woman, his arm around her waist. Jesse studied her, resisting the compelling, unexplainable urge to touch her image. She wore jeans and a Western shirt, blond hair spilling over her shoulders like spun gold. Her skin was fair, her features delicate, but it was her eyes that held him captive. Kept him riveted to her face. They were as blue as the sky, the brightest, most dazzling color he had ever seen.

A chill raced up his spine. That wasn't true. He had seen eyes that blue before. His brother's eyes sparkled like azure diamonds—just like the woman's in the photograph.

With a quivering hand, he turned the picture over. Would there be a note, a date, an indication of who she was?

Rebecca.

The feminine name scripted on the back jolted through him like lightning. Rebecca was his mother's name. Sky's mother's name. Sky, his brother with the bright-blue eyes.

Dear God. His heart pummeled his chest, threatening to pound its way out. Could it be? Could the woman standing beside Raymond Boyd be his mother? His Rebecca? Sky's Rebecca? She'd been a blue-eyed blonde, slim and pretty, he'd been told. A delicate fine-boned lady.

He looked up at Dillon. "Can I hold on to this picture for a while?" he asked, struggling to contain the fear in his voice. The despair. The rage that Boyd may have been associated with his mother.

Dillon nodded. "Sure, Dad. You can keep as many as you want."

"I only want this one," he answered. He would show it to Fiona. The older lady had been his mother's neighbor. She would know if the woman in the photograph was Rebecca Hawk.

Yes, Fiona would know. And then Jesse would know, too.

Thirteen

On Monday morning Patricia gazed out her office window. Boyd Enterprises had been bustling with activity: an early meeting, the closure of a profitable deal. She enjoyed the pace, the shift from fast to slow, noisy to quiet. An hour before, men and women in power suits had crowded the conference room. And now she stood alone, admiring the view from a third-story window, her computer screen glowing behind her.

The buzz of the intercom caught her attention. She turned and pressed the button.

"Yes?"

"Dr. Hawk is on line two."

"Thank you." Patricia smiled and pushed the second line. "Jesse?"

His voice rasped through the receiver. "Tricia, I need to see you. Meet me at Delany's as soon as you can."

"Why? What's wrong?" Delany's was a coffee bar located about two blocks from Boyd Enterprises, but Jesse's urgent tone didn't sound like an invitation to sample one of their international brews.

"I don't want to talk about it over the phone. Just hurry, okay?"

She stared at the screen-saver rolling across her computer. Apparently Jesse was already at Delany's, an odd place for him to be on a Monday morning. "Give me fifteen minutes."

She made it in ten, anxiety racing as fast as her car. She spotted Jesse immediately. He sat at one of the wooden tables, a frown furrowed deep in his brow.

Patricia took the chair across from him and noticed that his coffee appeared untouched, strong and black with steam rising from the cup.

"I was on my way to your office," he said. "But I decided to stop here instead. You know, take a deep breath, count to twenty, try to stay calm. Besides, I didn't want to take the chance of running into your dad. Not the way I'm feeling."

His expression was a combination of anger and despair, she thought, a devastating kind of rage. His hands were fisted on the table, but his eyes looked hollow, a dark empty gray. "Are you going to tell me what this is all about?"

He opened one of his hands and dropped a piece of paper onto the table. Patricia reached for it. It was a photograph, she realized, as she unrolled it to view the subject. Her heart bumped hard and fast. The slightly crumpled image depicted her dad many years before, standing beside a stunning blonde, an equestrian setting in the background. They looked like a happy couple, friends or maybe even lovers, their faces alight with radiant smiles.

"Why are you carrying around an old photograph of my dad?" she asked. A picture she had never seen before.

Jesse met her gaze, his voice rough. "The woman your dad has his arm around is my mother, Tricia."

Her heart thumped again, a violent knock against her chest. She glanced down at the photo. A happy couple. Friends or maybe even lovers. "That's not possible. What makes you think—"

"Damn it, I don't think it's her. I know it is. Even Fiona said so," he snapped back, then lowered his voice to avoid alarming the other patrons. "I tried to reach Fiona last night after I dropped Dillon off, but she wasn't home. So I showed that picture to her this morning when she came in to work. And she confirmed what I already suspected.''

Patricia moved her chair forward. "You're not making sense. Start at the beginning, please. I'm not following you."

He dragged his hand through his hair and explained in a shaky voice how he had come by the photograph the day before, and why he had chosen to remain silent until Fiona saw it. "Dillon doesn't know anything about this. Of course he knows I kept the picture, but he doesn't know why."

She struggled to grasp his words—Dillon hiding old snapshots of his grandpa, her father clinging to a woman named Rebecca, Jesse's odd sensation that he recognized the color of Rebecca's eyes.

"It can't be," she heard herself say, as she tried to make sense of the situation. Fiona was old, even a little ditzy at times. Her memories must be confused.

Patricia gazed at the lady in the photograph, at her pretty smile and bright-blue eyes. No, she thought, Fiona wouldn't forget someone like this, wouldn't mix her up with someone else. This Rebecca was too beautiful, too unique to fade from someone's mind.

"Oh, Jesse." She brought her hand to her mouth. Her father wouldn't have forgotten Rebecca, either. "My dad is at the office. I'll go back and talk to him. Ask him what you deserve to know." What they both had the right to know, she decided, fearful of the heartache Raymond Boyd's secret might reveal.

"Your dad threw it away," Jesse said, his voice hard. "Tossed it out like it was trash. If it wasn't for Dillon, my mother's picture would have burned at the city dump years ago."

"I'm sorry." Truly sorry for the actions of a father she couldn't begin to understand. Why would her dad pose for a picture, then dispose of it decades later?

She met Jesse's gaze and noticed how tired he looked, dark shadows revealing a long, sleepless night. "Go home and wait for me. Maybe close your eyes for a few minutes."

He shook his head. "I couldn't rest even if I wanted to. I've got appointments at the clinic."

"Fiona can cancel them," she suggested. "Say it was an emergency."

He released a heavy breath. "I'd prefer to keep busy. And besides, those animals need me."

And he needed them, she thought. Healing God's creatures made him feel whole, gave him a sense of purpose in this world. Patricia knew that part of Jesse's heart would always belong to his work, and she loved him for it. Loved him more with each passing day.

She swallowed around the lump in her throat. "I'll come by the clinic just as soon as I talk to my dad. I'll find out what this picture means, Jesse. I promise I will."

He nodded and rose to his feet, his coffee still untouched. He looked wounded, she thought, trapped between pain and anger—someone on the brink of destruction. She could tell that his mother's smile confused him, maybe even made him hurt inside. Patricia lifted the photograph. Her father, it seemed, was the recipient of that gentle smile. Her father, the one man Jesse Hawk despised.

Patricia entered her dad's office, the photograph in question tucked safely into her handbag. His office was similar to her own: lush carpeting, a slick black desk, contemporary chairs, a fully stocked bar. The modern artwork decorating the walls matched the decor, but the man behind the desk, the father she suddenly didn't know, wore a traditional gray suit and an understated tie.

"Are you on your way out?" he asked, taking in her appearance, her stiff posture and the handbag she clutched. "Did something go wrong after the meeting?"

Yes, she thought, something went dreadfully wrong. "I've already been out, but it didn't have anything to do with the Whitman deal."

Patricia stepped closer to his desk and sat when he motioned for her to do so. Smoothing her skirt, she took several deliberate breaths—inhale, exhale—a practiced relaxation method, slow and easy.

"There's something I need to discuss with you, Dad. It's highly personal and I'd appreciate it if we weren't disturbed." She had decided to handle this like a business meeting, hoping to keep her emotions under control.

He buzzed his secretary and told the woman to hold his calls. Afterward he sat forward in his chair, silent, giving Patricia the floor.

She reached into her purse and handed him the photograph, willing her hand to remain steady, her voice level. "I want to know about the lady in this picture."

Within a heartbeat, his expression went from shock to anger, then remained there, his lips drawn into a thin line, a muscle twitching in his cheek. "Where did you get this?"

She sat a little straighter. "Answer my question first."

He met her gaze, and she felt their defiant wills clash, collide as they so often did. "Her name was Rebecca."

"I'm aware of her name." Patricia took the photograph back. "It's written on the back. You know very well that I'm asking for more than that. I'm giving you the opportunity to defend yourself. Explain your side of the story."

"My relationship with her does not warrant a defense, young lady."

Patricia's pulse quickened. "How can you say that? She was Jesse's mother. His *mother,* Dad."

Raymond's eyes hardened. "She wasn't his mother when I knew her. Now where in the hell did you get that picture?"

"Your grandson gave it to Jesse. It seems you tossed it out years ago, along with some snapshots of your horses. Dillon fished them out of the trash, then hid them in his room for safekeeping."

"Oh, Lord." He reached for his tie, tugged at it. "I didn't realize. Did Dillon ask who Rebecca was?"

"No." Patricia shook her head, grateful her father's tone had softened. "He was more concerned about the horses. I guess he just assumed she was an old friend."

Raymond continued to loosen his tie. Clearly he needed to

breathe. "Rebecca was a waitress at the country club bistro," he said quietly. "And I fell madly in love with her."

Pain filled her father's eyes, an ache Patricia recognized all too well. The hurt that came with losing a loved one, she thought. The loneliness that followed.

"This was before you met my mother?"

"Yes, a long time before."

"Was Rebecca your lover?" she asked, believing Jesse had the right to know.

He shook his head. "Premarital sex wasn't as common then as it is today. And Rebecca was an old-fashioned girl, waiting for her wedding night, I suppose." He smoothed his sideburns and glanced away. "I wanted to marry her, but I didn't get the chance to propose."

"Why? What happened, Dad?"

"Michael Hawk took her away from me."

Michael Hawk. Jesse's father.

Patricia gripped her chair, despair clouding her vision. "Oh, Dad, no." Her father had taken his revenge out on Jesse. Punished him for being Michael Hawk's son. "How could you do that to Jesse? And to me?"

"Because you're too good for him, Patricia. He used you. And he's still using you. You're just too naive to see it. Too trusting."

"I love him," she shot back. "And he loves me."

"Does he?" Raymond leaned forward. "Are you certain of that? Has he asked you to be part of his life? Marry him? Share his future? Legitimize Dillon's birth?"

No, her mind said. Jesse had done none of those things. "I'm not naive, Dad. I know he loves me." He just hadn't said it yet.

Weary, she slipped the photograph back into her purse. She couldn't cope with the anger anymore, the resentment and bitterness. And she knew she'd never have a future with Jesse until her father's part in their past was resolved. She stood, ordering her legs to hold her.

"You owe Jesse an apology. What you did to him was despicable."

Raymond laughed sardonically. "You expect me to apologize to Hawk? For destroying you? For making promises he didn't keep? I can't do that. I won't."

"My heart's recovered," she said, knowing her statement lacked conviction. Her heart still waited for Jesse to bare his.

She turned away from her father so he wouldn't see the truth, the tiny fear that maybe she was wrong. Had Jesse fallen back in love with her? Or was it only hope on her part? Desperation?

She walked to the door, but before she could open it, her dad spoke, catching her attention.

"I know what love is, young lady. Rebecca was my world."

She turned. "Then why did you throw away her picture?"

"Because I was afraid Dillon would ask me about her, who she was and what she meant to me." He rose from his desk. "I have more photographs. They're at home, in my safe."

Understanding, she nodded. Her father couldn't bring himself to let Rebecca go, not completely. A part of him still loved her. Loved her the way Patricia loved Jesse. What a mess, she thought. What a horrible, soul-shattering mess.

Jesse sat in the break room at the clinic, scrubbing his hands across his jaw. A life-altering morning had turned into a humid, motionless afternoon. Energy-sapping weather, he thought, for an already tiring day.

He looked up to see Fiona enter the room, her signature hair teased into its dated bouffant, a big purple bow attached. Despite his emotional exhaustion, Jesse couldn't help but smile. His first patient of the day, a sweet but excitable poodle named Pudding, had bonded instantly with Fiona, straining its leash to reach her. And since Pudding had sported a similar hair bow, he assumed the pampered little poodle had viewed Fiona as a kindred spirit.

"Patricia just called from her car," the older lady said. "She's on her way."

His nerves leaped to attention, righting his posture. "Thanks. Point her in this direction when she gets here."

Fiona placed her hands on her hips in a strong female

stance. "You should eat something. It is, after all, your lunch hour."

Jesse decided not to argue the fact that he wasn't hungry. Fiona would only hover nearby—a self-appointed grandmother in a purple jumpsuit ready to spoon-feed nourishment into him if necessary.

"There's some yogurt in the fridge," he said. "Is that sufficient?"

"It'll do." She marched over to the refrigerator, removed the carton and handed it to him along with a plastic utensil and a napkin.

He lifted the top and took a bite, realizing he hadn't eaten since the day before. The yogurt adhered to his stomach like strawberry glue. He spooned in another mouthful and swallowed. "I guess I needed this."

"You need some sleep, too," she commented, studying the shadows beneath his eyes.

Sleep, he thought, produced dreams—nightmares. And his subconscious was primed, ready to distort that photograph of his mother and Raymond Boyd. His mother with Tricia's father—the image made him sick.

Fiona came up behind him and placed her hands on his shoulders. "Everything's going to be okay, Jesse."

He didn't think so, but he appreciated her attempt to comfort him. He feared the truth, the devastation Tricia's talk with her father might bring. Had his mother cared about Raymond Boyd? Had there been a relationship? A love affair? Had Boyd used her in some way? Flaunted his money to take advantage of an innocent young woman?

"Jesse? Fiona? Am I interrupting?"

He glanced up from the yogurt container he'd been staring at. Tricia stood in the doorway, looking delicate and tired. Fragile, he thought, like an angel who'd lost her wings. The weather had wilted her blouse, the white silk clinging helplessly to her skin.

"There was no one at the front desk, so I hope you don't mind that I—"

"Of course, we don't," Fiona answered readily. "You're

welcome anywhere in this clinic.'' She gave Jesse's shoulders one last squeeze. ''He's been waiting for you.''

The older woman exited the room quietly, leaving Jesse and Tricia alone.

She sat across from him. ''How are you holding up?''

He shrugged. ''I've had a busy morning.'' He turned and looked out the window, wishing for a breeze. Suddenly he needed air, the kind that rustled leaves on the trees and tousled a person's hair. The man-made gust from the air-conditioning unit wasn't the same. He turned back and searched Tricia's gaze. ''So what happened?''

''My dad opened up the best he could, I suppose.'' She unzipped her purse, removed the picture and placed it gently on the table. ''Apparently he knew your mother well.''

A knot formed in his gut. ''How well?''

Tricia touched a corner of the photograph. ''They weren't sleeping together, but he wanted to marry her.'' She expelled a heavy breath. ''He said that he was in love with her, that Rebecca was his world.''

Rage, confusion, disbelief, disdain.

Conflicting emotions warred within him. He didn't know what to do, what to say. The relief that came with knowing that Boyd hadn't been his mother's lover didn't loosen the knot in his gut. ''Your dad's lying. He didn't love her.'' Boyd couldn't have, he thought. Love was too sacred, too pure to be tainted by Tricia's father.

Her response slipped out in a broken whisper, a sound as frail as a baby bird falling from its nest. ''He wasn't lying. I could see it in his eyes.''

In the stillness that followed, the walls closed in. Jesse jumped to his feet and backed himself against the window, attempting to escape her words. It wasn't fair, he thought, that Boyd had known his mother well enough to love her.

''I don't remember her,'' he said, his chest constricting. Not one gentle memory or comforting image. He had nothing but a photograph of his mother being held by a man he despised.

''I know. I'm sorry.'' Tricia stayed where she was, although he could tell she wanted to reach out, hold him, protect him from the pain. Why didn't she? he wondered.

"There's more you haven't told me, isn't there?" Something that shamed her, Jesse decided. Something keeping her at bay.

She nodded. "My dad blamed Michael Hawk for taking Rebecca away from him. I think maybe our fathers were rivals. Or at least were in love with the same woman at the same time."

Jesse stepped forward, an immediate burst of fury racing through his blood. "Oh, God, that's it. The reason he tore us apart. Your dad hated me because he hated my father." He pounded his fist on the table, sending the yogurt spilling to the floor. "We didn't stand a chance, Tricia. He destroyed us because my father married the woman *he* wanted."

She picked up the photograph and brought it to her chest, protecting it from his wrath. "I know. I'm so sorry. I told him that what he did to you was despicable, that he owed you an apology, but he—"

Jesse stared at her in disbelief. Did she actually think he would accept an apology even if Boyd was willing to offer one? The storm brewing in his heart left no room for forgiveness. None whatsoever.

"I need some air." He turned and headed for the back door, his pulse pounding furiously in his head.

Once outside, the sweltering humidity hit him like a fist, a stifling, suffocating punch. There was no relief, he thought. No solace anywhere. Jesse sank to the ground beneath a gnarled old tree. Even Mother Earth had abandoned him.

Patricia covered her face, then burst into tears. Hatred could mutilate a person's soul, rip it to shreds. She had refused to let it happen to her, although she had been close many times. Loving Jesse, then almost hating him. Loving her father, then wondering this morning if he had ice running through his veins. What sort of man would threaten to destroy an eighteen-year-old boy's academic future? Then keep that grudge alive for twelve years?

One hell-bent on despising the boy—the man—who looked too much like Michael Hawk, her mind answered. Her father had crossed that fragile line between love and hate. He had loved Rebecca, yet he couldn't find it in his heart to embrace her orphaned son.

Michael's orphaned son.

Patricia wiped her eyes. "This has to stop," she said out loud. Raymond Boyd and Jesse Hawk were not going to live out the rest of their lives consumed with hatred. She was going to save them, no matter what the emotional cost.

When Patricia spotted Jesse beneath the tree, her courage almost faltered. He looked like a stranger, withdrawn and unapproachable, his eyes dark and cold. A contradiction to the sun's glaring rays, she thought, a defiance to the elements.

She took a direct path toward him, her chin held high, her heart hammering with anxiety. What if he turned away from her, refused to accept the love she'd come to offer?

She stopped in front of him, the fear of losing him more unbearable than the heat. A thin line of perspiration trailed between her breasts.

He gazed up at her from the dusty patch of earth he'd claimed beneath the tree. "You're not dressed for the farm, Tricia. You should go back to your office."

"Don't do this, Jesse."

"Don't do what?" He rose to his feet, but didn't dust his jeans. "Blame you for taking your dad's side again?" He pulled his hand through his hair. "Do you honestly think an apology is going to make what he did to me go away? I wouldn't accept one if he got down on his hands and knees and begged for my forgiveness." A sarcastic laugh barked from his chest. "Of course we both know that's not going to happen, don't we? Your dad isn't the least bit sorry."

Another line of perspiration rolled down her chest. She felt hot and sticky and so very alone. "My father's hurting, Jesse, just like you are. But you're right, he's not going to approach you and apologize. He's been carrying this bitterness around for so long, he doesn't know how to let it go."

Jesse leaned against the tree, his stance cocky and defiant.

A rebellious pose, she thought, like an eighteen-year-old mad at the world. Which, deep down, he probably still was. That boy her father had shunned remained inside him, a boy still struggling for acceptance.

"Do you think I give a damn how your dad feels?" he asked.

"You should," she answered sternly, battling her decision to enforce tough love. A part of her wanted to wrap Jesse in her arms and tell him whatever he wanted to hear. But she couldn't, because what he wanted to hear wasn't right. Wallowing in hatred would only destroy the good in him, the Godliness. "My father loved your mother. That should matter to you."

Before he could answer, she reached out and stroked his cheek, buckling from the urge to touch. Comfort. "You should go to him, Jesse, and ask him about your mother. He only threw that photo away because he was afraid of facing the truth in front of Dillon. He has more pictures of her. They're in his safe." A sign, she thought, that her father still needed Rebecca to be a part of his life. Something Jesse needed, too.

He jerked, flinching from her words. "You expect me to make amends with your dad? Go to him like some street urchin, begging for tidbits about my mother? I can't do that. I won't."

I can't do that. I won't. Her father had said the same thing when she'd asked the older man to apologize to Jesse. How alike they were. How stubborn and pained.

She grabbed hold of his hand and held tight when he attempted to pull free. "I love you, Jesse Hawk," she said, her voice quaking. "I've fallen back in love with you. I don't know exactly when it happened, I just know that it did."

Time stood still. Nothing moved. His hand froze in hers, lifeless and still, like his features. Like the fear stealing her breath.

Say it, her heart begged. Say you'll go to my father and prove to him that you love me, too. Prove, once and for all, that true love can abolish hatred.

Slowly, very slowly, he lifted their joined hands, then let

go, drawing his fingers back. "I don't want... I can't—" His voice broke a little, but his expression remained blank. The stoic warrior, the lone hawk. "Don't love me, Tricia. Please. Just don't."

Because he couldn't love her back, she realized, couldn't bring himself to love Raymond Boyd's daughter again. A part of Jesse was still locked in the past—the callous, distrustful side that was impossible to reach.

She wanted to run, cry, let her heart bleed into the earth, but she stood tall instead. Pride was all she had now, and she intended to hold on to it until the bitter end.

She lifted her chin, set her gaze directly on his. "There's nothing more I can say. What I wanted for us was peace, but you're not willing to let that happen. I can't have a relationship with you anymore, Jesse."

He stood as motionless as the air, looking as though his world had just died and he intended to perish with it. Allow his venom to consume him. "You're going back to your father, aren't you?"

She pushed her hair away from her face. "Yes, I am. And I'm going to tell him what I told you. I love him, but I refuse to have a relationship with him, either. Not if he continues to wallow in hatred."

She forced her tears back, forced them with all her might. Her dad still owed Jesse an apology. She would face her father at work every day, but she wouldn't condone his malice, just the way she wouldn't condone Jesse's. "You know, my dad kept calling me naive, and I kept arguing that I wasn't. But he was right."

A muscle ticked in Jesse's cheek. "Why, because you got involved with me again?"

"No, because I believed in you. Believed what we had could conquer the hatred."

"Don't you dare blame me, Tricia. Your dad started this. He's the one who ruined what we had."

"And you're the one who can fix it." But won't, she thought. Because he refused to love her. The love was there, a tiny seed deep inside him, but rather than nourish it, he'd decided to let it decay.

Jesse didn't respond, so she continued, saddened by the denial she saw in his eyes, the emptiness. "I won't take Dillon away from you or his grandpa. And I'll do my best not to influence him to choose sides. That's not what this is about."

She turned and rounded the building, heading for her car and hoping that he'd follow, but knowing that he wouldn't. Patricia Boyd had just lost the love of her life. The man who was her heart and soul. And tonight when she was alone, she'd allow herself to cry. Grieve for what could have been.

Fourteen

Jesse parked in front of Tricia's house and looked over at his son. "You rode well today." Better than expected, considering the circumstances and Dillon's sensitive nature. The child's parents hadn't seen each other in almost two weeks, hadn't spoken a word.

"I like riding. It makes me happy."

Jesse squeezed Dillon's shoulder. It probably helped the boy forget what was going on his world, too. Sometimes Jesse saddled Hunter for that very same reason. He'd ridden a lot in these past two weeks, blocking Tricia's image from his mind, trying to forget, forcing himself to go on with his life.

Tricia had kept her word. She hadn't taken Dillon away from him. Jesse suspected the boy was still visiting with his grandpa, too. And much to his credit, the child protected his mother's feelings, respected the choice she'd made by remaining silent. Not once in the past thirteen days had he tried to prod Jesse into a conversation about Tricia.

Dillon leaned in for a quick hug. "Bye, Dad."

"Bye." Jesse held on a little longer than usual, needing the closeness, the comfort. "I love you, son."

"I love you, too."

With a father's pride, he watched the boy open the truck door and walk to the house. *I love you.* Such easy words to say to his child. Easy to say. Easy to feel. Natural, like breathing.

Dillon waved, then disappeared through the front door, Jesse missing him already.

Instead of firing the engine, he sat in his truck and stared at the property. The gardeners had been there recently. The lawn, the flowers, the shrubs, everything was well tended, not a leaf out of place. Arrow Hill was like that, he thought. Pristine and white. Perfect. Overly manicured. He'd never been comfortable there. Jesse Aaron Hawk was far from being white or pristine, not with his sun-baked skin and faded denim clothes.

His gaze traveled from the lawn to the house itself. He couldn't see Tricia's bedroom from his vantage point, but he remembered every detail: the stained-glass window that illuminated color, the French door that led to a balcony, the full-length mirror that had reflected her beauty, her slim, sleek nakedness.

Was she home today? Sipping iced tea in her modern kitchen? Working on her laptop? Possibly curled up on a chair in her den, reading a suspense novel, those long, shapely legs tucked beneath her?

He pulled a hand through his unbound hair. How long would it be before she dated another man? Took him to her bed? She wouldn't love Jesse forever, wouldn't wait like before. There was no misunderstood promise between them this time.

His stomach tightened as he started the truck. Tricia with another man was an image he couldn't bear.

He headed down the hill, away from the heights of Arrow Hill and into the flats of Hatcher. God, he missed her. Missed the length of her body, the curve of her smile, the exotic fragrance she wore. Like a fool he'd taken to burning jasmine-scented candles, filling his home with a bittersweet reminder.

Jesse gripped the steering wheel. What good would it do to admit that the ache in his chest was love? Saying it out loud would solve nothing. Absolutely nothing. Love was not the cure-all, the magic formula for happily ever after. Jesse Hawk didn't believe in fairy tales. Life had dealt him reality—a strong, hard, lonely dose.

Unwilling to go home to the lingering jasmine, he continued to drive, passing other homes, other people. He turned to see a rugged old rancher schooling a young horse, then caught sight of two barefoot kids in a neighboring yard, lapping ice cream that had probably come from the local dairy. Familiar sights. Country folk in a country setting. They should have brought him comfort, yet they didn't. He felt more alone than ever.

Within twenty minutes Jesse found himself at a place he hadn't been to since his brother had come to visit. A quiet place with acres of grass and unseen angels whispering through the wind. The cemetery where his parents had been laid to rest.

He parked the truck and walked onto the lawn. Sporadic bouquets of flowers colored the terrain, and while some had wilted in the sun, others remained fresh. Recent gifts, he thought, Sunday offerings.

His parents had been buried near a tree, their graves marked with simple headstones, two flat rectangles side by side. No statues, poems or loving verses etched their memorial—only their names, the years of their births, dates of their deaths. Jesse knelt on the grass, the ache in his heart bleeding like an open wound.

Michael Aaron Hawk.

Rebecca Marie Hawk.

They'd married, made two children, then died together one tragic summer night when another vehicle collided with their truck. They'd taken their last conscious breaths while an elderly baby-sitter probably read fairy tales to their sons—two young boys, separated just days later.

"I'm sorry I didn't bring flowers," he said quietly, "but I didn't know I was coming here." He brushed several leaves away from the stone markers, then wondered if he should have left them instead. The leaves had fallen from the ancient oak that protected his parents, shaded them in the summer, watched over them on cold winter nights.

He fingered his mother's name and pictured her delicate features, her flowing blond hair. "I saw a photograph of you. You were with Raymond Boyd."

A man I hate, he thought. Tricia's father. The very reason he couldn't go to Tricia and tell her what she longed to hear. Loving her meant forgiving Boyd, something he refused to do. Boyd had tainted everything, even the memory of his parents.

"Why were you with him, Mom? Why were you smiling?"

When no answer came, he spoke to both of his parents, hoping to find a space in his mind that Raymond Boyd didn't occupy. "You have a grandson. His name's Dillon, and he's a terrific kid. Bright and sensitive."

But he's Boyd's grandson, as well, Jesse thought bitterly. Damn that old man. Almost everyone that he loved, Boyd had claimed, too.

Jesse heard a rustle in the tree and looked up. A red-tailed hawk had lit upon a high branch, its glorious wings fanned. He followed the bird's graceful movement, a lump forming in his throat. Hawks were messengers, couriers from the heavens. And this red-tipped angel had undoubtedly come with the tree—a beautiful spirit that belonged to his parents. His blue-eyed mother, his Creek father.

He scrubbed his hand across his jaw and closed his eyes, knowing that the hawk watched and waited, its message clear. Angels didn't send tidings of hatred.

What have I done?

He opened his eyes, heard his own voice—a low whisper—a disgraced confession. "I taught Dillon about the *busk*. The ceremony of forgiveness."

Yes, he'd taught his son about the Green Corn Dance. He'd spouted the words while storing contempt for the boy's grandfather. He had dishonored his son, he thought, shamed the child Tricia had given him. And he'd dishonored Tricia, as well, the gentle woman for whom his soul ached. He'd broken her heart once again, refused the love she'd offered, the peace and beauty. He stood motionless, their last conversation reverberating in his head.

Don't you dare blame me, Tricia. Your dad started this. He's the one who ruined what we had.

And you're the one who can fix it.

Jesse stared up through the branches of the tree and saw the hawk settle into its nest, certain now of what he must do.

A long private road led to the Boyd mansion. Jesse took the winding turns with ease since his truck had been built for a tougher terrain. As the hilltop estate came into view, his heartbeat quickened. The house sat like a proud monument. A bed of indigenous flowers lined a circular driveway, while white pillars supported the front door, tall round columns one would expect on a mansion. The grounds were exceptional, green and lush with a carpet of grass that went on forever.

Tricia and Dillon had both lived there, so he tried to accept the opulence, tried to make it feel homey by imagining them picnicking on the lawn.

He parked and rang the bell, then waited anxiously to announce himself to a butler or a maid. Would Boyd refuse to see him? Jesse stood tall and resisted the urge to dust his jeans. He didn't want to be caught fussing over his appearance, even though he probably looked more like a cowboy than a country veterinarian. He had dressed this morning for Dillon's riding lesson and still wore a simple ensemble of Western attire.

Boyd answered the door himself, a shock to Jesse's system. He stared at the other man, and before his mouth could form a word, Boyd belted out a gruff question.

"Is Patricia with you?"

"No. I came alone."

"What do you want?"

"To talk."

The older man scowled and stepped away from the door in a silent, unfriendly invitation. Jesse would have preferred to stay outside with the grass and the trees. Cowboy boots didn't belong on a marble floor, he thought, as he entered the mansion, feeling instantly out of place.

He followed Boyd into a room that boasted tradition and elegance: a crystal chandelier, a gold mantel over the fireplace, cream-colored sofas and ornate wood furnishings that had probably been in the family for generations. Words like Queen Anne and Chippendale popped into Jesse's head, antiques he'd heard of, but wouldn't recognize.

Once again, he tried to picture Tricia and Dillon there, tried to fill himself with their medicine—Tricia's feminine beauty and Dillon's youthful innocence—the warmth he felt for both.

Boyd pointed to a chair. "You came to talk. So talk. There's no one here but us. My staff has Sundays off."

Jesse sat, even though he would have preferred to stand. His towering height gave him an advantage over the other man. At six-two, he stood several inches taller than Tricia's father, the cowboy boots adding yet another inch.

He watched Boyd take a chair opposite him and realized how ridiculously macho his last thought had been. This wasn't about who had what advantage. So he was taller and Boyd had more money. So what? Neither one of them had Tricia in their lives, and loved ones mattered more than an intimidating stance or an overflowing bankbook.

"Do you miss Tricia?" Jesse asked.

"My daughter's name is Patricia. And if you came here to gloat because you finally managed to ruin her relationship with me, you can get the hell out now."

Prone to being hot-tempered, Jesse clenched his fists, then took a deep breath and relaxed his fingers. The hawk had sent him, the hawk and his lonely heart. Anger would only destroy what he'd come to repair. "She's Tricia to me. And believe me, I'm far from gloating. I miss her something awful."

Boyd sat upright in his chair. "She hasn't been here in two weeks, and she only speaks to me at the office when it's absolutely necessary. I never knew she had it in her to be quite this stubborn."

Yes, he missed her. Jesse could see the loss in the other

man's face, hear it in his tone. He inhaled another deep breath, then exhaled slowly, preparing his next words. "I'm in love with your daughter, Mr. Boyd. And I'm here because I want your blessing before I ask her to marry me."

"I should have known." Tricia's father tugged at his collar, the fear in his voice creeping into his eyes. "You're going to take her away from me. That's what this is all about."

Boyd's uncharacteristic burst of panic left Jesse momentarily speechless. Earlier the older man had seemed emotional but stern, impeccable in tan slacks and a matching pullover, as haughty and distinguished as the house.

Jesse glanced down at his hands, then back up, Tricia's words filling his head. *My dad blamed Michael Hawk for taking Rebecca away from him.*

"I resemble my father, don't I?" he asked.

The other man nodded, still struggling to maintain his composure. "Yes, you favor him. It's difficult to look at you and not see Michael."

Jesse steered the conversation down a road that made him as jittery as Boyd, as panicked, in a way. But he knew deep down that they both needed to travel that road, the painful highway leading to the past. "Will you tell me about my mother? Please," he added when the older man frowned. "It's important to me. I don't remember her."

"I..." Tricia's father hesitated, then cleared his throat. "I met her at the country club. She was a waitress at the bistro. She was new in town and didn't know anyone."

"I saw her picture. The one of the two of you together. She was beautiful. A lot like I'd imagined." Blond and delicate with a warm smile and bright-blue eyes. A mother other children would admire. The mother Jesse had always dreamed of having, someone angelic and caring.

"Yes. Rebecca was beautiful. Sweet and a little shy at times. I, umm..."

"Took one look at her and fell madly in love?" Jesse provided.

The older man managed a strained nod. "I began eating at

the bistro everyday. I was determined to get to know Rebecca. Figure a way to win her affection.''

Jesse remained silent while Boyd continued, surprised by his ability to listen without resentment. Maybe it was because he, too, had fallen madly in love the first time he'd seen Tricia. He understood masculine obsession.

''I learned that Rebecca adored horses, which was precisely why she had moved to Hatcher. She'd heard that Hatcher was an affordable cowboy town, a place where she might be able to board a horse for a reasonable fee.'' He smoothed his sideburns with edgy fingers, his composure not quite regained. ''She didn't have a horse, but she planned on buying one just as soon as she saved enough money.''

Jesse scooted to the edge of his seat. Boyd's hatred of horses was linked to his mother somehow. ''You owned several horses, didn't you? The ones from the pictures?''

''No. I mean yes, they were mine, but I bought them to impress Rebecca. And since I wasn't familiar with the equestrian world, I hired a trainer. Someone to teach me everything I needed to know, including how to ride.'' Boyd looked directly at Jesse, right smack into his eyes. ''I was a quick study, and the young man I hired was the best. Tall, good-looking Creek fellow. His name was Michael Hawk.''

Jesse held the other man's piercing gaze. ''My father.''

''Yes, your father.'' Boyd's voice went tight. He rose and stood beside the fireplace. ''We became friends, the three of us. We spent every free moment together—laughing, talking, riding. I didn't tell Rebecca how I felt about her, but I sensed that Michael knew. In the same way that I picked up on what was happening to him.''

They both loved her, Jesse thought. Friends in love with the same woman.

''It wasn't a deliberate competition, in fact it didn't seem like a competition at all. I felt brotherly toward Michael, and I was certain that he'd get over Rebecca. I intended to ask him to be my best man when I married her.''

''I'm sorry,'' Jesse said.

Boyd's stance went rigid. "You're apologizing for your father?"

"No." Jesse stood, resisting the urge to pace. The conversation had taken a turn he'd never expected. "I'm sorry that you got hurt. I know what it feels like to love someone. To hurt over them."

The older man sighed and made a humbling confession. "I was arrogant. So damn arrogant. Not once did Rebecca encourage me to be anything more than her friend. I'd see the way she would look at Michael and say to myself, 'But I have more to offer her than he does. I'm successful. I inherited a grand house.'" He gestured to the opulent surroundings. "Such an arrogant fool."

"You're not a fool." Jesse's eyes turned watery. "You've taken good care of Tricia and Dillon. And you cared about my parents. That makes you special in my eyes."

"How can you say that after everything that's happened?"

"Because it's time for forgiveness. And I want to marry your daughter and raise Dillon with her. I love them, Raymond," he said, using the other man's given name for the first time. "They mean everything to me." And he understood that Raymond Boyd had acted out of fear rather than true malice. He had been afraid of losing Tricia the way he'd lost Rebecca. "I want us to be a family. All of us."

Raymond stepped forward, shame etched upon his face. "Your parents wanted to remain my friend. They begged me to understand, to give them my blessing. And I should have. They loved each other very much."

"That means a lot to me." Jesse blinked back his tears. "I know so little about my parents."

"They would have been proud of you." Raymond extended his hand, his eyes as watery as Jesse's. "I'm sorry. So incredibly sorry for what I've done to you and Patricia. Maybe if I'd known how you really felt about her. Maybe…"

His voice trailed, taking the rest of his apology with it. For Jesse, it was enough. Raymond had wrestled with inner demons for far too long.

He clasped the other man's hand, then leaned forward when

he realized he was about to be hugged. It felt odd, wonderfully
odd to be embraced by Tricia's father.

Raymond stepped back a little awkwardly. "I have pictures
of your parents. Would you like to see them?"

Surprised, Jesse nodded. "You kept photos of my dad?"

"Yes, but I can't explain why I felt compelled to hold on
to them."

Because, Jesse thought, Raymond Boyd was an overly
proud, reclusive man who had mourned a lost friendship in
the only way he knew how.

Later that day Jesse waited at another door, nervous once
again. He brushed at his clothes. There he stood, empty-
handed, in old boots and worn denims. A man should propose
in a romantic setting with a diamond ring and a bottle of champagne. What was he thinking, showing up like this?

He glanced at the grass stains on his jeans. What if Tricia
didn't want to marry him? What if she'd fallen out of love
already? Maybe she hadn't missed him as badly as he'd
missed her.

She opened the door, and he stood like a scarecrow, afraid
he'd trip over his own feet if he dared take a step. She looked
soft and pretty in a pastel dress, a floral scent drifting around
her.

He hoped to hell he didn't smell like the hay he'd stacked
that morning. Or, God forbid, like his horse.

"Jesse," she said, "I don't think Dillon was expecting you.
He's at a friend's house."

"Actually, I'm here to see you," he managed, noting her
polite tone lacked the warmth he'd come to bask in. "I was
hoping we could talk."

She touched the top button on her dress in a protective manner. "I've already said everything that I intended to say, remember?"

Yeah, he remembered. The overwhelming loneliness had
made him do strange things, like hug his pillow at night and
wish the softness was her. "I just came from your dad's house,
Tricia."

Her eyes went wide. "Is everything...? You two didn't...?" She took in his down-home appearance as though checking for evidence of a scuffle. "What happened?"

He studied the sweep of her hair, the curvaceous lines of her body, the anticipation on her face. "Invite me in and I'll tell you."

Tricia stepped away from the door. He walked into the house and took her hand, felt it quiver in his. He decided she was nervous. Excited. Hopeful. The thought bolstered his courage.

"Let's sit on the patio." To hell with champagne and diamonds. That could come later. He was going to make this woman his wife the Creek way, providing she'd have him.

He chose the edge of a brick planter so they could sit beside each other, their shoulders nearly touching. Jesse turned to look at her. Elegant Tricia in her summer dress—flowing cotton and flawless skin.

Her breath hitched. "Please. Tell me what happened."

He held her hand and told her about the hawk at the cemetery, her father's confession, the embrace they'd shared, the emotion, the forgiveness, the burden that had been lifted from his heart.

She listened, her eyes filling with tears. "You made everything all right. You made the hurt go away."

"So did your dad. It wasn't easy for him." Raymond had opened a painful vein from his youth. It took courage, Jesse thought, for the other man to admit his mistakes, his loss and loneliness. "I think he really loved my mother. Letting his pain go after all these years must have been hard." He reached into his shirt pocket and handed Tricia a photograph that Raymond had given him, a gift he would treasure forever.

"It's your parents." She touched it with reverence. "Oh, my. You look just like your father. They're beautiful, both of them."

Yes, they were. Young and beautiful and madly in love. They stood side by side, their hair fluttering in a small breeze. His father's jet-black mane was banded into a ponytail, but several strands had blown free, indicating its length.

"Your dad took this picture, Tricia. He's a wonderful photographer." Raymond had captured his subject, the innocence of Rebecca, the strength of Michael. The sheer radiance of love and friendship.

Tricia dabbed at her tears. "This feels like a dream."

He smiled. He hadn't asked her to marry him yet, hadn't told her that he'd already received her father's blessing. The dream, he hoped, was just beginning.

Jesse tucked the photograph back into his pocket. "Wait here. There's something I need to do."

He scouted her yard, frowned at the short-cropped lawn. He needed reeds, two tall blades of grass with jointed stems. He continued to scan the flowers and plants, and decided his ancestors would forgive him for the compromise. He chose two long, green leaves from an abundant foliage and returned to Tricia, who sat quietly with a curious expression.

"I'm going to explain a Creek custom. It's simple, but extremely important." He pressed the leaves into the dirt, one in front of each of them. "When a Creek man chooses a bride, he builds a house and plants a new crop. I already have a home, and I intend to fill a garden with flowers that remind me of you." He swallowed his nervousness and met her gaze.

Fresh tears glistened in her eyes. "Are you asking me to marry you?"

He nodded, then motioned toward the leaves he'd pressed into the dirt. "All we have to do is exchange reeds. This gives the woman a chance to make her decision."

Without the slightest hesitation, she blinked through her tears, lifted the leaf in front of her and handed it to Jesse, her acceptance true and clear. He smiled and offered her his.

"I love you," he said. The sentiment was in his gesture, but he knew she needed to hear those three special words. Suddenly loving her had become so easy, so right.

She clutched the makeshift reed to her chest, her voice almost breathless—a soft feminine whisper. "Are you my husband now?"

"In the old way, yes." He still had flowers to plant, and they would both want a legal ceremony, a license to seal their bond, but they had just made a private commitment—a cherished vow beneath the sun.

He lifted her left hand, envisioning a ring there. "My brother and his wife are coming to visit in about six weeks. That's enough time to plan a wedding, isn't it?"

"That's perfect." In their hearts they were already married, Patricia thought, but a formal wedding would unite family and friends.

She touched his lips, felt them open beneath hers. Beautiful, rugged Jesse. Her Creek husband. Her lover. The father of her child. The world and all its glory was hers. He had just completed her life, her soul.

"When did you know?" she asked. "When did you know that you loved me?"

He closed his eyes as though savoring the aftertaste of her kiss. "I'm not sure I ever really stopped. I told myself I had, but..." He opened his eyes and took her breath away. "I couldn't let you go, not completely. I kept your hair in my medicine bag because I needed to keep a part of you with me even though it hurt."

The way her father had kept Rebecca's and Michael's pictures, she realized. "You forgave my dad so easily because you understood."

Jesse nodded. "Your mother and my parents died within months of each other. Can you imagine the grief he suffered?"

And the guilt. A combination that had led to an overly protective nature. Patricia didn't blame her father for having loved Rebecca in a different way than he'd loved her mother. Love came in many forms, and she felt certain her dad had been a good, caring husband. "We're going to be okay. All of us."

"Yes, we are. And Dillon's the link that binds your family and mine."

Patricia smiled. He was right. Dillon belonged to all of them. She looked around, thought about the wonderful changes ahead. "I won't miss this house, and I don't think Dillon will, either." Jesse's house had the wooden porch, the herb garden, the menagerie of animals that brought warmth and comfort.

His voice turned low and heated. "I'm going to put a stained-glass window in our bedroom, just like the one that's here. It's like making love to you inside of a rainbow."

Her knees went weak. She unbuttoned the front of her dress and brought his head to her breasts. He nuzzled, his mouth moist against her nipple.

"I want more children, Tricia. Sweet little babies."

"Me, too."

"Then don't take your pills anymore." He lifted his head and kissed her.

A soft breeze feathered his hair. She captured a strand and let it slide through her fingers. He took her hand and led her to the room that contained their rainbow.

She undressed before him, slipped the cotton off her shoulders and met his gaze, instantly losing herself in liquid silver.

He lowered her to the bed, to the prism of sun-washed color.

She arched her neck, felt him inhale the fragrance of her skin, touch and taste and relish the woman she'd become. There was no hurry, no anxious frenzy. His nakedness covered hers, and she smiled, welcoming his weight, warmth. The love she saw alight in his eyes.

Epilogue

Patricia Hawk. The bride tested her new name in her mind.

No, no, no. *Tricia* Hawk. She would think of herself as Tricia now.

Jesse's Tricia.

She stood beside her husband in front of the chapel where they had exchanged public vows. A thick carpet of grass surrounded the quaint little building. Red bricks made up the entryway, while a steeple provided early-American charm.

A professional photographer gathered family and friends, placing them just so, coaxing their smiles. Tricia wore her mother's wedding dress, a long, slim-fitting gown fashioned from white satin, pearls and lace. Her father had saved the dress for this occasion, a sentimental gesture that had brought tears to Tricia's eyes. Raymond Boyd had walked his daughter down the aisle as a proud but humbled man. That, too, had triggered tears of joy.

Jesse and Dillon, dark and handsome in traditional black tuxedos, sported simple white boutonnieres. Tricia's bouquet was made up of exotic blooms—jasmine and hothouse orchids—flowers Jesse had suggested.

A group photo was in the works, and Tricia watched as Jesse's brother, Sky, and his wife, Windy, were directed into place. Tricia couldn't help but admire the baby in Windy's arms, a delightful child with enormous blue eyes and ringlets of black hair.

"Can I hold Shawna for this picture?" she asked, eager to cradle the tiny girl against her.

Jesse smiled as Shawna was transferred into his bride's arms. "Practicing?" he asked in a hushed voice.

Tricia inhaled the gentle scent of baby powder as she adjusted the child's ribbons and bows. "We might have a girl this time," she whispered back, laughing as Shawna grabbed hold of Jesse's lapel and flashed him a toothless grin.

Dillon, who stood in front of his father, turned back to add his smile. Young Dillon Hawk had volunteered to announce his mother's pregnancy at the upcoming reception—a secret he couldn't wait to reveal. He was going to be a wonderful big brother, she thought, kind and protective.

No stone in their lives had been left unturned. Tricia's father had seen to that. He'd purchased the trailer park where Jesse's parents had once lived, promising to restore it in their honor, offering the current residents, including Fiona, an environment of which to be proud. Elda, Dillon's former nanny, had expressed an interest in managing the park, hoping to put her organizational skills to good use.

They were all there, everyone that Jesse and Tricia loved, gathered close for the photographer's critical eye. Tricia looked up and spotted a hawk gliding through the heavens. She whispered a prayer of thanks and smiled for the camera.

Her husband's guardian angel, in all its glory, had just arrived, completing the cycle of beauty and love.

* * * * *

Don't miss Sheri WhiteFeather's next
Silhouette Desire—CHEYENNE DAD.
Look for it this June!

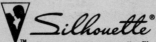

SILHOUETTE'S 20TH ANNIVERSARY CONTEST
OFFICIAL RULES
NO PURCHASE NECESSARY TO ENTER

1. To enter, follow directions published in the offer to which you are responding. Contest begins 1/1/00 and ends on 8/24/00 (the "Promotion Period"). Method of entry may vary. Mailed entries must be postmarked by 8/24/00, and received by 8/31/00.

2. During the Promotion Period, the Contest may be presented via the Internet. Entry via the Internet may be restricted to residents of certain geographic areas that are disclosed on the Web site. To enter via the Internet, if you are a resident of a geographic area in which Internet entry is permissible, follow the directions displayed on-line, including typing your essay of 100 words or fewer telling us "Where In The World Your Love Will Come Alive." On-line entries must be received by 11:59 p.m. Eastern Standard time on 8/24/00. Limit one e-mail entry per person, household and e-mail address per day, per presentation. If you are a resident of a geographic area in which entry via the Internet is permissible, you may, in lieu of submitting an entry on-line, enter by mail, by hand-printing your name, address, telephone number and contest number/name on an 8"x 11" plain piece of paper and telling us in 100 words or fewer "Where In The World Your Love Will Come Alive," and mailing via first-class mail to: Silhouette 20th Anniversary Contest, (in the U.S.) P.O. Box 9069, Buffalo, NY 14269-9069; (In Canada) P.O. Box 637, Fort Erie, Ontario, Canada L2A 5X3. Limit one 8"x 11" mailed entry per person, household and e-mail address per day. On-line and/or 8"x 11" mailed entries received from persons residing in geographic areas in which Internet entry is not permissible will be disqualified. No liability is assumed for lost, late, incomplete, inaccurate, nondelivered or misdirected mail, or misdirected e-mail, for technical, hardware or software failures of any kind, lost or unavailable network connection, or failed, incomplete, garbled or delayed computer transmission or any human error which may occur in the receipt or processing of the entries in the contest.

3. Essays will be judged by a panel of members of the Silhouette editorial and marketing staff based on the following criteria:

    Sincerity (believability, credibility)—50%

    Originality (freshness, creativity)—30%

    Aptness (appropriateness to contest ideas)—20%

    Purchase or acceptance of a product offer does not improve your chances of winning. In the event of a tie, duplicate prizes will be awarded.

4. All entries become the property of Harlequin Enterprises Ltd., and will not be returned. Winner will be determined no later than 10/31/00 and will be notified by mail. Grand Prize winner will be required to sign and return Affidavit of Eligibility within 15 days of receipt of notification. Noncompliance within the time period may result in disqualification and an alternative winner may be selected. All municipal, provincial, federal, state and local laws and regulations apply. Contest open only to residents of the U.S. and Canada who are 18 years of age or older, and is void wherever prohibited by law. Internet entry is restricted solely to residents of those geographical areas in which Internet entry is permissible. Employees of Torstar Corp., their affiliates, agents and members of their immediate families are not eligible. Taxes on the prizes are the sole responsibility of winners. Entry and acceptance of any prize offered constitutes permission to use winner's name, photograph or other likeness for the purposes of advertising, trade and promotion on behalf of Torstar Corp. without further compensation to the winner, unless prohibited by law. Torstar Corp and D.L. Blair, Inc., their parents, affiliates and subsidiaries, are not responsible for errors in printing or electronic presentation of contest or entries. In the event of printing or other errors which may result in unintended prize values or duplication of prizes, all affected contest materials or entries shall be null and void. If for any reason the Internet portion of the contest is not capable of running as planned, including infection by computer virus, bugs, tampering, unauthorized intervention, fraud, technical failures, or any other causes beyond the control of Torstar Corp. which corrupt or affect the administration, secrecy, fairness, integrity or proper conduct of the contest, Torstar Corp. reserves the right, at its sole discretion, to disqualify any individual who tampers with the entry process and to cancel, terminate, modify or suspend the contest or the Internet portion thereof. In the event of a dispute regarding an on-line entry, the entry will be deemed submitted by the authorized holder of the e-mail account submitted at the time of entry. Authorized account holder is defined as the natural person who is assigned to an e-mail address by an Internet access provider, on-line service provider or other organization that is responsible for arranging e-mail address for the domain associated with the submitted e-mail address.

5. Prizes: Grand Prize—a $10,000 vacation to anywhere in the world. Travelers (at least one must be 18 years of age or older) or parent or guardian if one traveler is a minor, must sign and return a Release of Liability prior to departure. Travel must be completed by December 31, 2001, and is subject to space and accommodations availability. Two hundred (200) Second Prizes—a two-book limited edition autographed collector set from one of the Silhouette Anniversary authors: Nora Roberts, Diana Palmer, Linda Howard or Annette Broadrick (value $10.00 each set). All prizes are valued in U.S. dollars.

6. For a list of winners (available after 10/31/00) send a self-addressed, stamped envelope to: Harlequin Silhouette 20th Anniversary Winners, P.O. Box 4200, Blair, NE 68009-4200.

Contest sponsored by Torstar Corp., P.O. Box 9042, Buffalo, NY 14269-9042.

PS20RULES

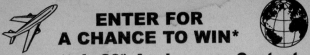

ENTER FOR
A CHANCE TO WIN*
Silhouette's 20th Anniversary Contest

Tell Us Where in the World
You Would Like *Your* Love To Come Alive...
And We'll Send the Lucky Winner There!

Silhouette wants to take you wherever
your happy ending can come true.

Here's how to enter: Tell us, in 100 words or less,
where you want to go to make your love come alive!

In addition to the grand prize, there will be 200
runner-up prizes, collector's-edition book sets
autographed by one of the Silhouette anniversary
authors: **Nora Roberts, Diana Palmer,
Linda Howard** or **Annette Broadrick**.

DON'T MISS YOUR CHANCE TO WIN!
ENTER NOW! No Purchase Necessary

Silhouette®
Where love comes alive™

Name: _____

Address: _____

City: _____ State/Province: _____

Zip/Postal Code: _____

Mail to Harlequin Books: **In the U.S.**: P.O. Box 9069, Buffalo, NY
14269-9069; **In Canada**: P.O. Box 637, Fort Erie, Ontario, L4A 5X3

*No purchase necessary—for contest details send a self-addressed stamped envelope to:
Silhouette's 20th Anniversary Contest, P.O. Box 9069, Buffalo, NY, 14269-9069 (include
contest name on self-addressed envelope). Residents of Washington and Vermont may
omit postage. Open to Cdn. (excluding Quebec) and U.S. residents who are 18 or over.
Void where prohibited. Contest ends August 31, 2000.

PS20CON_R